A **STAIN** UPON THE ROBE

ALSO BY TERRY DEVANE

UNCOMMON JUSTICE
JUROR NUMBER ELEVEN

A
STAIN
UPON
THE
ROBE

TERRY DEVANE

G. P. PUTNAM'S SONS
NEW YORK

This is a work of fiction. Names, characters, places, and incidents either are the product of the author's imagination or are used fictitiously, and any resemblance to actual persons, living or dead, business establishments, events, or locales is entirely coincidental.

G. P. Putnam's Sons
Publishers Since 1838
a member of
Penguin Group (USA) Inc.
375 Hudson Street
New York, NY 10014

Library of Congress Cataloging-in-Publication Data

Devane, Terry.
    A stain upon the robe / Terry Devane.
      p. cm.
    ISBN 0-399-15108-7
     1. O'Clare, Mairead (Fictitious character)—Fiction. 2. Gold, Sheldon (Fictitious
character)—Fiction. 3. Boston (Mass.)—Fiction. 4. Women lawyers—Fiction. I. Title.
PS3554.E923S73   2003   2003046912
813'.6—dc21

Printed in the United States of America
10 9 8 7 6 5 4 3 2 1

This book is printed on acid-free paper. ∞

IN MEMORY OF CLAUDE CROSS
AND LEONARD MATTHEWS

It was almost 4:00 P.M. on a June Monday when Mairead O'Clare came out of her law office in Sheldon A. Gold's suite and into its hexagonal reception area. "Billie, do we know who Shel's meeting"—Mairead checked her watch—"seven minutes from now?"

Billie Sunday swiveled in her reception chair from the dinosaur typewriter, which Mairead had learned was still the most efficient way to complete the many forms that Massachusetts courts insisted criminal defense attorneys submit. Billie shook her head, and Mairead thought the older woman appeared pleased, even in midlife, to have anticipated the cornrows-of-honey fashion statement by Serena Williams long before anybody had heard of the tennis sisters.

Billie said, "Shel just told me to hold the two-hour slot for a 'consult,' with you and me being available. And nobody else around."

Mairead felt a pang of disappointment. In the five months since she'd left the large, corporate law firm of Jaynes & Ward to join Shel in his Boston solo practice, he'd often had all of his "team" in together on certain client matters, with Billie as secretary taking dictation and Pontifico "the Pope" Murizzi serving as private investigator. However, Murizzi, having previously been a detective on the city's Homicide Unit, didn't usually help them on anything but murder cases, and even those only when he believed the suspect to be innocent.

Which prompted just one more question. "The Pope's *not* going to be with us, then?"

Another-shake of the cornrows. "Maybe Shel's afraid that spooky man would scare off any rational client who *hasn't* killed somebody."

Mairead, who thought of Murizzi as anything but "spooky," turned and went back into her own office, sinking into her desk chair. No murder charge, no quality time with the Pope.

However, there were three manila case folders splayed between her hands and arms, stained reddish-purple since birth with hemangioma from the fingertips past the elbows. Compulsive—like most attorneys she knew—Mairead believed she should work productively on at least one file during the short time until the four-o'clock "consult," but curiosity was trumping even compulsion.

Perhaps the person will be late, young lady, or you won't be asked to join the meeting, and therefore starting on something is better than waiting on nothing.

Mairead listened to the voice of Sister Bernadette, echoing in her head the same way the kindly nun's advice had echoed in the orphanage whenever Mairead needed—or the sister thought the unadoptable girl with the port-wine markings needed—some direction.

Okay, I agree.

Just as Mairead dragged one of the case folders toward her, the suite's door to the outside corridor opened and closed. She looked up, a female voice announcing herself to Billie too quietly for Mairead to hear the actual words. But there was something familiar about the tall woman's profile as she moved gracefully past Billie and extended a long-fingered hand to be shaken by Shel Gold, only an inch or two taller than their potential client. He was standing at the threshold of his office, as always a little rumpled in just suit pants, tie, and shirt, both sleeves rolled up twice. Shel shifted to the left with his own grace, the kind Mairead knew he'd developed in boxing rings, and then the woman was inside the older attorney's office, its door closing behind them.

Mairead came around her desk and noticed the generally unfazeable Billie Sunday staring after the woman no longer visible. "Billie, was that who I think?"

A nod this time, the cornrows not much involved. "The Honorable Barbara Quincy Pitt, judge of the superior court."

Mairead O'Clare found herself hoping that she'd be included in the consult even before she could accomplish anything productive on her own files.

Shelly, I must say you're looking well. Hair still sandy and holding its own against the ebbing tide of scalp, even the *Raging Bull* physique. But we really *must* introduce you to my family's tailor."

Sheldon A. Gold remembered another "introduction," to her family itself thirty years before, that had been less than a roaring success, but said, "Thank you, Judge. Why don't—"

"Please, protocol first. It's 'Your Honor' inside the courtroom, and 'Judge' most anywhere else, but still 'Barbara' between us."

Pitt blended into one of the two client armchairs in front of Shel's desk. Sitting behind it, he did a superficial assessment of his law school classmate cum superior court judge. Pitt had aged, necessarily, the blond hair going platinum either naturally or with chemical help. Her features benefited tremendously from a mainline Philadelphia gene pool that chiseled cheekbones like a fashion model's, no wrinkles except at the corners of the mouth and eyes. Hazel eyes—just as laser-like as Mairead's blue ones—that seemed to have passed the superficial stage and now were frankly appraising him, too.

Admit it: Just the way Pitt would stare at you in first-year Torts class, like she was making up her mind whether to ask you back to her apartment, in the fashion of the early seventies, for a little . . . afternoon delight.

"Well, Shelly, have we completed our respective window-shopping, or would you like to try kicking the tires?"

He had to smile. "I'm flattered, Barbara, but I'm also still married."

A look of concern clouded Pitt's face for a moment. "Is . . . uh, *she* any better?"

That surprised Shel a bit. Not so much that the judge would ask the question, but that she wouldn't have done some research to bring back that his wife's first name was Natalie. Of course, Pitt had called only that morning, asking to see him between four and six the same evening, for which there could be a lot of explanations. It had occurred to Shel that Her Honor couldn't get free until around four, but would rather *not* be seen coming into or leaving a law office at five, when a lot of curious people might be milling around.

On the other hand, Shel had found that if he overanalyzed something, time would usually prove him wrong.

"Shelly?"

"Sorry, Barbara. I zoned out a little. No, Natalie's not any better."

"Then I'm the one who's sorry."

Somehow, Shel drew the opposite impression, but said, "So, what can I do for you?"

"First, and I really should have begun with this, thank you for seeing me on such short notice."

Shel just shrugged, like what are old friends—or more than old friends—for? "There a reason you didn't want Pontifico Murizzi to be with us?"

The look of concern returned to Pitt's face. "Yes, but before that, you're aware of the trial I currently have?"

Shel felt a stinging in his heart just thinking about it. "The Catholic priest accused of raping children in his former parishes."

A sigh. "Just *one* of the priests, Shelly. But yes, the most notorious example of the current scandal—namely Cornelius Xavier Dooley, accused of attacking twenty-three different boys over the years. And it's a bear."

Shel tried not to picture the Magnavox screen in his small apartment in Brookline, the town due west of Boston. Nor the soul-numbing details replayed over and over again every half hour as successive pairs of news anchors took their chairs. Then he tried not to picture his own son, Richie, and what might have happened to him, well away from even any house of God.

"Shelly, are you 'zoning out' on me again?"

"Sorry, Barbara. Yes, I can imagine how hard that kind of case must be for you."

"Can you also imagine the reason I was assigned it?"

Shel shrugged again.

Pitt said, "The CJAM wanted somebody not male, and not Catholic."

Shel knew the Commonwealth's jargon for the chief judge in charge of administration was "CJAM." He said, "But surely they could find others among the several dozen superior court judges sitting in Suffolk County who were . . . neither."

A regal nod. "Yes, but it was vital for one of our best to be hand-picked for this ordeal, given the incredibly high profile, both locally and nationally."

Shel suppressed a smile: Pitt was never anything but positive in her self-image. "And so you were tapped for it?"

"Yes, which explains half my problem."

Sheldon A. Gold braced himself. "What's the other half?"

Another sigh before Barbara Quincy Pitt told him.

Billie Sunday heard Shel's voice behind her say, "Could you and Mairead come into my office, please?"

Billie noticed that the new child was halfway out of her chair before their boss's last words died in the air. She's a hard charger, no question, but a little tiresome to deal with in the energy department, like a puppy just beginning to realize why it has such big feet.

Billie watched Shel—a genuine Jewish gentleman—fetch an armchair from the empty office in the suite so that all three women now in his room would have a place to sit without him having to stand. Glancing around after the formal introductions, Billie nevertheless wished the "gentleman" had taken the trouble to straighten out his office. The first time her husband, Robert, Sr.—may God rest his soul—visited, the career Army sergeant said he'd seen less damage done by concussion grenades.

Shel settled back into his desk chair and cleared his throat, which Billie took to be a signal to get ready to start writing on her steno pad, and which fortunately the new child took as a signal *not* to start talking.

"First of all, I've assured Judge Pitt that we're all firmly within the circle of confidentiality for the attorney-client privilege, as will Mr. Murizzi be, should we call upon him as a private investigator. She has consented to your both being present on that condition."

If the client hadn't been sitting next to her, Billie would have said, "Huh!" out loud, because she knew it was more likely that Shel had told the lady that everybody participated, or he couldn't help her with whatever it—

"Judge Pitt is currently presiding over the *Dooley* trial, as I'm sure you know from the media coverage. Because she isn't Roman Catholic, the manager of Legal Research Services assigned her a specific law clerk who *is* Catholic. That young man's name is Charles Vah-*ray*-kah—spelled V-A-R-E-I-K-A." A pause. "However, he didn't appear at the courthouse for work this morning."

Billie looked up from her pad. Shel had done the same thing for Pitt when he'd introduced "Muh-*raid,* spelled M-A-I-R-E-A-D," to her. But it was the absence of the lady's law clerk from his job that caught Billie's attention now.

Shel said, "Judge?"

Now Pitt cleared her throat. "This is very . . . difficult to discuss. Mr. Vareika began working with me approximately six weeks ago, as the *Dooley* trial was starting, but for the . . . We have for the last month or so been . . . involved romantically."

Billie Sunday thought, The fan's been turned on high, and the shit is flying hard at it.

Mairead O'Clare was too stunned to think of asking anything when Pitt continued.

"I don't know anything about Chuck's—Mr. Vareika's—disappearance, except to say I had nothing to do with it. I expect you'll wish to ask me certain questions, but allow me to elaborate a bit first." She resettled her rump on the chair. "I've been divorced for ten years after a marriage of twelve, one daughter, now age twenty-one and a junior attending college in Maine. She was here in Massachusetts this past weekend, mostly visiting my ex-husband. I have always been able to keep my personal life separate from my professional one, both as a partner in a large firm and as a judge for the last decade. Recently, however, another member of the bench has been . . . pursuing me romantically, though unsuccessfully. I've given Mr. Gold a list of the names and contact information for all the foregoing people, and many others as well."

When Pitt paused, Mairead thought the woman might just be letting Billie catch up on the dictation, but then realized their apparent client was more bouncing the ball back over to Shel.

He said, "The obvious concern here is that Judge Pitt doesn't want to be drawn into a scandal like the one involving former Congressman Gary Condit and his intern, Chandra Levy, in Washington, D.C."

Mairead thought, Good luck on that score, you bed a lover probably half your age.

Young lady? said Sister Bernadette's voice.

Shel tented his fingers on the top of his desk. "Judge Pitt is also concerned about the impact such a scandal would have on the judiciary in general and female jurists in particular."

Mairead watched the woman take a deep breath before saying, "For the first time in a long while, the Commonwealth has a budget shortfall, made all the worse by the terrorist attacks of September eleventh. Courthouses across the state are literally falling apart, and employees have even brought lawsuits regarding those unsafe conditions. The legislature is locked in a death struggle over funding with the first woman ever to be named chief justice of our Supreme Judicial Court. A female judge of my own court is being investigated by the Judicial Conduct Commission regarding her supposedly 'lenient' handling of a child-molestation case. Thanks to the outcry over this, the speaker of the Massachusetts house has begun calling for the election of judges instead of our current, life-tenure appointments."

Pitt took another breath, and Mairead found herself actually starting to feel sorry for the woman.

"However," said Pitt, "it gets worse. There are allegations that attorneys on one side of a significant family-business lawsuit may have tried to 'turn' that judge's law clerk toward obtaining 'dirt' on his superior to use as leverage in the business dispute. And, as luck would have it, the female colleague involved is the same one who presided over the controversial child-molestation case I mentioned earlier."

Mairead thought, Well, better her than you, right?

Pitt groaned. "But now, in a high-profile, nationally watched clergy rape trial, with jackals from the press and conflicting personal interest groups howling incessantly in the corridors of justice, the law clerk assigned to the female judge—and who has been enjoying . . . assignations with her—has disappeared without explanation."

Pitt seemed to be finished, at least for a while, so Mairead said, "Judge, do we know if *your* clerk, Mr. Vareika, was 'approached' by anyone in the trial you're currently conducting?"

Sheldon A. Gold watched Barbara Pitt turn halfway, to get a better look at the female attorney who was probably about the age of his old lover's new lover.

Pitt said, "No, we don't. But the last time I saw Chuck—Mr. . . . . oh, hell, 'Chuck' it is—he did seem distracted by something."

Shel leaned forward. "And when was this, the last time you saw Mr. Vareika?"

Pitt moved a hand to her face and wiped her mouth daintily, as though she held a delicate hankie. "Saturday morning. Over breakfast in bed."

It seemed to Shel that nobody wanted to pick up on that one.

"I did try to reach Chuck on his cell phone, late Saturday afternoon, and last night, and again early this morning. Only his voice mail answered each time."

Now Pitt glanced around at all of them. "You do appreciate my dilemma? I'm presiding over a case that one newspaper columnist has decried as 'a stain upon the robe' of the entire Catholic Church, and here I am, arguably creating 'a stain upon the robe' of the entire Massachusetts judiciary."

"So," said Shel to Mairead and Billie, "here's *our* dilemma. Can we look into Mr. Vareika's disappearance without tipping anybody that we're representing Judge Pitt?"

Mairead raised her hand this time, more like a schoolgirl in a classroom. "Shel, am I right that the police won't act on a 'missing person' for forty-eight hours?"

Shel was thinking that the Pope—an ex–homicide detective—would know for sure. Which also made Shel wonder if the New England School of Law graduate's question might not be a pretty clever way of implying that Murizzi should have been with them from the beginning.

Admit it: You forgot to follow up why Pitt didn't want him here.

Shel said, "Judge, where does Mr. Vareika . . . uh, actually live?"

Pitt looked down at her hands, wrestling like snakes in her lap. "He shares an apartment with a roommate, though I've never visited it. We've spent most of our time together in my condominium near Harvard Square."

Mairead didn't raise her hand this time. "Did you call the roommate when Mr. Vareika didn't show up this morning?"

"My law clerk did. Chuck never returned to his place, either Saturday or last night."

Shel noticed Billie look up from her pad and say, "I thought this Mr. Charles Vareika *was* your law clerk?"

A certain smile from Pitt. The first time Shel had seen it thirty years before, he had thought it condescending, and he saw no reason to change his opinion now.

Pitt said, "Chuck was my 'research' clerk, a recent law school graduate on his first real job. My 'administrative' clerk is Florinda Altamira, a mainstay of the judicial system, rather like a career sergeant in the army."

Billie's husband, Robert, Sr., had been a "career" sergeant as well, and Shel felt she didn't like their client's choice of metaphor. "Judge Pitt tells me that nobody—not even Ms. Altamira—knows of her relationship with Mr. Vareika."

"Correct," said Pitt.

Frankly, Shel thought his former lover was relying more on hope than experience for that one, and he sensed similar feelings from both Mairead and Billie. "However," Shel holding up a sheet of paper, "the judge has provided me with this fairly long list of individuals we might speak to about Mr. Vareika's disappearance, including some of the rather vocal 'interest groups' pursuing their own agendas in and around the *Dooley* case. Copies will be made for all of us. But the question remains, can we investigate without tipping who our client is and why she wants to know these things?"

"With all respect," said Mairead, "I think the best person to decide that isn't here right now."

Sheldon A. Gold watched the Honorable Barbara Quincy Pitt begin nodding in agreement, though her eyes were squinched shut.

TWO

Mairead O'Clare walked downhill from Shel Gold's law offices on Beacon Street near the State House. Moving through the City Hall Plaza and then taking its steps to the Fanueil Hall level, she wondered what could have possessed a woman of Barbara Pitt's stature to enter an affair with a guy right out of law school.

People yearn for different things, young lady. Attaining one, like "stature," might just fan the flame for another, like love.

Mairead thought that was fair enough, and she'd certainly had strong romantic urges toward older men herself. But she believed a little more in daughters falling in love with father figures than sons with mother ones.

Yeah, right. Here I am, the girl raised in an orphanage, offering intra-family Freudian analysis.

Shaking her head, Mairead found a usable walkway through Boston's Big Dig—no mean feat, as the huge construction project's passages tended to change at least weekly and sometimes even daily. She came upon Christopher Columbus Park and the condo wharves and marinas extending into Boston harbor. Mairead spotted a restaurant as landmark, then went down the nearby stairs to a floating dock that would bring her to the blue-and-white houseboat of Pontifico Murizzi. From four slips away, she could see him sitting in one of the white resin chairs on his back deck, reading something. It was a warm evening, and he'd stripped down to just gym shorts and flip-flops, displaying his Richard Gere hunkiness in an offhanded way that reminded Mairead of why she'd nearly lost her heart to him when they first met five months earlier.

Before she really knew him.

"Hey, Pope," Mairead called out from ten feet away. "Don't you keep your cell phone on anymore?"

His eyes stayed glued to whatever he was reading. "Irish, how many times I got to say it? You want to sneak up on a guy, surprise him, you need to change your stride, so the rhythm of it doesn't bring back a memory of you moving toward him."

Mairead remembered the first time she "surprised" Murizzi, only to find herself staring down the muzzle of a gun. "Maybe I wanted you to know it was me. Same question on the cell, though."

"It's down below, getting recharged. What's your hurry?"

Mairead took out her own. "Shel's got a client who needs to speak with you." She hit the button for Phonebook, then scrolled down to Shel's office speed-dial.

"Now?" said the Pope. "I don't remember any recent homicides where the moke hasn't already lawyered up with somebody else."

"I think this is more a 'homicide-in-waiting,' but with an innocent client nonetheless." Mairead checked the face of her phone, be sure the call was going through. "Anyway, what're you reading that's so important?"

Murizzi held up a slick tear sheet. "Friend of mine gave me this, from *Boston Magazine*. Seems this kids' camp up in Maine, once school kicks back in, goes gay and lesbian, but for adults."

"A summer camp after Labor Day," said Mairead, deadpan until she was sure he was serious.

"Yeah. The cabins are named after famous gays like Elton John or lesbians like Melissa Etheridge. They've got all kinds of activities, too, from rock climbing and that kind of shit down to tea dances and drag shows. About half and half, men and women."

As Mairead said, "I thought you once told me you hated Maine," she heard Billie pick up the office phone. "I'm with the Pope. Ask Shel to get on the same extension, okay?"

Murizzi put down the tear sheet. "You still haven't nudged the boss into springing for a speakerphone?"

Mairead hoped the expression on her face was answer enough, then handed her cell to the Pope.

Into it, he said, "Hey, Shel, how you doing?" Now a frown. "Yeah, I know her all right, from back when I was on—" The frown deepened.

Mairead had trouble figuring out Murizzi's facial reactions.

"Shel," said the Pope, "I'm not sure it's such a good idea to talk about this over a cellular. I mean, probably nobody's trying to listen in, but these things aren't much more than walkie-talkies that use radio waves. . . . Fifteen minutes, if I don't have to shower and shave."

The Pope grunted out what seemed to Mairead a reluctant laugh, then said, "Right. See you then."

He handed the cellular back to her. "Sorry you had to play Pony Express here, Irish."

Mairead put the phone back in her handbag. "You and Judge Pitt have some . . . history, then?"

"Ancient history," said Pontifico Murizzi as he rose from the resin chair and handed her the tear sheet. "But you can read about my new adventure while I put on a shirt and get my own cell."

Actually, the Pope put on a shirt, slacks, socks, and shoes, "business casual," as he understood the term. And, Mairead preceding him into Shel's office, they upped the party's roster to five.

Murizzi could tell the guy was a little relieved to see his private investigator so well turned out. Shel, old-school, had on his typical parts of a suit and accessories, though he looked like he'd worn them for pajamas, too.

The Pope took his usual position, standing with his back against the old Wild West safe that had already been in the eleventh-floor office when he first visited it years before. The height and angle gave him a drop-dead view of the Boston Common, the Public Garden, and the Victorian neighborhood of Back Bay beyond them.

"Mr. Murizzi," said Her Honor, rather coolly to the Pope's ear.

And with good fucking reason. "Judge."

"Thanks for joining us," said Shel.

Murizzi nodded a couple, three times as Shel recited some details he hadn't given over Irish's cell phone. Then the Pope checked his watch. "I got five thirty-five P.M., meaning your clerk's been officially AWOL for almost nine hours, right?"

"No," said Pitt. "I haven't seen Chuck since early Saturday."

Chuck. "I said 'officially,' Judge. As his boss, you wouldn't know he's been missing that long until you got to the courthouse this morning, and your other clerk, Altamira, phoned his roommate."

Cool became a little frosty. "I suppose that is correct, yes."

"But still, Vareika's never bugged out before without notice, right?"

"Also correct."

"So, how come you didn't report him missing before this?"

A sigh. "You've already answered that question for me. Since my administrative clerk called Chuck's apartment, and his roommate said he'd not returned home Saturday or last night, I didn't see that he'd had an accident or any other mishap on his way to work at the courthouse."

The Pope shook his head. "Doesn't feel right to me. This honor student with perfect attendance breaks his record without letting anybody know, you need him on this heavy trial with the priest, and you don't call out the dogs?"

"Mr. Murizzi," said Pitt, icy now. "I am not on trial here."

"Not yet, maybe."

No one spoke for five seconds.

Shel finally said, "We might be getting a little ahead of ourselves."

The Pope was going to reply when Irish did.

"No," said Mairead. "I think it *does* look funny that there's been no follow-up at all. Would your administrative clerk still be at the courthouse?"

"I asked Flo not to leave my lobby until I called her."

Murizzi always thought it was screwy for the judges in Massachusetts to use "lobby" for what everywhere else was called "chambers," but he saw his opening. "I'd call her, then, and have her try the roommate one more time. If Altamira doesn't get a better answer, you or your admin clerk ought to call the police. Ask for Missing Persons."

"But—" began Pitt.

The Pope waved her off. "They're not going to do much, especially since it's hard to tell from what you know that Vareika's been gone long enough to file a report on him. But the point is, you tried. And got frustrated."

Pitt said, "I do not see how this plan puts me in a *better* position than I occupied two hours ago."

Shel leaned forward in his chair. "I think I do. You've already given us a long list of people who might have some impact on Mr. Vareika's life. That suggests that whoever investigates his apparent disappearance will have a hard time keeping the inquiring client's identity a secret. Mr. Murizzi's approach allows for a 'frustrated' citizen to turn to legal counsel and a private investigator when the formal system of justice, one she's a part of herself, simply doesn't address the issue promptly enough."

The Pope loved Shel. The lawyer knew Murizzi was right, but was smart enough to let the judge see it for herself without the shouting match the Pope figured would otherwise be necessary to knock some sense into the stubborn bat's head.

"So," said Pitt, after seeming to mull it over, "I hire you, Shelly, and you bring in your other staff, including Mr. Murizzi, to help the concerned superior find out what happened to her subordinate when the authorities are lax."

All the Pope could think was, Shelly?

When nobody challenged Pitt's statement, she said, "Very well. Where do we go from here?"

Shel said, "I'll offer a thought. After you call Ms. Altamira, Mairead will go over to speak with her about any other information she might have. The courthouse ought to be quiet enough this time of day, and young lawyers are always asking experienced administrative clerks how to get things done. Pope, if Ms. Altamira doesn't get a helpful response from the roommate, then you go over to Mr. Vareika's apartment."

"A suggestion?" said Murizzi. "Before I go anywhere, let me call in some chips at Homicide, have them do a slab-and-bed check on this Vareika."

As Pitt began shaking her head, Irish said, "A slab-and . . . ?"

The Pope nodded. "Morgue and hospitals, with emphasis on their emergency rooms."

"No." Pitt was still shaking her head. "I do *not* want the police involved. Or to know that I may *be* involved, however . . . innocently."

Murizzi heard that last as a code word, but didn't let go of his idea. "Judge, you want—and need—a cover story for our looking into your clerk's disappearance. If it turns out Vareika's worse off than just 'missing,' you'll look better to a homicide detective if I asked an old buddy to do the routine check."

Mairead said, "If Judge Pitt calls Missing Persons, though, won't they know about at least any hospital patients?"

"Only if the hospital thinks to call the John Doe in."

"Well, then," said Shel, kind of quickly. "Why don't we wait to hear back from Ms. Altamira—about the roommate and, if necessary, Missing Persons—before you call Homicide to request that check?"

Pitt nodded, so the Pope did, too.

Shel made three. "However, Judge, I do think that unless Mr. Vareika has returned to his apartment, Mr. Murizzi should at least go see the roommate to find out just what he knows."

"She," said Pitt.

Murizzi noticed that all four of Shel's team were looking at Her Honor. Fasten your fucking seat belts, folks.

"Chuck has assured me it's completely platonic, but his roommate is a young woman named Vivianna Klein. Their address and home telephone are on the list I've already provided."

"Judge," said Shel. "It would be a help to me, and possibly better cover for you, to stay here in my office for a while. I believe everyone else can get started, including Billie heading home to her family."

Shel Gold waited until Barbara Pitt used his office phone to call her administrative clerk, making the Pope's request of trying Vareika's roommate again, and, if no satisfaction, Missing Persons. When Pitt hung up on Florinda Altamira, Shel said to his new client, "Not the best of days, eh?"

"Nor the worst." The judge dropped her attitude. "Do you remember that time in Contracts first year, when Clark Byse called on me?"

Shel did. The terrifying-though-effective professor had been scanning his seating chart of names and photographs in the steep, amphitheater classroom for the next victim of his Socratic method of questioning students. Back then, Harvard Law School had been so overwhelmingly "male" that there were more black men than women of any color. Suddenly, Pitt coughed, and Byse snapped straight up like a hawk sensing prey, saying, "Who just coughed? Was that . . . was that you, Ms. Pitt?"

When she admitted it had been, the professor grilled her for the rest of the hour. But Pitt maintained her voice—and poise—amazingly, after every good question giving Byse a better answer.

Shel said, "That which does not kill us makes us stronger, Barbara."

"Tell me about it. No, don't. Just let me thank you for seeing me and . . . caring about me. Especially after the way we broke up."

Another memory, not so bad as instructive. Shel—the street kid and former boxer from Chelsea—had been dating Pitt for about a month back in law school when she decided to bring him to a "family outing" at her uncle's place. The "place" turned out to be an estate in Manchester-by-the-Sea, overlooking the ocean, large sailboats in full flight. His date had needed her drink freshened, and as Shel approached the bar, he heard her uncle say to another man, "Christ, Miss Barbie Q. Pitt. First a jigaroo from her college, now a kike from her law school. What'll she drag home next?"

"An Irish-Catholic?" said the man, reducing both to paroxysms of laughter to the point that Shel was pretty sure they'd never noticed him backing away. But Pitt didn't believe his lie of a splitting headache as the excuse for his bailing out of the "outing" shortly thereafter, and he'd told her the truth.

"Shelly?"

For just a second there, he was a first-year law student again, back at her uncle's estate, not in his spacious suite atop a building he'd owned mortgage-free for over a decade. "Sorry, Barbara. Do you have any more questions?"

"No, I don't think so. You—and your people—have come up with a workable plan, and you were right, we should have included Mr. Murizzi from the beginning."

"Why didn't we, then?"

Barbara Pitt looked the way she'd sounded whenever the Pope had asked her a question, but she now spoke in a flat voice. "I sat on some murder trials of his. Not all of them ended . . . successfully."

Shel thought about asking, "For whom?" but he had a different topic to raise now. "Another question?"

Even under the circumstances, a slight smile toyed with the corners of Pitt's mouth. "I think you've earned at least two."

"Why me, Barbara?"

"Meaning, why did I come to you about all this?"

"Yes."

Shel thought he might get a soft-shoe answer, like the one about her previous dealings with Murizzi. Instead, she said, "Three reasons, Shelly. One, we were classmates, and I trust your sense of integrity. Two, you went into criminal law while most of our classmates didn't, and I felt that specialty was what I needed the most."

When Pitt hesitated, Shel said, "And the third reason?"

The judge blinked a few times. "I'm not sure how well matched we were thirty years ago, Shelly, but I had the feeling we truly loved each other then, and therefore I thought you might work a little harder for me now."

Sheldon A. Gold nodded. But he couldn't help thinking there might be a fourth, even more Machiavellian reason for her choice: Asking a virtually solo practitioner of criminal law to check out her missing law clerk would look to the world as though Barbara Q. Pitt couldn't be deeply interested in Charles Vareika, especially since the practitioner himself was, after all, just a . . . "kike."

THREE

Pontifico Murizzi had walked to within sight of his marina when the cell phone bleated in his pocket and he took it out.

"Murizzi."

"Pope," said Shel, "we just received a return call from Ms. Altamira. She got no answer at Mr. Vareika's apartment, so she reported his name and description to Missing Persons."

"And?"

"Ms. Altamira was told they had no record of any patient with Mr. Vareika's identification, nor of any John Doe fitting his description."

"So I'm cleared to call Artie Chin at Homicide?"

"Yes."

"I'll do it on the way to the clerk's roommate."

"But there was no answer just now at their apartment."

"Shel, a lot of people don't answer the phone after work, but it's a bitch listening to the doorbell for half an hour."

Clicking off, Murizzi was glad to have given the lawyer a laugh, as Shel Gold had been dealt a hand in this life tougher than most had to play.

The Pope reached his Ford Explorer Sport in the marina's parking lot and climbed in, hitting Artie Chin's direct dial at Police Headquarters.

Murizzi had just pulled into the usual nightmare of Big Dig traffic on Commercial Street when he heard, "Homicide, Sergeant Detective Chin."

"Hey, Artie. How you doing?"

"Pope, better you asked me six months ago, before the commissioner hit the roof over our year-end."

The cumulative report on annual homicides. "What was the total again?"

"Sixty-eight. More than double the bodies two years ago."

"Yeah, but that's not your fault, Artie. Shit, we had a hundred fifty-two back in 'ninety, remember?"

"I remember," said Chin. "And, thanks to the fucking terrorists, New York City had almost three thousand more tacked onto its total. And who knows how many more in D.C., it wasn't for those guys on the flight that crashed in Pennsylvania." Chin paused, then continued in a different tone. "I got to say, Pope. I thought about you when it turned out one of that plane's heroes was gay."

Mark Bingham, and a little rush of pride surged through Murizzi again, despite the tragedy. "Yeah, Artie, but for Boston, we brought the stats down so far by putting away about a battalion of the gang-bangers who couldn't shoot straight."

"I know, I know. Only a lot of them were juvies then, and so the ones the Anti-Gang Unit could nail for only some kind of assault are back on the streets, older but no wiser. And the homicide numbers would be even worse, it wasn't for the great trauma units the city has now."

The Pope recalled a doctor once telling him about the "golden hour" after a vic got stabbed or shot, and how in that sixty minutes the intervention of a dozen trauma experts from EMTs to chest surgeons could give the poor fuck a real chance at survival. "Artie, speaking of hospitals?"

"Yeah?" a little wariness creeping into Chin's voice.

"Could you run a slab-and-bed for me on a guy?"

"What, you don't know anybody in Missing Persons anymore?"

"Client already tried them. No ID or physical description matches anybody in their system."

"And this can't wait till Missing Persons gets around to your guy themselves?"

"Artie, as a favor to me?"

"Okay, okay." The Pope could hear some paper rustling. "Start with the last name."

By the time Murizzi had finished the drill with Chin, thanked him, and hung up, the home address for Charles Vareika on Judge Hot Pants' list came into view. It turned out to be at the edge of Boston's South End, the neighborhood west of Bay Village and south of Back Bay. The Pope had taken his truck mainly because he figured to find a parking space, no problem. Except the South End had come up in the world since the last time he'd cruised it.

Back in the seventies, when Murizzi joined the force as a new uniform, the area had been a snake pit of abandoned cars—stripped of tires and chopped for parts—slumped at the curb outside burned-out husks of buildings with plywood for window glass and derelicts sleeping under the six to twelve-step stoops of the old brick and brownstone town houses. In the eighties, the South End just couldn't quite shake its rep as an outdoor, round-the-clock drugstore for scumbags who didn't have prescriptions to get the shit they bought for cash. But come the nineties, Murizzi had started hearing better things about the neighborhood. Gays coming in and restoring whole blocks, families of post-yuppies needing the public schools to get better and the streets safer, and the Cuban-Americans getting bolstered by prosperous Marielitos moving north after ten years in Miami to join their more-established, Castro-era relatives.

Now, as the Pope eased his SUV around the corner, he was having a hell of a time finding a parking space among all the Subaru Outbacks, Mazda Miatas, and even the occasional Lexus and Infiniti.

Jeez, where are all the poor people living these days, huh?

Murizzi finally found a spot just forward of a hydrant and walked back to Vareika's address, which turned out to be one of the nicer brownstones on a near-perfect block. The Pope looked up the twelve steps to the front entrance, but from his angle, he couldn't see whether anybody was in the foyer on the other side of the glass doors.

Murizzi climbed the stoop, almost more an exterior grand staircase, the edges of the steps all repointed, the iron railings on either side painted black with no rust showing. Even the casements for the bow window looked new. The Pope had read articles in the *Herald* about how lawyers coming out of school were making crazy fucking salaries—hundred to a hundred and a half per annum—at the large, traditionally Yankee firms, but he couldn't imagine the county or even the state laying out that kind of money for a kid who probably couldn't find the courthouse without a map.

At the top of the stoop, Murizzi still didn't see anybody, either in the foyer between the two doors or around the inner staircase leading up. There was a buzzer system, though, with a button reading "Klein/Vareika" as maybe the ground floor or basement. The Pope pushed, didn't hear anything, and so pushed again, this time rotating the button around in its setting, be sure to get a good connection. Still no sound, so he decided to give it a minute before following the observation he'd made to Shel Gold, about torturing a resident with the doorbell.

With maybe ten seconds to go by his internal clock, a young woman with black curly hair—plastered shiny, like from the shower—came out a door near the back of the first floor and to the side of the interior staircase. She used one hand to clutch a bathrobe around her, the other to shade her eyes like an Indian scout, trying to see through the glass doors. As the woman got closer, the Pope thought she looked kind of pissed.

But then, so did the Doberman pinscher that trotted alongside her. The dog had what Murizzi always thought of as the breed's classic characteristics: black-and-tan coat, ears clipped and tail bobbed, lots of teeth.

The woman opened the inner door, then stepped through, keeping it propped open by her back, bare foot, the Doberman slipping between her legs to stare up at the Pope. The woman was twenty-something, with attractive features.

And definitely pissed as she cracked the outside door. "I specifically told the company to send my package 'no signature required.'"

Murizzi looked down at the "business casual" he wore, not exactly his idea of a delivery uniform. "I'm not from the company, Ms. Klein."

"Oh." Now Vivianna Klein looked the Pope up and down herself, but with more an assessing look than a confused one. "Well, who are you, then?"

Murizzi took out the laminated copy of his private-eye license in its leather folder. "I've been asked to look into the disappearance of Charles Vareika."

The hand that wasn't holding the robe together raked through her wet, stringy hair. "So, you're from the court?"

"No. Like it says on the license, I'm a private investigator."

Now Klein actually read the thing. "Pontifico Murizzi." A flirty smile. "Come on back . . . Pontifico."

He followed Klein and the dog through the foyer doors, thinking for the hundredth time, If you knew what it was, you could maybe bottle it and make a fortune. Despite the sexual orientation that he'd sensed since kindergarten but fortunately had had the brains not to mention, much less act on, till way later, females of all ages and races had always found the Pope attractive. They'd sit next to him in school cafeterias, make room for him at sporting events, even ask him to save their seats in bars so they could have an excuse for talking after coming back from the toilet.

Okay, not exactly a curse, but a little bit embarrassing, considering Murizzi would usually have his own eye on the bouncer.

Klein reached her apartment door and went through, beckoning him to follow by doing pinkie-to-index rolls of her fingers, reminding the Pope of how a tarantula walked. Inside the apartment, she descended a half-flight of stairs with a sashay, like the belle of the ball at a barn dance. Then Klein plopped into a plum-colored sectional piece. The Doberman hopped onto another, did two three-sixties, and went down on its haunches, eyes on Murizzi.

He said, "What's the dog's name?"

"Miata." The creature lifted its head at Klein's voice, clipped ears standing up straight. "I named her after my car."

Probably one of the vehicles made you have to park a block away. "Easy to remember, but it must get pretty embarrassing, you yell, 'Miata,' and both a Doberman and a Mazda come running."

More suggestiveness seeped into Klein's voice. "I guess all three of us have odd names, huh?"

"What's so odd about yours?"

"Well, 'V-I-V-I-A-N' would be the typical spelling, but my mother spoke Spanish as her first language, and my father was Jewish, so it's not like I had to get a saint's name. And Mom had a friend named Vivian, so mine was run through the Spanish spin cycle and 'Vivianna' is what came out. My roommate's, like, Lithuanian, but at least he rated a normal first name." A grimace. "Only you got stuck with the guy who lives in the Vatican, right?"

Which made the Pope take in Klein's "chamber." The large living room had high windows overlooking a small, brick-based patio garden enclosed by a stockade fence. Long drapes picked up one of the many colors from the oriental rug centered in the room, the matching sectional furniture picking up another. Sparsely furnished with other shit like lamps, an oil portrait of a blond hunk over the mantelpiece, and some freestanding sculptures. All tasteful, both in size and hues.

"Nice place," he said.

Murizzi thought Klein might string out the flirting, but it was like she suddenly remembered why the Pope was visiting her. "Is there any word from Chuck?"

Same nickname for him the judge used. "Not that I know of," said the Pope. "I was kind of hoping he might have called you here."

A shake of the head, a few drops of water first beading at her hairline, then worming their way down her forehead until she swiped them away, the robe bowing outward at about breast level. "I'm sure he'll be okay, though."

"He's done this kind of thing before?"

A frown, two lines of flesh like vertical lips between her eyebrows. "What 'kind of thing'?"

"Staying out a couple nights in a row, no notice?"

A shrug, the lapels of her robe dancing a little more. "Like I said before, Chuck and I are just roommates, Pontifico."

She'd deflected his question, but Murizzi decided to follow up this line first. "Not a couple?"

"Not even a hookup."

Last few years, the Pope had heard the expression from people around her age. Hooking up for sex, not love or forever after. "Is Vareika 'hooked up' with anybody else?"

Klein wiggled her toes, seeming anything but childlike in doing it. "I'm not the type to . . . listen and tell, Pontifico."

"Even if the connection could help me find your roommate?"

She seemed to weigh something. Then Klein opened her hands so the palms were bookend clam shells to the air between them. "Look, you asked before if Chuck's stayed out all night—"

"Two nights—"

"—without letting me know. The answer is, we both have. And the one who didn't hear from the other gave the other hell for it. I mean, you want your parents to treat you like a grown-up, you have to treat your friends that way, too, right?"

The Pope pictured the judge's list. "Vareika's parents live in New Hampshire, right?"

Klein seemed to weigh that as well. "A little town on the beach. I think his old man has a service station or something."

The American Dream, thought Murizzi: from gas jockey to esquire in one generation. "They heard from him?"

"I don't know."

"Meaning, you haven't contacted them?"

"For God's sakes, Pontifico. Chuck's twenty-six years old, and he's been gone all of like, two days? Not even, maybe. He left me a message on our tape machine Saturday."

The Pope perked up. "You save the message?"

"No."

"You had any messages *since* his?"

Klein seemed uncertain now. "Why?"

"Because if you haven't, his might still be on there."

She became a weigher of things again. "We can try, you want to."

"Where's your machine?"

Klein got up, crossed the room past the fireplace, and pointed to a bizarre entertainment center/bookshelf thing that had no symmetry to it, for Murizzi the one sore thumb in the room. He looked at the machine, reading its labeled keys, then lifted the lid to read about its bells and whistles, of which there were few. Accordingly, he hit Play and heard the tape rewind. After ten seconds, he heard, "Hey, luv, it's

Chuck. I've got to see somebody, so I might not be back till way late. Don't wait dinner, and don't wait up. Bye."

As the machine stopped and rewound, a couple of things struck Murizzi. First, Vareika sounded in words a little closer than just a "roommate": "luv," "don't wait up." Second, while his tone seemed harried, there was no indication that he thought he'd be gone overnight. And, if that came about anyway, why didn't Vareika give Klein another call, ease her mind like this message was supposed to?

The Pope said, "He never called later?"

"If he did, I didn't hear it. But, like Chuck mentioned on the tape—about my not waiting up?—I had an early event yesterday morning."

Still didn't feel right to Murizzi. If Vareika wasn't coming back Saturday night, why not wish her luck on the Sunday event? "You have a cell phone?"

"Of course."

"Have it on this past Saturday?"

"No. I was home here, so that one there was good enough."

"Sunday?"

"Not in the morning, but I checked for messages both nights."

"Did you check it today, too, see if Vareika called you since?"

Klein stopped longer to weigh that question than she had the previous ones. "I checked my voice mail before lunch, and then again before I left work. Nothing from him either time." A head shake, the hair still wet enough not to move much. "But look, you're blowing this, like, way out of proportion. I mean, Chuck always thinks a thing through, makes up his mind, and then just does it."

The Pope figured Nike would be proud of the guy. "I'm told Vareika has a cell phone?"

"Well, duh, doesn't everybody?"

Murizzi thought of Shel as the exception that probably proved Klein's rule. "Have you tried reaching your roommate on his?"

"No."

"Why not?"

"Hey, why should I? I mean, Chuck's the one who should be, like, checking in with me."

Murizzi noticed Klein's expression change, as maybe she realized that last line was a reversal of her earlier stand on "just roommates," but all Klein did was flap her wrists outward and say, "Whatever."

"This Sunday morning event of yours. Where was it?"

"At the clinic."

"The clinic?"

"The Dufresne Institute for Holistic Health. We do work on body and mind interface and interweave."

Christ on a crutch. "What's your job there?"

"I'm a researcher."

"Anything in particular?"

Klein smiled, the flirty one again. "Human sexuality, Pontifico, and lots of our clients prefer to . . . come on Sundays. Care to volunteer for a study?"

Murizzi smiled back, took out a pad and pencil. If she thought he was calling her bluff, she gave no indication of waffling. "I'm gonna take down this tape message word for word. You have a photo of Vareika I could borrow?"

"A photo? I suppose I can find one, sure. But that's the best likeness of him, for both looks *and* personality."

The Pope was busy punching the Play button again, so he didn't get her drift. "Which is?"

Now he looked up as Vivianna Klein pointed, with some glitter in her eyes, at the oil portrait of the blond hunk hanging over the fireplace.

Murizzi said, "That's Vareika?"

"Yes."

Focusing on the thing, it seemed to the Pope that it was pretty well done. "Portrait like that probably costs a lot of money."

Klein smiled this time in a way Murizzi couldn't read, and he decided that he'd like somebody else as a quality control on her relationship with Vareika.

Then Vivianna Klein rolled her shoulders like a kitten who'd just awakened from a nap. "Chuck told me a *very* grateful friend sprang for it."

Pontifico Murizzi began writing down Charles Vareika's tape message, but the Pope was thinking, Judge, Judge, you've left one hell of a trail through the fucking forest of love.

Hey, Mom, what's for dinner?" said Robert, Jr., barely glancing up from his computer screen.

Her oldest was the second of her sons to ask Billie Sunday about that night's menu, and she was barely through the back door of their four-bedroom house. William, her youngest, had rattled on in the car all the way home from after-school straddle care on his personal favorites and dislikes, as gathered by the ripe old age of eight and a half. Her middle son, Matthew, hadn't chimed in, but Billie expected that was less because he didn't have a question on the subject and more that he probably wasn't home yet his ownself.

On the other hand, give thanks. For months after the World Trade Center towers fell, William—always a worrying child anyway—would ask whether terrorists were going to kill his momma in Mr. Gold's office building, too. Billie had sought counseling for William at school, but they said it was natural for kids his age to "localize" every danger, believe Godzilla or a tidal wave—or a guided-missile airliner—would automatically attack their own little part of the world next.

On the third hand, though, Billie had overheard Matthew telling Robert, Jr., that ever since September 11th, white people treated him differently. Like if he and some of his friends got on a subway, the white passengers would look up, scared as always, but once it was clear they were "just" black American teenagers, there were smiles and nods, even winks. "Robert," Matthew had said, "it's like the whites were relieved we were *only* gangstas, account of we'd beat the shit out of any terrorist threatening their asses because ours'd be in danger, too."

Think what it says about race relations in this town, you can call that a silver lining to what happened in New York City.

Leaving William to put away the canned goods under the counter where he could reach, Billie came up behind Robert, Jr., a riot of color and graphics slowly resolving on the screen in front of him. "What are you looking at?"

Over his shoulder, the athletic young man said, "College catalogs."

"On the computer?"

"They have them on CDs, too, but for skimming it's just simpler using the Internet than making my CPU become a DVD player.

Billie understood the individual words and acronyms, if not entirely how they fit together to make a sensible sentence. "Which places have you seen so far?"

"I'm working through the baseball factories that offer full scholarships."

Billie believed this son, just finishing his junior year in high school, was the brightest of her three, but wasn't sure she cared for what he'd just said. "Isn't that like letting the tail of sports wag the dog of education?"

"Education is what you work hard to learn, Mom, not the name of the campus or building where you do it. And if I can get a free ride after next year, it'll make it easier for you when it's Matthew's and William's time."

Billie blinked back a tear. Their father, her beloved Robert, Sr., had been taken from them by a drunk driver. Thanks to Shel Gold's lawyering, the insurance settlement had been enough to pay off the mortgage and set aside money for all three boys' college costs. At least until that same September 11th, and what had happened to the values in the mutual funds Shel had helped her choose as investments. Billie didn't blame Shel—or President Bush, or anybody else except those soulless terrorists—for what had happened to her country and her finances. However, the downward slide in the nation's economy and her stock holdings made Robert, Jr., sound maybe more right than wrong about his search approach.

Billie said, "You got any favorites yet?"

"The Arizona and Florida ones. Coach thinks I should aim high, though they'd be long shots for me."

And long distances for him to travel, there and back, meaning probably only summers and some major holidays with all three of her sons around her. "Anyplace else?"

"Louisiana State, Oklahoma State . . ."

Then again, you've got to let go of him sometime.

Billie Sunday, shaking her head after being sure her oldest child couldn't see the gesture, turned back to help her youngest put away stuff that belonged on shelves he couldn't reach.

Mairead O'Clare finally cleared security at the Congress Street entrance to the old federal courthouse that Suffolk Superior rented while its own, even older space was being renovated. The security line had been held up, as the uniformed officers couldn't figure out why a teenaged girl kept setting off the metal detector. At least until she stuck out her tongue, revealing a huge, stainless-steel stud through it.

Mairead thought, Ugh.

She made her way into the building's main lobby, the post office section already closed. The elevator—big enough to hold a VW bug—was slow, but it opened on the floor where Judge Barbara Pitt had said her courtroom and lobby would be. The tall, wide corridor of stone echoed as Mairead's heels tapped down the floor, nobody else in sight at that time of the evening.

Coming to the right door, Mairead entered the nearly empty courtroom, a lone bailiff jumping up from a chair on the right side of the bench area. Mairead guessed him to be about six feet and one-ninety, solid more than muscular, with hair—a shade darker than her auburn—cropped short. He was chewing on what looked like a Zwiebach, the hard and crumbly baby cookie.

"Can I help you?"

"I'm here to see Florinda Altamira?"

The bailiff nodded. "You're Ms. O'Clare?"

"Yes."

"The judge called us about you. I'm Tommy Flanagan."

They shook hands.

A powerfully strong man, young lady.

Which made Mairead unable to resist glancing at the half-moon cookie in his other hand. "You really like the taste of those?"

A sheepish grin, close enough to Shel's that she immediately liked the guy.

Flanagan said, "Actually, I can't tell the taste of anything, Counselor."

"I don't follow you."

"I used to play a lot of ice hockey, so when Rollerblading hit, I gave it a try. I figured, hey, no bodychecking, no helmet, right?"

Personally, Mairead thought that was like riding a motorcycle without one, but she just nodded.

"Anyway, I hit a bump or something, and down I went. Nearly fractured my skull, and when I woke up, my sense of taste—and smell—was gone."

"I'm really sorry."

"Self-inflicted wound. But now I go more for different textures in my food. Rippled potato chips, syrupy drinks, carrots"—now he glanced down—"even things they give teething babies, and I'm like a dog gnawing a bone and loving it."

"Makes sense."

"Yeah." Flanagan tilted his head toward the open doorway on the left wall of the courtroom. "But Flo needs to get home, and I'm holding you up, too, so come on."

Mairead followed him into the kind of anteroom that she always thought of as the clerk's "gate," because it seemed to be the buffer between the courtroom and the judge's lobby beyond.

A woman in her forties with olive skin and a dazzling smile looked up from some paperwork at the larger by far of two desks in the office.

"Flo," said Flanagan, "this is Ms. O'Clare. I'll leave you two alone."

Mairead thanked him, but studied Altamira, too. Her hair was dark brown and wavy, and only when Mairead reached across the desk to shake the woman's hand did the veining and boniness cause the young lawyer to up Altamira's age to more like Shel Gold's fifty-something. While the clerk stayed seated, Mairead noticed—and appreciated—that the woman didn't stare at the hemangioma nor flinch in taking Mairead's hand in hers.

"You are the attorney that Her Honor telephoned me about?"

Just a drizzle of Spanish accent on the English words. "Yes. Mairead O'Clare."

"Could you spell that first name for me, Counselor?"

Mairead did, then settled into a visitor's chair.

"Unusual," said Altamira. "But then, Florinda is, too, although back in Cuba there were many of us."

"When did you come to the States?"

"The year Fidel seized power at home. My parents were lucky to have a relative here in Boston, so he took us in until we could make our own way."

Young lady, note the pride in the woman's voice.

Coming from an orphanage herself, Mairead already had. "Ms. Altamira, I—"

"Oh, please, call me Flo. Everyone else does."

Mairead appreciated the easy way Altamira had about her, then realized she liked both the bailiff and this clerk better than the judge who was the actual client. "In that case, I'm Mairead, not Counselor."

The dazzling smile again. "Fair enough."

"Flo, Judge Pitt told us you called Mr. Vareika's apartment and spoke to his roommate?"

"The first time, yes. This morning."

"And Ms. Klein didn't know where Mr. Vareika went?"

"No, though it would be easier for me if we called Charles by his first name, as well."

Charles to Altamira, Chuck to Pitt. Levels of intimacy, I guess. "Is this the first time Charles didn't show up for work?"

"Yes. Oh, he has been late a few times, but I always assumed he might have been out carousing the night before, because he would look quite tired."

Mairead, barely a year out of law school herself, could identify with that. "Does he seem happy here?"

"Yes, most definitely. Typically a clerk will not be with one judge only for so long, but from the very first, Charles and Her Honor have been inseparable."

Mairead gave it a beat, trying to decide whether there was any double meaning in Altamira's choice of words that would suggest knowledge of the affair.

Then Judge Pitt's administrative clerk shook her head. "Though I must tell you, Charles was at first a little . . . reluctant to accept the assignment."

"The assignment?"

"Yes. Did you clerk for a court before you entered practice?"

"No, but I was a research assistant to one of my professors after my first year at New England."

"Similar job, I think, but a different process. Anyway, Charles is one of the many research clerks interviewed and hired for a year through a committee of our court administrators. The clerks form a pool, and the judges generally share them, with a rotation system of assignments so each of the judges gets some help from several different clerks and each of the clerks gets exposed to several different judges and types of cases—criminal versus civil, jury trials versus injunction hearings, and so on."

"But Charles is different, Flo?"

"Not in the beginning. When he came into the building on his first day in September, pretty much every female head turned. And—I'm progressive enough to say—some of the male ones as well. Charles is both a capable lawyer and a handsome young man. But when Her Honor drew the *Dooley* case, she and the chief judge realized she'd need research help virtually full-time on it, and they and the manager of such services did not think rotating different people in and out— only to force each new clerk to play catch-up—made much sense."

Mairead agreed with them. "Why was Charles chosen?"

"Several reasons, I believe. First, he is Roman Catholic, and Her Honor is not, so there was the advantage of having someone who knew that religion."

Mairead said, "Flo, are you Catholic, too?"

Altamira smiled. "Yes, but there was a second reason as well. I think Her Honor desired a young male's perspective on the case, about what it might be like to realize you were the target of an alleged pedophile like former-Father Dooley."

Mairead felt a little uneasy. "Are you implying that Charles *was* a target when he was younger?"

"Oh, no." Altamira seemed shocked. "Not at all. It is just that Her Honor perhaps felt she required something other than the female perspective in addition to the Catholic one."

Probably didn't hurt that the guy sounds like a hunk, either. "You mentioned before that Charles was a little 'reluctant,' though?"

"Yes." Altamira appeared to search her memory. "He was concerned about being 'typecast' by his experience, since he would be spending so much of his year with the court on a single case, and a criminal one at that. After his clerkship, Charles wants very much to enter a large firm and practice corporate litigation, you see, and, thanks to Her Honor, he has already interviewed with a number of them, which is quite a coup in this economic downturn."

Mairead thought back to her own experience at a "large firm," an opportunity arranged for her by the professor she'd worked with in law school. As far as Mairead was concerned, Vareika was welcome to that life and her share of it, but she also knew that Altamira was right about the "coup" part: Large law firms were laying off administrative staff and associates, even pushing out some partners, due to lack of business from the recession and September 11th.

Mairead said, "Did anything seem to be bothering Charles recently?"

"No. As you can imagine, he has been excited about his interviews for jobs. But if he was reluctant at first about the assignment to Her Honor and this case, he has certainly come into his own executing it. I recall Her Honor telling me that Charles is the finest clerk ever to work under her."

Mairead O'Clare clamped down on her teeth this time. For someone supposedly not aware of the affair, Altamira sure had a coincidental vocabulary.

"In Mr. Gold's office, Judge Pitt seemed to think Charles appeared distracted . . ." Mairead realized she couldn't say "Saturday morning in bed," so she repeated ". . . recently."

Altamira frowned. "He was a little agitated last Friday, in the afternoon."

Mairead leaned forward. "Agitated?"

"Yes, but I think it was just because the Commonwealth was finally about to rest in the *Dooley* case, and therefore he would have to be ready to help the judge with research on the defense by the accused."

Mairead, having been involved in two murder trials already with Shel, could identify with Vareika on that, too. She looked to the smaller desk in the room. "Is that where Charles does his work?"

Altamira turned her head, a little stiffly. "Yes and no. If he is looking at things already accepted into evidence during the trial, then yes, because while those exhibits can be viewed by a law clerk—or the attorneys involved in the case—the documents themselves do not leave this office until a convicted defendant appeals to a higher court. But if Charles is simply doing legal research, he would use the computers in the law clerks' office on the eighteenth floor."

Mention of the other law clerks reminded Mairead of a question she had meant to ask earlier. "Flo, you said before that many heads, male and female, turned when Charles began his clerkship with the superior court."

"That is correct."

"Any heads in particular?"

Altamira seemed to think about it. "You know we have a café on the third floor of this building?"

"Yes."

"Well, Her Honor does not go there often, because she finds the fried food not to her taste. However, before Charles began to work exclusively with us, I would see him sometimes eating with one of the other law clerks—a blond woman—in his group."

"Would you know her name?"

"Yes. Hughes, Leslie Hughes." Altamira then looked down at her watch. "If you do not need anything further, Mairead, I would like to catch my bus."

"Oh, sorry, Flo. I didn't mean to keep you even this long."

"That is all right." From under the large desk, Florinda Altamira pulled two metal braces, with handles pointing forward and encircling crowns at the forearms to help support the wrists. "Anything to help Her Honor. And Charles. People, them included, have certainly helped me over the years with my polio."

FOUR

G ood evening, Mr. Gold."
     Shel managed to smile at Doreen, a plump young woman with dull brown hair and thick-lensed glasses, dressed in the powder-blue jumpsuit of the summer season. He didn't need to read her name tag, since he'd met her several times over the last few years.

Of the nearly twenty Shel had been coming to the Estate. But the smile he gave Doreen at the massive, paneled-oak main entrance was the same one he'd mustered for the security camera, Shel figuring that if he had to visit from time to time because of his own demons, these poor people had to work at the Estate *all* the time.

And he was very grateful they were there.

Doreen led him down the corridors, making the small talk of weather and directions that was so standardized, Shel probably could have scripted it. But in some ways the routine reassured him, too, because it was normal.

And "normal" would soon be in short supply.

They reached the interior door both knew was Shel's destination, and Doreen, keying the lock, said, "I'll be just outside, Mr. Gold."

He thanked her. Sincerely. Then, taking a deep breath and squaring his shoulders the way he would coming off his corner's stool for the next round, Shel went into the room.

"Well, stranger, it's about time."

"Hey, Natalie."

She crossed the room to him from the sitting area, her chestnut hair swept back in the style he thought of as "post-Beatles." Her green eyes flashed, the glint in them easily mistaken for joy of life, until you looked deeper, and saw—

Natalie broke his train of thought with a fierce hug. "So, another long day at the office, eh?"

Shel managed to say "Afraid so" the same way he'd managed to smile at Doreen and the security camera.

Then his wife turned the hug into a bump-and-grind. "Maybe you need a little . . . diversion before dinner?"

Shel used his hands to tap her gently at the shoulders, feeling her bra straps beneath his fingertips. "I don't think that'd be a great idea, today."

"Oh, pooh," said Natalie, breaking the embrace entirely. "I'm afraid you're turning into an old fart, husband of mine."

"Probably right. Why don't we just sit for a while, catch up a little?"

They took the vinyl-covered barrel chairs, a plastic-protected hard-cover from the Estate's library on the small reading table between them. Shel told Natalie about one of his cases—a Latino accused of being the wheelman in a drug rip-off—just like he used to before . . .

Before his wife had left their toddler son, Richie, in his stroller outside a mall store those same twenty years before ("Just for a minute, Shel. Not even thirty seconds!").

Natalie listened intently to the wheelman story, then tsk-tsked with head shake and tongue. "Shel, Shel. When are you *ever* going to start taking the kinds of cases you went to Harvard to handle?"

A shrug, Shel feeling like he was magically speaking again with the woman he'd married. "I like criminal law, Nat. It makes me feel useful, valuable."

"The social engineer," she said playfully.

Shel smiled, this time genuinely. "Or the grease between the gears of his machine, anyway."

Then, like a change in the wind on a sunny day, a cloud bank rose over their horizon. "Only that didn't smell like grease on your collar when I hugged you."

Shel had reluctantly accepted an "air kiss" from Barbara Pitt as she left his law suite an hour before. On the subway ride over to the Estate, he'd debated within himself about mentioning his classmate's situation, ultimately deciding not to. "Nat—"

"Oh, no, Mister. *That* was perfume coming off you."

"Natalie, please—"

"Perfume from one of those *whores* you represent but *don't* mention when you 'come home to the wife.' Some brassy little bitch in purple hot pants who 'retains' you by dropping to her knees."

"It's nothing like—"

"Oh, you bastard. You *incredible* bastard. First you lose our son in that mall, and then you shoot your precious wad of manliness into the mouth of some hooker instead of saving yourself for the mother of your kidnapped child? Oh, goddamn you, Sheldon Gold, goddamn your eyes, and your cock, and your fucking soul to hell!"

Shel could hear the lock turning in the door behind him, so he didn't bother to yell for Doreen. Instead, he stood and went into Muhammad Ali's rope-a-dope mode, using his fists and forearms and elbows to absorb the pinwheeling punches his wife threw at him until a combination of her exhaustion and Doreen's restraint let him drop his guard again, hurt more thoroughly by his wife's flailing than by any shot he'd ever absorbed in the ring.

Admit it: She can still rip you to pieces just by using the love you'll always feel for her. And for what could have been your life together.

Driving north on I-95 and passing the exit for Topsfield, Pontifico Murizzi thought the evening's choice of assignment was basically a "no-brainer," as Mairead might say. From his time on Boston's Homicide Unit, he knew it didn't make a lot of sense to pursue the tangents in a victim's life—and you had to treat this Vareika kid as a vic, at least till you learned different—unless you'd covered the first circle, meaning family and "loved ones," who more often put people in the ground than acquaintances or strangers ever did.

So the Pope had looked at his copy of the list the judge had given them, and he saw the three "within the circle" in maybe ten heartbeats. First, you had the ex-husband of Her Honor, a guy who, regardless of the reasons for the divorce, probably wouldn't like that she was servicing a stud muffin half her age. Providing, of course, that said ex knew about said stud, while the judge maintained that nobody did.

Which to the Pope's way of thinking was bullshit: *Some*body always knew.

In second place, there was the judge's daughter, who maybe would take more than a passing interest in a guy around her own tender age who was banging Mom like a drum. Not to mention that Vareika might see a trophy-fuck in bagging two generations of the same bloodline.

And finally, there were the missing kid's parents, who maybe got wind of the May-December romance and thought their son had gone nuts. Risking his "promising" legal career—that they probably had to hock the family hearth to finance—by shtupping his boss-lady.

So, that was the circle of who to hit, but, in the end, logistics won out over logic. The ex-husband lived on the Cape, and there was no way Murizzi was going to fight the lemmings of the evening commute down the Southeast Expressway and Route 3 to drive eighty-some miles only to turn around and drive back north, not seeing his boat and bed until after midnight sometime. And that went triple for driving to Maine to see the judge's daughter at her college there, as the Pope had already driven through that state in his life, thinking maybe he'd somehow taken a wrong turn and was doomed to the Trans-Alaskan Highway for the next week and a half.

Which left the parents, who at least were within an hour of Boston up I-95, in one of those little towns shoehorned into New Hampshire's fourteen whole miles of coastline.

The Pope got off the interstate just after the most inefficient tollbooth in New England, then wound around some strip malls and marshlands until he could see the houses begin to clump together closer to the Atlantic. Soon Murizzi was passing blocks of bungalows squeezed into lots so small probably only natives could tell which crushed-gravel-and-shell driveway or parking pad belonged to which house. But the Pope had an address, and it was still early enough in the season that he could find a space on the street big enough for the Explorer only a few numbers below the Vareikas' place.

It turned out to be a cottage that probably started life as a tiny ranch, staying that way until somebody who thought he was handy with tools put in a couple of gables that weren't, to Murizzi's eye, exactly symmetrical. And, likely just before some kind of rational zoning became law, a ten-by-ten addition had been tacked on to finish off whatever charm the original place might have had.

One surprise, though: A beautiful Buick Riviera from the early seventies sparkled in the driveway. Then again, Vivianna Klein had said the father owned a gas station, and therefore maybe Vareika, Sr., had developed a love of cars, too.

The Pope walked up to the front door, having rehearsed his strategy during the drive north. His knock was answered by a woman's voice braying, "Eddie, can you get that? My hands are wet."

"Yeah, yeah, yeah," a guy now, with a voice like the crushed gravel in his driveway.

The door opened, a smell of some kind of cabbage getting pushed into Murizzi's nostrils by the bulk of the man standing there, in a strappy T-shirt and madras Bermuda shorts so faded the Pope had to believe they were the real thing from thirty years back, just like the Buick. Murizzi pegged "Eddie" at forty-five and obese by as many pounds, losing the fringe of wispy, blondish hair that lay like a horseshoe over his ears.

"Yeah?" said the guy, the Pope beginning to wonder about the extent of his active vocabulary.

"Mr. Vareika?"

"So?"

"My name's Pontifico Murizzi." The Pope held up the leather folder, showed Vareika his private investigator's license. "I wonder if I could speak with you and your wife about your son?"

Neither of the man's hands—stained permanently with grease and oil but huge—moved toward the folder. "Chuck? He's a lawyer, for Christ sake. He can't be in no trouble."

Chuck again, as with the judge *and* the roommate, so maybe it's just what the kid goes by. "I'd like to talk with you is all. Please?"

Instead of answering, Eddie Vareika yelled over his shoulder, "Lina, leave the dishes for a while, okay?"

Vareika turned, and the Pope took that as an invitation to follow him into the house. On the right was a small living room, jalousied windows open to catch the cool evening air coming off the ocean. The sitting furniture was all draped in slipcovers, but given how worn they were, the Pope didn't hold out much hope for the actual upholstery underneath. The "motif" was kitsch seaside, with a fishing net as wall hanging, buoys and shells hooked onto it, and a lobster pot under a glass top for coffee table. Photos of Charles Vareika crowded half the flat surfaces in the room, but they weren't as recent as the one Klein had given him of her "roommate." These were more like Mom and Chuck as a toddler, both parents with Chuck at nine or ten, Dad with his arm around the shoulder pads of Chuck in a high-school football uniform.

As Eddie Vareika and the Pope sat opposite each other, a woman came into the room, wiping her hands on a dish towel like she was trying to rub a layer of skin off them. She was slight and haggard, with mousy brown hair going gray without a dye job. However, the woman did match the younger "Mom" in the photos.

You didn't see the couple together, though, you'd say she was five, even seven years older than the "Dad."

Murizzi stood back up. "Mrs. Vareika?"

"Yes?"

He went through the ID process again, the wife actually reading the information on it, her husband saying, "He's here about Chuck."

"'Charles'," said the mother. "You know he wants to be called that, now he's a lawyer."

"Yeah, yeah, yeah. 'Charles.'"

Except, if the kid wants to seem like a grown-up, why are Barbara Pitt and Vivianna Klein still using the nickname?

The Pope folded his ID and took a seat again as Mrs. Vareika perched uncomfortably next to her husband. No holding of hands, not even an exchange of glances, both of them looking to Murizzi for the next cue.

"Your son never arrived home at his apartment Saturday or last night, and he didn't show up for work at the courthouse this morning."

Hit them with it, boom, just like that. See what happened.

Now the two finally looked at each other, blinked, and looked back at him. And in his heart of hearts, Murizzi knew the kid being gone was news to them.

The husband said, "You saying he's, what . . . missing?"

"His boss—the judge he works for—she's thinking that."

The wife said, "But he called us, just Saturday."

"What time?"

"Oh, I'm not sure I know." Turning to her husband, "It was during one of your baseball games, wasn't it?"

"Yeah."

The Pope looked at him, too. "Any kind of time frame?"

Eddie Vareika gave him a sour look. "Bottom of the fourth, Sox down three-zip to the Indians."

Murizzi knew he could check that, but it probably meant 2:30, 3:00 P.M. "What did your son say?"

The husband looked back to the wife, and the Pope had the feeling that at most the guy had answered the phone, then handed it to her.

Mrs. Vareika said, "Well, just the usual. Charles tries to call us every weekend." She got animated. "On account of with his cell phone, that's when it's free, you know?"

Murizzi nodded, encouraging her to keep rolling.

She nodded back. "Charles told us that the trial he was working on would be taking a lot of his time, even on Saturdays and Sundays . . ."

The Pope pictured "Charles," a few hours before calling his parents, feeding Her Honor a little Lithuanian sausage for her breakfast in bed.

". . . and that he couldn't really talk about it because it was very hush-hush."

"The trial was?"

"Yes."

Didn't figure, what with all the media coverage, but maybe that was how old Chucky was keeping his affair with Pitt a secret. "Mrs. Vareika, what else did your Charles talk about?"

"Saturday, you mean?"

"For starters."

She closed her eyes once, then opened them right away, and Murizzi got this image of the woman at, like, nine years old, asked by her grade-school teacher to recite a poem she'd read for class. "We talked a little about how his roommate—a very nice girl named Vivianna—was doing in *her* job."

The Pope decided to do a quality-control test. "And what job is that, Mrs. Vareika?"

"Oh, I'm not sure, really." She glanced at her husband, who just shrugged. "I think it's some kind of medical clinic, though."

Sounded to Murizzi like Chucky was keeping them mercifully in the dark about that, too. "Did your son mention anything else?"

"I don't think so. I mean, he said he'd had a nice dinner with the judge, who was treating him really well."

The Pope swallowed a grunt.

"Oh, and that he was feeling good because he was getting to work out a lot at his health club."

Mr. Vareika *didn't* swallow a grunt. "Health club."

His wife said, "Eddie, it's his generation. They want to stay in better shape than we did."

"Yeah, yeah, yeah. All's I can say is, at his age, I had better things to do than lift weights. And that's probably all this is, too."

Murizzi said, "I don't get you."

Vareika turned away from his wife. "Look, the kid's twenty-six his last birthday. He's been nothing but a student all his life, with no money. Now Chuck—Charles—has a little cash from work, he's probably just out feeling his oats. Get me now?"

"Something . . . romantic?" said the Pope with as straight a face as he could hold.

"Something female, anyway."

Mrs. Vareika sent one of her bony elbows into her husband's rib cage. "*Not* in this house with that kind of talk, Eddie."

"Yeah, yeah, yeah."

The Pope was getting a pretty good idea of who called the shots for the couple across from him. "Mrs. Vareika, has your son ever mentioned anybody specific?"

"You mean, like a girlfriend, now?"

"That's what I mean."

"No, I don't think so. More, 'I was talking to this nice nurse in a bar,' or 'I met a friend of mine's sister at a party.' Nobody specific, or even steady."

Provided you don't count his boss. "Anything else either of you can help me with?"

Eddie Vareika came forward, like his big, rough hands were blessing the glass-topped lobster pot. "Look, the way I see it, the kid got lucky last Saturday night, probably got hammered before or after, and he woke up with the kind of hangover makes him want to crawl off into the rocks and die. We've all been there, right?"

"Except he'd have had all of Sunday to recover, and he never blew off work before in the nine months he's been at the court, the last six weeks with the same judge on the same case. And he doesn't seem to be shy about using his cell phone to stay in touch with people."

Mrs. Vareika drew in a sudden breath, which was the effect Murizzi was hoping for. Take this seriously, maybe remember a piece of information that didn't seem important before.

She said, "You don't think something's happened to our son, do you?"

Before the Pope could reply, the husband said, "Lina, gimme a break, willya? He's six-two, two-ten, and strong as an ox. Plus, remember when he was nine, and that idiot Langley kid from the next street tried to take away his toy truck?"

Almost a smile from the mother. "The red fire engine you bought him."

"Well, then, remember right after that, how I taught Chuck to fight, too?" Back to the Pope with, "Our boy can take care of himself. I saw to that."

Lina Vareika didn't respond. In fact, she just brought her hands to her face, not even bothering to correct her husband on using "Chuck" instead of "Charles."

It had taken a while—years, to be honest about it—before Billie Sunday could go to bed alone and actually enjoy the silence filling her house.

After Robert, Sr., was taken away from her, she spent many a sleepless night, worrying over the future and listening for danger. When her husband had been next to her in their bed, Billie knew she could rely on his instincts and training from the Army, all the bad places he'd been—and survived—being all the "security" she needed. But when he died, their sons had been too young to step into that role, and so it fell to Billie to go around the house, checking doors and windows, before she climbed the stairs, her heart feeling as heavy as her legs, the pillow she clutched to her chest between the sheets spongy comfort compared to the strong shoulders and arms of her late husband.

Only now, so many years later, could she lie there and take some comfort from the pillow, even—if she was sure the boys were all sound asleep—talk into it a little from time to time, about the hopes for their sons that had been their hopes before they became hers alone. Or about some problem intruding on life after it, too, had become hers alone.

Like that high-and-mighty judge today in Shel's office.

Billie Sunday tried to understand people who acted the way Barbara Quincy Pitt did, but she just couldn't. Here was a woman that, from what Billie could tell, had just about everything in life handed to her on one of those silver platters you see in the stores where brides "register" their gift lists. But with all that, and a husband, and a daughter in probably a fine college, and a guaranteed lifetime job with no heavy lifting, the woman wasn't satisfied with what God already delivered to her doorstep as *life's* gifts. No, instead she gets divorced, then winds up looking for love in all the wrong places, like with a young lawyer working for her.

Billie had to laugh, though into the pillow, so she wouldn't wake any of the boys, especially William the Worrier, the youngest and the lightest sleeper of the bunch. Here you are, girl, going after that female judge for preying on somebody she should be teaching, just like that devil-priest preyed on those poor adolescents he was supposed to be mentoring, even ministering to. And yet, from the first day that Mairead walked into the suite, talking what sounded like nonsense about Shel offering her a job there, you've been kind of hoping something might work out between the two of them. That maybe the poor orphan girl with the radioactive arms might be the one to bring Shel out of the box he'd sealed himself into, long before even *you* knew the man, over his wife "losing" their son, and over him losing his wife to her own special, horrible kind of madness.

Then Billie felt a dose of reality settle in, something like an expression of Robert, Sr.'s, when he thought she was trying too hard to control life, instead of just going with it. He'd say, "It'll all work out, Billie, by and by." And it always did.

Almost.

But Billie was both too tired and too smart to start revisiting that tragedy in her own life when she knew she needed a good night's sleep toward what the morrow might bring.

And so Billie Sunday let out the breath she hadn't even realized she'd been holding. And, settling her head into the pillow beneath it, she slowly, softly kissed the pillow against her chest, said, "Sweet dreams," and drifted off, hoping to find some of her own.

T he next morning, Mairead O'Clare was watching the traffic be- fore crossing Cambridge Street on the way to the superior court. Next to her, Sheldon A. Gold said, "So, what do you think of our new client so far?"

Tread lightly, young lady.

Mairead agreed with Sister Bernadette, maybe because Shel's casual tone told her that he really *did* care about how his associate felt. "I guess I'd like to reserve judgment until after I've seen Judge Pitt in action."

"That seems fair," replied Shel, in a different tone that Mairead felt implied disappointment. "She said she'd leave word with her court officer that you were to be admitted to the gallery, no matter how crowded it might be."

"I met him yesterday. Tommy Flanagan. Seems like a good guy."

"They almost always are. Judges may decide the cases, but bailiffs run the courtrooms." Now a third tone from Shel, though a more normal one for him. "What did you find out from Florinda Altamira, the judge's administrative clerk?"

Mairead summarized both the facts as well as the "double entendres" she thought she'd caught.

Shel frowned as they reached Washington Street. "So, you think maybe our client's secret isn't as secure as she believes?"

"I think I agree with the Pope: There are a lot of names on that list we got from her, yet Leslie Hughes—the blond research clerk—wasn't even one of them. Seems hard to believe that Judge Pitt and 'Chuck' could have kept everybody in the dark."

Just a nod from Shel. "Well, maybe you'll be able to glean something from Ms. Hughes or from watching a part of the trial. What will you do after that?"

She told him about the call from Murizzi that had been on her home telephone tape, asking Mairead to see Vareika's roommate, Vivianna Klein, let him know "a woman's take" on her.

Shel frowned again. "Not like the Pope to need confirmation on a witness evaluation." Then the ghost of a smile. "You might be in for an interesting afternoon."

"Right now I'd settle for an informative morning. Where are you going to be?"

"Talking with the Honorable Bruce Rodrigue, our client's *other* love interest. At least, from his point of view."

Even without knowing that judge, Mairead O'Clare had *no* interest in changing places with her boss. Definitely.

As Sheldon A. Gold entered the empty courtroom on the second floor, a petite young woman in a pantsuit was walking out, carrying a legal pad and some documents.

A blond woman. Leslie Hughes?

Admit it: That would be something, in and of itself.

Shel asked the nearest bailiff if he could see Judge Bruce Rodrigue. The court officer escorted Shel to the lobby doorway, no administrative clerk in the anteroom office. Then the bailiff disappeared for a moment, came back nodding, and motioned Shel toward the inner office.

A short, dapper man, in just a tie and dress shirt, rose from a high-backed chair. Both his gray suit jacket and black robe were hanging on the coat tree behind his yacht of a lobby desk, a computer and telephone console on one corner of it.

Shel said, "Judge, thank you for seeing me like this."

Rodrigue simply smiled without showing any teeth, a reaction Shel had seen from other members of the judiciary many times before. That subtle, I'm granting you a great favor, Counselor, and I expect to be appreciated now and repaid later.

Rodrigue motioned Shel to take one of three captain's chairs in front of him before returning to his own with the springy ease of a gymnast. No more than five-foot-six and one-forty in Shel's estimation, Rodrigue still had most of his black, slightly curly hair, slicked on top from crown to back, cotton balls of white in front of the ears and enveloping the temples of his wire-rimmed glasses like snowbanks do fallen branches. "Distinguished" was the word that leaped to mind. Brown eyes, unlined skin, a bantam rooster who liked to fight, perhaps even lived to fight.

"So, Mr. Gold, what brings you to see me? Unless both my docket and my memory have failed simultaneously, we have no cases pending."

"No, we don't," Shel making the middle chair he'd taken squeak a little as he shifted to get comfortable. "But there seems to be a problem here at the courthouse, and I was wondering if you could help us with it."

"Problem here? And me help *you* with it?" Rodrigue picked up a brass—or, perhaps even . . . gold?—replica of a gavel from his desktop and began using it as worry beads. "Now I *am* intrigued, sir. Please, proceed."

Shel wondered if the man spoke this way over dinner as well, the way he would from the bench during a hearing. "One of the court's research clerks is missing."

"Ah, yes. I heard some scuttlebutt yesterday. The one who's working with Barbara Pitt on her priest mess."

"Correct."

"Horrible situation, that trial." More gyrations of the gavel. "Did you know I was Roman Catholic, Mr. Gold?"

"No, Judge, I didn't."

"No," that superior grin from the superior court jurist, now moving the gavel in short strokes toward Shel, as though Rodrigue were hammering a tack into the air between them. "But you did know I'm 'Portu-*guee*,' from the docks of New Bedford, correct?"

An unfortunate turn for the conversation to take, in Shel's view, Rodrigue using the slightly derogatory ethnic label, but not much the lawyer could do toward redirecting it. "I remember hearing that when you were sworn in, yes."

"And you also know we Portuguese are something like ninety-seven percent Roman Catholic, don't you?"

Shel wasn't quite sure why Rodrigue was taking him on cross-examination, but in the ogre's den . . . "All the men and women I've met who are Portuguese-American seemed to be Catholic as well."

Now the judge paused, cocking his head first left, then right before putting his gavel back down on the desk. "You must really want to find something out, Mr. Gold, letting me badger you like this without objection."

"Little standing *to* object, Your Honor."

Another of Rodrigue's smiles. "Very well. Tell me what your standing is, then."

"Judge Pitt became frustrated when the police seemed less than upset that her clerk apparently had been missing since sometime Saturday, so she turned to me."

"You engage in mostly criminal practice, correct?"

"Correct, Judge."

"Is that why she turned to you?"

"I think Judge Pitt might know better herself."

A pause before, "Undoubtedly." Then another. "All right, Barbara's asked you to look into the . . . 'disappearance,' if we can call it that?"

"Yes. Before the trail gets any colder."

Now Rodrigue pursed his lips, the way Shel imagined he might if a particularly nettlesome issue of evidence law were sprung on him during an important trial. "And the trail of this clerk . . . ?"

Shel thought he could answer the question not quite asked of him. "Charles Vareika."

"Vareika. This Charles Vareika somehow led you . . . to my lobby?"

Not to "me" as a person, but "my" chambers as a place.

Gambit time. "I thought maybe your research clerk might have mentioned something to you, Judge."

A wrinkling of the eyebrows, as white as the patches in front of the ears, so that the impression was of two albino caterpillars in a mating dance. "Have you spoken to her as yet, sir?"

The object of the gambit. "Ms. Hughes?"

Rodrigue cocked his head. "Yes, Ms. Hughes."

"No, I haven't."

The man picked up his gavel again. "Then why would you have any reason to think I know anything about this Vareika's disappearance?"

Shel shrugged in a way he knew that juries found engaging, a "can't blame me for trying" mode. "Just representing my client and running down all the possibilities that she . . . suggested."

"Well, I can't think why Barbara would have 'suggested' me, but your time has been poorly spent, as you've just 'run down' a dead end."

"Sorry, Judge."

Rodrigue tapped the gavel on its polished wooden base. "What's more, sir—and worse—is that *my* time has been poorly spent in speaking with you. Not only do I have to shoulder a disproportionate share of the caseload here in this county thanks to your 'client's' priest mess, but district attorneys in other counties are openly criticizing— even *suing*—the superior court system itself for not scheduling sufficient criminal sessions to process *their* caseloads. And, if that weren't bad enough, we have trial judges being threatened by defendants in their own courtrooms even as our departmental account to pay for interpreters is nearly exhausted, so that now my colleagues and I can be cursed and reviled in any of eleven foreign languages without knowing what's being said against us."

Shel didn't quite see his responsibility for that state of affairs. "Judge—"

"Look behind you. Go on, look."

Shel turned in his chair. On the wall, between bookshelves stocked with volumes of supreme judicial court decisions and Massachusetts form manuals, was a framed document, apparently attesting to Rodrigue's membership in the "Federalist Society."

Shel turned back.

Rodrigue said, "Do you know what the society stands for?"

The man wants to tell you a story, let him tell it. "Only vaguely, Judge."

Rodrigue tapped a little faster on the gavel pad. "We started twenty years ago as a reaction to the ultra-liberals who ran law schools with no respect for non-liberal views of certain documents, such as the United States Constitution. What began as a debating society to force these issues into the public eye has now grown to nearly thirty thousand members, with sixty attorney chapters and one-hundred-forty law *school* chapters. Imagine that, Mr. Gold, our organization can bring a bit of Libertarian dialogue to students on three-quarters of the law campuses in the nation."

Shel thought, Ducky.

Rodrigue stopped his tapping to say, "That's how I prefer to spend *my* time, sir, and yours with me is now over."

At which point the Honorable Bruce Rodrigue pointed his gavel toward the lobby door.

When Mairead O'Clare got off the elevator on the eighteenth floor of the courthouse, she saw a sign next to an open doorway directly in front of her. The sign said, SUPERIOR COURT LAW CLERKS. However, just before Mairead walked toward it, she noticed another open doorway on her right, with the same sign but an apparent reception or secretarial desk, unoccupied.

Not sure of the protocol, she turned right and stepped into the reception area, but nobody was in sight. Mairead tried a quiet, "Hello?"

No response.

She moved farther into the area, enough so she could see around a corner and into a large, airy room with tall windows giving a great city view and rows of computer workstations along the walls. Three twenty-somethings were fixated on their screens.

Wow. If I were a judge, this is where I'd want *my* lobby to be.

A short blond woman about Mairead's age carrying some documents and a legal pad under her arm came around the corner, nearly colliding with her.

"Who are you?" said the woman.

"Attorney Mairead O'Clare. I'm looking for Leslie Hughes?"

The woman seemed taken aback. "I'm Leslie, but I don't know you."

"One of the other law clerks seems to be missing, and we're trying to find him."

Now Hughes stiffened. "Charles."

"Vareika, right."

Hughes began to move around Mairead. "I don't know anything about that."

Mairead didn't exactly hip-check the woman, but did obstruct her progress. "Please, it's very important."

Hughes glowered at her, then glanced around. "There's no privacy in there with everybody on the computers, but our secretary called in sick today, so I can give you five minutes out here."

"Thank you."

They sat down, Hughes behind the reception desk, Mairead in front of it.

Best be efficient, young lady.

"Leslie, when did you last see Charles Vareika?"

"Friday. He didn't show up yesterday morning."

"What time Friday?"

"We usually knock off around four-thirty."

"So, here at work, then?"

"Here?" Hughes seemed confused. "Of course *here*. This is *where* we work."

Mairead decided to be blunt. "You didn't see Charles . . . after hours?"

"After . . . ? You mean, like, socializing with him?"

"Or whatever."

A stern look. "There hasn't been any 'whatever' between Charles and me. Period."

Seemed a little doctrinaire to Mairead. "Some people noticed you two eating lunch together."

"Oh, right. And if we're professionally friendly on the job, we must be hooking up afterwards? Real progressive, Mairead, especially from somebody, like, my own age."

"You don't find Charles attractive?"

An exasperated breath. "What I find 'attractive' is having a job. I went to law school out of state." Hughes named her university. "Not exactly an Ivy, or even top fifty. But I made law review, and because I graduated college here in the city, I wanted to come back to Boston to practice. Only with the recession and all, I didn't have a prayer with the good firms. At one interview, though, an alum from my college told me he'd clerked the year after law school, and it was a great stepping-stone to a mainline firm. But he went through the system before all the budget cuts. We pull down just over forty thousand in salary, yet we had to forfeit eight days of pay 'for the cause.' And we've been told there may not be money for us in the future, so if we can find an outside job, we should seriously consider resigning and taking it. Only most outside firms are laying off associates they've *already* hired."

Mairead said, "I'm sorry. I didn't know it was this bad for judicial clerkships."

Hughes relented a little. "Hey, the job itself is awesome. Doing interesting research on real-life cases, writing draft opinions. You're learning every day from really sharp judges, kind of like being a research assistant to four professors at once, and you're growing every day."

Mairead got the analogy, but was surprised at the number. "You work for that many judges at the same time?"

"It varies, but yeah, right now I'm doing assignments for . . ." Hughes reeled off four names, including Bruce Rodrigue.

Mairead figured to tell Shel about that connection, let him decide how to pursue it. "So, do any of the other clerks resent Charles Vareika's working for only one judge?"

Less relenting now, more a hardening. "We don't see that much of him. I guess Judge Pitt can be pretty . . . demanding. But at least she's set him up with some large-firm interviews, so he can't complain."

As Mairead said, "Is there some reason he *would* complain?" another woman's voice behind her intoned, "May I help you?"

Mairead turned her head. A brown-haired woman wearing a business suit and a pleasant expression stared at her.

"I think I'm okay, thanks."

"I don't agree. This is a restricted area."

Now Mairead stood. "I didn't see any 'Authorized Personnel Only' signs, like there are other places in the courthouse."

The woman's expression stayed pleasant. "You're an attorney?"

"Yes."

"Well, we can't have lawyers from pending cases engaging in ex parte communications with our judges' researchers, now can we?"

Mairead knew "ex parte" meant one-sided, without the opposing attorney being present. "But I'm not 'communicating on a pending case.' All we—"

"Sorry. I don't make the rules. I'm just the one who gets yelled at if they're not enforced."

Leslie Hughes said, "It's okay, Linda. We didn't talk about any cases. She's just here about Charles."

"Oh." Linda's face finally lost its pleasant expression. "Is there any word from him?"

Mairead said, "Not that I know of."

"Well, again I'm sorry, but I can't let you stay here. Perhaps if you go downstairs to the fifteenth floor, the court administrator can help you."

Sensing a brick wall, Mairead O'Clare turned back to the law clerk. "Good luck on the job."

"It'll take more than that," Leslie Hughes getting to her feet and plodding back toward the computer room.

When Pontifico Murizzi stopped for gas in the center of the right town on Cape Cod, he asked the guy taking money inside about Judge Pitt's ex-husband, Ugo Nagatami. The Pope had only the one address on his copy of her list, and it seemed to him that 14 Lilac Way would be residential, not commercial, though over the last twenty years, the Cape had gotten so fucking cutesy that a national bank might be on Dewdrop Lane, and the jaded blue-hairs that lived down there wouldn't bat an eye. Fortunately the guy handing Murizzi his change did some landscaping on the side, and he knew the street, but not the house, saying the company he moonlighted for didn't have Nagatami as a customer.

And yes, Lilac Way was all residential, the Pope now hoping he hadn't driven two fucking hours on a Tuesday morning only to find out he'd be stuck there till the ex decided to come home.

Leaving the gas station, the first thing that hit Murizzi was the traffic, almost worse than Boston's own Big Dig. One lane each way, bumper to bumper, denser even since he left the two-laner off Route 6, the Mid-Cape Highway that went kind of like a central spine all the way from the canal to Provincetown. The Pope had some fond memories of "P-town," the tip of Cape Cod doubling as the center of vacation life for gays in Massachusetts both before and after the Epidemic, despite the countless, senseless deaths of the eighties. Jeez, you couldn't equate the two—an opportunistic disease and crazy fucking terrorists—but Murizzi figured Provincetown must have lost nearly as many people over five years as New York City had on that one September morning.

After another fifteen minutes of clogged roads and intersections, the Pope reached Lilac Way. Turning onto it, he spotted number 14 about halfway down the block.

Murizzi stopped in front of the prior house, so he could do a windshield of Nagatami's diagonally from behind the wheel. Saltbox cape, cedar shingles weathered to that soft gray, like a seagull's wing. Pale yellow shutters and door. Window boxes under the sills with seasonal flowering plants. Lawn cut, edges trimmed, even on the driveway, which held a Toyota Camry convertible, halfway to the garage door.

The good news: Car means he's probably home. On the other hand, if the guy didn't hire out the yard work, he must spend a hell of a lot of time with his clippers and Weedwacker.

The Pope hopped from the Explorer, did a simple up-and-down visual of the street, all the houses roughly proportional. Established, but not ritzy, neighborhood. Murizzi looked once more at the judge's list, again sounded out the ex-husband's name—Ugo Nagatami— and wondered if he'd be as Japanese as his car before the Pope stuck the list back in his pocket and went up to the front door.

He pushed the button, and he could hear a set of chimes like the ones the wind blows against each other. Then a voice from behind the house called out, "I'm in the back."

No accent on the words, kind of a flat, newscaster's inflection, too. Murizzi was starting to get interested in meeting the guy.

There was a flagstone path around the right side of the house, so the Pope took that. And, clearing the back corner, got dropped into another world.

There was an arrangement of rocks that looked too perfect to be natural, but they were more like boulders, really, with a little bridge arcing over a pond showing flashes of orange-and-white fish, the colors in patterns like a pinto pony's. The plantings looked exotic, too, though there weren't so many of them. A sparse tree in the center held the garden together as a design, and some flowers in small clumps dotted the edges.

"Over here," said the same flat, male voice.

Murizzi turned. A muscular Asian guy in a T-shirt and blue jeans was coiling a hose around one of those holders advertised on TV during late-night cable shows. You could see only the salt-and-pepper sideburns, because he wore what the Pope always thought of as a coolie hat, which was kind of surprising, given the guy's ethnicity and all. Even more surprising, when the guy stood up, he was over six feet, which meant he had a few inches on Murizzi, who was more used to fireplug Asian guys like Artie Chin, his buddy in the Homicide Unit.

"Ugo Nagatami," said the man, wiping his right palm on his denimed thigh, then extending it toward the Pope.

He shook with him, Nagatami's grip like a vise, the bones feeling like they were coming through his skin. "Pontifico Murizzi."

A grin, the guy looking older in the face than the body. "Sounds like we both got branded early on with names."

The Pope found himself liking Nagatami—not romantically, just friendly—and he also found he had to remind himself that this was, after all, the client's ex, who might have it in for the client's next.

Nagatami said, "So, what brings you to Paradise?"

Murizzi glanced over at the garden. "You aren't kidding about that last part."

A shift in the eyes. "You enjoy gardens?"

"To sit in. Not to tend."

"Well, then, you going to be here long enough for me to drag out a couple of lawn chairs and beers?"

"Yeah, I think I will."

Nagatami nodded, then disappeared into a little shed abutting the house. He came back out with both the chairs and the bottles, Miller Genuine Draft.

The Pope said, "You've got a fridge in your toolshed?"

"Gardening shed, but yeah. Saves me having to track mud and grass and fertilizer into the kitchen. Sit."

Nagatami twisted off one cap, handed it to Murizzi, then did the same for himself before clinking neck to neck. "To simplification."

"I don't get you."

The ex took a swig, then pointed his bottle toward the garden. "It's beautiful, but still too complicated. I'm whittling it down to perfect simplicity."

Murizzi drank two gulps of his Miller, the golden liquid feeling just right after his long drive, even to a red-wine guy. "Hard to see how that could make it better, but good luck."

"Thanks." Then Nagatami set his beer on the grass at his feet, using his insteps to hold the bottle steady on the uneven ground. "So, Mr. Murizzi, what brings you here?"

The Pope felt pretty good about the situation, so he said, "How's about you just call me by my nickname?"

"Which is?"

Murizzi told him, and Nagatami grinned. "You did better than I have. People usually spell my first name like that lemon of a car, Y-U-G-O."

The Pope thought of a proverb his mother once told him: I cried because I had no shoes, until I met a man who had no feet.

Nagatami left his beer where it was. "Forgive me, Pope, but I get this scent of 'police' from you. Do you need to show me some ID before we go any further?"

Christ, thought Murizzi, this guy's had the drop on you, and you didn't sense it. Snap the fuck out of *Better Homes and Gardens,* huh?

"Mr. Naga—"

"Hey, it's Ugo, right?"

"Right." The Pope wanted to get back on the beam here. "Ugo, you know your ex-wife's been involved in this big priest rape trial?"

"Thanks to the little television I watch, yes."

"Well, the research clerk—guy just out of law school—working with her on the case has disappeared."

Nagatami's face did a flip of the easy grin into what Murizzi would have called a genuine look of concern. "That's terrible." A little jump in the eyes, too. "So, you're from the court."

Same assumption the roommate, Vivianna Klein, had made, and the Pope reminded himself to check with Irish on her impression of the woman. "The judge retained a lawyer about it because the police are kind of slow on these things. The lawyer brought me in for the legwork."

A careful nod. "Like coming to see the ex-husband of this clerk's . . . 'boss.'"

"Right," said Murizzi. "You ever met him?"

A laugh with more sadness than humor behind it. "Pope, Barbara and I have been divorced for a decade now. Other than the occasional stilted 'sharing' about Genna—our daughter—and her college education, we've entered the fourth stage of marriage."

"You'll have to give me one through three first."

Nagatami grinned again. "The engagement ring, the wedding ring, and the suffering."

Pretty good line. "How about the fourth stage?"

"The no ring, as in telephone, as in nothing. Barbara and I don't exactly have a relationship anymore."

But not exactly an answer to the original question, either. "So, you've never met her clerk?"

"No." Nagatami hesitated. "But Genna has, and she told me about him."

Murizzi remembered the photo of Charles Vareika in his pocket and found himself not wanting to ask Nagatami the next question. "Like what?"

"That he's working full-time on her mother's priest case. That he's over at the condo—Barbara's, in Harvard Square—a lot. Even on nights." Nagatami engaged the Pope with eyes Murizzi now noticed were black as fucking pitch. "And weekends."

So much for Judge Hot Pants' little secret. "You know I've got to ask how you feel about that?"

A sigh. "About the same way I'd feel if my daughter knew of an . . . affair I was having with a girl her age, I suppose. I'd think it sort of embarrassing, all the way around. Wouldn't you?"

Truth: If you'd had kids, yeah. But the Pope said, "So, no flame left to fan, no jealousy?"

A laugh this time with more humor than sadness behind it. "Barbara and I realized about two years before our divorce that things weren't working out. Which I think we took as kind of a . . . failed partnership? But we both also vowed we'd do nothing to harm Genna. So Barbara didn't object when our daughter decided to take only my last name, and I didn't try to gouge any of Barbara's family money out of her."

"Good of you."

Nagatami stared at him with those black eyes. "I'm from northern California originally, and my dad was one of the early Hewlett-Packard computer pioneers. I have family money of my own. Barbara and I just split up, pretty much taking from the marriage what each of us had brought to it, including the house Barbara owned outside Boston that Genna thought of as . . . 'home.' Then, when our daughter started college three years ago, Barbara and her family did some kind of swap, with the house going to a niece in exchange for that condo in Harvard Square going to Barbara. I don't really know the details, but I think it was a tax thing, so everybody got to hold onto more of the family money."

The rich stay richer. Then something else that both Pitt and Nagatami had said hit Murizzi. "Wait a second, Ugo. I thought your ex-wife said your daughter visited you down here this past weekend before going *back* to college?"

"That's right."

"Well, it's June. Aren't classes over for the year?"

"Mostly. But Genna's taking an extra course and working on a project up there, so she's staying in a dorm for the summer."

"And when did she leave here on Sunday?"

"Oh, I don't know, about . . ." Nagatami's tone suddenly turned cold. "Why do you want to know that, Pope?"

"Just my job, Ugo. Finding out the facts so the lawyer can sift them."

"Well, Genna couldn't have had anything to do with this Vareika boy's disappearance."

"So, your daughter mentioned the guy's name to you."

Nagatami seemed a little thrown. "I think you did."

"I think I didn't."

After a Mexican standoff—or maybe better, "stare-off "—Nagatami said, "Probably from the TV then, but we've talked long enough, anyway, Pope."

"Pity." Murizzi picked up his beer, slugged down maybe half of what was left in the bottle. "Pretty spot."

"That's always been my intention."

"You spend a lot of time here?"

"Most of my time, actually."

"Away from the job, you mean?"

Nagatami said, "I was downsized six months ago. This garden is my 'job' now."

The Pope looked up at the sky. "And when it rains?"

"I go inside, manipulate my bonsai."

"You do what?"

"B-O-N-S-A-I, the art of shaping trees. I start with a Japanese red maple, a firethorn, even a crab apple. Then I split, cut, and pinch to stunt their growth and turn them into very complex miniatures, often less than a foot tall."

Murizzi thought that was kind of contradictory: Garden outside to make big things simple, bonsai inside to make little things complicated. But instead he said, "Pretty tough to swing those tuition bills, you're out of work that long."

Nagatami gave the Pope a hard look. "Like I said before, my family has money. And, even if it didn't, Barbara's does. So, there is no problem. Not with me, and not with our daughter."

Murizzi stood up. "Thanks for the beer."

Nagatami's black eyes went back to the garden. "You can take the rest of it with you."

The Pope shook his head. "Open container in a moving motor vehicle? Not worth the risk. And besides, I don't want to get drowsy. It's a long drive to Maine."

Ugo Nagatami's flat voice finally grew an edge to it. "My daughter was the only lasting product from twelve years of marriage. Genna stays out of this, whatever 'this' might be. You understand?"

"Hey, Ugo. Enjoy the serenity your garden provides, huh?"

And Pontifico Murizzi strolled around the corner of the house, trying not to put too much of the cop-roll into his hips.

And so, if we have to clear the courtroom, you have to go, too, right?"

"Right," said Mairead O'Clare to Tommy Flanagan, Judge Barbara Pitt's bailiff.

He nodded once, then went through the low, swinging gate into the bar enclosure and up to the side of the bench near the empty jury box. Mairead was disappointed not to see the jurors, because their absence might mean just arguments between counsel and the judge. On the other hand, she might learn more about the case—and Pitt—that way, since the conversation would be less guarded with no jury to insulate from certain information.

Florinda Altamira smiled at Mairead from her kangaroo pouch in front of the bench. Flanagan turned around just as the courtroom door to the judge's lobby opened and Pitt, wearing her robe and carrying a sheaf of papers in one hand, strode out. He said, "Couuuurrrrt. All rise, please."

Mairead looked around on the way up and the way down. Based on her limited experience with high-profile cases, there was only a "second string" of broadcast media there covering that morning's proceedings. However, a number of people also didn't fit the usual gallery standards of retirees and court jocks. And one woman she was surprised to see: Gallina Ekarevskaya, an attorney who'd been a functional opponent in one of Shel and Mairead's earlier matters. Ekarevskaya seemed to notice the younger lawyer from the corner of her eye, but didn't acknowledge her.

Mairead looked back toward Pitt, now seated, referring probably to the papers she'd brought with her. "I understand we have a defense motion to be argued outside the hearing of the jury?"

"We do, Your Honor," said a tall black woman with a deep, resonant voice who rose from the counsel table farther from the bench. Beside her sat a slight man with very rounded shoulders. His hair was sandy like Shel's, but thinning terribly on top, and it was speckled with gray on the sides. From her seat, Mairead couldn't see his face, but given the two court officers positioned behind him, she assumed he was the defendant, former priest Cornelius X. Dooley.

Pitt addressed the black woman. "Very well, Ms. Yelverton. You may proceed."

"Thank you, Your Honor." Yelverton shook out her shoulders, something Mairead thought of as athletic preparation, partially confirmed by the woman's lanky build and close-to-the-scalp hair. "Our motion refers to three of the witnesses the prosecution has placed on her list of proposed. Based upon our investigation, these witnesses can be competent to testify only on supposed prior bad acts allegedly committed by Mr. Dooley during his tenure as a priest but *not* included within the present indictment. Accordingly, the defense moves to exclude such witnesses here and now on both the ground of unfair prejudice to Mr. Dooley's defense against the counts *actually* charged as well as the cumulative nature of such testimony and the resultant waste of the court's time."

"Thank you, Ms. Yelverton. Ms. Butler?"

"Yes, Your Honor."

As the defense attorney sat back down, Mairead saw a very short white woman stand. She had a braid of brown hair rolled into a knot at the top of her head, perhaps for a little more impression of height. Butler's voice was quiet but projected cleanly, to Mairead like rubbing the rim of a crystal glass.

The prosecutor said, "The issue is not whether Mr. Dooley committed the acts that the three witnesses alluded to will testify about.

Their testimony is being offered only to show a pattern of conduct by Mr. Dooley while a priest serving those parishes in the towns of Calem, Smithfield, and Weston Hills. And the Commonwealth believes we should be entitled to establish that pattern during the trial as a pre-dicate for the jurors recognizing the very similar—frankly, nearly identical—practices of the defendant in . . . 'grooming' his victims under the indictments currently before you."

Mairead liked Butler, the way she had more of a conversation with the judge and didn't let Yelverton's imposing presence overwhelm the issues.

Pitt looked to the defense counsel. "Ms. Yelverton?"

Butler stayed up as her opponent rose again, which Mairead thought—as an ice hockey player through high school, college, and beyond—was also just the right attitude to strike: I'll be standing till you knock me down.

Yelverton said, "Your Honor, the only possible reason for intro-ducing these three witnesses and their testimony will be to prejudice my client in the eyes of the jury as a 'bad man.' Not only haven't these alleged instances of sexual misconduct been included in this indict-ment, they are beyond the statute of limitations as it read at the time the alleged incidents took place. Therefore, they could not be charged in their own right, and they should not be included to muddy the wa-ters of *this* case."

Pitt looked to Butler, who said, "Your Honor, the Commonwealth will rest on its brief regarding the limitations issue."

Mairead liked that, too: Don't over-argue if you think you have the better side of a given point.

"Thank you, Ms. Butler. Ms. Yelverton, anything further?"

Defense counsel seemed to glance down at her client, who stayed staring straight ahead, giving her, Mairead thought, no clue or cue.

Yelverton said, "Not at this time, Your Honor."

The judge gathered up her papers. "Very well. I will take the de-fense motion under advisement, review your briefs, and render my decision before we begin hearing testimony again at . . . two P.M. Court to stand in recess until then."

As bailiff Tommy Flanagan bellowed and all stood up, it dawned on Mairead that three women were trying the case of one man. A trio of females, who couldn't "qualify" to be ordained under the Catholic religion, were determining this former priest's fate as a civilian.

At which moment the two court officers behind Cornelius X. Dooley turned him around, and he made eye contact with Mairead. She felt the breath go out of her, as it seemed for a moment he could see straight into her mind and heart. Then Dooley smiled, the teeth terribly stained from nicotine or worse, and placed one palm over the back of his other hand, nodding, Mairead thought, toward the hemangioma on her own. Then Dooley wiggled his fingers in a little puppet wave at her before the two bailiffs led him away past the table next to Altamira's clerk's pouch.

As Mairead tried to catch her breath, she looked to where Gallina Ekarevskaya had been sitting, but the other lawyer already had left the courtroom. Then Mairead felt somebody move up on the other side of her. When she turned, it was one of the gallery people she hadn't recognized as media, a man about forty-five with kind eyes behind horn-rim glasses and a ready smile. "You look like you could use a drink."

It sounded like a come-on, but, just as the first time Mairead met Shel Gold in the Boston Common, it didn't *feel* like a come-on. Still . . .

Go with your best instinct, young lady.

She said, "How about Dutch treat on sandwiches instead?"

"You're on." The man stuck out his hand. "Bill Sherden."

"Mairead O'Clare." They shook, then she began moving out from the pew-like bench and into the aisle to leave the courtroom. "Are you involved in this case?"

"In all of them, I'm afraid." Now a sad tone in the voice behind her. "I'm the executive director of an organization that tries to help the victims of priests like Dooley."

Billie Sunday had just rolled a district court Appearance of Counsel form she'd completed for the new child out of her typewriter when she heard the suite door open. Billie swiveled to the left in her chair to see Shel Gold coming through it, a bag labeled "Dunkin' Donuts" in one hand, his battered briefcase in the other.

She said, "Best not let Mairead see you with those heart darts in your office."

That little-boy smile the man had, like "what did I do?" "She'll be in court for a while, I think, though more as observer than advocate. And besides," he said, setting the bag on her reception desk, "half of these are for you."

Billie opened the top and saw one of her favorites—chocolate honey-dip. Casually as could be, she said, "You okay with this judge thing we're doing?"

No reply, so Billie looked up. "Shel?"

No smile, either. "I'm fine, Billie. Does it bring back memories of Richie, thinking about what that priest supposedly did to young boys under his wing? Sure. But every time I read a headline or watch a television anchor, that sort of thing happens."

"Only you can walk past a newsstand, or turn off the TV."

"And I can't turn my back on a client once accepted, you're right." He started for his office. "Or on all the other ones, waiting for me in there."

Billie Sunday wondered how the poor, saddled man made it through the night all by himself. "Shel?"

"Yes?"

"You forgot your doughnuts."

Pontifico Murizzi checked his trip odometer as he approached Marshfield, still well south of Boston. Having been reset at the fill-up on the Cape, it now read less than fifty miles, and the Explorer could comfortably range about three hundred on a tank. So the Pope figured he'd reach Genna Nagatami's college in Maine with three-eighths—at worst a quarter—to spare.

Which'd be good, let you stop at another gas station up there, get some reliable local directions again.

Even so, though, Murizzi asked himself why he'd agreed to help out Judge Barbara Pitt. Especially since there was no certainty her missing boytoy was a murder victim.

But "boytoy" yanked the Pope back to the case that started it all, made him leave the force in the first fucking place. The kid Murizzi and another detective in the Homicide Unit had made for a home-invasion felony-murder. The twenty-year-old—blond, slim, probably not a feather of hair on his chest—kept crying about how he was innocent, about how he knew the vic, would never have hurt her. But he was convicted and sentenced to life without parole. Thanks mainly to the case the Pope had built against him.

Only a couple months later, the kid hanged himself, leaving a note about how he couldn't face another day being passed around his cell block as a punk for every hard con with a hard-on. And then, two weeks after that, another home invasion gone sour produced a wounded moke.

With the keys to the first vic's car in his pocket.

Murizzi shook off the memory. But he knew that was why he'd taken on the judge's case.

Even particularly hers.

And so Murizzi settled back into the driver's seat, put the truck on cruise control at sixty-five, and popped a nice Puccini opera cassette into the tape player. A good seventy minutes of thinking music, counting the automatic click-over to side two.

Music to think about why daughter Genna, having the choice after her parents' divorce, went with her father's last name over her mother's or some hyphenated fucking hybrid.

How's the chicken salad?"

Mairead O'Clare looked up from her sandwich plate at Bill Sherden, sitting across the Formica table from her in the booth at the sub shop tucked into the shadow of the Old State House. "Good. And the smoked turkey?"

"Same," said Sherden, "but even better for my waistline. Kind of hard to get enough exercise in, especially these days."

"Meaning all the trials against the priests?"

A nod as the man chewed thoughtfully. "Plus the appropriate ancillary things that are happening." He set down his sandwich. "You've heard about the Survivors Network of Those Abused by Priests?"

Mairead thought back to the orphanage, where the only sexual predation was by the older kids, and one nun "from the dark side," but no priests. "Just because of the news coverage."

Another nod, even without chewing. "Well, the Survivors Network handles a lot of the national issues, like what the Conference is doing about both preventing abuse in the future and addressing abuse from the past, even the instances beyond the statutes of limitation, like the prosecutor and defense attorney were arguing about today."

Mairead wasn't sure she knew the answer to her next question. "And the 'Conference' is . . . ?"

"The United States Conference of Catholic Bishops. They established a new agency, the Office of Child and Youth Protection. The Survivors Network acts as kind of a gadfly on the Office, because the National Review Board—something the Church itself created to be a watchdog over the bishops—might have some conflicts of interest in making sure the Conference keeps its promises to weed out offending priests, and not just pass them on to other parishes."

Mairead tried to sort through all the overlapping bureaucracy. "And to contact with other kids."

"Right," Sherden taking another bite of his smoked turkey sub.

"So, where do you fit in?"

He held up his hand, then swallowed. "Some of the states—like Massachusetts—have a lot of civil cases filed by victims against priests who abused them. We needed our *own* specific organization to deal with the court systems, here within the Commonwealth, especially once the Archdiocese of Boston decided to rescind the settlement that many of our plaintiffs thought they'd reached."

"And that state-specific organization is what you're the executive director of?"

"Right," said Sherden, reaching into his pocket and handing her a business card with his name above an address and other information.

Mairead thought it would be very bad form to ask the next question, but Sherden answered it before she could. "And no, I'm not a potential plaintiff myself. In fact, I'm not even Catholic. But I look at all these kids—and, Mairead, while there are only so many offending priests, each of them imposed sexual contact upon dozens to hundreds of children. Of *both* genders, though many more boys than girls, nationwide."

Which made some sense to Mairead, given that only one gender was *allowed* to serve with the priests as altar *boys.*

Perhaps the single benefit ever bestowed upon you by sexism, young lady.

Maircad nodded. "So, Bill, you've been following the criminal prosecutions as well as the civil suits in Massachusetts?"

"As best I can."

Mairead tried to gauge whether to trust the guy, decided she could. "If I tell you something in confidence, does it stay between us?"

Sherden seemed to gauge her in return. "Yes."

Mairead believed him. "Have you seen the law clerk helping Judge Pitt with the *Dooley* case?"

Sherden seemed confused. "The Latina woman with the polio braces?"

"No. Her research clerk, a recent law grad named Charles Vareika."

Sherden looked away, then came back. "I remember seeing a big

A STAIN UPON THE ROBE

+

69

blond guy in the courtroom once early on, during the wrangling over seating the jury. He was sitting next to the bench, taking notes."

"Well, he's missing."

"Missing?" Sherden seemed shocked. "You mean, as in 'missing person'?"

"Functionally, if not legally technically. My boss and I have been asked to investigate, since the police won't act as yet."

Sherden now seemed more confused. "Why are you telling me this?"

"It's occurred to us that maybe somebody connected with the case would have a reason to make the trial turn into a circus."

"Too late." Sherden smiled grimly. "All of these trials turn into sideshows, anyway, either the priest or the victims being portrayed as . . . sexual freaks."

"Even so"—Mairead thought back to Judge Pitt's list having holes in its coverage—"you know the different interest groups?"

"The prominent ones, anyway. In fact, some of their 'champions' were in the courtroom with us this morning."

Mairead took out a pad. "Can you give me names and organizations?"

Shel Gold was sitting behind his office desk, putting the finishing touches on a motion to suppress in a bank robbery case, when he heard the suite door open and Billie say, "Welcome back."

Expecting Mairead's voice, Shel was surprised by, "Is our Sheldon available at the moment?" the formal English overlaid with more than a touch of Russian accent.

"Shel," Billie again. "You available?"

He did a quick scan of his desktop, to be sure nothing confidential was showing that another lawyer shouldn't see. "Ask Ms. Ekarevskaya to come in."

Given the carpeting in the reception area, Shel couldn't pick up Gallina Ekarevskaya's predictable heels clacking on the floor, but he wasn't disappointed in her appearance, tote bag slung over a shoulder, at his office door.

Mid-thirties and a willowy five-foot-six, she wore a light gray suit that contrasted with her waist-length, crow's-wing hair. The suit had a green pinstripe that matched her eyes, turned up just a bit at the corners. So like Natalie's.

The things you notice.

"Sheldon," said Ekarevskaya, extending her hand, Shel getting a little jolt of electricity from shaking it. "You are looking well."

"And you are looking more than well. Please, sit."

Ekarevskaya sat in the chair like a ballerina curtsying to royalty, and Shel immediately got the business-over-pleasure feeling.

She said, "I am not sure I ever thanked you properly for your role in our last case together."

Ekarevskaya hadn't, though Shel thought—even hoped?—that she might be saving that as an excuse for seeing him again. "I'm not sure any thanks are necessary, Gallina, but if you do, you're welcome."

"Sheldon, Sheldon." Ekarevskaya moved her head in a way that somehow was more exotic than a mere side-to-side shake. "I wish we could communicate in a language different from English, because I fear my formality with it seeps into your manner of speaking as well."

Shel thought again of Natalie, but now with a slight shudder that he tried to repress. "Let me know if you think of one."

A flash in the eyes. "I shall." Then business crept back into them. "But, unfortunately, not today. I wonder if I might ask what direction your interest in the *Dooley* trial might take?"

The warning bells sounded, but Shel knew he'd not said—even implied—anything about that to Ekarevskaya. "My interest?"

"Please, Sheldon. Do not be sly with me. It does not become you, and despite what others may have told you, it is rather transparent as well. Your Ms. Mairead was in the courtroom today for a rather routine motion in limine, and I doubt her attendance was part of some continuing legal education."

Shel felt himself smiling despite the gravity of Barbara Pitt's situation. "Assuming you were there as well, why didn't you ask her?"

Ekarevskaya made another ballet maneuver out of crossing her legs. "Perhaps because I prefer speaking with you, even in English and even about our professional efforts."

Shel decided he wouldn't be telling the woman any more than he'd already shared with Judge Bruce Rodrigue—nor more than the Pope and Mairead were telling anyone else they spoke to as well. "Judge Pitt's law clerk, Charles Vareika, didn't show up for work yesterday."

A widening of the eyes, too automatic to be acting, Shel believed.

Ekarevskaya said, "You think more is involved than just an unreliable employee?"

"Given his prior record with the court, yes."

She recrossed her legs. "I remember seeing a handsome blond boy of your Ms. Mairead's age once, near the beginning of the trial, but not since."

"So you've been attending the trial yourself, then."

"Upon occasion." Ekarevskaya sighed. "I represent civilly one of the many victims of Mr. Dooley."

You should have seen that coming. "Was this client part of the settlement that the cardinal rescinded?"

"No, but obviously it concerns me."

Shel nodded. "Gallina, can you tell me your client's name?"

Ekarevskaya seemed to assess something. "He will be testifying in the criminal trial, so yes, it is already on the witness list and need not be kept a secret. He is Hector Washington, a black teenager, though his mother, Ynez—spelled using a 'Y,' not an 'I'—is Latina."

Shel wrote those down on a pad. "Would you object if I or someone on my team spoke to them?"

More assessing. "Yes, as to Hector. Given your situation with Judge Pitt's clerk, however, I would not stand in the way of you alone personally speaking with Mrs. Washington."

Shel thought he ought not press his luck. "Thank you. Address and telephone?"

Ekarevskaya took out what looked to Shel like a small calculator, but when she began tapping it with a stylus, he realized it had to be one of those PDAs, a several-hundred-dollar item that supposedly would replace a $7.95 pocket calendar. However, after a short time, Ekarevskaya rattled off the requested information. She played with the device some more, then put it back in her tote bag before changing her tone, if not the general subject. "Sheldon, have you actually seen this Mr. Dooley?"

Shel realized that he really hadn't wanted to, given Richie's abduction and God knew what else. "No."

"He is repulsive, yet riveting. And such impression of mine is just from watching him sit in his chair. He appears never to communicate with his attorney, but he did take the time today to turn to your Ms. Mairead. To smile and even to wave at her."

Shel found that vaguely unsettling, probably again because of Richie, but said, "And you want to know why."

"Yes."

"Gallina, so far as I know, there is no connection between Cornelius Dooley and Mairead O'Clare. I think she would have told me."

Ekarevskaya uncrossed her legs and rose from her chair without using her hands on the arms of it. "May I make a suggestion, Sheldon?"

Straining a little in the stomach, he managed to do the same from his chair. "Certainly."

"Ask her?"

Sheldon A. Gold then watched Gallina Ekarevskaya spin on the balls of her feet and jounce out of his office, her shapely calves seeming to vibrate independently from the rest of her body.

Admit it: The woman can make an entrance out of an exit.

SEVEN

Billie Sunday had just settled into the chair next to Mairead's and in front of Shel's desk when he said, "I didn't have very good luck with Judge Bruce Rodrigue, I'm afraid."

Mairead nodded. "He denied having any romantic interest in our client?"

"Denied pretty much everything, but I had the feeling that he knew something more about Charles Vareika than he let on. In fact, looking back on it, I think His Honor was more interested in my questions from the 'what did *I* know to ask' standpoint."

Billie said, "If I hear from the Pope, you want him on the man?"

"Not yet. And besides, I imagine our investigator is still driving through Maine as we speak. Mairead?"

The child nodded again. "After our walk to the courthouse this morning, I talked with Leslie Hughes in the research clerks' office. She denies a romantic relationship with Vareika, but she envies Judge Pitt's intervening for him toward prestigious-firm interviews. And guess who she's clerking for now?"

Shel said, "Bruce Rodrigue."

Billie savored the dumbstruck look on the child's face.

"Well," from Mairead, "I also sat in on a motion hearing before Judge Pitt. And guess who I saw there?"

Shel, that ever-aggravating man, smiled this time before saying, "Gallina Ekarevskaya."

Mairead's jaw dropped even more, and Billie had to bite back a laugh.

"How in the world did . . . ?"

Shel, aggravating as he was, wouldn't keep anybody on the hook too long. "She came to see me, wondering why you were there. And why Cornelius Dooley seemed to take an interest in you after the argument."

"About Dooley, I don't know. He waved to me in a weird way, but I've certainly never seen him before. Believe me, I'd remember." Mairead seemed to recover a bit. "But Ekarevskaya . . . ?"

Shel said, "She's representing one of the victims, and she's given me permission to speak with the mother."

"You personally?"

Billie could tell their boss was pleased that the child listened to his every word, making sure how important each was. "That's right. Why?"

"Division of labor, mostly. At the hearing, I met a man named Bill Sherden, who's the executive director of a priests' victims organization." Billie watched her toss Shel a card like she was dealing poker. "He gave me some information on the interest groups and their . . . 'champions.' I figured we could divide up the most likely candidates."

"Who are they?"

"First is a woman, Am-ah-*lee* Car-*doan*."

Billie shook her head. "Can you spell that one for me?"

The child obliged with "A-M-E-L-I-E C-A-R-D-O-N."

Shel said, "And Ms. Cardon represents . . . ?"

"A priests' rights advocacy group called Save Our Clergy, or SOC."

Billie figured that would be better than Save Our Priests, or SOP, but she caught Shel frowning.

He said, "Wouldn't seem likely that such a group would be involved in foul play against a law clerk."

Mairead just stared at him. "Wouldn't seem likely that a state like Kentucky had one-hundred-fifty civil suits already filed against priests for molestation, either, or that the number of victims who've come forward in Massachusetts is approaching five hundred, but that's what Sherden told me."

Shel winced. "Point taken. Who else did he mention?"

"Donald Iverson. He represents one of the splinter groups that parted ways with the North American Man/Boy Love Association."

Lord in Heaven. Billie turned and stared at Mairead this time. "The what?"

She repeated the full name. "According to Sherden, the original group arose to lobby for changes in the statutory rape and other sexual practices laws."

Billie still couldn't quite trust her ears. "There is an actual . . . organi-*za*-tion that wants to make it legal for men to have sex with . . . boys?"

Shel said, "It's hard for me to believe, too, but I remember reading an article about them once."

Billie shook her head again, but wrote down "NAMBLA— splinter."

When she looked back up, Shel had turned toward Mairead. "Do we know why this smaller group broke off from the main one?"

"Not yet. But both Donald Iverson and Amelie Cardon were in the courtroom today. Sherden figured they're respectively milking the *Dooley* trial for all the free publicity they can, talking to reporters afterward, et cetera."

Shel closed his eyes, and Billie could only guess how this kind of talk must be stirring up memories of his own son.

Shel's lids suddenly flapped like shades on twin windows. "Mairead, I just don't think I'm up to speaking with both a victim's mother *and* this Iverson, or anybody else in his group. If you're troubled, too, I'd certainly understand, but if you could take him, I'll go see Ms. Cardon."

Mairead stood up. "I'll try for Iverson before he leaves the courthouse, since I told the Pope I'd visit Vareika's roommate tonight, give him my take on the woman."

Shel nodded, but Billie saw a loose thread. "Aren't you both forgetting someone?"

Mairead looked down at her. "Who?"

"This Bill Sherden."

Mairead appeared surprised. "But he's the one who told me about these other people."

"About these other 'interest groups,'" said Billie. "But it seems to me that your Mr. Sherden might have some issues his *own*self."

Billie heard Shel say, "I agree. Mairead, let's keep you his friend, and I'll ask the Pope to check up on Sherden when he can."

But Billie Sunday had been watching the new child, and it was plain as day that lawyer O'Clare thought investigating her new "friend" would be a pure waste of time.

M r. Iverson, excuse me?"

Mairead saw the man stiffen at first, then smile and almost relax as he stopped for her in the corridor outside Judge Pitt's courtroom. Iverson looked fortyish with black hair razor-cut like Mel Gibson's, and similar, probing eyes. About six feet tall and slender, he had that loose posture, even in a nicely tailored business suit, that she'd seen male athletes strike when they were comfortable with their quickness. "Yes?"

Mairead reached him and introduced herself.

"Well, Ms. O'Clare," Iverson shifting a black suede attaché case from one hand to the other. "I didn't know your name, but I certainly observed Father Dooley noticing you inside there earlier."

"FATHER" Dooley, young lady.

Mairead thought back to Shel's comment about Gallina Ekarevskaya and now wondered if anyone *hadn't* observed it. "I'd like to talk with you, if we can."

Iverson canted his head to the right. "I also observed you leaving the courtroom with, shall we say, my counterpart?"

Mairead said, "I'm not sure that's how Mr. Sherden would phrase it."

"Well, then, permit me the indulgence of equal time to make my association's points." Like Sherden, Iverson fished out a business card, though from the attaché instead of a pocket. "Do you think we might use a quiet courtroom for our little chat?"

Taking the card, Mairead wanted to take charge, too, so she said, "Let's see," and turned first, making Iverson follow her. They found a smaller courtroom down the corridor that was open but empty, not even a bailiff in sight. Inside the bar enclosure, Mairead pulled a leather-padded chair from one of the counsel tables to the opposite side of another, so she was facing the bench but also diagonally across from the seat Iverson had chosen.

A thin smile. "Keeping your distance, Ms. O'Clare?"

Mairead forced herself to smile back. "It seems professionally comfortable."

"Especially after what Wild Bill told you."

"'Wild Bill'?"

"My nickname for Sherden. Though perhaps an allusion to 'crusader' instead of 'cowboy' might be more apt."

Mairead thought of "Wild Bill Hickok" as a peace officer rather than a cowboy, but she let it pass. "Mr. Sherden didn't tell me anything beyond you heading a group that broke off from the North American Man/Boy Love Association."

"Ah. But not the reason for our little . . . schism?"

"No."

"Well, truth to tell, it was a clash more of personality than strategy, though those in my group believe a more public approach to the issues would better serve us."

"And that's why you're attending the *Dooley* trial?"

"Partly. You see, Ms. O'Clare, for thousands of years, young boys and men have been falling in love with each other, but heterocentrist societal norms weren't ready for that, any more than they were ready for adult women to enter blatantly lesbian relationships. Why, I daresay there was a time when that hemangioma stain on your hands—which appears to continue under your sleeves—would have been grounds for putting you to death as somehow 'marked like Cain.'"

Mairead found disquieting the memories of her "stigmata"—as characterized by Sister Angela, a cruel nun at the orphanage—but was more angry that Iverson had put her on the defensive so easily. "I think adults can make certain choices young boys and girls can't."

"You might be surprised, Ms. O'Clare. NAMBLA grew out of a 1978 gathering of men to discuss their relationships with boys. We wanted to bring into the open what historians—even ecclesiastical ones—had conceded was going on in seminaries and monasteries since the Year One, and before that in the pyramids and even the caves. It is a natural expression of love, not unlike the mentoring that I'm sure your own mother provided you when the first signs of your . . . maturing appeared."

"I was raised in an orphanage, Mr. Iverson."

He flinched, which Mairead didn't expect. "I'm so sorry, but perhaps then you have your own . . . experiences to go by."

Mairead pushed those—the predatory older boys *and* girls—out of her mind. "Children are curious, and they need to be taught. But not targeted."

"And why is that, Ms. O'Clare? Because sexual relations between men and developing boys is somehow harmful to the boys involved?"

Mairead felt her stomach turn. "You're not going to argue it isn't?"

"I would, but there are others who approach the subject more . . . scientifically, shall we say? Have you heard of the book *Harmful to Minors: The Perils of Protecting Children from Sex.*"

"This is a *book* book?"

"Published by the University of Minnesota Press recently. In it, the author—a woman, by the by—argues the same thing that we felt at that conference in the late seventies: What hurts a boy the most is what happens to him *after* the relationship is revealed. The 'shame,' the prosecution and even jailing of the one man in the world who truly 'loves' him."

"You can love an underage child without imposing sex upon him or her."

"It's hardly an 'imposition,' Ms. O'Clare. In most cases, the boy is as curious about the relationship's shared gifts as the man. And while a number of the children are homosexual, and hence man/boy is the route they choose, many others grow out of that phase of their development and go on to lead completely 'productive,' societally blessed, heterosexual lives."

"It's still rape."

"Only because a law makes it so. Look at that poor female schoolteacher in Washington State, wasting away in prison when her 'crime' was loving—and bearing the child of her union with—a twelve-year-old male student. Why, our own Supreme Court struck down the Child Pornography Prevention Act of 1996 as unconstitutional because productions of even *Romeo and Juliet* could be prosecuted for depicting 'underage love.'"

"You don't think it's simply immoral for a man to prey on a child, sexually?"

"No more than I find relationships between consenting adults, regardless of gender, race, or any other 'community-monitored' characteristic. The more we deny that which occurs 'naturally,' Ms. O'Clare, the more we condemn ourselves to casting the first stone in a landslide that would eventually bury us all for our own 'sins,' of whatever nature."

Mairead felt her lunch do a pirouette in the pit of her stomach and decided she'd ask the Pope to reciprocate on her going to second-check Vareika's roommate by having Murizzi meet with this guy, try to figure out what made him tick.

Then Iverson canted his head to the left. "However, Ms. O'Clare, while I'm certainly glad to debate these issues ad infinitum, I do wonder why you wished to speak with me at all?"

The man's right about that, young lady. You've gotten a bit lost in his cause.

Mairead nodded. "Mr. Iverson, does the name Charles Vareika mean anything to you?"

Iverson blinked. "I don't think so, yet . . ."

"Yet?"

"Well, it does seem to me that I've heard that somehow during the trial."

"You mean, Mr. Dooley's?"

"*Father* Dooley's, yes. You see, the Catholic Church is running from the poor man as though he has the plague. Defending oneself from societal onslaught is very expensive, so my organization has been helping to fund his war chest." Iverson blinked some more. "But yes, I know I've heard that name 'Vareika,' perhaps from the judge herself?"

"He's her law clerk, and he seems to have disappeared."

"Oh my." A frown. "But then, who's that woman sitting in front of the bench?"

As Mairead did for Bill Sherden, she explained administrative clerk versus research clerk.

Donald Iverson touched the tip of his index finger to his lips, then began tapping lightly on them. "Will this Vareika's going missing hold up Father Dooley's trial at all, do you suppose?"

"I don't know, but I'd guess not."

A smile again, only not the "thin" one. "Well, that's certainly a relief. His defense will begin shortly, and we'll want the jury's, and the judge's, undivided atten—"

Iverson suddenly looked over her shoulder, and Mairead turned to see a young teenager, no more than thirteen or fourteen, standing inside the courtroom's swinging doors. He wore a Ralph Lauren polo shirt and tailored slacks, but he had the look of harder times elsewhere, including an almost emaciated build, oddly dyed orange hair, and a bruised cheek.

"Ordell," said Iverson, "I thought you were going to wait downstairs?"

"And I thought we was gonna have lunch," an Appalachian twang in his voice.

"So I promised." Donald Iverson stood. "Ms. O'Clare, a pleasure."

"I wish I could say the same."

Mairead heard Iverson laugh heartily and watched him leave the courtroom, his arm around Ordell's shoulders.

Feeling dispirited, she gave them a two-minute head start, then went into the corridor herself.

"Ms. O'Clare?" from a different voice this time, resonant and somehow familiar.

Mairead turned toward its source: the defense attorney for Cornelius Dooley.

"I'm Kyra Yelverton."

Mairead remembered hearing the second half of that back in the courtroom. "How did you know *my* name?"

"I asked Tommy Flanagan, the bailiff."

Mairead said, "Because?"

Yelverton showed beautiful teeth, but in a sigh more than a smile. "Because for some reason my client wants to speak with you alone. And he won't cooperate with me any further in his defense until I arrange it."

. . .

"Y̵ou the other lawyer Gallina told me about?" from behind the screen door of the first floor of a three-decker, a wave of stale smoke coming through the mesh as the woman struck a match to light a cigarette at the corner of her mouth.

"Yes, Mrs. Washington. Sheldon Gold." He slipped one of his business cards through the crack in the door, studied her as she mouthed the words on it, though her voice had no trace of Spanish, despite her first name. Ynez Washington was around thirty-five, Shel guessed, but her latte-toned face and hands looked a generation older, and the smoking probably didn't help those aspects. She wore a cardigan sweater threadbare at the elbows and a shapeless housedress underneath, no stockings or even shoes, just shower flip-flops.

"All right," she finally said, "I guess you can come in."

Shel pulled open the door, on a strong spring, and got spanked by it when he didn't move quite fast enough into the cramped foyer. Washington gestured to the left, where a small living room held a couch and two easy chairs. The woman took the couch, pointing with his card to one of the chairs. The room smelled like chain-smokers had played cards in it every night for a week.

Sitting, Shel said, "I really appreciate your seeing me."

Washington nodded warily, releasing matching blue-gray plumes through her nostrils. "Gallina said the rules were only you and me, not Hector."

Shel nodded. "Is your son anywhere he could . . . overhear us?"

"No. Sent him to the store, and it'll take him a while. He's a little slow—one of the 'presents' that rat-bastard of a priest gave him."

"I'm sorry?"

Washington used the heel of her hand to whack the other one. "Hector said that if he didn't do the rat-bastard the way he liked it, the priest would cuff him in the head. Now my boy's slow."

Shel drew in a breath, nearly choking on the smoky air. "Mrs. Washington, I—"

"Gallina calls me Ynez. I guess one lawyer can, you can, too."

"Thank you. And I'm Shel, short for—"

"Sheldon, right. Like you said before and it reads on your card here."

"Right." Shel felt senile, realized he wanted out of that small, confining room as soon as possible. "Did Ms. Ekarevskaya tell you that the judge's law clerk is missing?"

"Yeah. The big blond kid."

"You've seen him, then."

"When the prosecutor was picking the jury. We had to be there, so they could tell whether any of them knew Hector. Or me. Or probably even Hector's father, though that'd be a trick, him in the ground almost ten years now."

"I'm sorry for your loss."

"Kind of late for sympathy cards," Washington waving Shel's business one around like she was trying to dry the ink on it. "The reason I let Hector get too close to that rat-bastard."

"Mr. Dooley."

"*Father* Cornelius Xavier Dooley, or 'Father Neil,' like he wanted Hector to call him. Oh, and Father Neil was a smoothy, too. Not a week after Paulie's high blood pressure blew the artery out of his head, that rat-bastard started sniffing around. I was drinking too much—grieving, you know?—when Father Neil stops by, asks if there's anything he can do, for me or for Hector. At first I thought it was nice of him, especially since we were black Latino, and he was Irish. Then it was a trip with some other boys for camping, only they came up one sleeping bag short, so Hector had to 'snuggle' with the rat-bastard. Then it was visits to the rectory—or the 'rectum,' I guess you could say, since that's all in the diary."

Shel had cringed at the play on words, but now said, "Hector's diary?" before he even registered it might be more than he'd want to know. Especially since his Richie was way too young to be able to write when he was . . . taken.

Washington, however, shook her head. "Not Hector's. Father Neil's. He kept one himself, the prosecutor says. Like a scorecard, maybe, or a scrapbook without photos." A different shaking of the head. "She also told me some of the priests, they'd take Polaroids of 'their' kids, for real scrapbooks. At least the rat-bastard didn't go that far. Hector's fifteen now, and Father Neil could have been photographing him since he was six. But even the diary don't stop that black bitch from defending him in court. She's a traitor, a traitor to her *race*." Now Washington raised her head, eyes fixed on Shel. "Only Gallina says we'll get good money out of all this, especially after the jury finds Dooley guilty."

A criminal verdict would be leverage toward negotiating a civil settlement. *If* by then the Church had any money left to offer. "But, Ynez, about the judge's law clerk?"

"Oh, right. The big blond guy."

"Do you know any reason he'd disappear?"

"Me?" Washington stubbed out her cigarette in an ashtray overflowing with its predecessors. "Why would I know?"

"Well, I thought you might have heard or seen something as you've been attending the trial, and—"

"Stop right there." Washington reached into the cardigan's pocket, dipping until she brought out a pack of cigarettes and hiked another one into her mouth. "Gallina said Hector and me have to be witnesses, so we haven't been there since the jury picking."

Of course, Shel thought as she lit up again. The witnesses would be sequestered so they wouldn't hear how prior ones had testified. Shel could feel the smoke from Washington's new cigarette invading his body, and the desire to run out of that room and that house almost overwhelmed him.

As he prepared to get up though, Shel heard the screen door open and then spank someone else.

Washington spoke around her smoke. "Hector? That you, boy?"

"Yeah," a weary voice.

"Why you home so early from the store?"

"Forgot what you want me to brung you."

Washington shook her head. "That why I give you the list. You can read, can't you?"

Something Shel had experienced before: Minority people speaking good English to whites, then lapsing into "street" when talking with each other. It also seemed to Shel that Hector Washington took forever to make it to the living room. His mother had said he was "slow," but did that mean the poor kid couldn't even walk and talk at the same time?

Then Hector shuffled into the room, coming to a full stop before saying to his mother, "I lost it."

"Lost what?"

"The list."

Shel Gold's heart went out to Hector. More tan than black—or even brown—in skin tone, he was tall for fifteen, but doughy, with a wispy mustache under baggy, sluggish eyes. Despite the warmth of a June evening outside, he wore a torn parka at least three sizes too small for him and a woolen watch cap.

Ynez Washington shook her head some more. "Well, you're here, say hello to Mr. Gold."

"Pleased to meet you."

"Same, Hector," replied Shel, thinking, My God, how long has he been like this?

"Well," said his mother, "you didn't buy us no food, you might's well go to bed."

Shel thought, She can't be serious.

"Okay," from Hector, shuffling off and out of sight.

Shel waited until he felt the poor teenager was out of earshot as well. "Ynez, I am so sorry."

A sly look from Washington. "Sorry enough?"

Shel blinked.

"You see," she continued, "you can't just apologize for breaking Gallina's rule. You got to make up for it."

Shel thought about correcting the woman's impression, explaining that he meant he was sorry about Hector's condition, not the technical violation by Lawyer A of the rules of engagement laid down by Lawyer B.

Particularly when the mother *told* her son to speak to you.

But the cigarette smoke was now so oppressive, Shel simply said, "Okay, what do you want me to do?"

Washington came forward in her chair. "See, I figure, if I do have to be a witness, might be a good idea for another lawyer to kind of hear my speech before I get on the stand."

"Ynez, your attorney probably wouldn't—"

"I answered your questions, and you broke Gallina's rule. So, how's about you just sit back and let me try out my lungs?"

Or cough them out. But Gallina Ekarevskaya didn't have to give Shel permission to see Ynez Washington, nor did Washington have to talk with him. So he dutifully leaned back in his chair.

Only to hear a litany of horror from Hector's mother that Sheldon A. Gold knew would give him nightmares for years, even if he could separate it intellectually from what might have happened two decades before to his own son.

EIGHT

I 'm so sorry you have to see me like this."

Mairead O'Clare stared through the reinforced screening over the picture window in the courthouse's "lockup" on the fifteenth floor. She shifted, somewhat nervously, in one of the mismatched chairs on the "Visitors" side of the wall. Mairead knew her nerves weren't from unfamiliarity with the surroundings, since she'd interviewed clients there before. No, her feelings flowed more from looking into the eyes of the man sitting atop the fixed chrome stool on the "Detainees" side of the wall. And, for the first time, hearing his voice: a mild, silky one, almost hypnotizing in its kindness.

God forgive me, young lady, but I believe we behold a monster.

Mairead cleared her throat. "Mr. Dooley, your attorney told me you wanted to see me?"

"Yes, but I'm afraid I . . . I don't even know your name."

His tone seemed to absolve any faux pas Mairead might have thought she'd somehow committed. "Mairead O'Clare."

A slow blink, done in time to a slow nod. *"That* was it. You were raised in a Catholic orphanage, correct?"

Steady, young lady. "Correct. Why?"

Now a self-deprecating grin and shrug, like Shel's, only with Dooley, it seemed learned, not natural, as though the former priest had perfected it in front of a mirror. "One of the nuns who served there, a Sister Angela, told me of the unfortunate little girl with the—her words—'stigmata blotching her arms.'"

Mairead could hear the old nun's voice now, shook it off.

Dooley leaned forward. "I chastised her, of course. You were no more responsible for the pigments in your skin than those of your hair or eyes. But her comment stuck with me, and when I saw you in the courtroom, the memory surfaced."

Mairead felt off-balance. "And that's why you wanted to see me?"

"That's why I *requested* Ms. Yelverton arrange it. But the real reason is that I wish to give you the opportunity to ask me your question."

Mairead tried to stay focused. "My question?"

"Yes, the reason you were sitting in that courtroom. The thing you need to find out."

Young lady, use even him as a resource if you can. "Mr. Dooley, I've been hired to—"

"No, no. Please, not yet." He sighed. "I'm afraid I require a nego-tiated exchange here."

"What kind of . . . exchange?"

Dooley pursed his lips. "I want you to promise that you'll first hear my story. Then I'll answer any questions you might have, young lady."

Initially repelled that he used the same phrase for her that Sister Bernadette always had, Mairead nonetheless tried to focus on Doo-ley's offer. "I sit here and listen to you, then you'll tell me what I want to know?"

A solemn nod.

She said, "And if I decline?"

"Then this very pleasant encounter will be at an end."

Mairead weighed the one against the other. *If I could tolerate Donald Iverson and his "man/boy love" pitch, I can stand anything.* "It's a deal."

"Excellent." A beaming smile, like a teacher rewarding an eager student. Dooley then held up his manacled hands, the chain's links clinking as they left the stool between his legs. "However, I could tell my story far more effectively without these absurd shackles."

"I don't have any control over whether you're restrained, but if I did, you'd stay that way."

Something passed over Dooley's eyes at that moment, and Mairead suddenly felt very chilly. She willed herself not to shiver, but instead locked her gaze onto his. "Okay, let's hear your . . . story."

Dooley's lips curled back from his stained teeth into something Mairead couldn't call a smile. "Despite those birthmarks, you would have been a poor candidate, young lady."

"Candidate? For what?"

"'Grooming,' as remarkably many of us seem to call it. You see, not long after I took my vows with the Church, I began to see the way our secular society utterly throws its unwanted children away. The ones from broken homes, the ones simply unloved. Or, as in your case, the ones who are . . . different."

Mairead was beginning to get Dooley's drift. "You'd look for the children who didn't have much going for them, with some kind of 'hole' in their lives."

Another teacher's smile. "You're a quick study, young lady. Yes, I'd watch for such, though as a priest, far more boys than girls came within my reach. Then I would test the child, make sure that he was trustworthy."

"Meaning, somebody who wouldn't tell a parent or schoolteacher."

"Precisely. And at first I was amazed by how many were in that category. I mean, I was saving them—literally—from a life on the street, being at risk of starvation, even murder, and so I suppose I *should* have anticipated their gratitude and discretion, but honestly, the depth of those traits in my little gentlemen came as a surprise to me."

Mairead thought back to the orphanage, how many of the boys there probably could have been "groomed" into being "little gentlemen." Then she wondered if the reason they hadn't been was because of the presence of nuns like Sister Bernadette, if not Sister Angela. "Mr. Dooley, weren't you afraid of being caught, anyway?"

He frowned. "A risk of doing business, young lady. And besides, who's the more credible truth-teller: a runaway waif, or a highly educated, respected member of the community?"

"The first time, maybe. But after the third or fourth child comes forward?"

"Oh, I'd usually be gone long before that." A laugh, polite enough, as if at a small joke. "No, the beauty of the archdiocese's rotation policy back then was that a capable priest—and I was that, a superb worker for all the Church's espoused goals—would be in demand. Other parishes clamored for someone who wasn't drowning in alcohol or lingering a bit too long on the skirt length of the attractive women in the congregation. I projected what we called *'bella figura,'* or 'a good impression,' a godsend wherever the archbishop or cardinal of the moment and his minions chose to send me."

"And the children in those various places. Were you a 'godsend' to them?"

"Quite frankly, yes." Dooley clasped his hands as though in prayer, the links of his manacles rattling more against the chrome of his stool. "Without me, who knows how many might have fought their sexual orientation, misunderstood tragically how to express it, perhaps even committed suicide over it? Believe me, young lady, they benefited from their exposure to me far more than I benefited from my exposure to them. Yet I persevered, despite the risk you mentioned earlier, for their sake, not my own."

Mairead began to feel that turning in her stomach, just as she had with Donald Iverson in the empty courtroom. "Mr. Dooley, why are you telling me all this?"

The eyes began to smolder and the lips to quiver, and Mairead thought for the first time that Dooley might be losing it. But when he began speaking again, his voice wasn't that silky, 'grooming' tone, but rather more like pulpit bluster, selling the congregation on a sermon's theme. "In Kentucky and Georgia, sheriffs are being murdered by their political opponents. In San Francisco, a woman whose dogs tore a neighbor to pieces got four years and a fine—a *fine,* young lady—of less than seven thousand dollars. In Great Britain, two eighteen-year-olds, who at age ten murdered a two-year-old toddler, will now be released from prison, and the media is forbidden even to report on their whereabouts."

Dooley raised his clasped hands now, the shackles shaking like a tambourine. "In this country, the authorities are going after every conceivable kind of clergy: Greek Orthodox and black evangelical,

Jewish rabbis and Lutheran ministers. In the Catholic Church alone, we've had archbishops resign, priests commit suicide, one even shot by an alleged 'victim.' The tragedy is not that we've taken desperate children under our wings and nourished them in mind, body, and soul. The tragedy is that we are being persecuted as though the supposed 'crimes' we've committed are worse than *murder*!"

Mairead had about had her fill of Cornelius Xavier Dooley. "You done?"

He lowered his hands, still clasped. "Meaning, you would like to ask your question now?"

"Yes."

"A final point, young lady, and then you may ask away." Dooley shrugged his rounded shoulders. "They took my diary from me."

"Your diary of . . . being in jail?"

"No. No, much worse. The diary I maintained about all our experiences, the ones with my little gentlemen."

He's serious, and I'm going to be sick. "You mean, the police seized it, and the prosecutor entered it into evidence?"

A dismissive wave of the manacled hands. "I'm not interested in the judicial details. I just want to read my diary again. It provides me great comfort."

Steady, young lady. He still hasn't helped you as yet.

"Mr. Dooley, perhaps your attorney has a copy of it, or can acquire one."

"I don't want a 'copy.' That's so . . . impersonal when we're discussing the product of my own hand."

Mairead thought back to something she'd been told by Florinda Altamira. "As far as I know, the original of an exhibit entered into evidence stays with the judge's clerk until the trial is completed, and an appeal is filed."

Dooley shook his head slowly. "That's what Ms. Yelverton told me as well." A sigh. "Earlier you asked about my little gentlemen coming forward to complain about me. Well, young lady, almost none of them ever did—never even considered . . . 'telling on' me." Another sigh. "Now it's rather like one of the hayrides I'd sponsor for them during our camping trips together: Everybody is trying to hop up on the wagon, see me in prison and then line their own pockets with the Church's silver. Disgusting, don't you think?"

A word that's sprung to mind a few times now. "Mr. Dooley, about my question?"

"Ah, yes. You are entitled. Please."

Mairead said, "Judge Pitt's research clerk, a young law graduate named Charles Vareika, seems to have disappeared."

A look of genuine concern? "Why, that's terrible."

"Do you know anything that might help me find him?"

Now Dooley's face went completely blank, like a passenger on a bus who knows his stop is a long way off. "And *that* is your question, the one you came into my courtroom to have answered?"

My courtroom. "It is."

"Well, then, I'm afraid I can't help you."

Just like that? "No information at all?"

Still a blank. "I've not even seen him since the beginning of my trial."

Which was what Mairead already had heard from Bill Sherden, the victims' group director.

However, something else still bothered her. "One more question?"

"Ask, young lady, but since it's beyond our bargain"—another shrug of the rounded shoulders—"I may not answer."

Mairead tried anyway. "Why did you want me to hear your 'story'?"

Dooley's smile returned now, a thousand-watt dazzler. "Did Ms. Yelverton tell you I'm being held in isolation?"

"No, but I'm not surprised, given the crimes you're accused of."

A nod. "Oh, I quite agree: It's a necessary precaution against possible vigilantism by my fellow detainees. But such absolute segregation carries its own terrible consequence."

"Which is?"

"I have no one to tell my story *to*." Dooley leaned forward. "And even in this perversion of a confessional, with a picture-window screen and bright lights instead of enclosed, contemplative darkness, I really enjoy telling it, young lady." Now Cornelius X. Dooley pressed his nose against the screen, distorting his face into a gargoyle's mask. "I really, really do."

. . .

Shel Gold knocked on the door with "Save Our Clergy" in calligraphic letters at eye level and heard a loud "Come in, please!" from a female voice, a slight accent to it that Shel thought might be French.

Twisting the knob and swinging it slowly open, he saw a woman in her twenties, streaked blond hair pinned up over skin so pale it was almost translucent, even minor veins in her forehead and jaw visible through it. Obviously flustered, she sat behind a cluttered desk, a telephone on a shoulder cradle squeezed under her chin while both hands collated documents and stuffed them into an envelope. Having filled it, the woman used the envelope to wave Shel in and then point to the door, which he closed behind him.

"Yes, Madame . . . Yes, I know it is a tragedy of 'biblical proportions,' but . . . Well, that is what we here at SOC are trying to address by . . . Yes, only—"

The woman—her accent definitely French—took the phone away from her chin and actually stared at it before setting it down on top of a stack of papers. "Another hang-up. The fifth this morning."

Shel wasn't quite sure what to do or say, so he just nodded.

"I am so sorry," said the woman, now standing and shrugging in a way Shel found charming before realizing that he had the same mannerism, and that their sharing it might be why he found hers so. "My name is Amelie Cardon."

"Sheldon Gold," he said, handing over one of his business cards again.

Cardon glanced at it, a lock of her hair coming undone and covering one of her eyes. She put the card under the phone, as though she didn't want to lose it, at least not right away. "Please, do not tell me you represent another victim of 'priest abuse.'"

"No, I don't."

Cardon puckered her lips and blew out a breath, pushing the lock of hair away from her eyes, as though her hands had more important things to do. "Well, then, sit please and tell me who you *do* represent."

Shel saw a chair against the wall with only a small cluster of papers on it, so he lifted them carefully, then set the cluster on the floor before he pulled the chair over to a conversational distance from her desk.

He noticed that Cardon, already seated again, used the time to stuff another envelope. "If I've come at a bad moment . . ."

A shrill laugh that Shel thought she bit off, for fear it would get away from her if she didn't. "Mr. Gold, we have no such thing as a *good* moment anymore."

He sat down. "The scandal."

"The 'scandals,' plural." Cardon waved at another chair, occupied by what appeared from headlines and ragged edges to be news articles torn rather than clipped from their pages. "Take your pick. We have clergy from virtually every major city in the country being charged by prosecutors or sued by victims, with even cardinals being subpoenaed—subpoenaed, *impossible*—to testify about how they 'handled' given rotations of their priests. We have bishops—*arch*bishops, for that matter—resigning, and monsignors being pilloried in their own parishes. We have priests supposedly paying for abortions, and some dioceses talking about selling Church real estate—even, in Chicago, the cardinal's *mansion*—to pay civil judgments in the millions of dollars." The lock of hair fell over her eye again, and Cardon once more blew it away. "So, yes, Mr. Gold, this is as bad a period as the Church has had since the Roman Empire fed our pioneering converts to the lions."

"I'm truly sorry."

Cardon seemed to deflate. "No, I am the one to be sorry. For venting at a stranger." She squared herself in the chair. "So, what can I do for you?"

"I understand you've been following the *Dooley* trial?"

"Daily."

Shel smiled in spite of himself. There's something about gallows humor that helps everyone get through the worst of troubles. "The judge presiding over the case has had a law clerk helping her with research."

Cardon shrugged again, bringing that errant lock of hair over her eye a third time. "I imagine that is sensible."

"Unfortunately, however, he's disappeared."

Cardon frowned, then shook her head, but still having to puff the lock away. "I do not understand."

"He didn't show up for work yesterday morning."

"No, Mr. Gold. I understand what 'disappeared' means. What I do not understand is why you are here to tell me this?"

Shel spread his hands, as though he were appealing to a jury during closing argument. "I was hoping you might have some information that would help us find him."

"Us? Who is this 'us'?"

Shel thought that an odd question somehow. "The judge he works with, the court system, me."

Another head shake, but now the right hand actually went up to tuck the straying lock of hair behind her ear. "There is something here that 'does not compute.' Why would I have any such information?"

"As you said, you've been attending the trial every day."

"Only because I must stay aware of what is attacking the clergy, as part of my job." Cardon gestured in a general way toward the mess on her desk. "These are fund requests, sent by me to a mailing list of prior contributors to Catholic causes." Now she gestured toward the news articles on the other chair. "Do you have any idea of the response rate since the scandals became this frenzy-feeding of media?"

"A lot less than it used to be?"

"Perhaps a tenth of that." Cardon held up both her hands, thumb and pinkie on the left ticking off points on the fingers of her right. "The faithful have lost their 'faith' in the Church's leaders. The rich parishioners have decided they prefer not to present five-figure, even six-figure checks, during communion breakfasts to bishops who turned prior contributions into 'hushed money' for settling sexual-abuse claims 'quietly.' Even the ordinary collections at Sunday Mass are declining. But worst of all is the situation for *new* priests. Last month, our cardinal welcomed to ordination only five seminary graduates, Mr. Gold. And the applications to Saint John's Seminary in Brighton and Blessed John the Twenty-third's in Weston? Half as many as were received by this time last year."

Shel thought he'd waited patiently enough. "Then you have no information about Judge Pitt's law clerk?"

Cardon seemed to deflate again. "The only person I have seen 'clerking' for the judge is a woman with the braces of one who had the polio." Then Cardon changed her tone. "Mr. Gold, may I ask *you* a question?"

"Certainly."

"You are Jewish, correct?"

Shel felt the old stiffening in his spine, fingers forming fists. "Correct."

A nod, somehow sad. "I accepted this job—I sought it *out*—because I wished to meet a good, Catholic man to marry. I have followed my religion's teachings to every letter. I may be the only twenty-six-year-old virgin in the city of Boston. But this . . . this devastation of the Church I have experienced, the clergy I have tried to save . . ."

And Shel saw the tears welling up as Cardon turned away from him, yanking open a desk drawer and stabbing at what he guessed to be a box of tissues, given the two she came away with in her hand.

Cardon said, "I am sorry, but can you leave me now?"

Shel stood up. "Thank you for your time."

She waved him off with the tissues the way she'd waved him in with the envelope.

And as Sheldon Gold went through the door, hearing Amelie Cardon snuffling behind him, he briefly wondered if the reason he didn't feel more sorry for her was because, given the reason behind her asking him if he was Jewish, she hadn't simply asked if he was not Catholic.

Well?" said Kyra Yelverton, standing with her arms crossed in the corridor on the fifteenth floor outside the lockup.

Mairead was still a little—no, more than a little—rocky from her session with Cornelius Dooley, and it took her a moment to even register the defense attorney's question. "Excuse me?"

"Why did my client want to see you?"

Mairead thought Yelverton was entitled to an answer. "To tell me his . . . story."

An expression of condolence washed over the black woman's features. "That's what I was afraid of." Yelverton uncrossed her arms. "My client mention a reason for picking you out?"

Mairead tapped each of her hands with the other's index finger. "Mr. Dooley saw these, remembered a nun once telling him about me."

"About your, uh . . . ?"

Mairead was used to people struggling to construct a politically correct phrase for her hemangioma. "No. About my being raised in a Catholic orphanage."

"Oh." Now Yelverton's features squeezed together. "God, I'm not doing a very good job of 'debriefing' you, am I?"

"Don't worry about it. You've got enough of a job in there," Mairead inclining her head back toward the lockup.

Yelverton glanced that way, nodding. "Student loans to pay and court-appointed cases to pay them. A combination the Devil himself must have invented."

Mairead empathized with her. "Ice hockey got me a scholarship through college, but law school was a whole different thing."

Yelverton grinned without showing the beautiful teeth. "Track for me—high and low hurdles. A million years ago." The grin faded. "Can I ask you another question?"

"Sure."

"I don't remember seeing you at the trial before."

"Today was my first time."

"Why come at all?"

Mairead couldn't see any harm in answering. "I'm helping Judge Pitt try to find her law clerk."

Yelverton's head snapped back like she was dodging a bumblebee. "What?"

"Charles Vareika, her research clerk. He didn't show up for work yesterday, and nobody seems to know where he's gone."

Now Yelverton chewed on her lower lip, but kept her eyes steady. "I hadn't heard that."

Neither had her client from his reaction, only Mairead sensed something different from the defense attorney. "Do you have any idea where Mr. Vareika could be?"

"Never met the man, unless he's the blond boy who sat in by the side of Judge Pitt's bench for jury selection and a couple of our motions."

"But not this morning's," said Mairead, still unsure about what was going through Yelverton's mind.

"No."

"Well, do you have any information that might help us find him?"

Yelverton shook her head. "Again, I'm sorry you had to suffer through my client's . . . 'story.'"

"Me, too," said Mairead O'Clare, definitely sensing that something about Charles Vareika was bothering Kyra Yelverton as the tall, slim defense attorney turned away and strode down the corridor.

NINE

Billie Sunday checked both the clock on her desk and the watch on her wrist. Within a minute of each other, basically saying 5:30 P.M.

And, of course, no word from any of the . . . "team."

The Pope? Well, he was so damned spooky, there was no predicting where that man might be or when he might call in, let a body know what he was doing. Billie seriously wondered whether, all the time he spent on the Homicide Unit, dealing with creatures who hunted at the bottom of the pond, maybe he'd picked up some of their habits, and that's what made him so strange to her.

But Shel certainly didn't fit into that kind of category. No, about him, Billie did a different kind of serious wondering. Like, how could a man go through all that education, including Harvard Law School, and still be such a . . . Billie tried to remember the name of a particular cartoon character, Gyro-something . . . Gyro Gearloose, that was it. This duck dressed like a World War I flier, only all confused about direction and what he was supposed to do next. That's the way Shel had struck Billie when she started working with him fourteen years before, the child who would always be late getting home from school, dawdling in mud puddles along the way. The man did know how to practice law, but basically he needed a valet, follow him around, clean up after him.

Billie glanced over her shoulder. Straighten out his office at least.

But the worst, to her, was the new child. Billie glanced over her other shoulder now. The young attorney who used to be in Mairead's office was a gentle, almost timid fellow named Vincent that Shel had taken pity on, brought into the suite almost like a starving cat caught out in the rain. Billie appreciated Shel's kindness that way, but it turned out to be worse than a curse, as poor Vincent didn't have the fortitude to practice law, especially not trial law, and most especially not criminal law. An image of Shel, with all the troubles in his own life caused by his crazy wife, having to help Vincent to another mental institution while Billie tried to raise the poor child's parents by telephone, let them know their son the attorney would be spending his days in a room horribly different from the court kind, one without jury boxes or witness stands.

Only that wasn't going to be the problem with the new child, uh-*unh*. No, if anything, they'd have to borrow a straitjacket from Vincent's asylum, slap it on her just to keep her in line. Billie wondered whether she'd ever calm down, whether maybe all she went through since birth about her atomic-bomb arms made her so hard to stop. Or even just to slow down, the child running before she could walk.

Then "child" and "running" made Billie Sunday think of her youngest, William the Worrier, and the fact that the five minutes she'd just frittered away wondering about things she probably couldn't change, much less control, would make her late in picking him up from his straddle care and taking him home to his brothers, and his house, and a more normal life—thank you, Lord—than any of the *other* members of Shel Gold's "team" seemed likely ever to enjoy.

Kneeling on an old towel, next to the flat tire on his Ford Explorer, Pontifico Murizzi for about the tenth time in the last seven hours asked himself why he *ever* agreed to drive again into the Heart of Fucking Darkness the map called "Maine."

The trip up from seeing the ex-husband/father Ugo Nagatami on the Cape to Boston hadn't been too bad, and the Pope had managed to stop for lunch at one of his favorite restaurants for a lobster-salad plate and a glass of bone-dry sauvignon blanc, even getting a table on the deck overlooking a tranquil cove. But as soon as Murizzi hit the merge for routes 3 and 128 in Braintree, the bumper to bumper had started, courtesy of the Big Dig.

The Pope went around the front of his truck, opened the hood, and took out the twisting rod for the jack. On Explorers, though, the rod pulled double duty: It also cranked down the lid on the under-carriage, which held the spare tire like a human tongue might a Life Savers mint. The feature was one that really sold Murizzi on the ve-hicle originally, since you didn't have to keep swinging the tire out of the way on a tailgate every time you wanted to load something in back. The downside, though, was that it took a while to get at the spare when you needed it.

As the Pope cranked the rod, his mind went back to the Big Dig. The project sounded great: to drop Boston's central artery under-ground, thus dismantling the elevated roadway's "barrier" effect and "rejoining" downtown with the waterfront through a twenty-seven-acre "necklace" of reclaimed land to be dedicated to greenspace. It all had sounded good when Murizzi first heard about it in the mid-eighties from a Transportation Department guy who had it on good authority that the project was the pork-barrel payoff by the Reagan Administration to then–Speaker of the House Tip O'Neill so that some of the Republican's conservative agenda could actually get de-bated, if not for-sure passed, by the Democratically controlled Con-gress. Only the original project budget was less than three billion dollars, and fifteen years later it had ballooned to something like six-teen billion, with no end of the actual construction in sight. You drove into Boston from any direction now, and what you saw was a Jurassic Park of cranes rising and dipping all over the fucking city, and ramps—even whole roads—disappearing and reappearing every week, sometimes every day.

Which, as he rolled the spare to the side of his truck and began to loosen the lugs on his left rear wheel, at least reminded the Pope of what he was trying to do for Judge Hot Pants on her missing law clerk.

The funny thing was, he'd managed to get through all the Big Dig potholes and uneven, metal bridging plates and sprinkled, tire-busting hazards like bolts and spikes in Greater Boston, only to pop on a tar-stripped section of narrow country road with orange-and-white-striped warning barrels in Maine, probably not five miles from Genna Nagatami's college. Except—surprise, surprise—his cell phone wouldn't work to call AAA from the bottom of whatever Valley of the Moon he was in right now.

And you actually seriously entertained driving to that post–Labor Day "summer camp" up here for gays and les—

"Fuck!" yelled Pontifico Murizzi, barking his knuckles on the wheel mount, then cursing, too, *any* job—any *thing*—that could take him into this godforsaken state.

Mairead looked at the woman about her age answering the door of the brownstone. "Ms. Klein?"

"Yes?"

Vivianna Klein's black curly hair looked carefully styled, but she was wearing just a tank top and shorts, barefoot and casual already while Mairead was still in office clothes, even after dinner. "I'm one of the attorneys trying to locate your roommate, Mr. Vareika?"

"God, now I'm starting to get worried," said Klein, but with less concern and more coyness in her voice. "First a private eye, now a lawyer? What's next, the 'Delta Force'?"

After 9/11 and Afghanistan, Mairead didn't think that was much of a joke, but she forced herself to nod. "May I come in?"

"Sure," with a head flip now, the hair resetting pretty much as it had been before. "Follow me, Counselor."

As Mairead did, Klein said over her shoulder, "Chuck tells me that his judge really calls all the lawyers that."

Chuck, Barbara Pitt's nickname for him. "'Counselor'? Yes, it's an easy way to treat everyone equally."

"Or," said Klein, reaching an open apartment door to the side of the staircase, "an easy way to cover the fact that you've forgotten their names."

Mairead truly had never even thought of that.

They went down half a flight of steps and entered a large living room, with high windows and drapes giving onto a ground-level patio. It was nicely appointed in Mairead's view, all the colors of drapes, oriental rug, and sectional furniture coming together to complement the fireplace and—

Which is when she raised her eyes to the portrait over the mantelpiece, and felt her heart just about burst, her knees go rubbery, and her breathing stop dead.

Young lady, this would be a very big mistake.

Mairead was vaguely aware of Klein walking into the kitchen, the woman saying, "Get you anything to drink?"

Mairead didn't reply immediately, but when her hostess turned around, the young lawyer forced herself to glance toward Klein. "Water?"

"Sure."

As Klein made noises of opening a refrigerator and dropping ice cubes into glasses, Mairead moved farther into the living room, centering herself on the portrait of the blond male smiling out at her. The artist must have had Leonardo da Vinci's touch on the *Mona Lisa,* this subject's blue eyes seeming to track Mairead as she moved, though it was more the smile, and the dimples, that told Mairead she'd just seen the man of her dreams captured on canvas.

Young lady, not to be rude, but snap out of it.

Klein came back in with two glasses. Mairead tore her eyes away from the painting to accept hers.

Klein looked up at the portrait now. "Guy really caught his charm, though I'm guessing you never met Chuck either, huh?"

"Either?"

"Well, that's what your Pontifico said."

Right, right, though Mairead never thought of their investigator by his real first name. She drank from her glass, glad for something to do but talk for a moment.

Klein took a seat on the sectional, and as Mairead backed up, she heard a slight growling from behind that caused her to wheel, sloshing some of her water.

A Doberman pinscher, black-and-tan, on its haunches on one of the sectional pieces, its growling causing the teeth to show, dimples at the corners of the long jaws that irrationally reminded Mairead of the man in the portrait.

Klein said, "Miata, clear."

The dog stopped growling and lay down, eyeing Mairead but otherwise seeming to relax.

Mairead took a deep breath.

Klein's tone had some laughter in it. "I hope you're not afraid of dogs, lawyer-girl?"

Mairead preferred "counselor" by a mile, but instead said, "No. Just a little surprised by yours."

"This apartment was mine before Chuck moved in, and I thought I needed some security, especially with the patio being so accessible to burglars and all. It's funny how most people are so afraid of Dobies, even though Miata is just as sweet as she can be, once you get to know her."

Mairead planned to leave well before that. Taking the sectional farthest from the dog, she held her water glass in both hands, willing her eyes not to stray toward the portrait. "So, you and Mr. Vareika haven't known each other very long?"

"Six, seven months. He answered an ad I put in one of the local throwaway papers, and we seemed a good fit." A coy smile now. "He liked this being a nice place, and I liked him being a big guy. And an attorney."

"That's refreshing," said Mairead, regaining a little composure. "Mind if I ask why?"

"All the lawyer-bashing, you mean? Hah, attorneys are still just people who went to law school. And I like knowing that if I have some kind of legal question, I can turn to him."

"Anything in particular?"

Klein smiled again, but not coyly. "Somehow I think that if Chuck was here, he'd say, 'Vivianna, you don't have to answer that.'"

And he'd be right: attorney-client privilege. "Mr. Murizzi already asked you a number of questions, but I was wondering if you'd heard anything more from—or even just about—Mr. Vareika?"

"No, and no."

Mairead felt as though the room's atmosphere had shifted, from two women kind of dancing around the disappearance of one very attractive man to something more . . . adversarial? "Well, have you thought of anything helpful that you might not have remembered when Mr. Murizzi was here?"

Klein used a finger to roll and twist the longest section of her hair. "Look, your Pontifico asked me everything under the sun about Chuck. But the problem is, I'm not his keeper, okay? So far as I can tell, he hasn't been here since sometime Saturday."

And now it's Tuesday night, three days later. "You're not worried about him?"

Klein let go of her hair. "Hey, lawyer-girl, Chuck's a big guy, like I said. If something was bothering him, he'd think it through, then fix it. He's probably just taken off somewheres."

"Any idea where that might be?"

"No."

Mairead couldn't see much else to ask. "Has Mr. Vareika ever been threatened in any way?"

"No."

"Fight in a bar, road rage?"

"No. Squared."

Dead end, young lady, though I can certainly see why Mr. Murizzi would have wanted a second opinion on this woman.

Mairead nodded as she rose from the sectional, Miata doing half a push-up on the other piece of furniture. "Well, thanks for your time, anyway."

Klein didn't stand. "Question for you?"

Mairead didn't sit back down, either. "Okay."

"Your legs. Ballet?"

Mairead knew the calf muscles could create that impression. "Good guess, but no. Ice hockey."

Klein seemed amused more than surprised. "And your hands thing?"

Mairead expected that one. "Hemangioma, a birthmark."

"So, not . . . contagious or anything?"

Mairead's turn to be surprised, if not amused. "No."

Klein rearranged her legs on the sectional seat like a cat looking to be stroked. "You have a boyfriend, lawyer-girl?"

"No."

"Girlfriend?"

"Never."

"Shame." Vivianna Klein now appeared to have lost all interest in Mairead. "How about closing the door when you leave, okay?"

Pontifico Murizzi stopped walking the macadam path on a grassy rise in front of a stolid, red-brick building. He took it for a dormitory, even though it overlooked what the Pope also took to be the faculty parking lot, as half the scattered cars in it were candidates for sticker-shock. He'd stopped because two preppy kids were coming toward him, and they were the first humans he'd seen since driving past the unmanned guardhouse at the campus entrance. "Excuse me, is that Gutterson Hall?"

One kid said, "Yeah, but school's, like, out of session now."

"I'm looking for a student named Genna Nagatami."

"Gen? Yeah, she's one of the few bunking there this summer."

The other kid looked down into the parking lot. "Only I don't see her car, do you?"

Murizzi followed the kid's gaze. "That's general parking?"

"No," said the first kid. "Just student parking. For those two dorms, Gutterson and Langley."

The Pope wasn't sure he'd heard the kid right. "But I see BMWs, Lexus SUVs, even a couple of Jags?"

Now the two kids looked at each other. The first came back to Murizzi with, "And therefore?"

The Pope shook his head. "If Genna Nagatami's *not* inside, what does she drive, and where might she be?"

In the elevator riding up to his apartment's floor, Shel Gold juggled the French baguette from the old bakery and the take-out bag from the new Chinese restaurant, both in Coolidge Corner. He always liked fresh, crusty bread with oriental food. Shel also thought that, given the number of Jews clustered in that neighborhood of Brookline, offering good Szechuan was just about a license to print money, though he hadn't tried anything from this place as yet.

However, he had tried a diet book on the remainder table at the Booksmith on Harvard Street, an independent store most everyone he knew preferred to the big chains. Shel had been intrigued by the volume's title because it implied that you should be eating certain foods, and avoiding others, based on, of all things, your blood type. No expert regarding things scientific in general, much less medical or nutritional in particular, Shel nevertheless thought the writer—a doctor himself—was pretty persuasive on how different blood types evolved over time in different geographic and ethnic enclaves, and that evolution was a function of the foods available to eat in those enclaves. If Shel was reading the book right, a Norwegian with Type A blood probably shouldn't be consuming the kinds of foods that Mexicans evolved Type O blood from eating.

The only problem for Shel was pretty much everything he liked was on the "Don't" list for *his* type and ethnicity.

Admit it, though: Unless you at least *try* to improve yourself, you stagnate, and die.

So Shel had substituted his usual "crispy beef" for a beef-flavored tofu dish. He wasn't sure about the consistency, much less the taste, of the stuff, but he also figured there'd be a silver lining: Moshe wouldn't be begging to share his dinner the way the little *momser* usually did.

At his apartment door, Shel juggled the bread and bag again to coax his keys from a pocket where one of the key snaps seemed to have become enmeshed in the pant lining. Resisting the urge to just rip the thing free, Shel finally had to set down his burdens and use both hands, hearing furtive scratching from the other side of the wood. Turning his key in the lock, Shel opened the door, Moshe scooting out to do the little victory dance he performed whenever Shel returned home. Lately, it had plateaued at careening once up the hallway and once back down, there to use the fronts of Shel's shoes as a scratching board for his own front paws.

Shel had just finished another book, this one by Thomas Cahill. The title of it was *The Gifts of the Jews,* and Shel was surprised to find that the name "Moshe," or "Moses," which the authors of the Book of Exodus took for Hebrew, actually was Egyptian, as one of Pharaoh's princesses had saved the child from the reed basket and named him. To Shel, the oddest thing about the linguistic correction was that "Moshe" in Egyptian means "he who pulls out," the opposite of the one-eyed Israeli war hero, Moshe Dayan, after whom Shel had named his also "dogged" one-eyed pet.

"Hey, Moshe, leave a little leather, okay?"

The cat decided it was time to abandon the shoes and cry expectantly at the smells coming from the bag.

Once inside the apartment, Shel set the bag down on the kitchen counter next to his microwave. The food itself was in a black plastic tray with a clear plastic top, meaning he just had to punch some small holes in the lid for venting, then slide it into the computerized oven. Shel wasn't sure how long one had to zap tofu to make it hot enough to enjoy without having it burn every internal tissue it touched, but he guessed at a minute and got things started. Then he walked into the living room to check his telephone answering machine, on its table near the BarcaLounger and TV tray, both across from the fifty-two-inch screen that he'd have to concede had become his central form of entertainment.

No messages. Good.

Shel went back into the kitchen, poured himself the single glass of red wine a day that probably dampened the antidepressant effect of the Zoloft he'd been on for the past few years. However, it was the one treat he allowed himself without burdening his doctor with the information, as Shel had read in a magazine that some red wine was actually good for the heart and some other organs as well.

The microwave binged, and Shel used an oven mitt shaped like a moose's head to lift out the plastic tray, sniffing—as though that could tell him what temperature his dinner had attained. Satisfied that it was at least hot enough, he used the mitt to carry the plastic tray to his TV one, which he'd decided over the years could probably have resisted molten lava without yielding too much.

Then Shel went back into the kitchen, got a steak knife and cut the baguette into four sections, putting three of them in a Ziploc and tossing it into the freezer. He took the fourth section, and the knife, and a fork, and a napkin, and his wineglass to the TV tray, adding them to the feast. Shel picked up the remote, slid into the Barca-Lounger, and kicked off his shoes. Moshe begged for some of the tofu by getting up on his hind legs and tentatively jabbing with his left front paw at Shel's knee.

Admit it: You feel really comfortable with all these little rituals, the cat's as well as your own.

Shel aimed the remote at his Magnavox, heard the baritone of James Earl Jones say "This is CNN" before the picture came up on the screen, and speared his first piece of tofu just as the phone rang. As usual during dinner, he let the tape machine take it.

But the message he heard being left, and, frankly, the tone of voice of the caller, told him that while he'd best finish his meal toward taking on fuel for energy, he probably wouldn't be giving the tofu a fair trial as substitute beef.

Pontifico Murizzi noticed a dozen luxury and sports cars in the parking lot of the bar the preppy kids had suggested for Genna Nagatami, but the Boxster they said she drove—a Porsche, for Christsake—

wasn't one of them. The Pope left his Explorer and went through the swinging doors anyway.

A band was banging away in one corner, the lead singer a scrungy beanpole doing a vocal in that kind of throaty, howling-wolf style that grated against Murizzi's ear. The melody didn't have a beat he could identify, and the Pope counted himself lucky that he couldn't make out a single fucking syllable of the lyrics.

The bartenders looked to be mostly college kids themselves, maybe some recent grads not real lucky in the shriveled job market since the recession of '99 and the terrorism of '01. Then Murizzi spotted a guy more his own age, looking managerial, so he walked over to him, saw his name tag read "Ralph," and said, "Hey, Ralph, how you doing?"

"What?" mouthed the guy over the din.

The Pope leaned into his ear. "I wonder if you can help me?"

Ralph shook his head, then motioned Murizzi to follow him. They ended up in a room behind the bar. Once Ralph closed the door, the difference, decibel-wise, was like night and day.

The room held some shoddy furniture, mainly a desk and a couple of beat-up office chairs. There were what looked like miniature mug books on the desktop, which Ralph shoved aside until he made enough space to rest his butt cheek on real wood.

Or real veneer.

Then the guy pulled flesh-colored plugs from his ears that the Pope didn't think were hearing aids.

Ralph palmed the plugs. "I didn't wear these things, I'd be as tone-deaf as that fucking band out there."

Murizzi wanted to keep the guy talking. "'Band' is generous."

"Yeah, but the fuck you gonna do? That's what these kids listen to. And at least this involves human beings, kind of. The other stuff is that techno-shit, not even real instruments, just electronic noise." Then Ralph folded his arms across his chest. "But I'm guessing you're here for something other than a music lesson."

"Looking for a college girl, last name Nagatami, first one—"

"Genna. Sure, I know her. Half-breed Jap, and a real piece."

The Pope nodded in what he'd learned to be a man-to-man way about grading females like cuts of meat. "Seen her around today?"

Ralph looked off into the distance. "Not for a couple of days." Back to Murizzi with, "Why, she done something?"

"No. A friend of her mother's didn't show up at work down in Boston, and we'd like to ask her about him."

Ralph shrugged. "Genna's a pretty straight kid, far as I can tell." He rummaged around on his desk, came up with one of the mini–mug books. "This'll have her picture from freshman year. She's put on some sass since then."

The Pope took the thing from him and paged through it alphabetically till he found the *N*'s. The young woman pictured above the caption "Genna Nagatami" was sweetly innocent. Murizzi got a fix on the things that don't change much—nose, eye-to-eye distance, ears—then looked at the front cover. "What is this?"

"Freshman class at the college from Genna's first year. Old president there was a good shit: She gave class registration books like that one out to each of the bars, so's we could run fake IDs through, see if a woman with a twenty-one-year-old's driver's license had an eighteen-year-old mug shot in this year or last year's freshman lineup. New president is a fucking jerk: So concerned about the 'privacy of student information' that he'd rather risk his kids drinking underage than give us a way to quality control what they show us at the door here."

The Pope nodded, kind of liking Ralph for trying to run a straight business himself. "Any idea where Genna might be, she's not at her dorm or here?"

"No. Don't really know her all that well."

A step ahead of me, pal: I don't know her at all. "No offense to your establishment, but is there someplace quieter I could get a beer and a burger before I start to canvass for the girl?"

Ralph nodded. "Levecque's. A locals' joint—as opposed to a college hangout, like this one. About a mile down the road, only . . ."

"Only what?"

"It's a lumberjack crowd. Quieter in the music sense, but watch yourself. They've been known to fight."

Finally, something to like about Maine. "Thanks." The Pope hefted the mug book. "Be okay if I took this with me?"

Ralph thought for a second. "All those kids, they're okay to drink now—agewise—so I suppose we don't need it for checking. But"—a sheepish grin—"it's nice to remember them before, uh, life spoiled their fucking hopes and dreams, you know?"

Pontifico Murizzi kind of liked Ralph for that, too. So, taking a long, last look at Genna Nagatami's face, the Pope laid the mug book back on the desk.

Tuesday night, Mairead O'Clare had a little anxiety attack over whether there was something more she could do for their new client before the next morning.

Swallowed up by the big—and only—easy chair in her Beacon Hill studio apartment, she was dressed in just sweatpants and a T-shirt. The arms of the chair were so wide, they were flat, and Mairead had a glass of chardonnay to her right and a bounty-hunter novel by Janet Evanovich, opened facedown, to her left. The novel was fun, even intriguing, but Mairead's mind kept drifting back to the female judge with the Bill Clinton problem.

Young lady, you've spoken with her bailiff, her administrative clerk, and another research clerk; "champions" for the good side and the dark side of "the Force"; plus the defendant in her current trial and his lawyer. You've even spent time with the missing boy's roommate.

"True," said Mairead, out loud. "And there's really not much I can do beyond that until I hear from Shel and the Pope about what they've found out, if anything."

Then Mairead thought again about the portrait of Charles Vareika over the mantelpiece in the apartment he shared with Vivianna Klein. And how nice it would be if "Chuck" were in Mairead's bathroom right now, showering and shaving toward joining *her* in the easy chair, and then in the . . .

But that's not going to happen, at least not tonight. So, I should just read my book, enjoy my wine, and turn in early enough to carpe diem tomorrow.

. . .

God, Shelly, thank you for coming right over."

He looked at the Honorable Barbara Quincy Pitt, decked out in a red nightgown, a crumpled white tissue in her hand. Though she was the wrong age and hair color, he couldn't help imagining the scene in *When Harry Met Sally,* where Meg Ryan calls Billy Crystal over to console her about an ex-boyfriend announcing he was getting married.

And, admit it: Pitt is still looking pretty good for a woman her—and *your*—age.

"Barbara, where did you keep the thing?"

"Upstairs. My night table."

"Let's take a look, then."

He followed her on the spiral stairs of the luxury duplex condo Pitt owned just off Harvard Square. Every time the woman climbed a step, the nightgown's hem rode northward to the point that Shel could see to mid-thigh.

He shook his head.

On the second floor, Pitt turned right into a master-bedroom suite larger than the entire first apartment Shel and Natalie had lived in with Richie. There were draperies of exotic colors that Shel bet would feel even more so to the touch. The carpet was deep enough to hide golf balls, and the expanse of bed and bedding made him think of all those rumors about the late Wilt Chamberlain's sexual escapades.

Okay, enough already. She's a lost love from law school, but now a client, even if the Zoloft didn't take the need to make an ethical decision from you.

"That table," said Pitt, pointing to the right side of her headboard. "Ugo told me to always keep it within reach."

Shel walked over to the charming nightstand, the top drawer with a protruding handle. He used a pencil near the telephone to trick the drawer open, then peered into it.

A cornucopia of condoms, a large tube of K-Y jelly, and some other devices the purposes of which Shel could only guess at and hope to be wrong. "What kind was it?"

"Smith & Wesson, a five-shot revolver."

"Chief's Special or Bodyguard?"

"I don't know."

Shel pictured the alternative weapons as he tried to stay patient with her. "Did it have a regular hammer sticking out the rear, or just a little, scored button on top?"

"A hammer. Yes, that you could pull back."

The Chief's Special, then. "And how did your husband come to have the gun?"

"*Ex*-husband, Shelly."

He just looked up at her.

Pitt wrung her hands a bit, then said, "Ugo told me a business friend from the Carolinas gave it to him as a gift, all the violence in Boston. This was years ago, when Ugo traveled a lot and the laws weren't quite so strict, at least in other states."

"Why didn't your former husband take the weapon with him when you two separated?"

A sigh. "Ugo was moving to the Cape, to 'get back in touch' with his feelings, and with nature, and with his feelings *toward* nature. He said I'd need the revolver more in my house, which I thereafter exchanged with another member of my family who owned and lived in this condo."

Shel wasn't sure he could question Nagatami's judgment on the gun issue. "Would your former husband have known it was here in your night table, even though you now live in this condo and not your old house?"

"Well, yes. That drawer's the only place I've ever kept the thing. But how could he get to it?"

A good point, for the moment. "When's the last time you saw the gun?"

"The last time Chuck and I made love. Saturday morning, after breakfast."

In bed, Shel remembered her telling them in his office, but he didn't append that. "So, the weapon was there *before* you made love?"

"Yes. My fingers brushed the handle as I reached for . . . for a condom."

"And was it there *after* Mr. Vareika left the condo?"

Pitt's chin fell toward her chest, almost a Desdemona mannerism from Shakespeare's *Othello*. "I don't know."

Shel tried to ratchet down a notch. "When *did* you notice the gun was missing, then?"

Pitt moved to a divan, a type of interior—indeed, *boudoir*—furniture Shel thought had bit the dust in the 1940s. Draping herself along it, she said, "Your Mr. Murizzi?"

"Yes?"

"He and I had . . . several cases together, as I've told you."

"Meaning, he was the homicide detective on them, and you the presiding judge?"

"Correct. Well, in one such, he was convinced that an irate husband had killed his wife's lover with a gun the husband's father had given her, his son traveling quite a bit, too."

Shel struggled not to lose the thread of Pitt's story. "And therefore?"

Another deep sigh. "And, therefore, when I actually *talked* to your Mr. Murizzi, I was reminded of that case we'd had together, and I checked on the gun Ugo had given *me,* and it was . . . gone."

Shel did a quick chronology in his head. "Barbara?"

"Yes?"

"The Pope joined us on Monday afternoon. Granted it wasn't till five-ish, why did you wait until tonight—more than twenty-four hours later—to look for this weapon?"

The deepest sigh of all. "Shelly, Shelly. Do you think Chuck's disappearance is the *only* thing on my mind? Even the only legally related matter? I made a mental note yesterday, in debriefing myself about the meetings in your office, to check on the gun. I didn't remember to do so until tonight."

"Because . . . ?"

"How the hell should I know 'because'?" Then a different, quieter tone, and maybe tack as well. "Shelly, a young man I fell in love with—one very much like you were back in law school, in that he's handsome, virile, exciting—comes into my life for a month or so and now seemingly has left it, suddenly. A gratuitous nod from my former husband about how women can't protect themselves without phallic substitutes like a gun wasn't exactly at the top of my 'to do' list."

Shel didn't speak. Or even nod or shake his head. He just closed his eyes and breathed deeply. In and out, in and out. He sensed Pitt was about to intrude upon him when he said, "Barbara, other than Mr. Vareika, who had access to the weapon?"

"Well, anyone with access to the *room*—or even the condo, I suppose. My cleaning person—who has never filched a dime or a piece of costume jewelry in the three years she's worked for me, for your information." Pitt clenched her teeth. "Who else. Chuck, obviously. Oh, and . . . Genna, I suppose."

Shel racked his brain for the exact words Pitt had used during the conference in his office. "I thought you said Genna had been visiting her father on the Cape this past weekend?"

"Well, yes, *officially.* That is, to satisfy the divorce decree's visitation provisions. But my daughter almost always drops in on me, even if just for a short time, before continuing on to college in Maine."

Shel tried to align all he'd learned. "So, basically what you're telling me is that the revolver could have been taken anytime from Saturday afternoon onward, by Mr. Vareika, your daughter, or—?"

"Ugo, if he could gain access here like some opportunistic stranger."

"Or, Barbara, yourself."

Pitt seemed to collapse inside the nightgown, almost as though a magic trick had been performed and she'd somehow been made to evaporate, the gown wanting from gravity to simply fall to the floor. Then Shel believed she recovered herself. "Technically, yes."

He said, "I'll need to have a copy of the formal registration on the gun."

Pitt just looked at him.

Shel tried to minimize her potential inconvenience. "I won't need—and we shouldn't open Pandora's box for—a *certified* copy from the Cambridge Police Department until a short time prior to any trial."

"Shelly?"

"Yes?"

"I don't think Ugo ever actually . . . registered the gun."

Shel felt a little off-center. "He'd have to have. You must know the law in this state requires—"

"Shelly, I'm just saying that I remember Ugo receiving the gun from a business friend down South. Ugo held onto it because the man died tragically in a car crash not long afterward."

Shel thinking, Nostalgia over a firearm?

Pitt said, "And I also remember Ugo saying he went into the police headquarters to register it and all, but he saw nothing but white males, in uniform *and* as supplicants, except for one poor black man who the police kept shunting around even though the man kept maintaining he owned a cash-basis convenience store in a dicey neighborhood and needed a gun for protection. And Ugo told me he just . . . well, left."

Shel could imagine the scene. "He didn't want to be one more man of color getting 'shunted around.'"

"Precisely."

Shel wanted to digest that, maybe run it by the Pope before actively looking into it. "Well, I don't see what more I can do here before meeting with my team, getting their input."

Barbara Pitt took a step forward, her hip swaying. "I can think of . . . something."

Shel felt the atmosphere of the bedroom shift immediately. "Barbara, I told you: I'm still—"

"Married, yes. But your marriage has become a phonetic namesake for you, Shelly: Just a 'shell' of what a relationship should be like. And"—Pitt came closer, raising her hand and running the back of it down Shel's cheek—"I have to admit, after a woman's gotten the best of it for a while, she wants more."

Shel felt as though he was being drawn and quartered, but the Zoloft spared him the moral dilemma, dictating only one answer to the invitation. "Barbara, no."

A bleak smile. "Not even for"—the back of the hand down his other cheek—"'old time's sake'?"

Strangely, that made Shel feel more resolved than conflicted. "Especially not for that."

. . .

Walking into the "locals" bar Ralph had sent him to, the first thing Pontifico Murizzi thought was, Your old partner from uniform would've called this place a bucket of blood.

The floor was dingy, peeling linoleum, impossible to tell what the original color might have been. The jukebox was spewing out an ancient rock anthem, and a pool table stood off to the right, only six or eight balls scattered on its green felt. The air smelled of fried grease, beer piss, and peanuts, enough cigarette smoke that the Pope's eyes began watering. He registered an assortment of guys at the bar, half of them doubles for Rudolph, the Red-nosed Reindeer. Given the crowd, Genna Nagatami, sitting at a back table, jumped out at you like a rose among thorns.

Or between them, the two guys in their thirties, both middling to husky, obviously hitting on her hard, one from each side, and pool cues in their hands.

Murizzi walked back toward them, catching one of the guys saying, "You are the most wicked cute thing ever walked in here."

"Thanks," said the Pope, loud enough to carry.

As Nagatami giggled, the guy who'd been talking cut a look at Murizzi from under an blaze-orange watch cap on his head. "What'd you say?"

The Pope hooked a chair leg from another table with his foot, spinning it near where Nagatami was sitting. Then Murizzi straddled the seat, settling down lightly, his forearms resting on the top of its back, the balls of his feet flexed against the linoleum. "I was thanking you, for the compliment on 'wicked cute.'"

The other guy, with a prospector's bushy mustache and sideburns to match, changed his grip on the cue from pool to baseball bat–style. And stance. "You making like we're queer or something?"

The Pope said, "I'm making like it's time to say good night to the young lady here."

"Good night, fellows," said Nagatami without moving to get up.

Blaze-Orange glanced down at her, then shifted his cue grip, more to the bayonet style.

Murizzi thought, He's the one you gotta take first. "Come on, guys. Let's be sensible, huh?"

Blaze-Orange said, "You didn't answer my friend's question there."

"About your sexual identities? I gave him the only answer he needs to hear."

Mustache turned to his friend. "Cop?"

Blaze-Orange shook his head. "Would've led with a badge, he had one. And listen to the accent. No, I say what we got here is nothing more than another Masshole."

Despite the circumstances, the Pope thought that was a pretty good line. "Why don't we just call it an evening, guys, okay?"

Mustache said, "What right you got, horning in on us?"

Murizzi looked up at him, but kept Blaze-Orange in his peripheral vision. "Let's just say I'm a friend of the family."

The Pope caught the telltale dip of the bayonet drill, and he was up and out of his chair by the time Blaze-Orange had fully committed to the lunge. Using the cue end of the stick like a pole-vaulter's fulcrum, Murizzi flipped the guy up and over his shoulder, then raised his chair by one of its legs in time to take most of the impact from Mustache's home-run swing. As the guy followed through, the Pope drove his left fist into Mustache's right side, sensing that satisfying tearing of cartilage between the ribs themselves. Mustache dropped the cue and doubled over onto his knees, coughing and yelling about the pain.

Blaze-Orange was back up, swinging a roundhouse left at Murizzi, who parried it with his right forearm, then locked the guy's arm at the elbow before breaking the nose with the heel of his left palm. Blaze-Orange got his right hand up to his face before the Pope felt the guy's knees buckle, and Murizzi let him just drop down to the floor as well.

The Pope took out each man's wallet without any resistance, checking and memorizing the names on their driver's licenses, in case he needed any follow-up on them. Then he took out a ten from each and walked over to the bartender. "For the damage to your furniture."

The keep just nodded.

Murizzi went back to Nagatami's table and said to her, "Let me introduce myself."

"You don't have to," lifting a cell phone in her hand, kind of a curious expression on her face. "You must be the 'Masshole' my father called me about."

The Pope glanced around. The two jerks were still on the floor, but a couple of other guys were giving him the evil eye. Like, One more beer, and I'll take a crack at you myself. "We ought to get out of here."

Genna Nagatami stood up. "Why don't you follow me in your car?"

Out in the parking lot, Murizzi watched her climb into—no shit—a Porsche Boxster, just like the two preppies had told him. She wheeled it out of the space and sent gravel flying like machine-gun bullets. The Pope derricked himself up into his Explorer and began to follow.

Though back in the bar he'd paid more attention to the two jerks, Murizzi now painted a mental image of Nagatami. Maybe five-four and slim, with a very pert ass swiveling under paint-on jeans as she crossed the lot. Hair black and past the shoulders, with a hank of it dyed a shade between pink and red, same color as her nail polish. But the face is what would stop you. Doe eyes, tipped up at the corners, finely sculpted nose that tipped up, too. And the kind of lips that said collagen really could improve on nature.

The Pope wasn't too surprised when she led him back to campus and pulled into the student lot in front of Gutterson. After he stopped beside her Porsche and got out, she beckoned him with her index finger. Murizzi followed her on foot, noticing there weren't many lights in the windows of the dorm on this side. At the main entrance, Nagatami swiped a security card vertically down a slot, and the Pope heard a buzzer that stopped as soon as she opened the door. Climbing one flight of stairs behind her butt, he found himself not really blaming the two guys back at the locals' place.

Nagatami walked to the end of the corridor, then used an old-fashioned key to open a door. When Murizzi walked in, though, he thought he was somehow trapped in a game of Clue, like when you yank on the bathroom door handle but instead step into a ballroom.

Or, in this case, a disco.

"What the hell . . . ?"

"This is my suite, summer through next year. It's a five-man—meaning three guys, two girls, though it's just me right now."

The Pope looked around the large space with five doors radiating off it, four of them closed, but he paid most of his attention to the tall DJ stand, the fully stocked bar, and the chrome pole that went floor to ceiling with an adjustable spotlight in a raised section near the corner. "This is your . . . dorm room?"

"My suite, like I said. The college lets us decorate the way we want, so long as we put it back together again before we leave. The guys did most of the construction, but . . ." Nagatami moving over to the pole and humping it subtly between her legs, ". . . *this* was my contribution to the decor. What do you think?"

The doe eyes asking him a different question, Murizzi believed. "I think I'd like to have a talk with you."

"Then let me change into something a little more comfortable. Help yourself to the bar."

She walked over to the only open door, went in, and closed it behind her.

Jeez, you could use a drink, less over the dustup back at the real bar, and more over what college kids could get away with these days.

The Pope poured two fingers of Jim Beam Black into a "sipping whiskey" glass and made a circuit of the "disco." The stuff on the walls at least seemed more like what he'd expect. Posters of John Belushi from *Animal House,* Bruce Lee from a kung fu epic, Mel Gibson from *Braveheart.* A couple of black bike racks, just a single mountain one hanging from the curved holders. Each bedroom door displayed collages of different-sized photos—some candid, some posed—from sports events and parties, school colors consistent across the shots. You looked at all the faces—sweet young things, male and female—and you had to appreciate why Ralph back at the college hangout held onto those innocent freshman mug books.

Nagatami's door opened behind him. When Murizzi turned, her "comfort clothes" amounted to a bra, thong panties, and four-inch stiletto heels.

Doing a prostitute roll to the DJ stand, she said, "You have any requests?"

"Yeah." The Pope watched Nagatami pick up an honest-to-God vinyl record. "Put some clothes on."

"That's funny," she said, wrinkling her nose over the album and choosing another for the turntable. "Usually guys tell me just the opposite."

Music began to surge from speakers, some kind of Latin beat.

Given the circumstances, probably the lambada. "I'm serious here." His voice sounded nervous to him. "Get dressed again."

Nagatami moved like a cat to the chrome pole, flicking one switch on and another off so that the only light came down as a shaft from the spot at the ceiling. "Are you sure?" Nagatami started to rub her breasts against the pole, one at a time, then between them, doing a little massage. Thanks to the spotlight, her nipples were prominently visible under the bra.

Murizzi said, "I'm sure."

"But you saved me from the brigands."

"The what?"

"The two guys in the bar. You were, like, the brave white knight, come to rescue the damsel in distress." Nagatami humped the pole now, a lot less subtly than before. "And she'd like to thank you, in her own very special way."

Embarrassment was taking over now. "Look, Ms. Naga—"

"Genna, or Gen." She started to lick the pole with the tip of her tongue. "Gen is what the guys I hook up with call me."

Embarrassment to something like exasperation, all of a sudden. "I don't know how to break this to you, but . . . I'm gay."

Nagatami froze, like she was suddenly stuck to the pole. "No?" Then she turned to him. "No."

"Yes."

"But the way you handled those guys back there?"

"I used to be a cop. What you saw comes from training and experience, not sexual orientation."

Nagatami now came completely off the pole and walked toward him, awkward in the heels now instead of seductive, and looking about twelve years old. "You're not kidding me. You are really and truly *gay*?"

The Pope nodded.

She huffed out a breath, looked down at herself. "Well, why didn't you tell me in the first place, save me all this . . . oooowh."

Murizzi watched Nagatami stalk off to her bedroom, close the door by slamming it, then reappear twenty seconds later barefoot, wearing now a pair of running shorts and a sweatshirt.

She said, "Better?"

"At least warmer. For you."

Another huff. "All right. Let's sit."

Nagatami went for one easy chair, started sliding it like a wheelbarrow across the dance floor. The Pope did the same with another until they were almost close enough to touch knees.

When they were both settled in, Nagatami said, "My dad told me you were down at his place on the Cape, asking about Chuck."

Chuck, not Charles, the Pope noticed. That makes the judge, the roommate, and the judge's daughter all using the guy's nickname.

Yeah, but Vareika's father, too, though son and Mom were trying to bring Big Eddie into the "Charles" fold.

Murizzi said, "Your dad also tell you why?"

"Yeah, that Chuck was missing or something, right?"

"Right."

"So?"

"So?"

A third huff. "So, what makes you think, like, *I* know anything about it?"

"Do you?"

"No."

"What time did you leave your father's place?"

"On Sunday, you mean?"

"Yeah."

"I don't know. Around three maybe? I wanted to get to bed at a decent hour for a change, and it's a hell of a drive up here from there."

The Pope thought, You're preaching to the choir on that score. "Did you see Mr. Vareika anytime over the weekend?"

Nagatami did a look-away.

"Genna?"

She came back. "Who are you working for in all this?"

"Your mother. She's worried about the guy being gone."

"Hah," Nagatami shaking her head. "That's a laugh. I'd think she'd be more worried about him not . . . coming."

Well, that confirms the hole in the judge's "secret." Murizzi said, "You think they were having an affair?"

"No, I don't *think* it, I *know* it. And I thought it was pretty disgusting."

The Pope nodded toward the pole. "Any difference if it was a younger woman and an older man?"

"That's not what I meant about . . ." The huff, which seemed to be Nagatami's wild-card safety valve for a lot of emotions. "Look, I can understand you probably think I'm a slut, with the outfit and the . . . performance and all. But I'm really pretty picky. And I know what you're going to say now, that Chuck's a hunk and so my mom was just being 'picky,' too. Only I don't think at her age I'd do *my* hunk on the kitchen table of my condo when my daughter might walk through the front door."

The Pope closed his eyes for a moment, then said, "She didn't see you?"

"I didn't even see *them*. And this was weeks ago, anyway. But I could hear them, loud and clear, all the way out in the living room."

"And you said something to your father about it."

"Yes," defiant now.

"But not your mother."

"No."

"You're closer to him than her?"

"Not that it's any of your business, but yes."

The Pope remembered a question he'd wanted to ask her, figured this was as good a time as any. "The reason you went with his last name over hers after the divorce?"

"No. It's because of these," pointing her index finger and pinkie at her own eyes. "I figured everybody would think I'm Amer-Asian, so why not let them know which part of Asia. And besides . . ."

"Besides?"

"Well, you look even just slightly Asian and you have a straight American name, like Pitt, people are totally going to think you're this poor orphan got adopted out of some mud hut in the old country."

The "orphan" part made Murizzi think of Mairead, him wondering if she'd have minded what people would "think," so long as she had parents who loved her.

But what he said to Nagatami was, "Chuck ever seem interested in you?"

Another look-away.

The Pope waited. When nothing came back, he said, "Or you in him?"

Nagatami turned to Murizzi, this time with a tear in her eye. "I met Chuck when he and Mom were 'working' at her place another weekend. Was he buff? You bet. Only when Mom left the room to make a phone call, Chuck started to feel me out."

Out, not up. "About what?"

"He asked whether I had a boyfriend, which I thought was pretty tacky, even if he wasn't boffing my own mother. I told him sometimes, and Chuck gave me this heartbreaker smile, then checked around, made sure he could still hear Mom talking. Old Chucky reached into his briefcase and took out this brochure. Told me I might enjoy joining, but that it was 'couples only.' Well, when I got back up here, I took one look at it, decided it was worse than my mom doing a guy half her age on the kitchen table."

The Pope leaned forward. "What was 'couples only'?"

Genna Nagatami stood. "Let me get the thing. I kept it." A hard smile. "Sentimental reasons, you know?"

ELEVEN

When Mairead O'Clare opened the door to the law office suite at 8:30 A.M. Wednesday to "carpe diem," Billie Sunday, sitting behind her reception desk, said, "We've been waiting on you."

Mairead just stood there until Billie got up with a steno pad in her hand and moved toward Shel Gold's door. Then the young lawyer followed her.

Only to see inside the office something she'd never seen before: Shel behind his desk, yeah, but Pontifico Murizzi sitting in the client chair Mairead always used instead of standing with his back to the old Wild West safe against the wall.

"Pope," she said. "You okay?"

He looked up at her, eyes red, bags under them. "I had kind of a long night, Irish."

Billie rightly went to the other chair in order to be able to take notes, so Mairead moved over to the safe herself, appreciating the view it provided (through the window behind Shel's head) of the State House dome, the Common, and the Public Garden, with Back Bay in the distance.

Shel said, "We've got some real problems on Judge Pitt's matter. Mairead, why don't you lead off, though, so we can see if there're any more?"

She bridled a little at that, as though the boss thought that keeping her in the dark was some sort of appropriate punishment for her arriving half an hour *early* to the office.

Young lady, he IS the boss, remember?

Mairead nodded, but decided to save her best till last. "I spoke with Donald Iverson, the head of the splinter group advocating for man/boy love." She thought Billie shuddered at that, giving Mairead a little revelation: I wonder if the Pope stands here all the time because it gives him a better look at the way the rest of us react to things?

"Mairead?" said Shel.

"Uh, sorry. Iverson basically pushed his group's position on me. Not much else, but"—she turned her head to face Murizzi at an angle—"Pope, you know how you wanted my take on the roommate, Vivianna Klein?"

"Yeah?"

"Could you do the same on Iverson?"

"Sure, you give me his contact info."

Shel said, "Mairead, do you think Iverson's hiding something?"

She paused, trying to be sure not to overstate her point. "I get the feeling he's pretty confident about the *Dooley* case, which from what I've seen, he shouldn't be."

"Have you talked to the prosecutor?"

"No, but I—"

Shel gave her one of his little smiles. "Think maybe you should?"

"Okay, but I did talk to the defense attorney."

Now Shel frowned.

What, he suggests I should speak with one side, then doesn't like that I've spoken with the other? "Did I do something wrong, Shel?"

He said, "We represent the judge presiding over the trial. I'd hate for us, in helping her, to be responsible for Barbara Pitt having to recuse herself and declare a mistrial."

Mairead still wasn't sure she saw a difference between contacting the prosecution and contacting the defense. "Well, if it matters, she—Kyra Yelverton—approached me."

Now the Pope said, "The defendant's lawyer came to you?"

"That's right."

"Why?" said Shel, the frown deepening.

What I thought was "the best" may turn out to be the worst. "Yelverton told me her client wouldn't cooperate with her anymore unless she arranged a meeting with him."

"A meeting?" Shel now folded his arms across his chest. "Between you and the accused priest?"

"Yes. And so I did. At her request."

Now Billie looked up from her pad, twisting her neck to face Mairead. "You actually talked with this Dooley?"

"More got talked to."

Shel's expression went from disapproval to curiosity. "How do you mean?"

"Dooley wanted to tell someone his story. Basically a stump speech about how his 'little gentlemen' benefited from him assaulting them."

Billie did shudder this time, no question.

Murizzi said, "But, Irish, why did this scumball want to talk to you in particular?"

"He saw me in the courtroom. Or, more precisely, he saw these," Mairead holding up her hands, "and he remembered a nun from my orphanage telling him about the poor little girl with the stigmata on her arms."

Nobody spoke for a few seconds.

Then, from Shel, "Well, what's done is done. Did you learn anything from either Yelverton or Dooley?"

"From the priest, no, except maybe what it's like to stare into the eyes of evil." Mairead didn't want to shiver, for fear it might seem theatrical to the other people in the office, but she couldn't completely avoid one. "I did have the feeling, though, that his attorney knew something about Charles Vareika."

"And what was that?" asked Shel.

"I don't know. It was less what Yelverton said, and more the way she reacted when I told her he was missing."

"Sounds thin," the Pope tick-tocking his head, "but I've sure followed up that kind of hunch myself."

Shel nodded. "Speaking of 'following up,' Mairead also had the idea that you should pay a visit to this Bill Sherden, the victims' association head."

As Mairead remembered it, that was Shel's idea.

Perhaps Mr. Gold is just making up for hurting your feelings earlier.

Yeah, if he was even aware he was.

But all Murizzi did was hold up two fingers. "So, Sherden and Iverson both?"

Shel said, "Yes. Mairead, anything else from your end?"

"Just Vareika's roommate. I had the feeling she wasn't worried about him being missing so much as miffed."

The Pope grinned. "Klein ask you any funny questions?"

Mairead felt herself being led into some kind of trap. "Questions?"

"Like maybe about your . . . social life?"

"She did want to know if I had a boyfriend. Or a girlfriend."

Murizzi went back to Shel. "What'd I tell you?"

Mairead said, "Mind letting me in on this?"

Shel nodded at their private investigator, who pulled out a brochure of some kind. "I drove up to Maine yesterday, talked with the judge's daughter." The Pope extended the brochure to Mairead, and she took it from him. "Genna Nagatami said Vareika felt her out about the same kind of thing, because the 'club' was couples only."

As Mairead scanned the brochure, she heard Billie say, "Please, Lord, not more of this man/boy horror."

God, the guy of my dreams? No, please. No!

Steady, young lady. This is a professional context now.

Mairead caught Shel looking at her strangely, but she answered Billie instead. "A different 'horror,'" her voice sounding uneven to her, "but it could be worse for our client."

"What could?" said Billie.

Mairead read aloud, a little shakily, from the brochure. "So, if you and yours are interested in first-class swinging, please contact us through the eight-eight-eight number above for an introduction to Loll, the best way to completely fulfill every sexual desire."

"Spouse-swapping now?" Billie shook her head again. "Worse and worse."

Noticing Shel again looking at her strangely, Mairead tried to recover by being more casual. "Doesn't say anything about holy matrimony being a prerequisite." Then she hit Murizzi. "You figure Vareika and Klein are . . . patrons of this swingers' bunch?"

"Yeah. And, based on the questions Klein asked me and you, and that the daughter says Vareika asked her, they recruit for it, too."

Now Mairead shook her head, saying, "Judge, Judge, Judge," but hearing in her brain, "Chuck, Chuck, Chuck."

Shel held up both hands like stop signs. "I'll tell our client about this . . . development. But we've got worse news."

Mairead snapped out of herself, then thought back on their division of labor. "The victim, Hector Washington?"

"No. That is, I saw him. He was, *is* pitiable, so broken in spirit as just a teenager . . ." Shel coughed. "I spent most of my time there speaking with his mother, who's fixated on getting at least financial justice for what happened to her son." Shel coughed again, Mairead figuring he was using it to cover his emotion over losing his own child. "And the Save Our Clergy person, Amelie Cardon, seems to be just a nice woman with an impossible job."

Mairead couldn't remember another possibility. "Then what's the worse news?"

Shel took a deep breath, then explained about Pitt's unregistered gun going missing like Vareika had.

"Jesus," Mairead realizing she'd hissed the word.

Young lady?

"Sorry."

Shel looked up at her briefly as Mairead realized she'd answered Sister Bernadette out loud.

Get a grip, girl.

Then Shel engaged the Pope. "How do we handle this?"

Murizzi bent forward in his chair, elbows on knees, hands moving as though he were lathering them with soap. "No easy way, Shel. Usually, somebody takes a gun from where it should be, they intend to use it. If that happens—or already has—and the gun's found but never been registered, the serial number will just bounce a computer search back to the gun shop in Dixie where the husband's friend bought it.

With luck, the friend being dead closes off that route. And, assuming the Smith has a checkered grip—like most of them do—a techie would have a hell of a job getting any fingerprints off that part."

Billie looked up from taking notes. "So far, that sounds like good news."

"Yeah, so far. But given where Pitt kept it, there'll be partial latents of hers—maybe Vareika's, even the daughter's—all over the frame and cylinder. And the shells, too, if anybody—including the father—ever reloaded it."

Shel said, "Add to that, her mother told me Genna was at the condo Sunday afternoon, and so could have taken it if Vareika didn't on Saturday."

Murizzi put in, "Or if the judge didn't herself, anytime."

"A possibility that I mentioned to Her Honor *my*self."

Mairead could feel the tension in the office, almost like the ozone atmosphere of a courtroom during a heated moment of trial. "So, Pope, where does that leave us?"

"Hoping that the gun's never found."

Shel said, "Or that those people's fingerprints aren't on file anywhere."

Murizzi shrugged. "The daughter's, probably not. But the father? Good chance he'd have been printed if he ever worked for any place needed a security clearance. And a lock on the judge, toward her being nominated for the bench. As to Vareika, I don't know how the court system checks out its clerks ahead of time, but if he ever got busted, even for something minor, his prints should be in the system, too."

"All right," said Shel. "Not much we can do about those possibilities, so let's focus on what we can do. Pope, you're going to visit Iverson and Sherden, see if anything helpful comes of either. However, do you think you also should recontact the ex and the daughter about the gun?"

Murizzi mulled that over, then an emphatic shake of the head. "No. No, that'd be like kicking the sleeping dog. And same for my people on Homicide, especially after I already asked Artie Chin to keep an eye out for a blond hunk showing up on a white slab."

Mairead shivered again, and she caught Shel once more eyeing her strangely.

But all he said was, "Mairead, you're going to speak with the prosecutor on the *Dooley* case, see whether there's some reason Iverson should be confident about the outcome." A hesitation. "Do you think you can get Yelverton to open up on what you feel she knows about Vareika?"

Mairead had been thinking about that. "Not with the little we've got so far."

Then she watched Shel glance from one face to another in the room. "Any other suggestions?"

The Pope said, "Be a good idea for the judge herself to call Missing Persons, follow up whatever her admin clerk did in terms of an official report on Vareika being gone now for way more than forty-eight hours."

Then Billie Sunday raised her hand. "Seems to me that a 'couple' of us ought to pay a visit to that 'swingers' thing, find out just how deep our Mr. Vareika was into the life."

Before Mairead O'Clare could reply, Pontifico Murizzi swung his face up to her, smiling through how tired he looked. "Hey, Irish. You free this evening?"

Shel knocked softly on the jamb to Mairead's open door. When she looked up from her phone with those laser-blue eyes, he saw in them the same thing he'd noticed during the conference in his office.

"Thanks, Ms. Butler . . . I'll see you then."

When Mairead hung up the phone, Shel said, "Butler's the prosecutor?"

"Yes. And I'm seeing her during the lunch recess today. I'm also going to revisit Leslie Hughes, the research law clerk who was somewhat friendly with 'Chuck,' see if he gave *her* a Loll brochure, too."

Shel nodded. "Okay if I close the door?"

A little blinking, but, "Sure."

He took the only chair in front of Mairead's desk. "You okay with this case?"

That troubled expression in the eyes again. "Yeah, why not?"

"Talking with this man/boy love guy throw you?"

Some relief in her eyes now, but more the kind you associate with a witness under cross-examination who suddenly felt steered down the *less* dangerous path. "Some. And the priest—former priest—Dooley? Even worse. But I'll get over both of them."

Shel nodded again. "Is there anything else bothering you?"

Mairead said, "Bothering me? No, how about you?" and Shel knew it was deflection more than banter.

He settled back in the chair. "Judge Pitt told me about a case she had with the Pope back when he was still on the force. It involved a 'family' gun something like ours here."

"So?"

"So," Shel clasped his hands behind his head, "I'm wondering if there's something—issue, history—bothering you about her?"

"No, other than I think she was stone stupid to get herself involved with Charles Vareika."

"Mairead," Shel not moving anything but his lips, "I think there is, and I want you to tell me about it."

She looked down at her desk, then out her window, which had more a view, Shel knew, of Beacon Hill than the one in his own.

Then Mairead came back to him. "It's stupider than even what the judge did."

Shel felt his heart rise in his chest, like a high-speed elevator.

Admit it: You were afraid something wasn't right with her reactions to Vareika and the swingers' club.

"Tell me?" he said. "Please."

"Shel, it's not just stupid." Her eyes went watery. "It's embarrassing."

"That makes the whatever harder to talk about, but maybe even more reason for me to know what's wrong."

"There's this . . . When I went to the apartment Vareika and Klein share, there was this . . . gorgeous painting of him—a portrait—over the fireplace. And I, well . . ."

Shel, confident that less on his part now would be more, stayed quiet.

Mairead bit her lip. "I got kind of a . . . crush on the guy."

Shel hadn't thought of that—moreover, couldn't have imagined it—but he also knew that if he didn't control his reaction, the poor, sincere young woman in front of him would feel even worse. *"Laura."*

The blinking again, then a deadpan, "Laura who?"

Shel dropped his hands to the arms of the chair. "A movie, from the 1940s that was shown on TV a lot when I was young. Dana Andrews plays a homicide investigator looking into the murder of this beautiful young woman, a shotgun blast having disfigured the victim beyond recognition. But her portrait hangs over the fireplace in *her* apartment, and he falls in love with her."

Mairead canted her head, as if Shel had just told her he'd once been abducted onto an alien spaceship. "This is a real movie?"

"Uh-huh. And it turns out Laura—the woman in the portrait— *wasn't* the one killed by the shotgun, that the real victim just resembled her. Well, first time I saw the movie, I fell in love with Laura—the actress, Gene Tierney, who played her—myself."

A half-smile now. "So, your point is that I'm not crazy."

"Or at least that you're not the only one in our suite who is."

A laugh now, and real relaxation as well. "Shel, I don't think my . . . crush will have any effect on how I deal with this case, especially after hearing about Vareika's 'swinging' attitude."

"And you're okay on going with the Pope to the club itself?"

"Absolutely. Not a problem."

Shel nodded, then thought of something. "This 'gorgeous' portrait of Vareika?"

Mairead seemed to grow wary again. "Yes?"

"Did it seem really professional to you?"

"Very. In fact, Klein also said it really . . . 'caught his charm.'"

"Sounds kind of expensive, then."

"Probably."

"Who do you suppose commissioned it to be painted?"

Mairead's face fell. "God, our client?"

Sheldon A. Gold realized there was one more "embarrassing" thing *he'd* have to be raising with the Honorable Barbara Quincy Pitt.

Pontifico Murizzi glanced at the business cards Irish had given him. Well, at least both guys live in the city, not up in the fucking tundra.

The Pope still wasn't over the effects of the night before. After the dustup with the hicks in that lumberjack bar, he knew the adrenaline would keep him wired for hours. And the attempted lap dance by Judge, Jr., back in her dorm disco didn't help matters any. Genna Nagatami had told Murizzi it'd be okay if he stayed over in an empty bedroom, but the Pope figured driving back to Boston and seeing the lawyers about what he'd found out was a better use of his time. And, going by the bombshells at the meeting in Shel's office, Murizzi had figured right.

Now he planned to hit the two guys Shel and Irish wanted a second read on, which meant choosing who'd be first. The Pope's mother always had a saying: Pontifico, you got a couple, three things to do, and one of them's tougher for you, that's where you start.

So Murizzi watched for Donald Iverson's address to come up on the trendy street in Bay Village, the neighborhood of Boston west of the Entertainment District and north of the Mass Pike. Twenty years before, New England School of Law—Mairead's alma mater—had moved there from over in Back Bay, and the Pope remembered some uniforms telling him how a thousand students kind of civilized what had been Dodge City, all the hookers shaking it on the corners and all the skels making it in the shadows. That civilizing effect brought in the gay community to kind of retake the housing stock, which was primarily two- and three-story attached buildings of brick like Greenwich Village in New York.

Iverson's place was a tri-level, the town house about twenty feet wide with red brick offset by white wooden shutters on every floor, curlicue carvings on them matching the brass holdbacks. Murizzi stuck his Explorer in an illegal space, put on his hazard lights, and pulled down the sun visor with the Policemen's Benevolent Association shield. At the front door of the town house, the chimes played several bars of a tune he couldn't quite place. Then the white six-panel door opened wide, and the Pope got a close-up look at man/boy love.

Or half of it, anyway.

The kid was maybe thirteen, with the kind of pretty face that'd make you look to hair and clothes, check on whether it was male or female. Here the hair was dyed some hideous shade of rust, the black roots showing under the bowl cut, so the kid looked like a punk-rock monk. He wore just baggy jeans, his upper body spare to the point of emaciated.

Bus-station runaway, especially with the fading bruise on his cheek. That or "Rusty" was one of the few males Murizzi had ever encountered who actually suffered from anorexia.

The kid said, "Help you with something?"

Hillbilly accent, the first word coming out "hep," and the Pope went with the bus-station scenario. "I'd like to see Donald Iverson."

Just a nod, then over the shoulder with, "Hey, Donald? Guy's here for you."

Murizzi didn't hear anything from inside, but Rusty nodded and said to him, "Second floor," hiking a thumb up the staircase. Then the kid just walked away into a living room to the left where a big-screen TV had a sci-fi movie going, volume low.

The Pope climbed the steps, trying to remember all the sections of the statutory rape laws.

At the top of the stairs, a guy appeared at the balustrade. Six feet, slim like Fred Astaire and limber on his feet, the kind of guy who'd surprise you with his quickness, you weren't ready for it, even in the pleated pants of a business suit, monogrammed shirt, and silk tie, a pair of suspenders holding the package together.

"And what have we here?"

"Donald Iverson?"

"Yes?"

"Pontifico Murizzi. I'm helping attorney Mairead O'Clare on this law clerk disappearance thing."

"'Pontifico'? Such an unusual name, but happy to meet you." Iverson extended a manicured hand to him, and the Pope shook with him, Iverson's eyes flashing as he held on for just a beat too long before saying, "We'll be more comfortable over there."

Murizzi followed him into a room with skylights across the south wall, admitting the June sun like there wasn't even glass in between. The Pope wondered how good that was for the oriental rug, fancy enough that it made the one in Vareika/Klein's place look like a dust rag. The walls had bookshelves, some framed portraits of Iverson in posed publicity shots, a couple of bronzed plaques that seemed to be patent approvals, and some techy gadgets sprinkled around the books like somebody might display Hummels.

"You an inventor?"

Iverson glanced at the shelves as he went behind his desk. "More a venture capitalist. Electronics, mostly."

Murizzi wondered if that was how the guy's association got funded.

Iverson waved him to a sling-backed chair. "So, I already spoke with Ms. O'Clare at the courthouse. What is it now?"

"The judge's clerk's still missing."

The guy sat down. "Charles something-or-other, correct?"

"Correct."

"Well, I'm afraid I've no more to tell you than I did your colleague."

The Pope thought, Then why waste your time seeing me? "You're involved pretty deep in the only case the kid's been working on."

A smug smile. "Pontifico, it's my understanding that this 'Charles' is a law school graduate. That makes him at least mid-twenties, and therefore hardly a kid."

"Not like the lapdog downstairs, no."

The smile widened. "Ah, near-record time to come around to my . . . specialty, shall we call it?"

"Actually, when I was on the force, we had a more technical name for guys like you."

"Pedophile."

"No. Baby-raper."

A laugh now, with a wagging of the head. "You know who are *the* most sanctimonious of all that I try to reach?"

"I'll bite."

"Closet gays like yourself."

The Pope reacted in fight-over-flight mode, stiffening, then cursed himself for letting Iverson fuck with his head so easily. But give the guy credit: Hitting you with it like that, out of the blue, was a smart approach. "You're assuming I'm homosexual?"

"Oh, my dear Lord," more laughing, "even the way you pronounce that word. 'Ho-mo-sex-you-all,' like it's so foreign to you."

Murizzi figured he had two options here. One, slap the guy around a little. Two, go with him on his rant.

Try the second, at least for now. "What does my sexual orientation have to do with being 'sanctimonious' over what guys like you do to young boys like Rusty downstairs?"

"Rusty? Ah, of course, his hair. You mean Ordell."

Ordell. "Yeah, him."

Iverson leaned back in his chair, actually hooking his thumbs in the straps of his suspenders around nipple level, like the lawyers in black-and-white films. "When I met Ordell two weeks ago, he was starving, hustling his poor little ass at the mouths of alleys for nickels and dimes, half the time giving value without even receiving the agreed-upon exchange."

"I thought we were talking about you and statutory rape, not the plight of street urchins."

"They're often one and the same, Pontifico. Something which your prior police affiliation—and current sexual insecurity—won't allow you to see."

"What I see is you taking as much advantage of the kid as the other sparrowhawks would, with maybe just a warm bath and clean sheets added to the 'agreed-upon exchange.'"

"And what I see, Pontifico, is a gay male *so* insecure also regarding the gains *his* kind have made in the civil rights area that he's happy—nay, enthusiastic—about casting the first stone our way."

The Pope had read news articles about gay priests. One outside study had estimated some thirty percent of the Catholic priests in the U.S. of A. were gay. He'd also spoken over the years with several gay priests himself, who'd put the percentage at more like seventy, especially among the younger ones. In Murizzi's view, the young gay priests had saved the Church—keeping failing parishes going, doing *good* works for troubled kids in particular and the poor in general. But those same priests would be tarred by the brush of perverts like Cornelius Dooley, even though the Pope's time on the force convinced him of two things: Most pedophiles were hetero, preying on both boys *and* girls, and most gays really felt about this man/boy stuff pretty much the same as the "normal" heteros did.

But, with Iverson, not a debate you're going to win. "Okay, then tell me this: How come your group's backing a shitbird like Cornelius Dooley, who wasn't exactly playing sugar daddy to his victims?"

A smile more smarmy than smug. "An organization—a crusade—finds its . . . posterboys where it can, Pontifico. The media fury over priests engaging in sex with young men under—"

"Try eight- and nine-year-olds—"

"—his 'tutelage,' shall we say, is the best 'pulpit' we could hope for toward presenting *our* position, which is that the sexual love between a man and a boy is no less 'worthy' than the paternal love between a father and his son. In each pairing, the older generation is teaching, acculturating, and maturing the younger, like experienced women in African tribes 'initiating' pubescent male warriors to the joys—and techniques—of heterosexual intimacy."

"And you really expect to sell this . . . justification through Dooley's trial?"

A shrug. "I've sold a lot of justifications over the years, Pontifico. On theories of science and applications thereof that I barely understood myself. But my investors always realized a return of three hundred to one thousand percent on their capital." Now Iverson came forward in his chair. "And I believe we have a solid way of selling this one, too."

"Being?"

"Why, the heartwarming tale of Father Dooley and his 'little gentlemen,' the unfolding of which I really should be getting back to attending. Care to join me?"

"No, thanks. I need to take a couple showers before I mix with real people again."

The smarmy smile returned, and Pontifico Murizzi thought, You haven't laid a fucking glove on Donald Iverson, baby-raper-at-large.

After buying a sandwich and Diet Coke from the café on the third floor of the courthouse, Mairead O'Clare picked a banquette booth where she could see the entrance. Leaving her drink unopened and her food in its bag, she settled onto the blue leatherette bench and waited.

About ten minutes later, Leslie Hughes appeared in the line waiting to go past the cafeteria-style offerings. Mairead got up and approached her from the research clerk's blind side, tapping the petite blonde on the shoulder.

Hughes turned and seemed to recognize Mairead. "Not again?"

"I didn't want to get either of us in trouble by trying to see you up on eighteen this time."

"And I don't have anything more to say to you."

Mairead looked around at the others on the line, some feigning disinterest while obviously straining to hear what appeared to be some sort of spat. "Tell you what, Leslie. We can discuss a certain 'brochure' Charles gave you right here and now, or at that booth over there. Your call."

"Brochure?" Hughes stayed still, but her eyes were backpedaling. "I don't know anything about—"

"Fine. Tell it to the Homicide Unit then. But I've talked with them some, and they're not much fun. Nor very . . . discreet."

Mairead returned to her banquette without looking back at Hughes. Within twenty seconds, though, the law clerk left the cafeteria line and slid aggressively onto the other bench in the booth across from Mairead.

"Good decision, Leslie."

Hughes glanced around them once, then in a tone etched with acid said, "Why are you doing this to me?"

"Doing what?"

The woman lowered her voice, but the acid drip stayed on it. "I told you: I'm trying to use this clerkship as a stepping-stone to a permanent job, just like everybody else. Linking me to Charles and that . . . club would royally fuck me over."

"I'm not trying to ruin anything for you, Leslie. I just want the truth."

"The truth." Hughes lowered her face now. "Okay. After Charles snowed me during a couple of lunches in here, we *did* do the deed, but just once, at my place."

Mairead thought, Am I the only woman in the city Chuck *hasn't* had?

Hughes sputtered. "Before he leaves, though, the shit gives me this swingers' thing, tells me I'm good enough—'Looks as well as overall talent, Les'—to join up, but I have to find somebody else because it's 'couples only.'"

"What did you say back?"

"I told him to stay the fuck away from me. I mean, *drugs* would be safer, what with AIDS and who I might see there—or be seen by. And that was it between us. The end."

"Charles didn't haunt you about it?"

"Haunt me? More like shunned me, acted like we'd never even met."

"And that's all?"

"Read my lips. And I don't know jackshit about him being missing. Now," Leslie Hughes looked down again, this time at Mairead's lunch bag, "can I go eat, too?"

TWELVE

Billie Sunday probably would never say it to Shel or Mairead, and definitely not to the Pope, but she really enjoyed being in the law suite by herself. There was a certain peacefulness that descended on the place when the lawyers were off to court, and the investigator was out poking around in other people's lives. Billie felt she could order her tasks, control her day the way it's tough to do, three boys at home and spread enough in age that no two would be doing the same thing at the same time, except maybe eating. Of course once Robert, Jr., went off to college, things might be simpler at home, but not, Billie believed, better.

For all the helter-skelter of the three added together, the time she enjoyed the most was being with one of them for something important to him. Billie really felt she understood then what people meant by "living in the moment."

Lord, I will miss having that good, smart oldest son around me.

Then she felt a small tear tickle the nose side of her eye, and she wiped it away abruptly, angry with herself for letting family creep in on business, the same way she'd get angry if business crept in on family. A soul has a life with both, she ought to be able to keep them straight and separate.

And so Billie Sunday inhaled a deep breath, scooped up the assorted pieces of paper Shel and Mairead had heaped onto her desk, and began to prioritize the rest of her day.

. . .

Getting off the elevator at Suffolk Superior, Sheldon A. Gold saw a burly uniformed bailiff leaving the courtroom where Barbara Pitt had said she was sitting.

"Excuse me?"

The officer, with what appeared to be half a baby carrot between his thumb and forefinger, turned to him. "Can I help you?"

At least the man eats healthfully. "Yes. I'm here to see Judge Pitt."

"Ah, Mr. Gold, right?"

"That's right."

"Tommy Flanagan." The bailiff popped the other half of the carrot into his mouth. "Her Honor told me you were on your way over. This way, please."

Shel walked with Flanagan back into the session, empty thanks to the noon recess. They moved together to the lobby door next to the bench.

The bailiff said, "Flo?"

"Yes?"

"Her Honor's visitor's arrived."

"Send him in, please."

Flanagan motioned Shel to go past him, the bailiff backing out into the courtroom again.

Shel saw an attractive woman in her forties, maybe low fifties, sitting at the larger of two desks in the anteroom. "I'm Flo Altamira, the judge's clerk."

Shel nodded. "She's told me a lot about you."

Altamira smiled in a way that suggested he'd confirmed the expected. "Judge Pitt also indicated that she'd like a little extra privacy," reaching under the kneehole of her desk and coming up with two polio braces, "so I'll be off on break for a while."

"Can I give you a hand?"

"No," Altamira rising in a series of Erector-set mechanical movements, "but thank you. Just knock: Her Honor is already inside."

Shel waited until the woman had crab-walked out into the courtroom before doing just that.

"Come in."

He opened the inner door. Pitt's lobby was larger than Bruce Rodrigue's, with more personal than professional touches. Vase of flowers, photos of the judge with a young Amer-Asian girl that Shel guessed to be her daughter.

None of any man. Not her ex, and not her clerk-lover.

Barbara Pitt turned to him from her computer monitor, but didn't rise. "Without Chuck, doing research is a bear." She pushed a button that made the screen fade to black. "So, Shelly, do you have some news for me?"

"I'm afraid so," he said, closing the door behind him this time.

Mairead O'Clare had been to the district attorney's office at Bowdoin Square before and thought again how cool it would be to have a major health club as your basement neighbor. Tough day in court? Just pop down to the cardio room, burn off the aggravation in a spinning class, then tone up on the Nautilus and Cybex machines, maybe even do some yoga.

A club doesn't have to be that conveniently located in order to avail yourself of its advantages, young lady.

Mairead nodded. Her ice hockey league wouldn't be gearing up again until September, which meant she'd have three months without competitive skating. And which meant in turn that she'd have to come up with something to replace the endorphin lifts and calorie burns.

But not today.

Mairead went into One Bulfinch Place, took the elevator to the third floor, and gave her name to the nice woman behind the thick glass, who told her that Assistant District Attorney Deborah Butler was expected back from court any minute. Mairead exchanged her driver's license for a laminated VISITOR badge, and took a seat next to a rack of brochures, which made her remember the one for the swingers' club, Loll, that she and the Pope would be hitting later on. Then she noticed that the displayed brochures dealt with "Abuse Prevention" in about five different languages, which reminded her of why she was visiting ADA Butler. That message was pounded home when Mairead looked up at the dull pink walls of the reception area, framed drawings by public-school students hanging in every open space.

I wonder how many of the artist-kids have had to deal with their own brand of sexual—

The elevator doors opened, and Mairead turned to look, seeing the diminutive prosecutor, medium-brown hair down today a bit past her shoulders. She wore a simple tan suit and brown shoes, and Mairead suddenly had the impression that Butler mirrored Shel as to dress code: Don't be flashy, let the jurors focus on the witnesses and believe in their answers.

"Ms. Butler?"

"Yes, and you must be Ms. O'Clare. How are you?"

Butler extended her hand and shook Mairead's without looking down at the hemangioma. Mairead felt even better when Butler said, "Let's get acquainted on the way to my office."

Butler grabbed a sheaf of phone messages from the receptionist, then riffled through them as she walked to the elevator, Mairead tagging along behind with the lunch she'd bought at the courthouse cafe. As the doors closed, the prosecutor pushed a button on the control panel. "First names okay with you?"

"Yes, fine."

"Mairead, I saw you auditing my courtroom yesterday, but not before, and not today. What's up?"

Mairead explained about Charles Vareika being missing.

As the elevator doors opened again, Butler stepped out and to the right, but frowning. "I heard somebody—it was Tommy Flanagan, Judge Pitt's bailiff?"

"I've met him."

"Tommy said that Judge Pitt's clerk wasn't around. I didn't think much of it, until Her Honor announced this morning that it'd be a few days before she'd rule on that motion you heard us arguing, and I asked Flo Altamira—the session's administrative clerk?"

"Met her, too," said Mairead.

"Flo told me that nobody's seen or heard from this Vareika since—what, sometime Saturday?"

"That's my information as well."

Butler threw a sidelong glance at Mairead as the prosecutor entered an office stacked high with files on the floor, making getting to the desk nearly a matter of trailblazing. "You seem like you're playing this pretty close to the vest. You think it's worse than a boys-will-be-animals long weekend?"

"Deborah, you've had more contact with Mr. Vareika than I have."

A warm smile, despite the next comment. "Should poor little *me* start playing my cards close, too?"

Veiled by the smile and the self-deprecation, but a direct question nevertheless. As they both sat down, Mairead said, "Guy has a near-perfect attendance record, then doesn't show, doesn't call work, doesn't even contact his roommate after one message Saturday afternoon of 'don't wait up for me.' We're just trying to figure out what's happened to him."

Butler seemed taller in her chair. Maybe a fanny cushion? "The 'we' being . . . ?"

Mairead told her about Judge Pitt retaining Shel's team because the police brushed off the initial complaint.

"The initial, maybe," said Butler. "Only now it's Wednesday. Are the police involved yet?"

"I think that'll happen this afternoon."

Butler folded her hands on top of the desk like a schoolgirl. "Well, I may have to repeat myself then, but you're already here, and I have to eat. Let me clear some space for us."

Mairead noticed the two file cabinets, wondered if they already were full of paper or if, like Shel, Butler preferred to be able to "see" her caseload just by looking around her office.

When there was enough room, the desktop became a lunch counter, Butler bringing out a salad in a clear plastic container, Mairead her sandwich. After a couple of bites and silent chewing, Butler said, "So, ask your questions."

Mairead nodded and swallowed. "We don't know if Mr. Vareika's disappearance is innocent, or, if not, whether it's foul play from his professional or personal life."

"Fair enough."

"Professionally, your *Dooley* case is the only one he's been working on for quite a while now, so naturally . . ."

Butler tamped an errant chunk of tomato into the corner of her mouth. "Naturally, you want to talk to all the players in it."

"Right."

"Well, I only saw the guy a few times. Model-quality looks, but I'm not even sure I heard him *talk,* except for identifying himself to the jury array, see if anybody in it knew him." Butler now cocked her head. "Not that I'm insulted, but how come you took this long to get around to me as a 'player'?"

"I got kind of channeled toward the defense side of things by Bill Sherden."

A nod. "Good man. Doing things for these kids that their own parents can't get it together enough to do themselves." Now Butler stopped the plastic fork halfway to her mouth. "What connection do you have to Dooley himself?"

"None, until he finger-waved to me, then asked his lawyer to have me visit him."

"In the lockup."

"Where else?"

"I just meant, you've never seen his cell, then?"

"No."

"His 'supporters' send him magazines. Innocuous enough, until you realize that most of them are catalogs for boys' clothing."

Mairead felt what she'd eaten of her sandwich lunch in her stomach. "Say no more."

"It's public knowledge, so I'm not exactly telling secrets here, but the guy kept a diary, too."

Despite already having heard about it from Dooley himself, the thought . . .

Butler let out a breath. "As a piece of evidence, it's a real help. Especially toward figuring out the statute of limitations issues, and the ones in this mess are incredible. Some of the rapes go back twenty years, which means we have to determine date of last incident, then try to identify the boy, then calculate when he hit majority, and then how many years after that we are now. The whole thing is like score-cards in baseball for compiling Dooley's 'statistics' over the course of his 'career.'"

Mairead willed her stomach to get a grip. "Couldn't you just sub-poena the archdiocese records on complaints against him?"

Butler frowned again. "We found that typically the local 'record keeping' left a lot to be desired. There was an attempt by the United States Conference of Bishops back in 'ninety-four to survey abusive priests nationwide, but it ran into the same local problem, and the bishops themselves scuttled the whole idea because they feared the survey would just create evidence for victims to use in presenting civil cases for damages against the Church."

Protecting the purse over the victims, young lady, both past and present.

Mairead nodded. "Dooley told me that you provided his attorney with a photocopy of the diary."

"We did, but it wouldn't surprise me if the guy asked her for it. To relive his past glories, no doubt."

"Actually, Dooley asked me if I could get the original back to him."

"Huh, fat chance. Even if I had it, I wouldn't. But that's not up to me now. We introduced it into evidence already, so Flo Altamira's got the original."

"That's what I told him." Then, very casually around a small nib-ble of bread, Mairead said, "You keep a copy?"

Butler cocked her head the other way now. "You want a look at it."

"Yes."

"Mind if I ask you why?"

Mairead didn't reply.

Butler smiled. "Okay, mind if I *tell* you why?"

"Go ahead."

"You want to know if your Charles Vareika is in Dooley's diary, don't you?"

"Actually, Deborah, I'd think you'd want to know that. Because if he is, the research clerk of the judge presiding over your trial might have a real reason to be less than evenhanded in helping her make decisions about how the defendant should be treated."

Butler seemed to appreciate Mairead's logic. "Shit." She dropped her fork into her salad and delved into her handbag, coming out with a ring of keys.

Shelly, would you do me a favor, please?" said Barbara Pitt, leaning back in her lobby's desk chair with a sigh. "Don't make this into a 'good news, bad news' joke."

Shel sat across from his long-former lover, debating internally which piece of "bad news" to spring on her first. "Barbara, Charles Vareika has a portrait of himself over the fireplace in his living room."

Pitt looked confused. "A photograph, an oil painting?"

Shel tried to assess his client's reaction. "You've never seen it, then?"

Another sigh. "Shelly, Shelly. I told you, back in your office. Chuck always visited *me*. I've never been to his apartment."

"It's a painting, I'm told. A very good one, and accordingly pretty expensive."

A blank look. "And therefore?"

"And therefore I'm wondering who commissioned it."

"You're . . . ?" Now Pitt's face clouded over, and she looked down at her desk more than at Shel. "You've come here to find out if *I* paid for the portrait?"

"Yes."

Pitt looked back up at him. "I didn't."

"Any idea who might have?"

"No." Now her face grew stern, as though about to lecture a litigator over some transgression committed in her courtroom. "Do you?"

"His roommate told Pontifico Murizzi that 'a very good friend' arranged for it."

"Well, I certainly have no idea who that could be. And, for all we know, it could have been 'commissioned' long before Chuck and I began to work together, couldn't it?"

Shel nodded. "Except that the roommate claimed it was a 'very good likeness,' too, implying it's pretty recently painted. But you understand why I had to ask the question?"

Pitt set her jaw. "You think that if I didn't pay for the portrait, another 'rich, doting' lover might have."

Admit it: This next part will be even more cruel, but you need to know.

"Barbara," said Shel, reaching into his suit jacket's inside pocket and taking out the Loll brochure, "have you ever seen one of these before?"

Pitt pointed toward her desk, and Shel slid the thing toward her.

She picked it up, glanced at the front and back, then slid the brochure back a little too hard, so that it sliced through the air and fluttered to the carpet.

Pitt spoke now behind clenched teeth. "A 'couples-only' swingers' club? Of course I haven't seen this."

Raw emotion, and for that, all the more sincere. She really has no clue.

Shel bent over in his chair, retrieved the brochure. "The Pope also visited Genna, at her college in Maine. Your daughter says Mr. Vareika gave her this. In your condo."

"That's . . . absurd. No, it's *beyond* absurd."

Shel tilted his head toward the console on Pitt's desk. "Call Genna and ask her."

Pitt's eyes went to the telephone, then came back to his. "Shelly, this can't . . . be."

"Mr. Vareika's roommate, Vivianna Klein, asked both the Pope and Mairead if they had current partners, and when each said no, she seemed disappointed."

Now Pitt's eyes fluttered like the brochure had. "Do you . . . Are you telling me that Chuck—and this Klein woman—actually have gone to this . . . 'club' as a couple?"

"I'm not sure. But I am sure of one thing."

Pitt couldn't seem to focus. "What?"

"Your Mr. Vareika isn't quite the person you thought him to be."

Pitt's eyes welled up, tears brimming over the lower lids.

"Barbara?"

"I'd like you to leave now."

Nearly the same reaction as Amelie Cardon at Save Our Clergy, if for nearly the opposite reason. "Barbara."

She looked at him, using her right index finger to whisk at her tears.

Shel said, "There is one phone call we think you need to make, as soon as possible."

"To?"

"The Boston Police. Missing Persons."

Mairead O'Clare tapped the first photocopied page of cramped, precise handwriting and said, "What do those initials centered at the top stand for?"

Deborah Butler now sat next to Mairead at a table in one of the district attorney's small, windowless conference rooms, the air hot and stuffy. The prosecutor angled the binder containing the pages so Mairead could see them better. "The church Cornelius Dooley was assigned to."

"And those numbers down the left-hand side are dates?"

"Month and day. We had to interpolate the years based on when his assignments to the various parishes began and ended."

Mairead riffled quickly through the diary, beginning to end. "How many years' worth, Deborah?"

"Twenty-seven."

Mairead hung her head, then shook it. "I'm told Vareika is my age, twenty-six."

Butler consulted a typed paper next to her, which Mairead guessed to be some kind of translation table for the parishes and years. "Okay, let's start when he would have been . . . six?"

"Six?" Mairead's stomach twisting, the stuffy air in the conference room not helping it any.

Butler looked at her. "That's the youngest one we've found that Dooley ever actually raped."

Mairead closed her eyes, vaguely aware of the woman next to her paging through the diary.

"However," said Butler, "we can stop when your law clerk would have reached thirteen."

Through still closed eyes, "Why thirteen?"

"Because by then, his victims seem to have 'aged out' of his target range . . . Okay, here we go."

Mairead opened her eyes again.

Butler pointed. "The church in Calem, the beginning of Dooley's second year there, when your Mr. Vareika would have turned six."

Mairead forced herself to look down at the page, follow Butler's finger tracing the middle column of handwriting:

Billy C.
Matt M.
Kevin O'B.

and so on.

Mairead said, "Did Dooley ever use the full last name?"

"No. And I don't know why, since everything else is pretty obvious."

Mairead thought she knew.

God forgive him, young lady, but he didn't NEED to write them out because he knew he'd remember each well enough from just first name and last initial.

She nodded. "I think we should be searching for 'Charles,' but also variations, like 'Charlie' and 'Chuck.'"

"Okay."

Mairead looked at the other margin of the page. "What do the letters to the right of the names stand for?"

Butler shivered, though the air hadn't suddenly cooled down. "That was Dooley's code for what he did to the boy involved on that date."

Mairead didn't really want to ask the next question, but knew that Shel, despite losing his own son, would somehow find the courage to do so. "Deborah, explain the code to me, please."

Mairead listened as closely as she could to phrases like "genital fondling," "digital penetration," "oral satisfaction," and worse.

When Butler finished, Mairead forced herself to begin scanning the middle column, for the names. "There's a 'Chuck,' but wrong last initial."

Butler nodded and turned the page, her finger now tracing a little faster. "Zip on this one, too."

Another turn. "A 'Charlie,' only not a 'V,' either."

After two more pages, Mairead's eyes began to move ahead of Butler's finger. "Another 'Chuck,' but an 'L.'"

They went on like that, through the rest of Dooley's time in Calem, then the periods when Dooley "served" in Smithfield and Weston Hills. All the way through the year that would have been Charles Vareika's thirteenth birthday. Mairead began to see the pattern of Dooley's abuses, how he began "grooming" the boys, their names alternating as he slowly escalated the level of imposition on each to the . . . "ultimate."

Butler looked up at Mairead. "I counted only six variations on 'Charles.'"

Mairead rubbed her eyes now. "Same. And no 'V' last names."

"Something else I thought of."

"Being?"

Butler said, "You have any reason to believe your law clerk ever lived in any of these three towns?"

Shit. "No. In fact, his parents are somewhere in New Hampshire."

"Well, then. I'd say this is a dead end for you. *And* for me, in terms of your Mr. Vareika tainting my trial, thank God."

Mairead O'Clare nodded slowly and didn't feel the least regret about Deborah Butler closing the photocopied binder that reflected, one step removed, a monster's own, handwrought chronicle of sin and crime both.

THIRTEEN

Pontifico Murizzi checked the address on the other business card Irish had given him. Bill Sherden's building read like it'd be halfway up Beacon Hill, on the south side, so he left his Explorer in the garage below the Common, took the elevator to the ball-field level, and began walking up the macadam path toward Beacon Street.

The Pope had gotten about fifty strides through the big park when he noticed what he thought was a large seagull, standing in the tall grass and kind of mashing its feet, like a cat will its paws before lying down on a rug. It seemed pretty strange until Murizzi, drawing closer, realized it wasn't a gull but a hawk, the first one he'd seen in the city since he was a boy, though he remembered news articles about peregrine falcons now nesting in some of the skyscrapers and taking pigeons on the wing. When the Pope moved closer still, the thing finally took off, flapping hard to get enough lift from the ground, seeing as its talons were gripping the shoulders of a rat that would have gone fourteen inches easy. The hapless rodent now just dangled, its head at that impossible, broken-neck angle Murizzi had witnessed at crime scenes over the years.

Nice fucking segue from talking with that "sparrowhawk," Iverson, and his latest lovebird, Ordell.

The Pope shook his head and walked on, finding what he thought would be a pretty nice if small town house was instead a grand mansion. He checked the card again, then rang the bell.

A few seconds later, a tall woman with a pleasant face smiled out at him through the windowed panels in the huge entry door. She opened it wide for him. "Are you Mr. Murizzi?"

"Yes," the Pope taking out his ID.

The woman never even glanced at it. "I'm Molly Sherden, Bill's wife. Come in, please."

Murizzi followed her, thinking, Maybe I should call ahead more often. Then he thought about the kind of people he usually visited, and the Pope decided that his typical practice of just popping up probably made more sense in the long run.

After climbing a half-flight of stairs, Molly Sherden turned right into a beautiful, mahogany-paneled library big enough to serve as a men's club back in the nineteenth century. The guy himself was sitting in an easy chair off the desk. Dressed casually, a notebook computer in his lap, a mustard-patched cocker spaniel drowsing at his feet. When he saw Murizzi, though, Sherden pushed a button on his computer, then lifted it off his lap and onto the desk. As he got up himself, the dog came over to sniff the Pope's feet.

The wife said, "Bill, this is Mr. Murizzi. I'm going to head back upstairs to make sure the boys are ready."

"Fine, honeybun."

As she left them, the spaniel in her wake, Murizzi shook the guy's hand, no lingering squeeze like with Iverson.

Jeez, get over it. You're among human beings again.

Sherden made his way back to the easy chair, its mate a nice conversational distance across from it. "Please, have a seat."

The Pope sank in the leather, brass tacks holding the piece together so well, he couldn't guess whether it was brand-new or a hundred years old. "Thanks for seeing me."

"When you called, I said 'sure' kind of automatically, but thinking about it since, there isn't much I can add to what I told Ms. O'Clare."

Meaning, maybe you're interrupting a family outing he wants to get under way. "I don't think this'll take too long, Mr. Sherden."

"Please, it's Bill."

"And call me Pope. Everybody else does."

"Okay, Pope. What are your questions?"

"Well, I think you've kind of answered the first one. You haven't come up with anything else about Charles Vareika?"

"Your missing law clerk? No, nothing more."

"The address on this card you gave Mairead is for the victims' organization."

"Right."

"So, you run the operation out of your house here?"

"Yes." Then Sherden seemed to sense something. "Pope, how much did Ms. O'Clare tell you about me?"

"As much as she thought was important, I guess."

A smile, but a friendly one. "Well, whether hers or yours, that's a pretty good answer."

At which point, there was the thumping of multiple feet down some stairs, and Murizzi turned to see the wife and two boys come into the room. Both kids were wiry and athletic, one maybe twelve, the other fourteen. When the two boys saw the Pope, he thought they were looking at him, politely, the way he remembered first looking at the animals in the Franklin Park Zoo.

Molly Sherden said, "Bill?"

"Yes?"

"Before we go, could the boys meet Mr. Murizzi?"

Standing up, the Pope beat him to the punch. "Sure."

They came over, exchanged names, and shook hands. Then the older one said, "You used to be a homicide detective, like on 'NYPD Blue'?"

"Right."

The younger said, "And now you're a private eye, like those old reruns of 'Magnum, PI'?"

The Pope heard "old" the loudest. "That's right."

The two kids looked at each other, the taller saying "cool" like it had seven syllables in it, the shorter "awesome."

The wife and mother said, "Okay, that's it. Dad and Mr. Murizzi have business, and we're going to be late."

They said their thank-yous and good-byes, then left.

Bill Sherden waited until the outer door closed, then said, "Off to the Red Sox at Fenway Park."

"Am I keeping you from joining them?"

"No." An unusually sad smile. "We had a former neighbor—a good friend for ten years—who moved out to the suburbs. As will happen, we didn't stay in touch, and pretty soon I hadn't thought of him for a long time. Then we saw in the papers that he was on his way to Los Angeles on September eleventh, to arrange early retirement, be able to spend more time with his teenaged boys."

The Pope just nodded.

"Well," said Sherden, "Molly and I talked about it. She was a partner in a large law firm, with intellectual property clients she could still represent on her own. And given all the projected layoffs of personnel due to the recession *and* nine-eleven, we both thought it would be good for her to be here rather than making hard decisions about people there. I'd run a consulting business from home for a long time, but I began paring that down, too. We're comfortable, thanks to high-income years and good investments, so now I focus on charitable efforts, like the victims' organization." Sherden looked over Murizzi's shoulder, back toward the door. "And on our sons."

The Pope didn't nod this time. "I don't want to sound critical here, but wouldn't that argue for *both* Mom and Dad bringing them to Fenway?"

The sad smile again. "After the terrorist attacks, we thought about how one parent might have to perform double duty. So we started criscrossing the stuff we'd do with the boys. If Molly took them to the symphony, I would instead. If I took them to a ball game, she would instead."

The Pope didn't believe he'd ever have thought of it, but, once explained, the plan made a lot of sense. "So, if anything happened to either one of you, the sons wouldn't feel so odd about going to everything with only one parent."

"Our approach, anyway. And scaling back on our professional lives has let us both spend more quality time with the boys in so many ways."

Jeez, talk about a different world from the one you were in less than—what, an hour ago? "Tell me about this Donald Iverson."

The jump seemed to surprise Sherden, though he then nodded.

"Independently wealthy thanks to investing in high-tech start-ups. Runs his . . . 'association' from his home, over in Bay Village some- where. In a lot of ways, Donald Iverson's my parallel."

"That's pretty magnanimous of you."

A shrug. "We live in a democracy, Pope. That creates some strange . . . tolerances, even within the unthinkable. I mean, before my namesake Clinton, did you ever imagine 'President of the United States' would appear in the *New York Times* within the same sentence as the word 'fellatio'?"

Good point. "What if I told you that Iverson seems to have a youngster around your sons' ages living with him now?"

A look of pain crossed Sherden's face. "I'm involved mainly with the priest victims, so I don't know much about the law-enforcement side in general. Did you ever work Vice?"

Sherden phrased it like he had himself.

Murizzi said, "No."

"Well, I've spoken over time to some who have. I ask them, 'Why can't you arrest a man who's obviously living in a sexual relationship with an underage boy?' Their response?"

The Pope could guess. "No complaining witness."

"Exactly. So long as the man is careful not to involve anyone else—"

Murizzi's brain flickered on the "swingers' club" brochure.

"—and the boy is being treated by the man in virtually every *other* way far better than any adult ever has before, who's going to call the police?"

"Neighbors," said the Pope, "but I know what'll happen then, too. The man and the boy both deny anything inappropriate, and even if Child Welfare does a house inspection, nobody catches them in the act, there's not enough evidence to file charges, much less convict."

"Exactly again." A shake of the head. "No, when it's completely consensual, even when the *law,* as I understand it, says the boy by def- inition is too young *to* consent, there's not much we can do." Now a little fire. "But there is about these priests, Pope. And the way to change the system that first permitted, then covered up the scandal, is through criminal prosecutions, as educational publicity and legal springboards for damages in civil suits. Once the church has to go public and sell off its acquired property, it will police itself a lot bet-ter." Fire gave way to determination. "I intend to get these injured kids as much compensation as I can, both for their past humiliations and to prevent something like that happening to future boys, who but for 'the grace of God' were born into a religion that allowed them to be abused."

The Pope nodded.

The guy came forward in his chair now. "I mentioned my name-sake before? Well, I will make the Church pay and change, even if we have to auction off everything in *your* namesake's Vatican Palace."

Pontifico Murizzi thanked his host for his time, and once outside on the sidewalk again, was more than a little relieved that Bill Sher-den wasn't coming after him for anything.

Walking back toward the office from the district attorney's build-ing, Mairead O'Clare checked her cellular's voice mail. There was a message from Shel, and, given the background noise, he was calling from a pay phone. For the umpteenth time, Mairead wished her boss could enter the twenty-first century by ponying up for a cell himself.

But the message was clear enough: Judge Barbara Pitt denied commissioning the portrait of Charles Vareika. Mairead dialed the office, leaving a message of her own with Billie that their client's lover had also tried to "recruit" one of his fellow law clerks for the swing-ers' club, but that Vareika's name was not in the priest-rapist's "diary" of victims.

Mairead stopped for a traffic light on Cambridge Street, then steeled herself toward a decision. Walking a few blocks more, she bought a disposable flash camera at a CVS drugstore, then went up and over Beacon Hill. She cut across the Common and the Public Garden, skirted Back Bay, and continued into the South End. After a total of thirty-five minutes, Mairead stood in front of the brownstone where Vivianna Klein shared an apartment—and maybe a swingers' club membership—with Charles Vareika, a man Mairead had irra-tionally fallen for without even meeting, a crush she wasn't over yet.

As luck would have it, an older woman was leaving the building just as Mairead mounted the last step of the exterior stairs. The young lawyer said a thank-you as the woman held the otherwise locked entrance doors for her. Once inside, Mairead moved to the back right corner, knocking on the apartment door.

It opened to show Vivianna Klein, evidently expecting someone else.

At least based on the black leather outfit and Catwoman mask, multi-lashed whip in hand and Miata the Doberman on studded leash, collar, and harness.

Jesus Christ Almighty, said Sister Bernadette's voice, the first time Mairead could ever recall the nun taking the Lord's name in vain.

Klein's shoulders dipped, and her face came forward in a "duh?" kind of way.

Mairead said, "You're sure home a lot for somebody with a job." As she took a step inside the apartment, the dog growled, baring its teeth.

Klein said, "Get out of here, lawyer-girl, or Miata will—"

But after her first visit, Mairead was ready for that. "Be awfully noisy, don't you think? And," bringing her cell phone from her handbag, "how would you ever get out of that costume and into real clothes before the police arrived?"

Klein now put her hands on her hips, even the dog, Mairead thought, sensing the argument was over. "Come in, then. Quick."

Klein let Miata loose, and the Doberman hopped up onto its apparently favorite sectional piece, did two circular walkarounds, then plopped down, gnawing on the leather leash. Mairead moved into the living room, Klein slamming the door shut behind her.

Mairead took a different piece of furniture across from the dog. "I don't want to wreck whatever party you're about to host here."

Klein stayed standing and glanced up at the mantel, but whether at the clock or the portrait, Mairead couldn't be sure. In fact, she was almost afraid to look at Vareika's likeness herself, for fear she wouldn't stop.

Klein said, "It's not a 'party,' lawyer-girl. It's a 'part' of my job."

Mairead felt a "bullshit" expression crossing her own face.

"Truly," said Klein. "My work at the institute involves empirical research into sadomasochism and domination, trying to determine how people who are oriented that way can have alternative, safer outlets for their desires."

Mairead was about to mention the swingers' club as an "alternative outlet," but then decided to just nod.

Klein's voice lost its defensiveness. "What do you want this time?"

"Everything you know about that painting."

"The painting again." Klein shook her head. "I do not, like, believe this."

"You haven't heard word one from Chuck Vareika, have you?"

"No, I haven't. How many times do you need to *hear* that?"

"Who was the artist?"

"I don't know, and I don't care."

Mairead rose again, noting that the dog, despite her owner's tone, didn't seem to mind. "Can you help me take it down so I can look at it?"

"Will that get you out of here?"

"Faster, anyway."

Klein stomped off in six-inch heels, having to swing her legs unnaturally, like a stilt-walker in Boston's First Night parade on New Year's Eve. Mairead gazed up at the face that had touched her so deeply, so immediately.

Klein came back from the kitchen with a green stepladder. "Here, lawyer-girl. You do it."

Mairead opened the ladder, made sure it was sturdily grounded on the floor, then climbed to the second step. Up close, the painting lost its power, going from an overall impression to individual components of color and stroke.

The frame was heavy, the dimensions of the thing making it awkward, and Mairead silently blessed the time she spent in the weight room toward building upper-body strength for ice hockey. When she finally cleared the hanging wire from the hook it had rested on, Mairead backed down to the floor carefully. Walking to a patio window, she held the portrait up to the outside light. In the lower right-hand corner was what looked to be a signature, but illegibly written except for an "x" in the middle of the single name.

Mairead said, "Chuck never mentioned the artist to you?"

"No," in a flat voice.

"Maybe the address, for the studio?"

"No," the voice growing an edge.

Mairead supported the bottom of the portrait on her thigh as she turned it around. There was a small label on the back.

Not the artist's, but, from the name, the shop that framed the painting. She memorized the address, then set the portrait down in the light from the windows.

"Aren't you at least going to put it back where it belongs?"

"In a minute." Mairead took out the disposable camera.

"Hey, don't ruin the thing."

"I'm just going to take a couple pictures of it."

Then Mairead, not very familiar with cameras in general, shot without the flash going off. Figuring out how to activate that, she photographed the portrait from as many different distances and angles as she could until the tiny counter above the viewfinder told her only two were left.

Which is when Mairead turned and took a photo of Klein, Miata blinking in the background.

"Hey, what the fuck do you—"

Mairead dropped the camera back into her bag. "I can either help you rehang the painting, or leave sooner, so that your . . . expected guest doesn't see me."

Klein's eyes blazed in the mask's slots. "Give me that camera, lawyer-girl."

"No."

"Give it to me, or I'll take it from you."

"Without resorting to 'guy rules,' Vivianna, I don't think you can, and if you sic Miata on me, again I just hit my speed dial for nine-one-one, and the emergency dispatcher's tape will hear me yelling out your name and address." Mairead looked toward the sectional, the dog's tongue slobbering between teeth like tusks. "And I don't think the police will take many chances with a Doberman in gladiator armor."

Klein was seething, but she managed to say, "Get out! Get out and never come back!"

"Thanks for all your help."

Mairead opened the apartment door herself, heard it slam behind her after only a few steps. She continued to the main entrance, taking the stairs to the sidewalk, then moving down a few buildings until she could comfortably lean against a wrought-iron fence. Mairead brought the camera out again, clicking off the flash function before cupping the small device in the palm of her hand. She began checking her watch every few minutes, pretending to wait for a cab or other ride.

Young lady, you don't think Ms. Klein will have called whoever her "expected guest" was, to warn him off?

Mairead grinned. "Him or . . . her."

She felt a little shudder inside her head.

Then Mairead noticed out of the corner of her eye a taxi pulling up several houses to the far side of the one she'd visited. A man Mairead didn't recognize got out. He was shorter than medium height, wearing a nice business suit.

As the man paid the fare through the driver's-side window, Mairead debated whether to use her last photo on him or not. After all he might not be bound for the right building.

Or he might have had the cab stop a short distance away, so the company's records would show a different destination than Ms. Klein's address.

Mairead nodded.

The taxi moved off, the man fiddling with his wallet until the driver reached the end of the block and turned. Then the man walked quickly toward the building Mairead expected. He merely glanced at her without a smile and climbed the first step.

Mairead lifted the camera and got what she hoped was a good profile shot even as the man continued up the stairs and used a key to unlock the front doors before disappearing inside.

Billie Sunday watched Shel Gold enter the suite from the corridor and had one of the most outlandish visions she'd ever experienced.

The poor man looks like the Savior climbing Calvary, the burden of his own cross pushing him down.

"Shel, you all right?"

He gave her his sad smile, not the little-boy one that said he was putting something over on somebody. "Better than some, Billie."

"You want anything? Coffee, soda?"

"No, thanks. I just had a difficult talk with one person, and no talk at all with another."

Now the man was barely making sense. "I think maybe you ought to go home for the day. There's nothing else on your calendar here."

"In a little while, Billie, in a little while."

And she watched that poor, good soul—too sensitive for this kind of work: He could do it, but it hurt him so bad sometimes—shamble into his office like a tired stable horse into its stall, hoping it wouldn't have to go out again that day.

Wow." Mairead O'Clare suddenly realized she must have sounded like a little kid, but the sixtyish man who occupied the magnificent loft smiled and told her his name was Jaxon.

The sun streamed in brilliantly through a greenhouse of glass on the south wall of his space, the ceilings at least fifteen feet high. The carpeting was drop cloths under easels where there was work in progress. A skull rounded out on one canvas, the features of a face on another, all but clothing painted in on a third. There were at least four finished, or what Mairead assumed were finished, portraits on a display wall. Some of families, some of children, all with that same essence—Mairead thought it might be brush stroke, or sense of color— that the painting of Charles Vareika radiated.

And the eyes, like Mona Lisa's, follow me as I move.

Jaxon himself was potbellied, but with a kind face and thinning gray hair trailing down his back in more a braid than a ponytail. He wore cargo pants and an old denim shirt, both torn and spat- tered. His hands had paint on them, too, and so Mairead understood that him not offering to shake might have nothing to do with her own stains. Most of the places to sit were stools rather than chairs, even at a makeshift desk with a computer and telephone on it. Jaxon pulled one stool over, checking it for paint before he bade Mairead to sit.

He took another, but rested just his butt cheek on it. "So, Mairead, your first time in the Collaborative?"

"Yes."

Jaxon looked up at the ceilings, especially the glassed-over part. "This was an old warehouse. When the Fenway district declined during the Great Depression, it closed. For a while after the Second World War, the area came back, but not so much as to need this derelict. Decades later, a bunch of us got together, somebody knew how to write a grant, and the foundation of a wealthy art lover refurbished it for us."

"All painters?"

"Oh, no. We have sculptors, metallurgists, fabricists who work in collage . . ." Jaxon suddenly stopped. "Could you turn your face just five degrees toward the windows?"

Mairead tried to do that.

"Hold it . . . back a little . . . perfect." He moved his own head around, left-right but also high-low. "If you've come to me for a portrait yourself, I think I can do you justice."

Mairead felt complimented, even though the rational part of her identified his remark as the opening line of a sales pitch. "Actually, I'm here about a portrait you've already painted."

A warm smile. "Ah. You saw one of my works, and a former client referred you." Now Jaxon swept a hand around the studio. "As you can appreciate from the finished ones here, the painting you saw was no fluke. And, while the total time we'd have to spend together is considerable, I can be flexible. As those in progress suggest, we can arrange a sequence of sittings to suit your own, no-doubt-busy schedule."

Well, I hit the "sales pitch" nail on the head. "I'm sure you could, Jaxon, but that's not why I'm here." Mairead reached into her handbag, took out the best three of the photos she'd had printed at a one-hour shop on Boylston Street. "I took some pictures of the portrait involved, and I brought them to the framing shop whose label was on the back of the original. The woman there told me it was you, no question, and she even had your address here."

Confused now. "Why would you do that?"

"Because I couldn't read your signature on the painting, except for the 'x' in the middle. The woman at the shop told me you go by just the one name professionally."

"No, no." Jaxon shook his head. "I mean, if you're not interested in a portrait, why did you want to find me at all?"

"Please, just take a look at these?"

Mairead handed him her photos. Jaxon stared at one without even glancing at the others.

Then he handed all of them back to her, his face without expression. "So?"

"So, you did paint the original portrait?"

"Why do you want to know?"

"Because the young man pictured in it has been missing since Saturday."

Mairead wanted to hit Jaxon with it like that, because the Pope often told her that was the best way to get a sincere reaction.

And this reaction was surprise, even shock. "Missing? From where?"

Note, young lady: Not "I've never seen him before in my life."

Mairead nodded. "His job."

"Who . . . who are you?"

And now, not "What job?" Mairead said, "I'm an attorney, and my firm's been retained to find this man."

"I have nothing to tell you."

"You won't even admit the portrait's your work?"

"I don't have to answer any of your questions."

"That you don't recognize somebody who must have sat for you over a 'considerable time,'" motioning around the studio, "perhaps at many different sessions?"

"I'd like you to leave now, Ms. . . . ?"

"O'Clare. Mairead O'Clare, remember?" She dipped into her handbag, came up with the last photo she'd taken. It hadn't turned out quite as well as she'd hoped, but the nice guy at the one-hour shop had enlarged and reprinted the shot so she thought the face in it identifiable. "Or maybe you remember this man better."

Jaxon's lips went to very thin, horizontal lines. "Leave now, or I'll call the police."

"I doubt it, but I'll leave anyway." Mairead put the photos back in her handbag, got off the stool, and headed for the door. Opening it, she turned back and said, "Jaxon, you really might prefer a talk with me rather than the police."

He already had one hand to his face, covering his eyes, as he waved her away with the other.

Mairead went through the door into the empty hallway of old, re-finished wood she'd used to walk to Jaxon's loft a few minutes earlier. She clacked briskly down to the staircase that would lead to the street, passing another closed door with metal-on-metal shaving sounds coming through it.

At the head of the stairs, however, she slipped off her heels and tip-toed as fast as she could back to Jaxon's closed door. Unlike the metal shaving from his neighbor, she couldn't hear anything, so she dropped to push-up position on the hallway floor, her ear at the crack of the threshold.

Now she could hear Jaxon's voice, evidently on the phone and in mid-sentence.

". . . missing since Saturday, she said. . . . O'Clare, an attorney . . . No, I didn't see it spelled *out*. But she showed me photos of that por-trait you commiss— Let me finish, all right? It was the one I did of Charles. And then she showed me a candid, not a very clear shot, but good enough so I could recognize the person in it. . . . Who else? You! Now I need some— Hello? . . . Hello? Oh, damn you to hell!"

The sound of a phone being slammed back into its cradle.

Mairead got up and brushed herself off, really looking forward to telling the Pope what she'd accomplished. Even if the circumstances probably *would* be a bit strange.

Young lady, the word "understatement" may never be better applied.

FOURTEEN

No," said Pontifico Murizzi, handing back the profile photo Mairead told him she had snapped of the man going into Vareika/Klein's building. "I don't make the guy. But you did real good to think of taking his picture, Irish."

"Thanks."

He could feel her blushing as she put the print back in the bag on her lap in the passenger's seat of his Ford Explorer. The Pope tried to remember if he'd ever seen Mairead in real party clothes before. She went with basic black slacks, tight enough across her rump to show the heft back there was more playing sports than Play-Doh. A blouse in a pattern of blue swirls, one shade picking up her eyes just right. Light jewelry—Mairead hadn't made herself into one of those retro-punk pincushions of a dozen earring and nose and lip studs. She'd done something different with her hair, though. Not color so much as style, sort of a barbaric-slave-girl look. The kind he figured might catch the eye of another swinging couple.

Murizzi turned the wheel to make a dogleg right. "You didn't happen to get the commission number of the cab that dropped him off, did you?"

"No. Didn't think of that."

"Not a problem." The Pope did a little projecting. "I can still call the taxi company, goose the dispatcher for where the fare dropped off there was picked up and around what time."

"Which will tell us where the cab was requested as a starting address?"

"Maybe, but our party boy's smart enough to have the driver stop a few doors down when he's visiting Klein, he probably just hailed the thing at a busy intersection. You got anything else?"

Murizzi liked more what Irish was telling him now, about over-hearing the artist guy do a panic call to whoever paid the freight for the missing kid's portrait. "You did even better on that."

"I was trying to think of how you'd handle it."

More blushing. You didn't even have to glance at her, because it came through in the voice. Jeez, figure what Mairead would have been like, she'd had a decent family like you did, praising her when she came through something with flying colors?

The Pope said, "But I like best of all the way you handled that Klein in her dominatrix get-up, especially with the dog."

"Pope?"

"Yeah?"

"I've been thinking about her. A lot. I get the sense that Klein really is just a part of the furniture on this one. Kind of a strange part, like a couch on one of those TV commercials that has a fold-out cup holder on the side and a pull-out hassock underneath. But not really involved directly in whatever's happened to Charles Vareika."

Murizzi's view, too. The problem for an investigator who ignores weird connections, though, is that sometimes they're like traffic ro-taries: You enter at six o'clock, thinking your turnoff's going to be at three because twelve just weirds out of the formula, but as a result you never do a drive-by of nine, where a lead might appear, take you someplace closer to clearing the case.

And, speaking of closer. "You see that sign up ahead?"

"The one with just 'Club' on it?"

"Yeah," said Pontifico Murizzi, checking the address he'd written on the brochure that afternoon after dialing Loll's toll free. Then, re-membering the contrast of the Sherdens, the best couple he'd met in a while, the Pope reached his right hand over to cover Mairead's left. "That's our den of iniquity for the night, honeybun."

. . .

Sheldon A. Gold said to the back of the powder-blue jumpsuit leading him down the wide, familiar corridor, "I'm really sorry to disturb you so late."

An over-the-shoulder flip of the bangs this young woman wore to her eyebrows. "No problem, Mr. Gold. That's what we're here for, and we understand our visitors' schedule problems."

Conserving a voice he increasingly couldn't trust, Shel just nodded.

They reached the right door, and the woman—Shel hadn't caught her name—unlocked it, then stepped aside in the corridor as he knocked and entered the room.

"What . . . Who is it?"

He saw his wife, eyes muzzy with sleep, sit partway up in bed, using her elbow for support. Natalie's chestnut hair splayed against the pillow one moment, then lifted off it the next, like a dark waterfall capable of flowing uphill as well as down.

"It's me, Nat."

"Shel? What time must it be?"

"Late. But I've . . ." His voice started to wobble, and he moved closer to her bed. "I've had kind of a bad time."

"Here?"

Meaning at the Estate, his wife's voice growing stronger in sympathy to his own faltering. "No, on this new case." Recent memories flooded his mind. Of Barbara Pitt and Bruce Rodrigue, stories about Charles Vareika and Vivianna Klein, but most of all the painful interlude with Hector Washington, and the descriptions by his harsh mother, Ynez, concerning what the boy had gone through.

What Shel and Natalie's son, Richie, might have as well.

Shel said, "The people I've had to deal with, Nat. The . . . hollowness of what they call 'love.'"

A wise smile. "Our love's never been that."

He sat on the comforter, not making contact with her body in any way, just sharing her bower. "I'd really like it if you'd just hold me for a while, tell me it's all going to be okay."

"Oh, of course, my darling, of course. Come to me. Come."

Shel hitched and shifted a little, his wool suit pants not sliding too smoothly over the bedding. He felt his wife close on him from the rear, press her breasts into his shoulder blades and wrap her arms around his neck, like he was to stand up and take her for a piggyback ride. And then Natalie cooed into his ear, telling him what a strong and wonderful and brave man he was, to help all the miserable people who came to him as clients and dampened his spirit, even broke his heart.

Now Shel could feel the first few tears roll from the corners of his eyes down the sides of his cheeks. He sniffled, tried to hold back the tide, but pretty soon was crying in great gulps of air and salt-tanged liquid as the wife he so often visited toward giving her a few minutes of normalcy managed to muster at least the same dose of warmth and sympathy and blind, simple, consoling love for him that night. Shel couldn't predict how long it would last, didn't want to waste even one second of living in that moment to try calculating when Natalie's psychosis would abruptly end the good part for him.

But admit it, said a small part of Shel's brain as he gave in to the overwhelming relief of human contact based on love: You come here more for you than for her, anyway. Every time.

That will be seventy-five dollars, please."

Mairead watched the Pope's smile dazzle the woman sitting at the Art Deco counter next to the Tyrannosaurus rex of a bouncer standing between them and the inner door to Loll. Originally afraid that Murizzi might show up for their "big date" looking like something out of that campoid disco movie *Saturday Night Fever,* she was impressed that he'd dressed in a tailored casual shirt; conservative, pleated slacks; and slick loafers. And as always, he looked his cool, macho self. Trim body, great buns, a look in his eyes of "I might show you something new" that Mairead thought was probably the motivation for people to come to a place like this.

After the Pope got his change from the cashier woman, the bouncer stamped the backs of their hands with some kind of invisible ink. Murizzi tilted his head toward the strings of beads that curtained the entrance.

As Mairead parted the strings, they tinkled like chintzy wind chimes, and the interior of the place sort of cascaded over her.

An assault on all the senses, young lady.

Mairead just nodded, because she didn't think she'd be audible even talking to herself. The music—some kind of relentless, house/techno mix—filled the ears, but instead of tacky disco, the overall impression was of the banquet hall of a heavily upholstered, medieval castle. The eyes went up to ceilings that rose twenty feet high in the center of the room, where a circular dance area of parquet wood was laid over rough stone flooring. Tapestry was draped from beam to beam, creating a warming effect on the otherwise five-degree-too-cold air. Walking farther, Mairead noticed a bar to the left, the topless young men there spinning and juggling liters of alcoholic beverages like Indian clubs to the pantomimed applause of couples on the stools awaiting their drinks. Mairead's right hand brushed a stack of large cushions, vinyl to the touch but buttery soft, too.

There was a long buffet table at the far end of the room, with snacks like cheese wedges, baguette sections, and sliced melons. Mairead looked down at a little end table near one of the cushion stacks. Under a small, oddly glowing lamp, it had a quart-size ceramic bowl containing a paella of assorted condoms, single-use K-Y jelly packets, and some vials marked "herbal enhancers." Looking around, Mairead could see a half dozen similar outposts of stacks and tables, lamps and bowls.

Just then the dance music stopped, and the Pope picked up one of the vials. He whispered into her left ear, "Viagra wannabes, no prescription required."

Mairead said, "I guessed that," but she envisioned Chuck Vareika, "the man of her dreams," sampling one of them.

Some smooth jazz or New Age instrumental came over the speakers now, and Mairead noticed several of the couples who'd been on the dance floor leave it. A woman in one made eye contact with a man in another, though, and he smiled back, whispered into his dance partner's ear the way the Pope had into Mairead's. The man, still smiling, walked over and took the eyeing woman's hand in his, giving her an air kiss. The woman patted *her* dance partner on the shoulder, and he grinned and let her go off to the floor with the smiling guy. They began to dance very slowly and very closely.

"You guys LVs?" said a smoky female voice.

Mairead turned, but the Pope replied first. "We don't even know what that is, Ms. . . . ?"

"'Ms.'? Here? No, you pick a name you like, first ones only, kind of like AA. You know, 'I'm Shanna, and I'm an alcoholic.'"

"So, Shanna," Mairead rallying from her thoughts of Vareika's "picking a name" by leapfrogging over the Pope to the next question. "What's an LV?"

A saucy smile from the woman, a bottle blonde with the brown roots showing a quarter-inch up from the scalp. The dye job made Mairead think Shanna had heard it was a signal that she was pretty hot even without the unnatural color. The dress wasn't a really expensive one, but it showed off good breasts and blurred what Mairead would have called heavy thighs. And Shanna definitely had a sexy way of shooting her hip when she shifted stances, as if to say she enjoyed doing things in a variety of ways.

Young lady, I'm closing my eyes now.

"An LV," said Shanna, "is a Loll Virgin. I'll show you." She took the Pope's hand in both of hers, Mairead watching the long, manicured nails sinking like tent pegs into his palm as the woman drew the back of his hand under the strange little lamp. In the glow, you could see a clear, mercury-colored "V" against the skin.

Mairead admired the way Murizzi was playing his role, not in the least making as though his hand was unhappy in Shanna's claws.

He said, "Let me guess. You've been here before."

"A . . . faithful customer." Shanna put her own hand under the light, a mercury "M" visible. "But the 'virgin' part just means management hasn't had you screened for STDs, the hepatitis alphabet, et cetera. It's a warning to the rest of us members—what the 'M' stands for—to maybe stick to lighter games until you decide whether to join up."

Shanna turned to Mairead. "So, what should I call you?"

She pretended to think about it. "If I pick a name tonight, am I stuck with it forever?"

"No, of course not. My husband's used Errol, Rock, and Harrison, depending on his haircut and body conditioning."

In honor of her "date," Mairead said, "How about Gaye, then? With a 'y' in the middle."

Over Shanna's shoulder, Murizzi grinned. "And call me Lex, with an 'x' at the end."

Mairead's turn to grin. The Latin word for "law."

"Gaye and Lex it is, then." Shanna began to scope the room. "Let me introduce you around."

"Before you do," said Mairead, "a couple of questions?"

"Sure, though I think I can give you the answers first." Shanna glanced over to a corner where a couple was making out on one cushion while another was just sitting, drinking and talking, on the next. "To start with, you don't have to play anything you don't want to. If just necking floats your boat, no pro-*blame*-oh. And you don't have to do anything, period. A lot of couples, they just come here to get turned on for each other back home later."

Mairead tried to see why you'd spend $75 plus drinks to do that rather than just pick up a female-sensitive erotic video for three bucks.

Shanna now looked over at another corner, the sectionals wider and—

Jesus Christ.

Young lady?

Keep them closed, Sister.

Shanna said, "They're really into the 'grand' play. As you can see, nudity is fine, and intercourse of any kind is fine, too, so long as you do it in the 'play' areas of the club. That part of our philosophy keeps people from getting pushed into a game they don't want to play or somebody they don't want to play with. Anything like that starts to . . . go down, and a dozen of us would be on them, pulling the guy or woman . . . off."

"Woman?" said Mairead, trying to ignore the increasingly audible sounds of pleasure from a certain corner. And images of Chuck Vareika and Vivianna Klein comporting themselves there on earlier occasions.

"Sure, Gaye. Hot guy like your Lex here? A girl could easily get a little too drunk and a lot too bothered, want to be on him when maybe he'd like to save his energy for somebody else." Shanna curled a long finger around the back of Murizzi's right ear, then probed the opening just a bit, in and out. "Our way at Loll, everybody gets what they want."

The Pope said, "That's what our friend told us."

"Who's your friend?"

It sounded to Mairead that Shanna was asking the question in a completely "Welcome Wagon," not suspicious way, and when the young lawyer reached into her bag to bring out the photo she'd taken of Vivianna Klein in costume, she could see Murizzi nodding his agreement. "We were warned not to use her real name here."

"Like I said, that's our policy." Shanna looked at the photo and laughed. "God, I didn't know Yvette was into the heavy stuff, but even with the mask, no way you can mistake those legs and boobs, huh?" Then Shanna scoped the room again. Mairead followed her eyes, willed them to continue past the couple grunting and shuddering in the corner, although four other people had gathered closer to admire their technique.

Shanna said, "Funny, I don't see Billy Ray, either."

Murizzi winked at Mairead. "Billy Ray is what Yvette's big blond partner goes by?"

"Right, right." Shanna came back to them. "After Billy Ray Cyrus, the country singer with that 'Achy Breaky Heart' hit a while ago."

Mairead thought, Terrific: My whole relationship with Chuck Vareika can be summed up by a too-dumb-for-words C&W song.

Shanna said, "Neither of them's here tonight, though, and come to think of it, I haven't seen him for a few days now."

"When did you see Billy Ray last?" asked the Pope.

Shanna shrugged. "Oh, maybe . . . Hey, wait a minute. What difference would that make to you guys joining Loll?"

Mairead showed her the photo of the man outside the brownstone. "Recognize him, too?"

Shanna glanced at it. "You cops?"

"No," said Murizzi. "But this Billy Ray didn't show up for work on Monday, and we're worried about him."

Shanna looked from the Pope to Mairead. "Let's go back to the office."

"The office?" said Mairead.

"Yeah," Shanna heading off but motioning them on. "I'm not just a Loll member. I'm also the owner."

They followed her to a narrow hallway with a closed door at the end. Mairead watched Shanna take a key from inside her bra and unlock the door, all in one practiced motion.

As offices went, Mairead thought it pretty cushy. Desk with an elaborate telephone, credenza holding a computer and fax machine, but also a glass conference table with four caned chairs in one corner and a leather sofa against one wall.

Not to mention, across from the sofa, another wall sporting a dozen television monitors, each showing "streaming videos" from different parts of the club's "play" area.

Shanna closed the door, but despite all the seating options, she stayed standing. "Just what do you two want?"

Mairead said, "Lex already told you."

Shanna took in a deep breath. "Look, I run a good, clean place here. All the right licenses for the buffet, the booze. What we do is legal, because nobody gets paid for anything sexual."

Murizzi hiked a thumb over his shoulder. "Once you get past the cover charge to Beauty and the Beast out there."

"Any two adults who want to get it on and need a hotel room would have to pay twice that in this town. And here at Loll," Shanna tilted her head back toward the video wall, where the couple from the corner appeared to be hurtling toward the gates of heaven at about a hundred miles an hour, "there's the additional advantage of learning by both doing *and* watching." Now she fixed both of her "virgins" with a steady gaze. "It's all free, it's all up front, and it's all consensual."

Mairead said, "Yet you use medical screenings."

"To protect our clientele's health, Gaye."

"And phony names?" said the Pope.

"*Play* names, Lex. To protect our clientele's privacy as well."

Murizzi nodded. "You recognize the guy in the close-up photo, too, don't you?"

Shanna folded her arms under her cleavage. "Like I told you, we pride ourselves on maintaining our members' privacy."

"So," said Mairead, building on that, "he *is* a member, then."

Shanna seemed to get a little of her verve back. "Gaye, we provide a valuable . . . service in this club."

From the combined reactions on the monitor of the corner-couple and their well-wishers, Mairead felt certain one more such had just been . . . performed.

God, I have had enough of puns and buns. And reminders of what Chuck Vareika would have done here.

The Pope said, "Shanna, you won't ID the guy for us?"

"Not on your life. So, please, just leave me in peace and don't come back?"

Mairead O'Clare looked at Pontifico Murizzi, and, thankfully, he nodded.

Sheldon A. Gold turned out the reading lamp over his bed because he knew that it bothered Moshe's one good eye. The cat had hopped up into bed with him after a late dinner of deli sandwich and a glass of red wine, then slowly insinuated himself to the point where his head under Shel's book was like the nose of a camel under the tent. The novel was a good one—Dennis Lehane's *Mystic River,* an Irish version of the same kind of tough neighborhood Shel had weathered in Chelsea. With guys like Big Ben Friedman and other Jews who'd gone into the rackets in one capacity or another. So Shel would have liked to continue reading for another hour or two, get a little of the distance provided by distraction that often carried with it the gift of perspective.

Like perspective on why he'd gone to see Natalie again so soon.

Simple really, thought Shel, stroking the fur between Moshe's ears as the cat settled into purring. You're spending time dealing with the people who in turn deal with the sexual abuse of children, and no matter what your shrink tells you about the benefits of Zoloft, and the counseling, and the passage of time, Billie Sunday was right: It's one thing to see an isolated story about it for fifteen seconds of sound bite during the evening news, and another to spend entire workdays on it, one after the other. Richie can't stay . . . buried safely that way. Not your memories of him, not your nightmares about what might have happened to him at the hands of God knows who, and for God knows how long.

No. And it's only going to get worse, until this case for Barbara Pitt is resolved.

Which made Shel think of another woman he loved—not only *once* loved, but still loved—and how, despite her madness, Natalie had been able to comfort him earlier that night. To hold him, and shush him, and just let the goddamned dam break for a change, not hold back all that water until he thought he'd burst. A good cry can't cure many things, but it can relieve some of the pent-up infection.

Shel gradually began to be aware that Moshe had devolved from purring to snoring. And so, shifting only slightly so as not to disturb the little mop, Sheldon A. Gold pulled the covers up a mite higher, relaxed his neck with a couple of head rolls, and decided to join his pet in the relative sanctuary of sleep.

FIFTEEN

I t had begun raining pretty hard by the time they were leaving Loll, so Pontifico Murizzi offered to bring the Explorer around, keep Mairead from getting drenched. But she told him they could both just sprint across the lot for it. Arriving at the truck and getting behind the wheel, the Pope said, "So, you have as good a time as I did?"

He watched Irish close her passenger's door a little harder than was, strictly speaking, necessary. "Not much of a run."

"I meant more in the club there."

A sideways look. "I thought it was a nightmare."

The Pope grinned, on account of he actually did kind of enjoy himself, then put his key in the ignition and turned it. "What, that people like to act out in semi-public things they usually do only in the privacy of their own bedrooms?"

Mairead drew her seat belt across her chest before jamming it home. "If I want group calisthenics, I can sign up for an aerobics class."

Murrizi felt the grin spread across his face as he retrieved his cell phone from the center console under the armrest. "Hey, different strokes, right?"

Mairead cut him another look, this one clearly disgusted, then asked, "You going to call Shel?"

"Yeah," said the Pope, pushing the Power button and waiting for the thing to fire up. "I don't know if we found out much that helps, but maybe he'll see more in it than— Shit, missed a call."

Murizzi pressed the Phonebook option, then hit his own number.

After the usual half-ring, he punched in his password—pass numbers, really, but the nice lady's atonal voice wasn't programmed to say that—and heard the "you have one new message" announcement. The message itself sounded like a flashback to the old days: "Pope, it's Artie, eight-thirty in the P.M. You get this before ten, meet me at . . ."

Murizzi listened to the specifics, then pressed End before checking his watch. Seventeen minutes until Artie's deadline.

Irish said, "Anything wrong?"

The Pope shook his head. "Don't know, but okay if we take a little detour before I drive you home?"

Mairead O'Clare still couldn't quite push the sights—and sounds, even *smells*—of Loll out of her mind. Nor the images she kept getting of Chuck Vareika—her love-at-first-sight dream boy—cavorting there. But she tried to focus on where Murizzi was taking her, despite how confusing it seemed. Almost like a bizarre form of race-car driving, in which the object of the game was to slalom the sport utility vehicle around as many ramp-and-roadway pillars for the Big Dig as possible. Then, up ahead, Mairead could make out through the night what looked at first like one of those small carnivals that tour rural areas, all the different colored lights flashing. Once they got closer though, she recognized the patterns.

Police cars, ambulance, and maybe worse. Like the medical examiner's white van.

A uniformed police officer wearing a luminescent vest materialized out of the darkness, waving the Pope to pull over. Before the Explorer came to a stop, Murizzi said to her, "Irish, you might want to stay in the car."

The Pope's features flickered and distorted like a child's kaleidoscope in the strobing lights coming through the rain dappling the windshield. "Like hell," said Mairead.

He glanced at her. "That call was from Artie Chin, my old partner in the Homicide Unit. If this is what it could be . . . Well, your law clerk's been missing long enough to lose his good looks."

She willed herself to swallow before saying, "I want to be there."

Murizzi nodded. "Just explaining the options. I got an anorak in the back and an umbrella. Take your pick."

As he exited his side and started talking to the officer, Mairead went around to the back and opened the hatch door. She saw an orange anorak and sniffed it. Mairead didn't think her stomach could take the eau de dead fish, so she opted for the umbrella.

Coming around to the driver's side, she held the anorak out to the Pope, who pulled it over his head and squared it away, hood up, before unzipping the front pocket and taking out a plastic vial like 35mm film comes in. He dipped an index finger into it, then daubed the tip of the finger below and around both his nostrils with some kind of glistening jelly before offering the vial to Mairead.

She said, "What is it?"

"Vicks VapoRub. Even with the rain, the uniform told me the corpse is pretty high."

Mairead didn't think Murizzi meant altitude. "You use this when you were on the force?"

"Yeah. Some guys prefer gasoline or kerosene, even perfume. But I liked the Vicks better. If I was still in the unit, though, I wouldn't apply it till after I was on-scene for a while."

"Because the stuff would affect your initial sense of smell, maybe cost you a clue?"

"Basically."

Mairead took some of the goo, applied it to her nose as the Pope had to his, the pungent smell transporting her back to the orphanage, Mairead at age eight with a bad cold, Sister Bernadette gently layering facecloths slathered with the jelly on the girl's chest.

And I'm still here, if you need me.

Mairead returned the vial to Murizzi, saying "Thank you" once but meaning it twice.

He shook off some rain. Then, ultra-casually, "Just watch your step, so you can find your way back to the truck, you want to leave the party a little early."

Mairead swallowed hard again, opened the umbrella, and began to follow him.

The ground was cluttered with chunks of cement and blacktop over gravel, all made slippery by the rain and hard to see by the conflicting lights. Plus, Mairead wasn't exactly wearing hiking boots. But even in his dress loafers, the Pope seemed to pick his way like a mountain goat behind the lumbering officer leading them down the slope to a pile of debris against an abutment. Five or six people in all-weather gear were huddled around the pile, those white-hot, steady lights Mairead always associated with TV shows and fashion shoots illuminating all the garbage.

And some of what was in it, looking more like cloth than food wrappers and wax soda cups.

Their guide yelled ahead with "Sergeant?" A shorter man rose from his haunches, then walked partway up the slope to meet them.

Mairead heard Murizzi say, "Artie," and the shorter man, thanking the uniformed officer, just replied, "Hey, Pope. Who's Mary Poppins?"

Wanting to correct her status immediately, she said, "Attorney Mairead O'Clare. We sort of met a few months ago, on the Irish Hermit case."

Up close now, she could see Chin's features clearly, but his poker face didn't tell her much, and when she looked down at his hands, she saw he was wearing some kind of lab gloves. "You the attorney the Pope's working for?"

"One of them, anyway."

Murizzi said, "Artie, what've we got?"

"Maybe you can tell me. Come on."

Mairead didn't feel completely invited, but nobody had told her expressly that she wasn't included, either, so she followed behind them toward the strong lights.

The others huddled around the pile of debris glanced up, then went back to their observations. A male voice asked nobody in particular, "Now that the Pope's here, can we get on with it?"

Mairead thought Chin kind of ignored the question, then stepped forward to what at her distance of now only about five feet appeared to be part of a spring jacket, like the Nautica yacht parkas some of the associates at Jaynes & Ward would wear over their polo shirts and khaki slacks on the firm's casual Fridays.

Chin said, "There was a stop-work order on this area of the Dig for the last few days while they dealt with some underground flooding. Then nine-one-one got a call from a guy said he was a laborer, just walking by here, but noticing some strays—dogs and cats—were paying more attention to this spot than before the flood."

Murizzi said, "You find the laborer?"

"No. Anonymous, called it in from a pay phone."

The Pope shook his head. "Lot of guys on-site now carry cellulars. You see them gabbing into them, lunch break."

"So maybe this guy didn't have one. Or didn't want us tracing his, he was off on a frolic of his own when he passed by, since the construction company responsible for this section told me their crew isn't due back here till tomorrow night."

Shifting the umbrella to her other hand, Mairead thought she felt what Murizzi did: Conscientious citizen doesn't have a cellular, or doesn't call on it, but instead walks on in the rain till he finds a pay phone, just to report some odd animal activity?

Chin said, "Or maybe the guy actually saw the corpse, and he just didn't want to get involved."

The Pope nodded, and Mairead believed that sounded more likely, too.

Now Murizzi motioned toward the pile and squatted down on his haunches the way the others had been postured. "You had a look at him yet?"

"Why I called you." Chin moved toward the jacket material.

The Pope said, over his shoulder, "Irish?"

"I'm okay," not really meaning it.

Steady, young lady. You've been through this—and worse—before.

Mairead nodded.

Using his gloved thumb and middle finger, Chin pincered the edge of the cloth and lifted it very slowly, as though undraping an underlying art treasure bit by bit.

"Oh, God," said Mairead, turning away from a torn and gory right side of a human face. The wet and stringy hair around where the ear would have been was darker and shorter than in the portrait over the mantel.

Murizzi said, "That's probably from the animals, scavenging."

Then, the water streaming down her face making her realize that she'd dropped the umbrella, Mairead picked it up and, steeling herself, turned back toward the pile.

Chin was gently lifting the corpse's jaw. To the Pope, he said, "I really think this is his better side, don't you?"

Murizzi nodded before twisting his own head toward Mairead. "The hair's wrong, probably from the dirt and rain. But I'd say it's him."

"Same," she managed, Shel's story about that movie, *Laura,* intruding upon her. "Only this time, we know who the real victim is."

"What?" said Chin.

"Never mind," Mairead starting to feel very cold inside.

"Okay," Chin lowering the face to its original position. Then, to the others around the pile, "Get started." He began walking upslope again. "Pope—and Counselor—you, with me. Now."

Murizzi rose, and Mairead looked into his eyes. Not at all sure how well she was gauging things at that moment, she seemed to detect a little softening through the hardness that must have come from visiting places like this as a career.

He said, "Irish, it could have been worse."

"I'll take your word for that."

"Hey?" from Chin, ahead of them.

"Coming," said Pontifico Murizzi, and Mairead O'Clare felt his hand close gently on her elbow to steady her toward their climb.

The telephone rang twice in Shel's dream, Natalie from the next pillow begging him to answer it, before he registered the third ring, mostly awake in his own bed. As he shook out the cobwebs, Moshe bailed off his chest. Not knowing what time it was, Shel debated whether to let the machine just pick up a message. He heard his outgoing tape activate in the living room, then recognized the Pope's voice after that. Shel fumbled as he lifted the extension from its cradle on his night table.

He caught, "—her home, but I think you need to—"

"Pope?"

"Hey, Shel. You okay there?"

"Yes. Just asleep."

"You hear what I said so far?"

"Not really. Can you take it from the top?"

Shel listened for a solid two minutes, sitting straight up after about thirty seconds. At what seemed like a good breaking point, he asked, "Is Mairead all right?"

"Yeah. Like I said just before you picked up, I drove her home after Artie took us to school on why we should be cooperating more. She's shaky, naturally, but Irish held up solid."

Shel pictured that morning, when she admitted having an irrational crush on the now-dead man. "Chin's upset, then?"

"Upset? Yeah, I think you could call it that. You could also say he's fucking batshit about my having asked him to run a slab-and-bed check on a 'husky blond male' named Vareika, Charles, just days before said male turns up with three bullet wounds in him, contributing his bit to the garbage heap under a bridge abutment."

Shel homed in on the "bullet wounds" part. "Any weapon found?"

"Not that Artie told us, but from what I could see at the scene, your clerk might have been shot someplace else, then dumped there. And, since you're probably wondering, we'll have to wait for a while to even know whether the slugs could be the same caliber as Pitt's missing Chief's Special."

"What did you tell Chin about why you were looking for Vareika in the first place?"

"We stonewalled him, Mairead and me both. No name of client, no details, period. But Artie's right to be batshit here because he's got a real problem, too."

"His name's on that morgue-and-hospital check you requested."

"For our purposes, Shel, close enough. Artie's not just a thorough cop, meaning he'll squeeze me any way he can to find out facts about a murder he drew. He also has to cover his ass on the paper and computer trail his doing the check would leave, maybe even handing the case over to another detective in the unit with the specifics of what I asked him to do for us."

"Which will shortly put you in the vise."

"Yeah, but I think we can wait till tomorrow A.M. to worry about that part, and to fill you in on what Mairead and I turned up before we went to the crime scene. Right now, I think you're going to have to contact your judge with some basic bad news before she sees it sandwiched between a couple of car wrecks and house fires on her local news."

As Shel thanked Pontifico Murizzi and hung up, he couldn't imagine any alternative. So, reaching again for that day's suit but a clean shirt, Shel called for a cab. And then, more or less dressed, he trundled downstairs, only to have to jog back up, two steps at a time, when Sheldon A. Gold, Esq., saw how hard it was raining outside.

SIXTEEN

Lying under her comforter in the studio apartment on Beacon Hill, a few blocks from Shel's office building, Mairead O'Clare could hear the rain against the windowpanes like someone was spraying sand at them. Occasional gusts of wind rattled the old frames, too, but when she got up to check, no water was on the sills.

Resettling herself—with goose bumps—in bed, Mairead knew that her feeling cold had more to do with the crime scene itself than the June weather through which she'd visited it. She also seemed unable to stop picturing Sergeant Detective Artie Chin, holding Charles Vareika's lifeless corpse at the jaw, tipping the head so that the unruined side of the face could be seen. Mairead had been present at another crime scene when a hastily buried body was found, but that was more like . . . archaeology? The human body as artifact.

She'd also been present when people—even some she'd known—had been killed, brutally if . . . well, necessarily, given the circumstances. But all that had happened so fast that there weren't many images to register. And remember.

Also, young lady, you didn't have a . . . crush on any of them.

Nodding before turning over, Mairead briefly wondered what it would have been like to bump into Charles Vareika when he was alive, in a bar or even just a coffee shop. Would she have had the same reaction to him live as she had to his portrait over the mantelpiece? Would he have approached her, despite the hemangioma? If not, would she have approached him?

Yeah, right. And become another Vivianna Klein? No way.

Klein claimed to be just doing her "job," an extension of the research at the sex clinic where she worked. Well, Mairead had done some of her own research, though not "empirical," and she'd found an article about sex addicts. Given the sadomasochist outfit Klein had been wearing, she seemed to be a "paraphiliac," somebody who got off on deviance, and not just sex. Vareika, on the other hand, seemed to have what the doctors in the article called a "paraphilia-related disorder," or PRD, basically such a high sex drive that his whole life would revolve around satisfying it.

And probably, given the portrait he persuaded someone to commission, a bit of a narcissist as well.

Mairead nodded. At least one doctor quoted by the reporter felt that while ninety-five percent of paraphiliacs and people with PRDs were male (and of course both men *had* to add that ninety-five percent of people with eating disorders were female), it wasn't a testosterone surplus that drove them. No, the doctor believed it was a serotonin deficiency, and so he gave his patients antidepressant drugs that effectively killed their sex drive, but seemed to make them happier and more functional in every other way.

Rather a dilemma, young lady: one malady or the other.

Now Mairead just shook her head and rolled over one last time, thankful that she'd dodged the poison that Charles Vareika would have been for her. And thankful also that nobody she knew was truly depressed, so that they had to take pills that killed *normal* sex drives.

Knocking on the door to Barbara Pitt's condominium near Harvard Square, Sheldon A. Gold decided he should have taken a supplemental Zoloft before coming over. He hated to take more of the antidepressant than prescribed, but his psychiatrist had told him that, if life threw you a nastier-than-normal curve, it was okay to up the medication temporarily to deal with a short-term situation.

And this case seemed to fit that bill.

Then the door opened, and Shel's heart went out to his former lover because the bad news obviously had preceded him. Pitt looked terrible, hair suffering from bed-head, eyes and cheeks and nose all red. Dressed in a green terrycloth robe tonight with white tissues peeking out of the pockets, she had balled a handkerchief in one fist. Pitt threw her free hand up and over his shoulder and pulled him tight against her.

Shel wished he'd thought to take off his raincoat first.

"Oh, God, Shelly. What's happening to the world?"

He figured she meant to "her" world, but all he said was, "Barbara, I'm so sorry."

Her lips were blubbering against his ear, making it wetter than the weather had. "I got a call . . . from my court officer, Tommy. He said the police . . . called his chief because they found . . . Chuck's ID as a law clerk for the court . . . and he . . . oh, God, Shelly, oh, God."

Shel thought they'd be better off completely inside her apartment, so he led her like a dance partner a few feet, then reached his right hand behind him and swung the door shut. Now Pitt changed her grip on him to one of a wounded soldier being helped by a comrade toward the couch. When they got there, her weight and his awkwardness basically pulled him down next to her.

Pitt buried her face in the valley between his shoulder and neck. "Shelly, Shelly. What am I going to do?"

Admit it: You don't have a good answer, certainly not as a lawyer. What she needs is a magician, somebody who can just wave a wand over the last week, make it all go away.

"Shelly?" into his shoulder, more a vibration than a sound.

He refocused on what he could do. "Have you had any calls yet from the police themselves?"

"Just Tommy."

They're cutting a judge that much slack, anyway: Give her until morning, at the courthouse. "How about the media?"

"No." Pitt lifted her face a moment. "My number here is unlisted."

Buys some time, anyway. "Our first decision is what you say when the media does contact you. I would advise 'My heart goes out to Mr. Vareika's family, but this terrible tragedy is under investigation by the police, so I have no further comment.'"

Pitt nodded into his shoulder now.

"The second issue is tougher. The police have already been talking to my associate Mairead and the Pope."

"But . . . why?"

"They were asked to go to the crime scene. Toward identifying Mr. Vareika."

"Oh, God, no."

"The Pope tells me that they both refused to answer any other questions, including the identity of the client who asked them to investigate Mr. Vareika's disappearance."

"But, I thought your people were admitting—"

"To the people they contacted that you'd retained us to look for him, yes. And they did. Therefore the police will find that out within the first or second person they talk to, probably his parents or his roommate."

"The . . . sex-club person."

Shel thought, The swingers' club partner of your lover. "So now the question becomes, do you cooperate with the police, or take a Ramsey-family posture?"

"A Ramsey . . . ?"

She really is in shock. "The mother and father of JonBenet Ramsey, the Colorado case?"

"Oh, God." Pitt now lifted her face from his shoulder, speaking to him with a sour scent on her breath. "Shelly, are you telling me to . . . plead the Fifth?"

"I'm telling you that refusing to answer police questions on the ground that you could incriminate yourself is an option."

Her eyes widened. "What the hell kind of 'option' is that? For God's sake, Shelly, I'm a judge!"

He realized she needed it spelled out for her. "Barbara, you made every effort to keep your personal relationship with Mr. Varcika a secret. However, our investigation indicates that at least your daughter and ex-husband—and probably Vivianna Klein, the roommate—have reason to believe that Mr. Vareika and you were sleeping together. With a disappearance turning into a homicide, the police will probably uncover the relationship, too."

"Exactly what I didn't want to have happen, why I turned to you in the first place." Pitt hung her head, then wagged it, side to side. "Gary Condit and Chandra Levy."

"At least we have to prepare for something similar. And once the police find out, the media could, too."

Pitt didn't look up. "And my gun is—" Now she jerked her head up. "Wait a minute. Did the police say Chuck was shot?"

Good: She's starting to think again. "The Pope told me there were three bullet wounds."

Pitt's eyes went left-right-left. "And nobody except your people know about my gun being missing?"

Not, "Poor Chuck. I hope he didn't suffer too much." Shel just said, "Yes."

"So if . . ." Pitt stopped, then shook her head. "So, if it wasn't my gun, or if the police don't find my gun—"

"Barbara—"

"—or even if they do, since it's never been registered, I—"

"Barbara!"

She stopped cold this time.

Shel tried to leaven his next words. "We may have better information on those things before the police contact you. If they haven't been here already, I think they'll probably wait until tomorrow, at the courthouse."

Pitt nodded, her eyes a little vacant. "Of course. Businesslike."

Shel said, "But we have to go through the possibilities now, determine whether you need to start by refusing to cooperate."

"But, Shelly, how would that look?"

You'd hoped she'd gotten beyond that. "Barbara?"

"I'm a judge, remember? If I don't cooperate in a homicide investigation, the Judicial Conduct Commission will— No. No, first the chief justice will suspend me. But can she do that? Can she just . . . *do* that?"

"I don't know, Barbara. But I do know that we need to have a talk, right now. You must have a strategy in place before the police see you tomorrow."

A bleak smile. "Then can I make a . . . request?"

"Sure."

"Can we do it in bed?"

Shel closed his eyes.

"No," said Pitt quickly. "I don't mean make love, Shelly. I just mean . . . I need somebody to hold me tonight. We can talk until dawn about strategy and posture, if that's what you think is best, since I don't trust my own thinking very much right now. But I can't be alone tonight, not imagining poor Chuck . . . dead and alone himself."

Shel tried on his part to imagine what it had been like for Mairead O'Clare, to see the young man she'd—however irrationally—been infatuated with from a portrait, lying lifeless in the rain.

"Shelly?"

Then he pictured himself, just hours before, crying his eyes out on Natalie's shoulder at the Estate, the depressive husband turning to his psychotic wife for comfort. And receiving it when he needed it.

"Shelly, please?"

And now a former lover needed it, too. "All right, Barbara."

She took his left hand in both of hers and kissed the tops of his knuckles.

Admit it: This is going to be one time you're glad for the Zoloft. And the drug's lock on the libido.

Pontifico Murizzi, pouring himself a last glass of Petite Sirah—a nice one, from the Guenoc Winery—listened to the rain pelting the deck above him and the wind rocking his boat, even in the relative protection of Boston Harbor.

Good fucking thing you battened down the hatches before going off to pick up Irish.

The Pope hadn't liked the way the sky looked at the horizon that morning, so he'd tuned in the Marine Channel on the radio, keep abreast of the forecast. The one thing you don't want, you live on a boat, is to get the inside wet. The dampness is bad enough, the hull sitting in the water, the heavy sea air coming through the windows— Murizzi could say "hatches" without blanching, but "portholes" always struck him as a little too cute.

He crossed from the living area into the bedroom of the house-boat. Until a month ago, that berth had been shared many nights by a "boat-jolly" from England named Jocko, a beautiful boy of maybe twenty who was smart, funny, and incredibly sexy. But the British walrus whose sailing yacht Jocko maintained had returned to claim it, vessel and crew leaving the harbor for the Mediterranean. The Pope still felt a pang every time he thought about losing Jocko, then decided he'd worry a lot more about himself as a person, he *didn't* miss the guy.

Murizzi set his drink down in the little crater carved from the nightstand to keep wineglasses from shifting and tipping with the motion of the boat. Plumping a couple of pillows behind him, he started to read an old paperback by Nathan Aldyne entitled *Canary*. The Pope had found it in a used bookstore, and he was surprised when the back cover told him that the mystery novel involved a mur-der set in the wildly sexual gay community of Boston, before the Epi-demic. Usually, he couldn't stand "homicide-lite" books because the authors just got so many things about police investigation so wrong. But this one he wanted to read more for the "community" than the "murder," because in the pre-AIDS period, Murizzi had still been on the force and staunchly in the closet, and he'd only fantasized about what went on at parties for those already "out."

Fantasy, though, brought him back to how he'd spent the evening before getting Artic's call about the corpse. The Pope hadn't been kidding with Irish: He really did enjoy himself at Loll. But how in the fucking world even heteros could still be promiscuously sleeping around—or, at the club, not even *sleeping*—was beyond him. Murizzi figured either they couldn't read, or they had a death wish, because the last time he checked, most condoms had a failure rate of maybe three percent, which might be "who cares?" territory if you're the one wearing it, but not so great for the other partner receiving the bodily fluid directly. And, unless human anatomy had changed radically since the Pope's tenth-grade biology class, it was the woman who ran the most risk as the "receiver" from the male as "fire hose."

Which brought Murizzi to another thing he could never figure out. The Pope was raised Catholic, but even without discovering his sexual orientation, he figured he'd have fallen away from the Church at some point, with monsters like this Cornelius Dooley moke accelerating the process. But Murizzi still believed in some kind of God, and whenever he thought about it, he decided that the Supreme Being just had to be a male. The concept came up once in conversation, this big-breasted blonde trying to score him in a bar. When she asked why the Pope believed that, he remembered saying, "Because I've met so many more smart women than smart men in my life, I figure the Big Fella has to be male, because we could never still be on top, power-wise, without a supernatural being of our own gender tipping the scales toward us."

Well, at least the blonde had made a face and turned away from him. But when applied to that swingers' club, Murizzi had to question his view on women as the brighter bulbs.

Then the Pope realized that he was getting a little too tired to read, so he downed the rest of his wine, turned out the miniature reading lamp over his berth, and decided that Shel Gold probably had the right idea: You have such terrible luck that the woman you're absolutely crazy for goes absolutely crazy on you, it'd be better to always sleep alone, regardless of any opportunities that might present themselves.

SEVENTEEN

The first two things Shel became aware of were thanks to his sense of smell. Slowly awakening, he registered the sharp pong of fresh-brewed coffee. Then he rolled his head on the pillow and caught again a scent of the perfume Barbara Quincy Pitt had worn to bed the night before.

Admit it, though: You're not sure how you feel.

After they'd talked through the strategy of dealing with the police, Barbara had insisted on a little brandy. He'd joined her, but when she poured a second dram for herself, he said he'd had enough, and, after that next one, so had she.

Then it came time for the level of clothing—or absence thereof—for sleeping. Shel hadn't wanted to take his pants off, Pitt cajoling, saying he didn't want people to think he'd *really* slept in his suit. Shel remembered replying that people already were convinced he did, so what was the harm? Eventually, though, he agreed to swap his slacks for some sweatpants that Charles Vareika had left in her closet. Which meant that Shel went to bed topless.

Once under the covers, however, it became evident that Pitt had chosen bottomless for herself.

"Come on, Shelly, what can it hurt?"

"Barbara, I'm still married."

"And still grieving. As I am now over Chuck. Why can't we comfort each other?"

"The deal was we go to bed, and we talk strategy, and I hold you so you're not alone."

Her right leg slid over his left thigh. "So, I'm suggesting a slight . . . modification of that contract."

"And I'm declining, Barbara."

A little bump-and-grind, so like Natalie's typical greeting that he nearly—

Pitt said, "Truly not interested?"

"Truly."

A sigh. "Shelly, Shelly. How could I *ever* have let an honorable knight like you get away in law school?"

Thinking back on the "family outing" their first year, he had no reply that would make her feel better, and he didn't want to make her feel worse.

So, the bottomless Barbara Pitt backed off on the seduction, and, probably with the help of her brandy, fell asleep before Shel did. He asked himself whether the reason he'd stayed awake longer was the old "male protective" mandate, or just curiosity, after so many years, about what it *would* feel like to sleep—even *just* sleep—with a desirable woman again. Shel was surprised, given the Zoloft, at the stirring he'd sensed down there when Pitt was urging him with her leg and groin, but he'd played the fool often enough in other contexts that he had no desire to embarrass himself in this one.

And then also, you are still married.

Which meant Shel drifted off, occasionally awakened when Pitt shifted in a way that carried more heft than Moshe, and in those moments wishing he really did have someone of his own species to help him through the night.

Then Barbara Pitt's voice at the doorway to her bedroom brought him back to the morning and real-time living. "Shelly, I have some coffee brewing, unless you'd prefer decaf?"

He rolled over, noticing that she was in jeans and a long-sleeved T-shirt from some kind of rowing competition on the Charles River. "Regular is fine, thanks."

"Feel free to use the bathroom, and come down when you're ready."

"Right."

Even though he was still wearing his—or Vareika's—sweatpants, Shel nevertheless waited for Pitt to pad her way down the upstairs corridor before he threw back the sheets and got out of bed.

He was sitting on the john in Pitt's incredibly feminine master bath when he heard chimes sound as though someone was at the front door of the condo. He'd had to be buzzed in downstairs first, so Shel cracked open the bathroom door to hear a little more clearly.

PITT: Yes?

MALE VOICE: Judge Pitt, we've met before on a couple of cases. I'm Sergeant Detective Arthur Chin, and this is—

PITT: Detective Marjorie Tully, I remember. Homicide Unit.

Shel thought, Oh, shit, recalling both of them from earlier trials as well.

TULLY: I take it you know why we're here, then.

PITT: I do. But I'm not exactly dressed for—

CHIN: Oh, no, ma'am. Only we were thinking. To get to the courthouse, you generally take the Red Line into Park Street Under, correct?

PITT: Correct.

TULLY: Then why don't we wait for you in our car downstairs? That way, you can tell us what you know as we drive you intown, and you won't lose any valuable time on the *Dooley* trial.

Shel had to nod his head. Smooth: Jump on the case before Pitt has much time to think it over, then interrogate her in their car, unfamiliar surroundings without the trappings of authority in her lobby.

PITT: Fine. I'll meet you downstairs in, say, half an hour?

CHIN: Thank you, Judge.

Good thing you came here last night after all, map out the client's strategy. Even if it *did* turn into . . . pillow talk.

TULLY: Just one more thing?

PITT: Yes?

TULLY: Could I use your rest room before we leave?

Shel froze, the seat under him feeling cold as a gravestone.

PITT: Uh, certainly. It's this way.

A bad ten seconds passed before it dawned on Sheldon A. Gold that in a condo as swank as Barbara Q. Pitt's, there would also be a bathroom on the first floor.

. . .

Billie Sunday's immediate thought at the beginning of the meeting was, Well, at least Shel changed his shirt from yesterday, if not his suit.

The team was in her boss's office, Billie and the new child seated in front of his desk, the Pope standing against the safe.

Billie watched Shel slump back in his old and cracked high-bustled leather chair, some of the white stuffing poofing out beside his ears. "Judge Pitt . . . contacted me this morning. It appears the Homicide Unit was aknocking on her door around eight."

Murizzi said, "Artie Chin?"

"And Jorie Tully."

"Uh-oh."

Mairead turned to him. "She's the detective we kind of teed off during the *Friedman* trial, right?"

"Right," said the Pope. "But she doesn't partner up with Artie to work cases. Which means our dead law clerk is being shifted over to her because of Artie's initial involvement, doing the run-down favor for me."

Billie noted that on her pad, then heard Shel come back in. "Well, we expected something along those lines. I assume this means no more cooperation from your contacts in the unit?"

"I'd say that's a safe bet. And they're going to be all over Irish and me on why we were investigating Vareika's disappearance for two days before he turns up dead."

Billie thought the new child shivered a little at that, but then gave her the benefit of the doubt: Who wouldn't be shaky, they get dragged out in the rain by a bunch of hard-assed men to see a dead body on a trash heap?

"Shel," said Mairead, "were you and Judge Pitt able to talk last night?"

Now Billie noticed her boss had a funny look on his face, like one of her sons when the boy was guilty of something.

Shel said, "Yes. And we went over it this morning as well before she was driven to work by the police."

"Smart," said the Pope. "Both them and you."

The child started to ask something else, but Shel overrode her. "Judge Pitt and I agreed that she would admit to having 'worked with' Charles Vareika at her condo for several hours on Saturday morning before he left, not to be seen by her again."

Billie heard a grunt from the Pope on the "worked with" part.

Shel said, "I had a call here from Judge Pitt a few minutes ago. That's the story she told them, and, at least for now, they're buying it."

The Pope asked, "What did Her Honor say about the portrait of Chucky in his apartment?"

"That she'd never been there, never seen the portrait, and certainly didn't commission it."

Mairead said, "Well, somebody did. I went to visit Vivianna Klein, the roommate, again." Then Mairead paused, and Billie had the feeling she was skipping something. "Through the frame shop address on the back of the painting, I traced it to an artist named Jaxon, J-A-X-O-N, and went to see him."

Billie took that down, kind of hoping the man wasn't another black show-off who couldn't spell.

Mairead continued. "This Jaxon got real antsy when I showed him the photos I'd taken of the portrait. The frame shop said it was his work, and the style matched a lot of the paintings-in-progress around his loft."

Shel frowned. "Did he admit painting it, though?"

Billie caught the new child smiling. "Not to me, but after I left him, I doubled back and listened under his door to part of a telephone conversation. I could hear only his end of it, but he was going ballistic on whoever *did* commission it."

The Pope said, "We get as far as trial, you can subpoena the local logs from the phone company, find out what number this Jaxon called."

Shel nodded. "Good work, Mairead." Then Billie thought he squirmed a little. "How did you do at the, uh, swingers' club?"

The Pope said, "I had a little better time than Irish."

The new child blushed. Funny, thought Billie, you'd think there

A STAIN UPON THE ROBE

wouldn't be enough surplus color in her body to do that, given her arms and all.

Mairead said, "I have to back up a step. Remember I mentioned visiting Vivianna Klein again?"

"To trace the portrait," from Shel.

"Yes, but this is how she greeted me at her door."

Mairead took a photo from her handbag and set it down on Shel's desk, angled so both he and Billie might see it.

Disgusting was about all she could think, but guessed that might be what the child had skipped earlier.

The Pope said, "And the owner of the swingers' club recognized Klein as a member, 'play' name of Yvette."

Shel cringed. "Was anyone else at Klein's apartment?"

"Not right then," said Mairead. "But I had the feeling she was waiting for somebody . . . special, so I waited around outside the building for a while, and I took this shot of a guy acting like he didn't want to be caught climbing up its steps."

The child set the second photo down the same way, and Billie joined their boss in looking at it.

The Pope said, "I don't make the guy, Shel."

"I do." Shel leaned back in his chair again, the thumb and index finger of his right hand massaging the inside corners of his eyes at the nose. "The Honorable Bruce Rodrigue."

Billie said, "*Another* judge?"

Mairead nodded. "And the one hitting on our client."

Not wanting to believe it, Billie nevertheless took all that down, too.

"But then it gets better," said the Pope. "When Irish and I hit the swingers' club, I'd bet my boat the owner recognized Rodrigue, too, and she wasn't real pleased that we were poking around her clients who 'play' there."

Inwardly, Billie now groaned. Judges were people, too. She just never thought they were *that* kind of people.

Shel reached for the photo of Rodrigue. "I'll go see him about this, maybe beat the police to the punch."

Another grunt from the Pope. "With Jorie Tully on the case? Good luck."

Shel sighed, then looked around at all of them. "So, do we have anything else new?"

Murizzi said, "I paid a visit to Donald Iverson, the baby-raper's best friend. Seems he has a new playmate himself, young teenager named Ordell, from Appalachia via the Greyhound station, I'm guessing."

Billie wrote, *Ordell, bad to worse.*

Mairead shook her head. "I saw him, too. Meeting up with Iverson at the courthouse for a late . . . lunch."

The Pope nodded. "I'm also guessing there's not much we can do about that, other than to keep an eye on the scumbag. Then I went to see Bill Sherden, the victims' advocate?"

Shel said, "And?"

"Clean as a whistle. Nice house about five blocks from here on the Hill, nicer family living there with him."

"So, a scratch from our list of possibles?"

"I'd say so."

Finally, something Billie was happy to enter in her notes.

Shel sighed again. "Okay. I go see Judge Rodrigue. Mairead, can you start doing some legal research on just how protected the Pope's investigation will be if the Homicide Unit, or the district attorney, comes after him?"

Billie thought Murizzi would make a wiseass remark, as usual, but when she glanced back at him, he was frowning.

The new child said, "Shel?"

"Yes?"

"I thought you told Judge Pitt when we first talked with her here that everything would be within the attorney-client privilege, and therefore not anything the police or the prosecutor *could* find out about?"

A small smile, like one of her sons caught in a scam but *not* feeling guilty about it. "I've been wrong before."

Then Billie watched Shel look to her and the Pope. "Are we missing anything here?"

Murizzi said, "Given what we know about how Vareika died, might be a good idea for me to visit Pitt's ex again, button down the fact that the gun he gave her never *was* registered."

"Do it."

Billie had saved what she was wondering about till the end. "One other thing. If I got all this right, the dead research clerk and his roommate were both members of the swingers' club, right?"

"Right," said Shel.

"Did you ask our client if she was, too?"

Shel closed his eyes, then opened them again immediately. "Sorry. I did, when I asked her about the portrait. She was insulted I'd even suggested it, and I thought her reaction was sincere."

Turning to the Pope, Billie felt like she was on a roll. "And her daughter says she didn't go for it either, right?"

"That's what she told me, and I believe her, too."

Mairead said, "Same on the other research clerk, Leslie Hughes."

"Okay then," Billie checked back over her notes, "seems to me that this club wants couples only."

The child nodded. "That's what everybody's told us."

"Well, if our Judge Rodrigue has to be coupled up to go to the club, who's his girlfriend?"

The Pope slapped his hand on top of the safe. "Or boyfriend?"

Shel and Mairead said, almost like a chant, "The portrait."

Billie Sunday folded up her pad. "I'd sure think about it, I were you."

Mairead O'Clare, at her desk and already deep in researching attorney-client privilege, looked up when she heard a light rapping on her doorjamb. "Shel, come on in."

He did, closing the door behind him. Which was unusual. In fact, the only other time she could—

"Last night," he said, sitting down across from her, "the client came first, in terms of what I had to do."

Mairead thought it an odd way to phrase counseling, but she nodded.

Shel pursed his lips. "However, I remember us talking about the way you felt toward Charles Vareika after seeing his portrait, and I wanted to make sure you were okay after seeing . . . well, the crime scene."

Young lady, Mr. Gold is a genuine prince.

Agreeing with the voice in her head, Mairead said, "Shel, I won't say it was easy. But given the kind of guy our client's clerk and lover is turning out to have been, I'm okay. Not completely over it, maybe, but getting there."

"Good, good. These kinds of things . . . they can be really hard on the professional side, sort of eating through the walls we put up, keeping the personal side from . . . well, you know."

Mairead thought she did. But she also had the crazy impression that Shel had come into her office less as a boss offering comfort and more as a friend seeking it, though Mairead O'Clare couldn't imagine why.

EIGHTEEN

Pontifico Murizzi had figured it was easier to walk to Shel's office that morning than drive, so he'd left his Ford Explorer in its space at the marina.

Maybe not thinking about vehicles is why you didn't spot her car. Or maybe she had somebody else drive it around the corner, wait you out.

Because when the Pope hit the floating dock, or "camel," that led to the stern of his houseboat, he could see he had a visitor, sitting in one of the white resin chairs on his back deck, reading what he recognized also as the *Boston Herald* as he got closer.

Murizzi said, "Anything interesting on the cop beat?"

"Yeah," replied the voice of Detective Jorie Tully from behind the paper. "Seems this law clerk you've been asking about all week turns up dead. And when Artie Chin calls you, it also seems you were close enough to where they found him to arrive shortly thereafter."

"Just coincidence, Jore." The Pope carefully considered Tully's other choice of words. "By 'where they found him,' I take it Vareika was killed someplace else?"

As Murizzi hopped over the gunwale and landed lightly on the decking, Tully lowered her paper. With pale, pale eyes he always thought looked kind of like a wolf's, she gave him a cold, level stare with tone to match. "I told you the last time, Pope. No more favors."

"The last time you thought I'd gotten somebody killed. Then you found out I didn't. How's about we go back to normal?"

"Normal." No inflection on that word, either.

"Hey, Jore. Ease up, okay?"

Tully gave an abrupt nod, folded her paper, and put it on the table, next to her handbag. "Okay. You first. Why did Judge Barbara Pitt hire you?"

Thinking, Here we go, Murizzi pulled the other resin chair to conversational—as opposed to interrogational—distance away from his visitor. "Her Honor didn't. She hired Shel Gold."

Now Tully shook her head. "Then why did he hire you?"

"As I understand it, the judge was concerned that the system she was part of wasn't acting fast enough on the apparent disappearance of her law clerk."

A thin smile. "Practically word for word, Pope."

"I don't get you."

"I think you do. That little speech was almost word for word what 'Her Honor' told us about two hours ago."

"So maybe it's the truth."

"Oh, I don't doubt that. I'm just wondering if it's the *whole* truth, like the oath says."

"Jorie, we're not in a courtroom.

Murizzi gave her credit that she just let that hang in the air, imply the return threat instead of make it out loud.

Tully waved at her newspaper. "Charles Vareika took three bullets from a thirty-eight, Pope, up close and personal."

Murizzi thought, Unburned powder, stippling the guy's clothes or skin. "You have the murder weapon?"

Instead of answering him, Tully said, "Vareika was working with a judge presiding over the most current of the media-crazy priest rape cases. Said judge does *not* call in any chips she might have earned with the formal authorities, like, say, our department. Instead, she hires a criminal defense attorney, who, if I have my dates right, was a classmate of hers in law school. And then he hires a former homicide detective to help her out. Is it me, or does this feel like protective overreaction from our lady in the black robe?"

"Hard for me to speak for her on that one, don't you think?"

A little flare. "Then how about you speak for me, Pope?"

"According to Shel Gold, I'm inside the attorney-client privilege on this thing."

"Maybe—*maybe*—as to what the client told him, and he told you. Or she told you. But how about the people you talked to yourself, and what they told you?"

Murizzi spoke quietly. "Not my call, Jore."

Tully dropped her head, spoke to her knees. "You were a good cop, Pope. A role model even, at least for me when there weren't a lot of those wearing makeup around yet. But you're on the other side now, and I think you have information that could help the Homicide Unit on an open investigation."

Murizzi could feel it coming, could have mouthed the words along with her, but the prospect didn't make him feel any better.

"And so," said Tully, reaching into her handbag, "you leave us with no choice but to serve this subpoena on you, commanding your appearance before the grand jury for Suffolk County, sitting in Boston. Appear, and testify, or you can be held in criminal contempt. And jailed."

Standing, she handed him the piece of paper, folded in threes. He'd seen enough of them, he'd have to read it just for the date and time, but he wasn't looking forward to doing even only that.

"Pope, I'm really sorry it's come to this."

"Me, too." Pontifico Murizzi heard the off-key tone in his voice, tried to put a little more camaraderie into the next sentence. "Take care of yourself, and give my best to Artie, will you?"

"If he'll take it," said Jorie Tully, not even a note of triumph in her own voice, as she slung one leg over the rail before dragging the other after it and then doing what the Pope considered her own version of a resigned copwalk back up the camel toward the staircase to the street.

Judge," said Sheldon A. Gold with a nod as he closed the lobby door behind him.

"I have a very busy morning," said the Honorable Bruce Rodrigue from his desk chair, "but when my court officer passed your note to me on the bench, I felt I owed it to a colleague like Barbara Pitt to see you. Briefly."

"Thank you." Shel took a seat in front of the desk, noticing that the short, intense man had kept his robe on, perhaps to emphasize that the conference would be short, too.

If not sweet.

"Judge, I take it then that you've heard about Mr. Vareika?"

Rodrigue picked up his brass-colored gavel, probably just a habitual prop. "I became aware of it last night, from the late news. I tried to call poor Barbara at home, but got no answer, and I didn't wish to impose on her today, given the priest mess she's handling."

Shel thought that a rather long explanation for someone with a "very busy morning," but instead said, "I understood Judge Pitt's home number is unlisted."

From behind the eyeglass lenses, Rodrigue blinked at him.

"Judge, somehow I don't think she would have given that out to you."

"I . . . I'm not sure now how I came to obtain it."

"Perhaps through Mr. Vareika himself?"

"What?" Rodrigue shook himself, like a dog throwing off a bad dream. "Why in the world would he have given me—or I have asked him for—Barbara's number?"

"Maybe he let it slip during one of his . . . portrait sessions."

The color drained from Rodrigue's cheeks, and Shel found himself almost feeling sorry for the man.

Almost.

Rodrigue said, "I don't know what you're talking about. Now, if—"

"My associate traced the portrait to the artist, Jaxon, and then overheard a rather panicked phone call he made to you."

A sneer to accompany a jab of the gavel in the air. "She couldn't have."

"Judge?"

"What is it now?"

"How did you know my associate was a woman?"

"How . . . ?" Rodrigue seemed to go inside himself, scanning the archives. "Yes. Yes, when your associate spoke with my own law clerk, Ms. Hughes, who then advised me—"

Give him a little head fake. "How did you know it was my *female* associate who spoke with Jaxon, though?"

No reply, just the jaw muscles, working under the skin like the man was chewing gum.

Shel said, "The same associate who snapped a photo of you, climbing the rather long stoop to the apartment Mr. Vareika rented in the South End."

Rodrigue dropped his gavel, and not onto its wooden pad.

"The one, Judge, that he shared with Vivianna Klein, for whom Halloween isn't the only day for elaborate costumes. Nor for attending parties, especially at a club called Loll, where the man depicted in that photo is a rather regular customer." Shel gestured to the Federalist Society document framed on the wall behind him. "Some might say you've gone from 'Libertarian' to 'Libertine.'"

Rodrigue's right hand fluttered to his forehead and skittered down over his glasses. "What . . . what do you want?"

"The truth, please."

"But you can't . . . you can't *tell* anyone else about this."

"I'm not sure I'll have to. Ms. Klein was at least the 'roommate' of a homicide victim, and you know her better than most. How long do you think she'll stand up under police questioning?"

Rodrigue closed his eyes. "It was never . . . This wasn't supposed to happen."

"Judge?"

He just shook his head, a few tears seeping from his still closed eyes.

Shel felt sick about what he was doing, but he also couldn't take a chance on losing the man who had information he needed. "Judge, this is a capital case. They'll put you in front of a grand jury."

"Oh, God."

"Tell me, please. What was your relationship with Charles Vareika?"

"I'd been . . . I'd been trying to get into Loll for weeks after I discovered it existed a few months ago. I used a 'play' name as they call it, 'the Professor.' But their rule was 'couples only.' I even tried to . . . enlist my law clerk, Ms. Hughes, in attending with me. But she declined." A deep breath. "Then, a few days after that, Charles Vareika approached me. He said he understood I might like to attend a club event, and if so, he could arrange a . . . date for me. I was fascinated by the possibility, and my date turned out to be Ms. Klein. It was the most fantastic night of my life, sexually. Being a part of Loll gave me so much confidence in myself, in my . . . capacities, that I even found the courage to pursue Barbara, though she wasn't interested. Which made me all the more eager to return to Loll's diversity of experience."

"And the portrait of Mr. Vareika?"

"Our bargained-for exchange. Charles is . . . was very narcissistic, and with good reason. He could have had any woman in that club, and probably did, though those would be the nights he'd attend with Vivianna, and I wouldn't. To make up for the lost opportunities, I'd spend time with Vivianna at their apartment. I even went there . . ."

Rodrigue stopped, and Shel suspected something else had suddenly occurred to him.

Then the judge said, "Wait a minute. I continued to see Vivianna, even after Charles had failed to appear for work on Monday." A wheedling note in the voice now. "It would have been madness for me to do that if I'd been involved with his death, wouldn't it? So, I couldn't have killed him."

Shel knew what Rodrigue was doing, had seen it a hundred times over the years with his own clients. Coming up with "evidence," however embarrassing otherwise, that might create reasonable doubt in the minds of jurors. But the fact that Bruce Rodrigue had done the same so abruptly, so obviously sincerely, in the middle of what had to be a wrenching confession for him, persuaded Shel of something else.

This man really didn't kill Barbara Pitt's clerk.

"Judge, do you have any idea who might have had a reason to take Mr. Vareika's life?"

Something like self-possession had re-entered the quivering jurist, and Shel could sense he wasn't going to get any more useful information from him.

The Honorable Bruce Rodrigue stood behind his desk. "Now, I have to return to my work, Mr. Gold, and I suggest you do the same regarding yours. And, if you *ever* breathe a word of what I told you this morning, I'll have your head on a platter."

Sheldon A. Gold stayed seated, and he yielded for once to the temptation of gratuitous cruelty. "I'm not planning on going to the police, Judge. But I'd bet your pension they're planning on coming to you."

Billie Sunday picked up the telephone next to her reception desk and answered as usual, "Law Offices."

"It's the Pope."

Better a call from the strange man than a visit. "Shel and Mairead are both gone."

"Any idea where they are?"

"Him to the courthouse, like he said, to see the judge. Or judges, maybe. Mairead just told me she had 'an idea.'"

"Well, let them know that I'm scheduled to go before the grand jury this afternoon, two o'clock."

"Huh," said Billie, jotting that down. "Not wasting any time, are they?"

"No, and Jorie Tully—the homicide detective—told me that Judge Pitt's late law clerk took three thirty-eight-caliber slugs, up close and personal."

"Same as our client's?"

"Same caliber. No indication the police have the murder weapon to compare ballistics. But I'll go over it with Shel and Mairead later. I just want to make sure we're all on the same page of the prayer book for the grand jury, so have them give me a call about when they can see me."

"Meaning here, at the suite?"

"Unless the three of you want to catch lunch from the harbor."

Billie tried to imagine actually *visiting* with the Pope on his ground, some fish-smelly ship, and didn't have to think twice. "Make it here, then. I'll call you on your cellular. What're you going to be doing?"

A grunt on the other end of the line. "Enjoying what might be my last day of freedom for a while."

As she hung up on her end, Billie Sunday thought there was a pinch of something other than wise-guy humor in the Pope's voice, something she couldn't ever remember hearing from the man before.

A little—even if just a little—fear.

Mairead O'Clare's idea was simple, really: Surprise the roommate, Vivianna Klein, while she's still shaken up over Vareika's death, see if something new emerges.

For a change, that June Thursday was a sunny one, temperatures in the mid-seventies, so Mairead decided to walk over to the South End, organize her approach along the way. When she arrived at the old brownstone and rang the doorbell, though, she got no answer. Taking out her cell phone and trying the apartment number for Vareika/Klein given to her by Judge Barbara Pitt, she got an atonal. "This number is temporarily out of service. No further information is available."

First thought, young lady: Ms. Klein has run away—or disappeared—herself.

Mairead liked a second thought better: that Klein might be hunkering down, not answering the door and yanking her phone jack from the wall, to more privately mourn the loss of both a roommate and a lover.

Then Mairead pictured the apartment from the inside looking out.

She walked to the end of the block and entered the alley. Counting buildings from their backs, she walked along the individualized privacy fences enclosing rear gardens. When she got to the one that matched up to Klein's address out front, Mairead peeked through the tiny gaps between the upright, stockade-style pieces of wood. She couldn't see much, but she did make out a thong bikini bottom, rump up, on some kind of unfolded beach lounger.

Mairead knocked on the fence door. No movement from the rump. She knocked louder, really hammering her fist. Still nothing.

And, oddly, no sound of the Doberman pinscher, Miata.

A little concerned now about a third possibility—that somebody had visited Klein with bad intent—Mairead looked up at the top of the fence. The pieces of wood were pointed, but not exactly sharpened stakes. And there were trash cans in the alley, several tall enough to give her the necessary initial boost.

Nothing ventured, young lady.

Mairead brought over the sturdiest of the cans, a plastic barrel. Taking off her sensible heels, she scrambled onto the lid, got her balance, then rose up until her hands could comfortably grab the tops of the fencing wood. Careful of splinters, she did a pull-up.

Vivianna Klein lay flat on her stomach and squarely in the sun, her face toward the apartment windows. She wore Walkman earphones, a wire trailing down to a CD player under the lounger. Off to the side, Miata was stretched out on the flagstones, inert. From Mairead's position, she couldn't tell if the dog was breathing, but she also couldn't imagine how her knocking and climbing wouldn't have alerted Klein's pet.

If Miata was just sleeping.

Mairead eased herself back down onto the lid of the plastic barrel. Looking up and down the alley, she saw no one, so she hitched her skirt up over her waist, sticking the hem inside her panty hose. Then she did another pull-up and swung her right foot over the top of the fence, feeling the stocking mesh tearing on the pointed wood. Hoping for no blood, she got herself into a saddle position straddling the fence, then brought her other leg over and dropped down eight feet onto the flagstone near Vivianna Klein's head.

Which jumped up about six inches off her lounger and whipped around to face Mairead.

"What the hell are you doing?" Klein yelled, a bit too loud from either fear or the competition from her headphones as she pulled them down around her neck.

Mairead rearranged her skirt. "I rang your bell, tried your phone, then knocked on the fence door. When I didn't get any response, even from the dog, I climbed over to be sure everything was okay."

Klein's face turned back toward the house. "Yeah, well, it is, so get lost."

"What's wrong with Miata?"

"Nothing. She kept barking every time the phone rang, then she didn't stop, even when I, like, yanked that alligator thingie out of the wall. It happened before—when Chuck was away for a while—and I got a prescription to knock her out."

"You drugged your dog?"

"Hey, lawyer-girl, you try sleeping with the thing yowling and the neighbors banging on your walls and doors, which only set her off more. I couldn't even sunbathe out here until I gave her a date-rape mickey."

Mairead tried to take a breath, found it hard, even in the open air. "Vivianna, I'm guessing the police have spoken with you."

"Yeah. They're almost as much of a pain in the ass as you are."

"Your roommate was found dead. That's their job, even if you don't seem all that broken up about it."

Now Klein turned back and levered up on her elbows. "Yeah, right. Let me guess: Every guy you've boffed has been, like, 'true love,' huh?"

"I've never had one killed on me."

"Okay, I'll give you that: This is a first for me, too. But you got to understand, lawyer-girl. Chuck and I were great sex partners, only as much for other people as for us. Maybe even more."

"I'm sorry, Vivianna. I don't get that, any more than I get your lack of . . . emotion about his being killed."

Klein did a full push-up now, swinging her own legs around to put her feet on the flagstones and come to a sitting position. "Look, lawyer-girl, I live with sex all the time. At work, at home, at play, like being a member of a swingers' club. Chuck wasn't just buff *and* hung like a horse. He was also slow to cum, and I've been around long enough to know that's rare in a young guy like him. Did I enjoy Chuck fucking the shit out of me? Yeah. Christ, there were nights I came three times with him inside my 'tunnel of love.' Then I'd bring him off, and after half an hour, a glass of wine or a little toke on some weed, he was ready to go another three of *my* rounds. That's what made Chuck such a hit at the club, especially with the more— shall we say, mature?—women members. But there's no way Vivianna is gonna, like, lose her heart to that kind of guy. I mean, would you?"

Mairead didn't care for how her truthful answer would sound. "What did you tell the police?"

"What they asked me: Did I fuck him, did he fuck anybody else, did we fuck other people together."

So, young lady, the homicide detectives knew about that Loll club before interviewing Ms. Klein, possibly from Ms. Hughes, the other research clerk.

Mairead decided to gamble. "Did you mention the judge?"

"Which . . . ?"

Gotcha, thought Mairead.

Klein tried to back and fill. "Oh, you mean Chuck's boss?"

"Or Judge Bruce Rodrigue. He takes a nice photo, even just a candid one. On your front steps?"

Klein made a disgusted face. "That asshole. He had his cell phone on in the cab, I could have warned him off. But no, he likes to 'play' at cloak-and-dagger as well as S and M."

"And likes to commission portraits, too?"

Klein looked genuinely surprised. "Huh, that was from him? Chuck never told me."

"Really?"

"Chuck never told me anything about the judges he worked for. Said it wouldn't, like, be very smart of him, careerwise. I thought he was right, so I never pushed it, even with 'the Professor,' which was asshole's play name at the club."

Mairead realized that with all the sexual activity involved in the case, she'd simply assumed that Klein would have known about Vareika and Pitt's relationship.

But maybe not.

"Now, if you don't mind, lawyer-girl, I'd like to catch some rays before the weather turns back into fucking March again."

Mairead looked over at the stockade gate, a combination lock on it, hasp closed. "Can you let me out of here?"

"Why should I?" Klein returning to prone on the lounger.

"Because, concerned about you, I left my shoes out there to climb over and check on you."

"God leaves no good deed unpunished, lawyer-girl."

"Okay, then how about this? I roll you off that lounge chair and use it as a battering ram until it or the gate breaks."

"Oh, fuck you." Klein levered up on her elbows again. "If you're not, like, a bull dyke, you ought to be."

"Your furniture or your gate . . . Yvette."

"Okay, okay."

Klein went up to the gate, blocked Mairead's view, and spun the combination dial until the hasp clicked and opened.

Turning, Klein said, "Satisfied?"

"Unless there's anything else you can think of?"

She actually seemed to weigh the question. "Yeah. One thing, actually."

"What's that?"

"She's not really my type, but I bet she'd go over big at the club."

Mairead was drawing a blank. "Who?"

"This one cop-girl," said Vivianna Klein. "Had eyes like a werewolf."

I'm sure Jorie Tully would love to hear that description of her.

Mairead O'Clare picked her barefoot way over to where her shoes still sat at the base of the plastic barrel. In a casual voice, she said, "You be sure to ask her, next time she comes by."

Outside Judge Barbara Pitt's lobby door, Shel Gold watched bailiff Tommy Flanagan snack on what appeared to be rippled potato chips.

So much for the health-food impression.

The court officer said, "You want to see Her Honor?"

Shel Gold nodded. "If I can."

"I think so, since we're in recess, but let me check. Why don't you come inside?"

Shel patiently waited for Flanagan to open the door, then watched him cross the outer room to the inner one. Shel forced himself to smile at Florinda Altamira, sitting behind her desk.

"Mr. Gold," she said, whether as greeting or absence of surprise, Shel couldn't tell.

"Ms. Altamira, how are you?"

"Better than some," she replied, then returned to paperwork on her desk.

Shel thought, Just the way you yourself answered Billie in the reception area yesterday.

Flanagan said, "Her Honor will see you now."

Shel moved past him, the court officer closing the door solidly, as though to emphasize he was creating privacy.

Barbara Pitt looked up. Her eyes were still red, despite what Shel knew had been some attempt at makeup before she went off with the police from her condo that morning. And maybe more makeup by remedial application thereafter.

Shel said, "How are you faring?"

"Oh, just swell."

"Have you remembered anything else from the police interview?"

Pitt tossed a pencil over a stack of papers on her desk, a miniature pole-vaulter trying a new stunt. "That's what they called it, too. An 'interview.' Somehow that made it all the more sinister, and I'm beginning to understand why some criminal defendants are intimidated by even the lighter side of police questioning."

When she seemed to envision that tangent, Shel said gently, "Barbara?"

"What?"

"My question? Have you remembered—"

"Oh, of course. Sorry, Shelly. No, I think I gave you a pretty full account of what we discussed. I'd say they were allowing me the chance to tell them all I wanted to, whereas I stopped after praising Chuck as a fine clerk—even willing to make 'house calls' on the weekends, hence my last seeing him on Saturday—and that I really knew nothing of his personal life." She brought her hand to her mouth and seemed to be trying to stifle something, a sob, maybe. "Which certainly *was* the truth."

Then Pitt squared her shoulders and engaged his eyes. "Do we know anything more about Chuck's . . . activities?"

"Just that the portrait was commissioned by another member of the club who . . . admired him."

Half a laugh. "Thank you, Shelly. For trying to spare my feelings. If I have any left to spare after this morning."

Shel wasn't quite sure that he got her drift. "You mean, riding in with the police?"

"No," a full laugh now, but shrill, even tinged with fatigue. "And not our rather platonic 'pajama party,' either. No, as we resumed the trial of *Commonwealth versus Dooley* this morning, I was informed by the defendant that after yesterday's court session, he discharged his attorney."

Shel couldn't believe it. "Dooley is firing Kyra Yelverton and—"

"Continuing *pro se,* which will make my life even more miserable. I'll have no law clerk to do research for me, no defense attorney to rein in her client, and I'll have to bend over backwards to be sure the 'process' Dooley receives is 'due.' Not to mention the added media frenzy over a murder possibly connected to already the most circus-like trial in town."

Shel made a mental note to have Mairead contact Kyra Yelverton as soon as possible.

"And," said Pitt, handing Shel a telephone message slip, "this just in from the front."

The slip read:

To: B.Q.P.
Fr: Flo
Re: Sheldon A. Gold, Esq.
    Please tell Mr. Gold that Ms. Sunday called to say that Mr. Murizzi must appear before the grand jury today (Thursday) at 2:00 P.M. Ms. Sunday will call Ms. O'Clare toward a 12:30 P.M. meeting at Mr. Gold's office.

Admit it: Sooner rather than later.

"Thanks, Barbara," Shel pocketing the message, "but as I said, I really did come over just to see how you were faring."

Pitt looked at him differently. "Oh, Shelly, I'm sorry. I never even asked: You were able to get out of my place this morning without incident?"

Meaning, he thought, without anybody spotting him. "Yes."

Then she seemed to look inside herself. "You know, there is one other thing the police and I discussed."

"Being?"

"They told me Chuck had been shot, obviously, and by a thirty-eight-caliber gun, like my missing one."

Shel experienced a severe anxiety flash. "You didn't tell them about yours not—"

"Of course not, Shelly." Pitt's face didn't match the strength of her words, and Shel believed she was about to burst into tears. "But I did ask that Chinese detective whether he thought Chuck . . . whether in his experience, dying that way could have been . . . painful for the victim."

Well, she finally thought of it, though asking the police that question might have been revealing too much, given her own experience as a judge with gunshot cases.

But, try to be supportive. "What did he say?"

Pitt reached for some tissues in a desk drawer, again so like the gesture of Amelie Cardon at the Save Our Clergy office that Shel almost jumped in his chair.

Pitt said, "He didn't answer me. The female detective, Tully, told me . . ." The judge wiped her eyes and swiped with the tissue under her nose. ". . . told me, 'Not as painful as it's going to be for whoever shot him.'"

Sheldon A. Gold couldn't think of anything to say, supportive or otherwise, so he just nodded and stood to leave.

NINETEEN

Behind her reception desk just after lunch, Billie Sunday thought to herself, I truly believed I would never see the day.

She didn't mean so much the Pope coming to the law suite dressed in an actual business suit and tie, which he did once in a while when he helped Shel Gold with a case. And not even him knocking—*knocking*—on the corridor door instead of slipping into the reception area like a teeny wisp of smoke from a stranger's cigarette.

No, it was seeing the spooky man spooked his ownself.

"Billie, how you doing?"

She felt her eyes were playing tricks on her: As he tried to adjust his tie, both hands were shaking.

Billie said, "Fine, Pope. You?"

"I been better, tell you the truth. Shel and Mairead ready for me?"

"They're in his office. Told me to send you right to them."

"Fine. Uh, thanks."

As Pontifico Murizzi went past her desk, Billie Sunday came to a conclusion. This is *not* going to be a stellar day for the Law Offices of Sheldon A. Gold, Esq.

Uh-oh, said Mairead O'Clare to herself.

The Pope looked both the best dressed and the most nervous she'd ever seen him. And he sat down next to her in what was usually Billie's chair, instead of standing against the big safe.

Shel seemed concerned as well. "You okay?"

Murizzi nodded. "Just kind of a new experience for me, you know?"

"How so, Pope?"

"Back when I was on Homicide, I'd be going in to the grand jury to tell them enough to think the skel we thought did the victim was the right guy."

"And now?"

"I'm going to be trying *not* to tell them anything."

Mairead had a thought, something that might help Murizzi get over his jitters without embarrassing him about having them. "Shel?"

He turned to her. "Yes?"

"I don't know very much about grand juries. Can you kind of fill me in, so I can do a better job on the brief we figure I'm going to be writing afterwards?"

Shel looked at her, and Mairead wondered if he got why she'd asked the question.

Her boss said, "The grand jury was originally meant as a protection against the power of the state for the average citizen suspected by the police of committing a crime. The idea was that the Commonwealth, through a prosecutor, had to produce enough evidence before the grand jurors—average citizens themselves—to justify arresting the target defendant."

"So," said Mairead, stealing a glance at the Pope, "like a probable cause hearing?"

"Not exactly. At a probable cause hearing, the standard of proof before the judge is technically higher: The Commonwealth has to show there is sufficient evidence—though not necessarily evidence beyond a reasonable doubt—to prove the target defendant committed the crime."

Mairead nodded, but without thinking Murizzi was loosening up much. "So just that the defendant is kind of guilty, not trial-jury almost certainly guilty."

"Correct," said Shel. "Also, at a probable cause hearing, the target defendant is allowed to ask questions of the witnesses, though generally that just gives the assistant district attorney ammunition for the trial itself. At the grand jury stage, by comparison, the attorney for the target defendant can be present during the client's testimony, but can't do anything but assert a privilege or confer with the client if the client needs counseling on a question from the prosecutor. Or one of the grand jurors."

"So, in addition to the ADA presenting the case, the jurors themselves actually get to ask questions?"

The Pope suddenly said, in an almost natural tone, "When the prosecutor's finished with the witness. But it happened to me as a witness only after the jurors were sitting for maybe a month, starting to feel comfortable in the role, you know?"

Mairead didn't want him to stop. "Even if you're *just* a witness, and not the target defendant, can one of us be in there with you?"

Murizzi nodded now, easing back into his chair. "Yeah. Which used to frost the ADAs I worked with, let me tell you. The Commonwealth in its wisdom says a citizen's entitled to the lawyer being there whenever the citizen's 'involved in a criminal proceeding.' The prosecutors would tell me what a pain it was, they ask a question, and the witness says, 'Hey, can I talk to my lawyer about this first?'"

"However," said Shel, "while I can be there, and confer with the Pope outside the grand jury chamber, I can't object to most questions."

"Or ask any yourself," from Murizzi, now in what Mairead thought of as his normal voice. "Like we said before."

She remembered it as more like "Shel" said before, but Mairead was happy that her ploy of making the Pope less nervous about feeling like a turncoat and more "comfortable in the role" seemed to have worked. And she was even more happy that Shel Gold was now nodding himself, at her, as if in approval for what she'd thought to do for their beleaguered private investigator.

Chaos.

That was the first thing to strike Pontifico Murizzi as he and Shel Gold walked into the corridor outside the grand jury room on the fourteenth floor of the courthouse. At one end of the not-so-wide hall were people who looked like victims—or vics' survivors—on benches. At the other end, what looked like suspects, milling about, some lawyered up.

Like you, one part of the Pope thought, a trickle of sweat worming its way down his spine.

But in between the taunting and jeering from the two camps were fifteen, twenty detectives, some from the various police districts, a couple Anti-Gang Unit guys, everybody with badges on their belts and the new Glock .40-caliber semis on their hips. And all of them acting kind of like UN peacekeepers, the buffer between two warring fucking factions.

The Pope said, "Chock-full of Glocks."

Shel looked at him kind of funny. "What?"

Get a grip on yourself. "Nothing."

His lawyer pointed Murizzi toward an open doorway, and they made their way through the crowd. A few of the detectives said, "Hey, Pope," or "How's it going, man?", but most, even ones he'd had cases with, studiously ignored him.

The word is out: Pontifico Murizzi isn't here today in a coplike way.

"This is us," said Shel, entering a room maybe twenty by twenty, a court officer at one wall, sitting behind what looked like an old booking counter from one of the district stations. Wooden benches were against the other three walls, but all of the seating span was taken, so the Pope stood next to Shel, waiting to be called inside the next room. When Murizzi glanced around, find a clock, he didn't see one until another standee shifted. There, on the floor and leaning against the baseboard, was an old, round thing, with Roman numerals for the hours, but both hands broken off.

Message to the masses: We've been here forever, and we got all the time in the fucking world, so you wait on our pleasure.

Then a connecting door opened, and a woman with chopped brown hair and a jovial face stuck her head through the gap. "Pontifico Murizzi?"

Shel said, "And his counsel, Sheldon A. Gold," giving the woman what looked to the Pope like a business card.

"I'm ADA Tina Murphy. Come in, please."

As Murphy held the door for them, Murizzi thought back to the old grand jury chamber at Pemberton Square, before the Commonwealth decided to renovate that courthouse and began renting space from the feds in the building he was in now. More like a courtroom itself, the old chamber had a high ceiling and dark wood paneling. As a witness, you came in from a secure waiting area—not the chaos in that hallway—right near where you'd testify. The prosecutor's beautiful oaken table stood mid-room, the jury foreperson and clerk just past that. Across from them, on the long right wall, the grand jurors would be sitting like a trial jury, although there'd be so many of them (a max of twenty-three, the Pope seemed to remember) that they needed three tiered rows of chairs, nicely upholstered in blue.

Now being shown by ADA Murphy to a cruddy table with a microphone and a box of tissues on it and two mismatched chairs behind it, the Pope almost couldn't believe his eyes.

Murphy went to her table, here along the left wall and next to a man and a woman the Pope figured to be foreperson and clerk. And, like the old chamber, this room was stifling on a June day, area fans on the floor angled up forty-five degrees.

But the room itself was only twenty feet wide by forty feet long, and the poor grand jurors—Murizzi head-counted nineteen of them as today's quorum—were sitting in the back of the room and against the right-hand wall in more mismatched chairs.

The Commonwealth's budgetary crisis, coming home to roost.

As ADA Murphy began some formal identification recitals for the record, the court reporter repeated her words into what looked like a beige stereo headphone with black baffling. The Pope noticed half the jurors using six-inch-by-nine-inch steno pads as fans against the hot, sour air. Murizzi felt the soggy cloth of his shirt plastering itself against his back.

The foreperson administered the oath to him (including the "so help you God" part from his old days on the Homicide Unit). Then ADA Murphy asked him to state his name.

"Pontifico Murizzi." He thought his lips kind of smacked against the mike, so when Murphy asked him to spell both first and last, he backed off a little.

"And your current profession, Mr. Murizzi?"

"Uh, private investigator."

"Your prior profession?"

"Boston Police Department."

Murphy moved out from behind her table. "Your rank there?"

"Well, I started out as a patrolman"—shit—"patrol officer, like anybody else. Then I made detective, and eventually sergeant."

Murphy walked slowly toward the jurors in the rear of the room. "And your last assignment as a sergeant detective?"

"Homicide."

"And for how long on that unit?"

"Nine years, give or take a month, maybe two."

Which was when Murizzi realized that, despite the heat and mustiness in the room, he wasn't actively sweating anymore. Somehow, the familiar process of foundation questions from an ADA—any ADA—brought him back to his days of testifying as a detective. Calming down, the Pope began to make actual eye contact with individual jurors, the way he'd been taught.

"Very well, Mr. Murizzi." Murphy now stood way back in the corner, maybe to be sure her questions and his answers could be heard by all the jurors. "Did you at some point have occasion to investigate the disappearance of one Charles Vareika?"

"I did."

"Could you explain to us how that came about?"

"I don't know how he disappeared," said the Pope, as carefully as he could word it, "but Mr. Sheldon A. Gold, Esquire—the attorney sitting next to me right now—asked me to come in for his client."

Murphy's face became even more jovial. "Mr. Gold is representing both you and that first client?"

Shel didn't tap his arm or give any other signal, so Murizzi said, "That's my understanding."

"And do you know who that first client is?"

Still no signal. "Yes. The superior court judge that Mr. Vareika worked for as a law clerk, the Honorable Barbara Pitt."

Murphy turned so she seemed to ask her next question to the row of jurors along the right wall. "And, on Judge Pitt's behalf, whom did you speak with about Mr. Vareika's disappearance?"

Now a tap from Shel, who said, "The witness respectfully declines to answer on the ground that any response by him is protected by the confidentiality provision of the Commonwealth's private investigator licensing statute as well as the attorney-client privilege and the work-product doctrine."

The Pope noticed a couple of the grand jurors perk up a little, some starting to write on their steno pads instead of using them as fans, others looking to ADA Murphy, who both frowned and nodded. "Mr. Murizzi, did you receive or gather any documents in the course of your investigation?"

Another tap as Shel said, "The witness declines to answer for the reasons already stated."

Murphy's frown became a scowl. "Mr. Murizzi, is it your intention to decline to answer any further inquiry from me about persons you contacted during your investigation on the grounds of the alleged privileges and/or protections cited by Mr. Gold?"

The Pope waited a few seconds, make sure Murphy was asking him what he thought she was. "That's right."

"Mr. Murizzi, do you realize that Mr. Gold may have a conflict of interest here, advising *you* not to testify when that course may somehow advance Judge Pitt but harm you?"

"I realize that, yes, but it doesn't bother me."

Murphy now faced three-quarters to the jurors at the back of the room. "Does it bother you that you could be jailed for contempt, should a different judge rule that you must answer my questions?"

"I understand that."

"And that your term of incarceration, should you *still* decline to answer my questions, could be for the duration of the three months this grand jury sits, or any further judicial extension of its sitting?"

"Yes, I realize that, too."

"Very well," Murphy walking back to her table. "Ms. Foreperson, do any of the grand jurors have a question to ask?"

The Pope watched the foreperson look around the room just as an elderly black male raised his hand in the back. She said to him, "Yes?"

"My question is, do you mean they can make us sit in this sauna even after August?"

ADA Tina Murphy hung her head, a few of the other jurors laughed, and Pontifico Murizzi wanted to kiss the old guy on the spot.

Following the Pope out of the grand jury room, Sheldon A. Gold was sorry Mairead couldn't have seen what he felt was the product of her clever, "break the ice" maneuver back in his office, because Murizzi had appeared personally comfortable and professionally appropriate during his "testimony." But Shel also knew that they might need the brief she'd prepare toward a possible contempt hearing pretty quickly, and so it made sense for her to stay back at the office. Now all he had to do was return there, share the questions asked by the prosecutor and *not* answered, and then plug those into the brief at the appropriate points.

Staying silent in the if-anything-more-crowded corridor and then elevator of the courthouse—because you never knew who might be around to hear things—Shel waited until the Pope and he were outside the Congress Street entrance and on the sidewalk before saying from behind him, "You did a good job back there."

"Thanks, but you might be the only one who thinks so."

When Shel fell in beside Murizzi, he expected the Pope's face to be turned toward his own. Instead, though, the private investigator was looking at a woman walking briskly toward them, a cell phone in her hand.

Shel recognized her just as she said into the device, "I'm five feet from him, Tina, even as we speak."

"Jorie," said the Pope, kind of sadly to Shel's ear.

"Pontifico Murizzi," Tully taking a folded document from her handbag, "you are to appear before the first session of the superior court tomorrow at ten A.M. to show cause why you should not be held in contempt for refusing to answer questions during your grand jury appearance today."

Shel wondered if the Pope's former colleague in the Homicide Unit would have recited the whole litany if an outsider—and a lawyer at that—hadn't been there to spoil their "mini-reunion."

Murizzi accepted the summons. "Jorie, like we were saying this morning, I'm sorry it came to this, and I'm even sorrier it had to be you."

Tully glanced at Shel, then said, "You know, Pope, it's gotten to the point where I'm not," and wheeled like a soldier on a drill field, marching back toward the passenger side of a brown four-door sedan waiting for her at the curb.

TWENTY

As Billie Sunday proofread the affidavit she'd just typed for Shel to sign, "establishing the arising of the attorney-client privilege," she could hear her boss and the new child squabbling over lines in the brief. Near as Billie could tell, Mairead had shown Shel her work, and he'd suggested where they should plug in the questions the Pope had refused to answer. The tone of their voices, back behind her in Shel's office, sounded like what Billie remembered of her aunts in North Carolina, pecking at each other like hens over which patch of bright cloth should go where to make the best quilt possible. It kind of amused Billie that it didn't matter the project, or the race, or even the educational level of the participants. You put two or more human beings together to work on something, and they are not going to agree on much of anything.

Then she heard their suite door opening, and she was surprised to see a certain woman come through it for the second time in the same week.

As she smiled at Billie and fussed just a little with her scarf, the receptionist called out, "Shel?"

"Yes?" from his office, back turned toward her by the way his voice bounced.

"Ms. Ekarevskaya's here to see you again."

Pontifico Murizzi had figured that on a Thursday, there'd be less traffic heading to the Cape, even on a nice June afternoon. And he'd been right. Barely an hour and a half after the Pope left Boston, he was sliding the Explorer against the curb near Ugo Nagatami's salt-box house, the Camry convertible reassuringly snubbed tight to the garage door.

If only going to Maine to see the daughter again would be so easy.

This time Murizzi didn't bother with the front door. He strolled around to the back, kind of slowing, if not stopping, to smell the flowers along the way.

Give the guy this: He's "simplified" his garden, all right.

The Pope couldn't have begun to explain to somebody what Nagatami had done to change things, but the little dell was definitely more spare than on his last visit just two days before.

So spare, in fact, that Murizzi didn't see even Nagatami himself.

"Hey, anybody home?"

The Pope heard clumping footsteps, like somebody wearing boots, but was kind of surprised to see that instead of Poppa the Gardenmeister it was daughter Genna, the "Sex in the College" girl from Maine, in a pair of those enormous black, platform clodhoppers. Going northward, she had on tight black jeans and a black-and-white leopard-pattern blouse, maybe silk. Her hair was tied up on top of her head in a samurai ponytail, one thatch now dyed silver against the rest.

Nagatami said, "What are you doing here?"

"Let me guess: They're remaking *Bride of Frankenstein* on the Cape, and with that hair and those boots, you figure to be a shoe-in for the part."

"'Shoe-in'?" Nagatami huffed, sort of her trademark reaction to things back in her dorm room, too. "Pun bad, brain hurt. Now, what do you want?"

"Talk to you and your father about something that happens to rhyme with 'pun.'"

She seemed just confused.

Murizzi said, "Meaning 'gun.' As in the one your father gave your mother in the long ago."

Changing tones, the daughter yelled, "Daddy!"

A softer but quick stepping sound through the house and out-doors. Nagatami, Sr., was dressed in garden clothes again, even if they were different ones and without the coolie hat. Usually the Pope preferred to interrogate witnesses separately, so they wouldn't blend their recollections and couldn't cover each other's gaps. But he decided togetherness might work better here.

In that flat voice of his, the father said, "I thought we finished our business the last time."

"Me, too," said Murizzi. "Then our business changed after Chuck Vareika became not-so-clean fill on a Big Dig construction site, three bullets in him."

"So I heard," said the father, still flat as a pancake in tone.

The Pope nodded toward the daughter. "That why you pulled her out of school?"

"Noooooo," Nagatami, Jr., kind of stamping her foot like a twelve-year-old told she can't have another pony-back ride today. "My car needed servicing, and I, like, trust the guys down here to work on it right."

Murizzi processed that. "You drive seven hours to get an oil change? Even on a Porsche, that's kind of stretching the TLC, don't you think?"

The father said, "It needed a lot more done than that. But why don't you just get to what you're here for, and then leave us alone?"

Somehow the Pope didn't think he was going to be offered another beer, so he took a lawn chair already out of the shed without being invited. "The gun used to kill Vareika was a thirty-eight caliber."

"So?"

"So, the same kind you gave your ex-wife."

"How many thousands, even millions, of thirty-eights are in this country, Mr. Murizzi?"

What, not "Pontifico" anymore? "I don't know. But I do know of one that was in Judge Pitt's bedstand, at least until your daughter here visited Mom last weekend."

"This . . . is . . . ridiculous," the daughter seeming to play down in age from when the Pope had seen her at the college, and especially in the dorm after the dustup at the lumberjack bar with Beavis and Butt-Head. Murizzi thought it might be because of her father being present, kind of a reversion to the role she played when she was growing up.

Nagatami, Sr., said, "Genna is right. It's patently absurd to think *she* took the gun, much less would shoot this young man with it."

The Pope decided to show an ace. "That's what I think, too. It's why we haven't told the police about the gun, or about Genna having the opportunity to lift it. But I'd be curious to hear what you two have told them."

"The police?" said the father, exchanging glances with his daughter. "They haven't questioned us."

"Not yet, maybe. But if they run into the same brick walls I have, they'll start expanding the circle of folks to talk with, especially if they find out that their decedent was romantically involved with your ex-wife, and that he came on to your daughter."

"He came on . . . ?" Now Nagatami, Sr., turned to her. "Genna, is that true?"

A huff. "Yeah, only not exactly personally. It was more like, 'Hey, come join this club I belong to.'"

"What kind of club?"

Murizzi said, "A swingers' club. And in case you're still hoping for good news, we're not talking Glenn Miller here."

Nagatami closed his eyes and moved his head slowly from side to side, like a horse resigned to flies gathering on it. "What the hell did Barbara get herself—and us—into?"

"More than you'd want to know. But for now, I'm going to ask just one question: Did you ever register that gun?"

"Did I ever . . . ?" A different shake of the head, emphatic. "No, I could feel the wave of racism coming off—"

"You're sure about this? The guy who bought the revolver down in Dixie and gave it to you is dead, and you never went official with the authorities up here."

Nagatami didn't answer right away, the Pope figuring it was the guy's way of showing he didn't like being interrupted during a complaint about discrimination. "No."

Murizzi turned to the daughter. "When's the last time you saw the gun?"

"Never did. Why didn't you just ask me that in the first place?"

"Any idea who might have taken it?"

"None. Zero."

"Who had access to the thing?"

"Ask Mom, since Chuck'll probably clam up about it."

"Genna," said her father. "Don't get too cute."

A third huff. "I am, like, so out of here. Daddy, can you drive me to pick up my car?"

The Pope said, "I could give you a lift."

"No, thanks," said Ugo Nagatami. "You've already helped our family enough."

As Pontifico Murizzi made his way back around the house and toward the curb, he wondered if the Nagatamis believed that sarcasm was lost on him.

No, Sheldon," said Gallina Ekarevskaya as she moved into his office, her skirt and blouse on the yellow side under a brown blazer and print scarf. "I think perhaps Ms. O'Clare should stay with us."

Shel hadn't figured on that.

Admit it: You were looking forward to talking with this woman alone again.

Then he sensed Mairead sensing something herself just before she said, "Actually, Shel, if it's all the same to you, I think we should get Billie started on these corrections."

"Uh, yes. Good idea."

"Are you certain, Sheldon?" Ekarevskaya moved to one of the client chairs in front of his desk. "What I have to say will not take very much of your time, and since Ms. O'Clare has seen the subject of my concern, she might be helpful to your understanding of it."

Shel knew he should make a decision here.

Mairead relieved him of it by taking the other client chair. "Okay. We'll trust your judgment."

A bit shaky, Shel went around the desk to his own high-back, remembering to settle in gently so the stuffing wouldn't waft out of the cracks by the bustle.

He said, "So, what's the 'concern' that you have?"

Ekarevskaya crossed her legs, Shel noting this yellow skirt was the shortest she'd worn in his presence. "I have attended as much of the *Dooley* trial before your client Judge Pitt as possible, due to my representation of Hector Washington."

Shel just nodded.

"You are aware, Sheldon, that Mr. Dooley discharged his attorney yesterday?"

Shel nodded again.

"I believe that the man is more clever, in the diabolical sense, than even I would have imagined. And I also believe he is about to attempt some sort of . . . coup in that courtroom."

Shel didn't nod. "Violence?"

"No." Ekarevskaya did something he couldn't recall her ever doing before, though he could empathize with it: She squirmed in her chair. "There is something in his eyes, Sheldon. Or behind them."

Mairead said, "I know what you mean on that one."

Ekarevskaya pursed her lips. "Dooley behaves before the jury as though . . ." She shook her head now. "As though he is the kindly clown at a child's birthday party, with a big surprise he is saving for the right moment."

Shel thought about that, how Barbara Pitt would have to try to handle it, with the jury present and no defense attorney to "code talk" the situation away from a mistrial. "Any idea what kind of 'surprise' he's planning?"

"None." Ekarevskaya allowed herself—or him—a small smile. "But since in this situation you and I are not exactly adversaries, I thought you should know, for your client's sake."

"Thank you," said Shel, sincerely.

She turned to Mairead. "Because you have seen Mr. Dooley, perhaps you can puzzle his secret for Sheldon."

"Perhaps," said Mairead, in that deadpan tone he'd heard her trot out from time to time.

Ekarevskaya came back to him. "Well," standing, "I must now pursue other avenues. A pleasure, as always."

She extended her hand, and—as always—Shel felt that little tingle of electricity from touching it.

"Ms. O'Clare."

"Ms. Ekarevskaya."

Shel watched the Russian lawyer leave the office and waited until he could see the suite door open and close before speaking from the corner of his mouth. "What did you think?"

Sheldon A. Gold heard his associate reply, "I'd ask her out for dinner."

He turned to her, his mouth now open completely.

Mairead got up. "And soon, Shel. Before she asks you."

At her reception desk, Billie Sunday listened to Mairead's explanation of where to insert in the brief the questions their private investigator had refused to answer before the grand jury. Billie spotted a couple of bad transitions in the following paragraphs, and she and the new child hashed them out. Since Shel's office door was closed now, Billie decided to test the waters.

"Did that Ms. Ekarevskaya have anything helpful?"

Mairead said, "More a warning than anything."

"Warning about what?"

"About what the priest in the rape case might do in the courtroom."

Billie could only imagine, but preferred not to. "Anything you can do about it?"

"Probably not. I told Shel I'd try to run it down, though."

"Meaning talk to that . . . man again?"

Mairead made a face, like Billie's youngest, William, when asked to taste a brussels sprout or other healthy vegetable he already knew he wouldn't like. "Only if I have to."

Pontifico Murizzi fumed in his Ford Explorer, inching his way north toward Boston. It was the part of Route 3 that runs through the town of Plymouth. Even without traffic, it always seemed to take forever. In his view, the reason for this was that the Pilgrims must have anticipated how every Tom, Dick, and Carrie would want to develop the picturesque area, so the original colonists staked out the town to be the size of a county in its own right.

Only that Thursday afternoon, when there should have been absolutely *no* fucking mass migration heading north toward the city, the Pope found himself in a bumper-to-bumper jam that, according to his dashboard's trip odometer and clock, had allowed him to travel 2.3 miles in just under an hour. To make matters worse, he was angled uphill on a sloping part of the highway, with nothing on either side but scrub pine and bushes, so he couldn't see what the problem was, nor even ask somebody along the shoulder of the road.

Okay, you're stuck. Getting to see the judge's daughter on the same trip as the ex-husband was a nice piece of luck, logistically speaking. So sublimate this horseshit delay: Has to be an accident, and a bad one, far enough ahead that the staties and locals haven't figured out how to siphon the poor fucks like you stuck on the highway off onto secondary roads to get around the bottleneck. And that means they're probably eyedroppering the cars just behind the accident one at a time over the shoulder, even the bushy median, while waiting for the tow trucks.

Which also means there's no way you're going to be able to reach even New Hampshire tonight by a reasonable hour. But you don't have to drive to Maine tomorrow, thanks to killing two birds with one stone on this trip to the Cape. So you go to the contempt hearing tomorrow morning, then hit the Vareika kid's parents during the afternoon.

Pontifico Murizzi took a deep breath, pressed Shel's office number on the cell phone's speed dial to report that Ugo Nagatami had confirmed no registration of the judge's gun, and noticed his truck's odometer telling him he'd gained another tenth of a mile while thinking about his plight.

TWENTY-ONE

H ello, Flo."

"Ms. O'Cl— Sorry, we decided on 'Mairead,' did we not?"

Mairead nodded at the woman's elaborate syntax, then glanced around the anteroom to Judge Pitt's lobby. "I'm sorry to disturb you, but I didn't see Tommy Flanagan around."

"He is with Her Honor," Altamira tilting her head back toward the inner office, a tired expression on her face. "I am afraid we had to call another recess."

"Mr. Dooley giving you trouble?"

"Yes, but not . . . intentionally? At least, I do not believe it is intentional on his part. He simply does not know much more about courtroom practice than you might learn from television, despite his having sat at that defense table while Ms. Yelverton was representing him."

Mairead tried to decide whether she should share with Altamira what Gallina Ekarevskaya had told Shel and her about Dooley preparing a "surprise."

I'd say no, young lady. That's more for Mr. Gold, or your client, to decide.

Agreed. "Can I sit a minute?"

"Certainly."

Taking a chair, Mairead said, "I want to go back to that afternoon, last Friday?"

Altamira seemed to grow more solemn. "When I last saw Charles, you mean."

"Yes. You told me he asked you about the case, but was agitated."

"He did, and he was, as I already have told you."

"But you couldn't determine why."

"No."

Mairead decided to take another tack. "I know that sometimes when I'm having trouble remembering something another person said, it helps for me to close my eyes and picture him or her, as they were talking to me."

A kind smile. "Mairead, I believe that holds true for virtually all of us."

"Good. Can we try that now?"

"I already have, believe me."

We'll see. "You were sitting there when you spoke with Charles, right?"

"Right. He came through that same door to the courtroom you just used."

"Could you close your eyes, and I'll do exactly what Charles did?"

A glance around her desktop, cluttered with papers. "Really, Mairead, I have a lot of work to do."

"Flo, please? This could be awfully important."

"Very well." She closed her eyes, reclined in her chair, and crossed her arms flat against her chest.

Not the best of body language. "Okay," Mairead getting back to her feet and walking to the door. "This opens. Did Charles bang it against the wall?"

Eyes closed. "No."

"Slam it behind him?"

"No, no. He was agitated, Mairead, not violent."

"What were his first words?"

Eyes still closed. "'Flo, I have to know some things, for the *Dooley* trial.'"

"And you said . . . ?"

"'Such as what, Charles?'"

"Not, 'Certainly, Charles'?"

"Well, no." Some eye movement behind the lids. "He already had asked me many questions, as I told you earlier."

"About trial procedure."

"Yes. Who sits in which seats, the party allowed to challenge the jurors first, those kinds of things."

Mairead harked back to her Evidence class at New England School of Law, where the professor had made a point of explaining all that so a student wouldn't feel stupid on his or her first case in the real world.

I guess that's not the practice at every law school, young lady.

Mairead said to Altamira, "Yet Charles seemed agitated."

"Yes. As though he really needed to know the answer right away."

"The answer to what?"

"Which affirmative defenses could be raised by the accused's counsel."

"Even though the prosecution hadn't even rested yet, correct?"

"As I told him. But Charles just kept crushing . . ." More eye movement behind the closed lids.

"Flo, Charles kept 'crushing' what?"

The eyes didn't open, but a smile crossed Altamira's face, and she unfolded her arms. "Very good, Mairead. Your little process here has made me remember something."

"And what's that?"

"He had an envelope in his hand. Charles was quite a strong young man, and he seemed to be crushing it."

"Like in his fist?"

Altamira demonstrated just that with her own hand.

Mairead said, "Was there any writing on the envelope?"

"Not that I could see."

"Anything in it?"

Just a shrug.

"Flo, what did you tell Charles?"

"In answer to his question, you mean?"

"Yes."

"I told him the raising of affirmative defenses usually depended on the testimony and exhibits the prosecution had introduced during the Commonwealth's case-in-chief, but that in any event which specific defenses were actually pursued would be up to the attorney for the accused."

"And what did he say to that?"

Altamira finally opened her eyes. "He did not, in words. Charles simply looked down at the carpet, right where you stand now, and nodded, somewhat stiffly."

Mairead looked down at her own feet.

Florinda Altamira said, "Has this exercise in memory refreshment been any help to you?"

Mairead O'Clare brought her face back up. "I'm not sure, Flo. I'm not sure."

When Sheldon A. Gold stepped out of the elevator into the first-floor lobby of his office building, he had to blink at what he assumed was a mirage.

Shel was carrying his old bookbag-style briefcase, the documents for the contempt hearing in it toward reviewing them that night. One document was a photocopy of the brief, enlarged slightly on the Xerox machine by Billie as always. Shel liked the enhancement so that he would have more room in the margin to write, in red Flair pen, the buzzwords he'd want to see if he needed to glance down at the written version of the argument while presenting the oral version to the judge who'd decide the issue. The marginal notes also let Shel cite the exact page and paragraph of the brief where a given point was made, for later reference if the judge decided to reserve the decision, which Shel thought was likely here.

Then the mirage in the building lobby spoke to him. "Sheldon, you are surprised to find me waiting here for you."

"Yes, Gallina, I am."

Ekarevskaya canted her head. "Surprised, but not, I hope . . . disappointed?"

"No. No, of course not."

She smiled. "I thought we might share dinner tonight."

Mairead predicted this, and you were too dense to see it coming. "I'd like to, Gallina. Truly. But I have to prepare for a contempt hearing tomorrow."

"Contempt?"

Shel summarized what had happened before the grand jury.

Ekarevskaya nodded toward his briefcase. "And your preparation is in there?"

"Yes."

"And how long is your brief, Sheldon?"

For just one mad moment, he thought she'd said "briefs," as in—"Uh, ten, twelve pages I guess."

"And for how many years now have you practiced law?"

"Twenty-some."

"Soon to be thirty, if I am correct in my calculations."

A second surprise: Shel found himself enjoying this little exchange. "So?"

"So . . ." Ekarevskaya took a swaying step toward him, then a second. "It should not take an experienced attorney like yourself all night to prepare an oral argument from a 'ten-, twelve-page' brief. And you also have to consume some food. For . . . energy?"

"My cat," said Shel, too quickly, he realized.

A slightly stunned expression on her face. "Your food, your . . . cat?"

"No, no. I have to feed my cat. I always do, as soon as I get home."

The stunned look slid away, replaced by a more poker face. "Sheldon, I have no desire to make a fool of myself. Do you wish to have dinner with me, or not?"

"I do, Gallina," again too quickly, he knew. "But maybe . . . maybe not tonight."

She canted her head the other way now, her eyes so like Natalie's, both the color and the slight slant at the corners. "I will accept that, Sheldon. Not as a rejection, but rather as a . . . What is the American idiom, when the ticket to a baseball game cannot be honored due to bad weather, but the ticket-holder can attend another time?"

"A raincheck."

"Yes, though I have never been able to understand the derivation of that phrase. Why is it not 'rain-ticket'?"

Shel gave her his "in front of the jury box" shrug, accompanied by, "Not everything in life is logical, Gallina."

Ekarevskaya reached her hand up to the lapel on Shel's suit jacket, just straightening it perhaps, but somehow so intimate. "No, Sheldon.

Much in life is illogical, which is the way it should be. And I would very much like to explore some of that with you."

She drew back her hand and turned toward the doors to the sidewalk. Then over her shoulder with, "When you feel comfortable doing so, of course."

Sheldon A. Gold watched Gallina Ekarevskaya move more like a dream than a mirage through the doors before losing her in the two-way pedestrian traffic on the sidewalk.

Admit it: You really *should* have asked first on the dinner thing, just like Mairead said.

Finally pulling into the parking lot by his marina, Pontifico Murizzi thought about the poor devils in the accident, which he had pegged just about right. A rental truck, probably the biggest fucking thing the kid driving it had ever tried to handle, was sprawled on its side across both travel lanes, a Chrysler convertible and a Nissan minivan also involved. There'd been shards of glass everywhere, and from the windshield of the van, that driver had gone into it, hard. There was more blood, though, by the convertible, and the Pope was really glad he'd never had to deal with traffic accidents much, other than the occasional fender bender on a clogged city street, back when he wore a uniform.

Maybe it was thinking about being on the force, or maybe it was Jorie Tully paying him a visit that morning, but getting out of the Explorer in the marina lot, Murizzi saw an unmarked, maroon Crown Vic that he thought he recognized from the Homicide Unit. He walked over to it, and sure enough, the plate matched his memory.

Well, no sense putting it off.

Walking to the floating camel, the Pope could see somebody on his fantail, sitting in one of his white resin chairs, just like Jorie had been. Only when Murizzi got a little closer, he recognized Artie Chin, with some brown bags on the table that smelled a hell of a lot better than the harbor. When Chin saw him coming, he reached down to the deck and lifted up a six-pack of beer or ale.

"Hey, Pope, where the fuck you been?"

"Eating fumes on Route 3, accident in front of me."

"I've been sitting here an hour easy, torturing myself with the pride of China's best cuisine."

Murizzi vaulted over his gunwale like it was a gym-class horse. "We celebrating something?"

Chin tossed him a bottle, then took one for himself, both Molson Golden.

"Good choice, Artie. And thanks for waiting on the beer, too."

"*No* choice, Pope. These aren't twist-offs, and I didn't bring a church key."

Murizzi twisted his top off.

Chin stared at the one in his hand. "But they're Canadian, and they don't say anything about—"

"Sometimes you just have to take a chance, Artie."

Chin opened the other beer. "Which could explain this situation."

The Pope dipped the neck of his bottle in a silent clink, then took a swig in unison with Chin. "Tell me about it."

A measured look on the guy's face. "I want to clear the air with you on this law-clerk thing."

Murizzi leaned back against the gunwale and crossed his ankles. "While the investigation's still live?"

Chin said, "We go back a long ways, Pope, you and me. Jorie still thinks you screwed her somehow on that case with the dead juror."

"I didn't."

"I said that's what she thinks."

"And what do you think, Artie?"

"About that one, I don't know, frankly, and I didn't want to get between the two of you on it. As you may recall."

Murizzi nodded, took another sip of his beer. "Do you think I screwed you on this one?"

Chin paused with the bottle halfway to his mouth. "No. I don't see you asking me to use the official system if you thought something was rotten in what you were investigating."

The Pope looked inside himself, wasn't sure he could completely agree with the guy, these days.

Chin drank a little more. "But the thing with the law clerk has gone as rotten as it can. We released the body back to his parents, and Jorie has her ass in gear."

"I've noticed," said Murizzi. "I'm going in tomorrow morning on a contempt citation."

"That's Tina Murphy, the ADA who caught the killing, but Jorie probably goosed her on it." Chin looked at Murizzi. "You and Detective Tully have some other issues, I'm guessing."

Murizzi thought back to Jorie, coming on to him after he'd left the force, thinking they'd make a good couple. "We have had. The dead-juror case pretty much did that in."

"Maybe from your standpoint, Pope. Not from hers."

Murizzi drank some more beer. "So, you're here to, what, apologize for Jorie?"

"You know better than that. And I'm too polite to mention just how badly you're fucking up our homicide statistics for the commissioner." Chin pointed the mouth of his bottle at the brown bags. "I was just thinking the condemned man might want a good last meal before he starts eating jail chow."

The Pope felt himself grinning. "Thanks, Artie."

"I also realized that it's been a while since I shared the bounty of my homeland with a fucking wop/former cop."

Murizzi felt the grin grow wider. "Always the wordsmith."

"So," said Artie Chin, tearing open the nearest bag, "you got a microwave on this tub?"

Mairead O'Clare knocked at the door of the three-decker on the Dorchester/Roxbury line, her cabdriver no doubt drooling over the twenty she'd given him to wait for her at the curb. It took a while for someone to answer her knock, though, and so during the interim, Mairead was glad she'd kept the taxi.

When the door opened, Kyra Yelverton stood in a sleek sweatsuit, her figure backlit by an overhead light in the hallway. A hoarse, male voice called her first name from somewhere up the stairs behind her while Alanis Morissette sang from somewhere closer.

"What are you doing here?"

Mairead said, "This is the address on the appearance slip you filed with the court in the *Dooley* case."

"I mean, what are you doing here at dinnertime?"

The male voice cut in again before Mairead could answer. "Kyra girl, where the fuck are you?"

Yelverton's facial features squeezed together. "I'm sorry. My father's sick, and I—"

"Go on up to him, please. But if you'll talk to me, I'll release my cab."

Yelverton glanced over Mairead's shoulder. "All right. But not for too long."

"Kyra! Answer me, girl!"

"Thanks," said Mairead as Yelverton yelled, "Coming!"

Mairead went down to the taxi and settled up. Then she made her way back to the front door and entered the house.

To her left was a small living room, the furniture looking very old-fashioned, even some doilies—

Antimacassars, young lady.

—on the headrests. But there also was one of those new Bose radio-CD players on a table, and some other modern artists' names beyond Morissette on the jewel cases scattered around the player.

Mairead heard slapping footsteps on the stairs, looked up to see Yelverton, her feet bare under the sweatpants' elastic cuff.

Halfway down, the woman said, "He'll be okay for a while. You're a little young yet," Yelverton's eyes drifting to the second floor again, "but it's a bitch, becoming the parent for your parents."

Then she snapped her head around toward Mairead. "Oh, I'm sorry. You told me you were an orphan, right?"

May as well use her embarrassment, young lady.

Mairead nodded. "Raised in an orphanage, actually. My real parents abandoned me there. Because of the hemangioma, I'm told."

"Oh, God." Yelverton brought her hand up to her forehead and swiped, almost like she was whisking sweat from her skin. "I really have *not* been my best around you. Let's sit in here. Coffee?"

"Only if it's made."

"It's not, but I can—"

"Soda?"

"I have just diet. Dad's a diabetic, and—"

"Diet anything is fine."

"Be right back."

Mairead looked around the room a little more carefully now. The one thing that stood out was a photo of two young black people, him in a uniform, her in a wedding gown. Like the furniture, it seemed old-fashioned, and the colors seemed unrealistically bright.

Yelverton returned with a Diet Pepsi and two glasses, cubes of ice in each. "We split this, it'll stay colder."

"Good idea. Your father was in the Army?"

"Yeah." Yelverton poured the soda carefully. "After Korea. Became kind of a family tradition. My only brother's stationed on Okinawa, so it's just me."

"To take care of your dad?"

"Right. My mom died six years ago. Heart attack."

Mairead thought of Sister Bernadette's last illness, how the cancer slowly eroded even her strong body and spirit, like somebody dripping acid on steel. "Sometimes quicker can be better."

A nod from Yelverton as she handed one glass to Mairead and sipped from the other. "You go through something yourself?"

"With an older nun. The sister who kind of raised me, at least in the orphanage sense."

Another nod, Yelverton now perching on one of the old couch cushions. "When Dad got so bad, I was over here enough, keeping my apartment didn't make sense. Then I moved my office here, too. Save commuting time *and* money."

"You're good to do that for him."

A shrug. "Kind of thought it was part of the contract." A pause, then a change of tone. "So, seriously, what brings you here?"

Mairead had rehearsed her opening during the cab ride from the courthouse. "When I first talked with you—after Mr. Dooley told me his 'story'?—I got the impression that maybe you knew more about Charles Vareika being missing than you told me."

Yelverton paused longer this time. "What do you mean, 'knew more'?"

"It was just a sense I had. You seemed shocked that Mr. Vareika had disappeared, when I can't see a way that you'd even have known him very well."

"I didn't." Yelverton looked down at her knees, jiggled the glass up and down on them. "But you were right. I did hold something back because I didn't want him to get in any trouble, though I can't see how it can hurt him now."

Mairead felt that surge of excitement, like going over the boards and onto the ice to start a sudden-death overtime. "What do mean?"

Yelverton licked her lips. "Maybe a week ago, I'd just gotten home here, and the phone rang, my business line. It was still before five, though, so I picked up. It was your Mr. Vareika."

"What did he say to you?"

"He wanted . . . He told me Judge Pitt asked him to give me a call, lay out the affirmative defenses I was going to raise for Dooley after the prosecution rested."

Mairead's mind rocketed back to her Professional Responsibility course in law school. "But that's—"

"Unethical, right. Ex parte communication from the court about litigational strategy of the defendant. Which is what made me realize your Mr. Vareika was also lying to me about Her Honor asking him to make the call."

"What did you do?"

"Kind of pulled rank on the boy. I said no judge I'd ever been before would dare ask that, and that he was on shaky grounds himself for even bringing it up."

"Vareika have an answer for you?"

"No. He just apologized for bothering me and hung up. And, like I told you a few minutes ago, I didn't want to get him into trouble over his question, so I didn't mention it to you when we talked at the courthouse."

"Back to the phone call. What was Vareika's tone like?"

"His tone?" Yelverton seemed to think about that. "Kind of . . . excited, but impatient, too."

"Agitated, even?"

"I'd say that, yes."

"Kyra, could this call have been Friday of last week?"

"Could have been." Yelverton started a bit. "In fact, it was, because I'd just gotten Dad's medicine from the VA—they call it something other than the Veterans Administration now, but I had to wait on a very long line for the drugs, and I remember being ripped about it when I spoke to Vareika."

Mairead tried to think of an ethical way to put her next question. "Kyra, I've talked with your client, and I've thought about his case. A lot."

"Join the club, though frankly I'm glad to be quit of it now."

"Just what 'defenses' does Dooley think he has?"

Yelverton stiffened, and Mairead was afraid she was going to be kicked out of the house for saying face-to-face effectively what Vareika had asked over the phone.

Then Yelverton sighed. "I think I owe you one, so long as there's no attribution."

"No one will hear anything you tell me."

"And I'm not going to share any client confidences with you. But, again frankly, I haven't got the foggiest idea what the man thinks he *has* by way of a defense."

Mairead wanted to know if they'd ever discussed his strategy, but that would so clearly be a "client confidence" that Yelverton would find the question insulting. "When I was in the courtroom Tuesday, he didn't seem to be communicating with you at all."

Yelverton hesitated, maybe trying to determine whether even that aspect was over the "confidence" line she'd drawn in the sand. "I'll tell you the level of his 'communicating' with me in the courtroom, because the jury and everybody else could see it, too." Yelverton blew out a breath now. "I'd made the usual barrage of pre-trial motions, including one for change of venue."

Made sense to Mairead: With all the scandals involving priests in the Boston area, maybe get Dooley's trial moved to Worcester, even Pittsfield, the latter a hundred miles away and nearly in New York State.

"Well," continued Yelverton, "the venue one, like most of the others, was denied, but I gave copies of Judge Pitt's rulings to my client, which were just her decisions handwritten on each."

Having seen a number of her own motions denied over the months working with Shel, Mairead could picture that.

Yelverton said, "Dooley seemed to fixate on the venue decision, though, to the point that he kept writing it over and over."

Now Mairead was confused. "Writing what?"

Yelverton looked around the room before saying, "Just a second," and left. She came back with a pad and pencil, and then jotted something on it. "Here," handing the pad to Mairead.

Yelverton had written in script, *Defendant's Motion for Change of Venue is denied.*

Mairead looked up. "You mean he just kept repeating this one line?"

"Over and over, on a pad at the defense table. I mean, can you imagine? Here Dooley's on trial for something that he doesn't deny doing—revels in *having* done—but he doesn't plead guilty. Instead the man insists on a trial, basically daring the judge to max out his sentence for wasting everybody's time. And then, while I'm doing my best to save his sorry ass from sitting in a cell for probably the rest of his *un*natural life, there he is sitting next to me, copying that same line over and over and over again, like a fourth-grader in detention who has to write 'I will not talk during class' a hundred times."

Mairead listened carefully, but now was lost again. "I don't understand why Mr. Dooley would do that."

"Same here. When I first noticed what he was writing, the man just looked at me, like I was interrupting him as he was trying to compose a difficult poem. Then, when I asked what the hell he was doing, Dooley . . ."

Yelverton petered out, a frown spreading over her face.

Mairead pressed on. "What did he say, Kyra?"

"No." She shook her head. "No, I just realized, that *would* be revealing a client confidence."

Mairead tried to keep the edge of frustration out of her voice. "Kyra, please? What could Dooley have said about it that could possibly hurt him?"

Yelverton kept her frown, deepening it when her father's voice yelled her first name again.

Mairead quietly echoed it. "Kyra?"

"I've got to go help my dad."

"Kyra, please tell me—"

"Look, I'm sorry for all this, but I now have to go up those stairs and wipe the ass of the poor old soldier calling me. Can you understand that?"

"I can even identify with it. When that nun I mentioned was wasting away from cancer."

Yelverton squeezed her features together again, as she had earlier in the courthouse and then on the stairs of her father's house when Mairead first arrived. The younger lawyer's heart went out to the slightly older lawyer for what the last month or so must have been like for her, both professionally and personally.

Then Yelverton stood and left the room.

Mairead followed her to the foot of the staircase. "Kyra, please?"

Yelverton turned about halfway up the steps. "All right. Man would probably tell you himself, if you'd just agree to listen to his 'story' again." A deep breath. "When I asked Dooley what he was doing, writing that line over and over, he said, 'Unfortunately, I'm missing a letter.'"

Mairead blinked. "What did he mean by that?"

Yelverton turned back and continued climbing the steps. "Beats the shit out of me, girl. Beats the shit out of me."

TWENTY-TWO

On Friday morning, Sheldon A. Gold stood, like the few other people in the first session, as he watched the Honorable June Smith ascend the bench. And "ascend" was the right word, since the session occupied the old federal Court of Appeals cavern on the fifteenth floor, and the bench was twice the height of a typical one. The room's dark wood paneling and red carpet always reminded Shel of a medieval banquet hall, down to the brass-tacked, blue leather chairs.

Once the judge sat, Shel and Mairead did as well. At the next table, on the other side of the podium, was ADA Tina Murphy, looking less jovial and more stoically ready for battle. Shel twisted around far enough to see Pontifico Murizzi sitting in the gallery behind him. Given that a secret grand jury matter constituted the topic of the moment, the first session had been cleared of everyone except bailiffs, administrative clerks, and the "voice-talking" court reporter.

Shel turned back toward the bench as the clerk intoned, "*In the Matter of a Grand Jury Investigation,* Commonwealth's Motion to Show Cause Why a Witness Should Not be Held in Contempt."

Judge Smith, a slim, refined woman with black hair, riffled through the papers in front of her. "Ms. Murphy, I take it you appear for the district attorney's office?"

"Yes, Your Honor," Murphy coming halfway out of her chair before sinking back into it.

The judge nodded. "And Mr. Gold for the witness, Pontifico Murizzi?"

"Yes, Your Honor," parroted Shel, standing. "With my associate, Mairead O'Clare."

As the judge nodded once more, Shel glanced down at the pad in front of his "associate." Mairead seemed to be writing *Defendant's Motion for Change of Venue is denied* over and over again.

Shel shook his head, but retook his chair.

Smith said, "I've had time only to skim counsels' affidavits and briefs. Ms. Murphy, I'll hear you first, but no need to use the podium."

"Thank you, Your Honor," the ADA getting to her feet again and staying there. "As indicated in the affidavit of Detective Marjorie Tully of Boston Homicide, her unit and our office are investigating the shooting death of a Mr. Charles Vareika. Until his death, Mr. Vareika worked as a research law clerk for this court, specifically under Judge Barbara Q. Pitt."

Shel watched Judge Smith close her eyes for a moment, as though trying to conjure up the face of the decedent.

ADA Murphy chose a paper from the table in front of her. "Sergeant Detective Arthur Chin of the Homicide Unit became aware that Mr. Murizzi, in his capacity of private investigator, had been looking into Mr. Vareika's failure to report for work at the court on Monday of this week, four days ago. Mr. Murizzi was investigating at the request of Judge Pitt. As this is a capital case, Massachusetts Rule of Criminal Procedure Four requires submission of the facts to a grand jury, and accordingly Mr. Murizzi was subpoenaed under Rule Seventeen to appear as a witness before it. However, Mr. Murizzi refused to answer questions put to him by me at that time, and therefore we've brought the current motion."

"Thank you, Ms. Murphy. Mr. Gold, I suppose my first question would be why you didn't file a Motion to Quash the original subpoena, as Mr. Murizzi seems to fall under Supreme Judicial Court Rules Three-point-oh-seven and Three-point-eight (f), which—as interpreted in the 1990 *Grand Jury* case—ethically bar a district attorney from subpoenaing an attorney *or* the attorney's agents before the grand jury?"

"Three reasons, Your Honor," said Shel, standing and feeling better, finally getting to throw some punches. "First, while we could and did raise several privileges in refusing to answer certain questions before the grand jury, I did not believe Mr. Murizzi could refuse to appear altogether to testify about *un*privileged matters." Shel thought about the judge mentioning she'd had little time to review the motion documents. "Therefore, I wanted to save this busy court the burden of having to hold two hearings."

"Thank you for your consideration, Mr. Gold."

Shel thought he caught a whiff of sarcasm from that comment, but plunged on. "My second reason for not moving to quash was that, while the subpoena demanded Mr. Murizzi bring any documents with him, there were no documents in his possession connected to Mr. Vareika's death, other than one composed for me by Judge Pitt herself, which is clearly within the attorney-client privilege. Third, and probably most telling, Mr. Murizzi was summoned by in-hand service of the subpoena yesterday, only hours before he was to appear before the grand jury, and thus I really had no time to file a motion to quash on *any* ground."

"Very well," the judge sending a look toward Tina Murphy that Shel hoped meant, Why the rush? "As appears from the minutes of the grand jury session excerpted in the briefs, three distinct reasons were raised why the witness could refuse to answer the Commonwealth's questions. Mr. Gold, the first is the private investigator licensing statute, which imposes a duty of confidentiality upon the investigator regarding things learned in the course of working on a client's case, correct?"

"That's correct, Your Honor."

"However, that duty is not a privilege, and the same statute provides that such duty can be overcome simply by a court order, one I could issue today. Accordingly, let's focus on the other two reasons. Regarding the attorney-client privilege as raised by your affidavit, explain to me if you would why Judge Pitt, as the 'client' involved, doesn't want your investigator to tell the police who he talked with and what he learned about Mr. Vareika?"

Uh-oh, cutting to the car chase. "If Your Honor please, the attorney-client privilege exists exactly for that reason: To reveal communications between attorney and client would chill the free flow of information to the attorney and advice to the client which the privilege is intended to promote."

"I don't think you've answered my question, Mr. Gold. But let's assume that I'd be willing to include Mr. Murizzi, as your agent for investigation, within the circle of confidentiality regarding the privilege itself." Smith turned toward the other counsel table. "Ms. Murphy, why do you wish to break that circle?"

"I don't, Your Honor," Murphy sounding comfortable now, conversational instead of formal, like "We're all on the same team, Judge." The ADA picked up another paper. "The Commonwealth is *not* trying to pry any secrets Judge Pitt might have confided in that document Mr. Gold alluded to, nor any information revealed during any meetings or telephone conversations or even e-mail exchanges she might have had with Mr. Gold or his 'agent.' But a young man— in fact, a court employee—has been murdered here, and thanks apparently to Judge Pitt's understandable concern about his earlier disappearance, Mr. Murizzi enjoyed at least a two-day investigative 'head start' over the Homicide Unit before the body was discovered Wednesday night. As the case of *Three Juveniles* established twenty years ago, every person has a duty to respond to a grand jury subpoena and to answer all questions relevant to the investigation of a crime. Here the crime is homicide, and it's quite likely that the people Mr. Murizzi spoke with during his investigation of Mr. Vareika's *disappearance* could be helpful to the police during their investigation of his *death*."

"Mr. Gold," Judge Smith now leaning forward on her elbows, lightly tapping her fingertips together, "what argument do you have against that? A simple listing of names, addresses, telephone numbers, et cetera, of the persons Mr. Murizzi reached—or tried to but didn't—including accompanying documents?"

"Your Honor," said Shel, struggling to buy a few more nanoseconds to think of a better answer than the one at the front of his brain, "the police can simply do that themselves, with far greater resources than Mr. Murizzi had at his disposal."

"True, Your Honor," Murphy sounding awfully magnanimous in her concession. "But as I pointed out before, Mr. Murizzi had a head start in speaking with these persons, and there's no reason the police shouldn't gain from that in trying to find and arrest a killer."

Shel registered that Murphy had adopted Smith's verbiage: "persons" instead of "people." Smart.

"I agree with Ms. Murphy on the attorney-client privilege analysis," said Smith. "Mr. Gold, your third argument for why Mr. Murizzi could refuse to answer the questions before the grand jury?"

"The work-product doctrine, Your Honor." Shel took a breath. "Since Mr. Murizzi was investigating on behalf of an attorney for that attorney's client, the results of his efforts should remain confidential."

"Ms. Murphy?"

"Two problems with that argument, Your Honor. First, work-product protection is generally extended to efforts by an attorney or that attorney's agent toward anticipated future *litigation*. Here, there is no reason to believe that Judge Pitt, as the client, was expecting any litigation over Mr. Vareika that might involve her, and so the doctrine doesn't apply to the facts here. Second, even if it *did* apply, it is only a relative 'protection,' not an absolute 'privilege,' and here the police should not have to undergo the hardship of compiling their own 'list' of persons when Mr. Murizzi could save them that time and hopefully effect the arrest of the killer sooner."

All Shel could think was "persons" again.

"Mr. Gold?"

"Your Honor, my client's dollars should not provide a free ride to the police, who are perfectly capable of—"

"Mr. Gold," Smith now actually clapping her two hands together, "we're not talking about a civil case, where Adversary A is trying to ride the hard work of Adversary B's attorney for free. This is a homicide investigation, and certainly Judge Pitt is no 'adversary' in it, is she?"

Shel knew he dare not answer that one.

Now June Smith nodded. "Ruling from the bench, accordingly: Witness Pontifico Murizzi is to appear again before the grand jury on Monday, at a time to be designated by ADA Murphy, and there testify as to each and every person he contacted in any way on the question of Mr. Vareika's disappearance *or* death, including any information, oral or written, that such persons provided him dealing with any aspect of Mr. Vareika's life, whether professional or personal in nature. Should Mr. Murizzi maintain his refusal to answer any such questions, he shall be held in contempt and jailed for the balance of the grand jury's sitting—or any extension thereof—until and unless he does answer such questions. Anything else?"

"No, Your Honor," said Murphy. "The Commonwealth is content."

"No, Your Honor," from Shel as well, feeling anything *but* content.

So, I guess I'd better pack my toothbrush on Monday, huh?"

In the corridor outside the first session, Pontifico Murizzi put a little more pep into his comment than he could justify. But it got something like grins from both Shel and Irish. Then Jorie Tully approached them, extending another folded paper to Murizzi.

She said, "Have a nice weekend, Pope."

He took the paper. "You, too, Jore."

Tully copwalked away from them.

When she was out of earshot, Mairead said, "Another subpoena?"

Murizzi held it out to her. "I don't think you could find anybody who'd bet the other way."

As she unfolded the paper, Shel said, "Judge Smith didn't give us much time for an appeal to the Single Justice Session, but frankly, I don't see much ground for one."

"Me neither," the Pope looking at his two lawyers. "Hell, Shel, I'd have ordered the same thing as Her Honor there. When I was on the unit, I'd have jumped at the chance for a 'road map to the stars' from a private eye who'd been on the case before me." Then Murizzi shook his shoulders and loosened his tie. "Never was crazy about wearing a business suit on the job, even when it was what we all had to do. Shel, check me on this, but if I don't answer Murphy's questions come Monday—"

Irish looked up from the paper. "At nine A.M.—"

"—then I'm in the slam by what, ten?"

"Yes," said Shel. "Since you were on the police force, though, you shouldn't go into General Population."

"No shit," the Pope trying to keep his voice light, casual.

"I can speak to the Sheriff's Department, get you Administrative Segregation."

"Great. They'll treat me just like the baby-raping priest, right?"

Mairead said, "Or, you can answer the questions Murphy puts to you on Monday."

"Even better. Expose Pitt to everything she hired us to prevent, even though she had nothing to do with Vareika's getting killed."

After a moment, Shel said, "Either way, it's your call, Pope, not ours. Not when it involves jail."

"Well, then," Pontifico Murizzi tugging the tie completely off. "Jorie said to have a nice weekend. I think that's what I'll try to do."

As Mairead O'Clare and Shel Gold moved toward Judge Pitt's courtroom, she heard her boss say, "What were you doing before the argument just now?"

Mairead shrugged. "Working on a hunch."

"That's a relief," said Shel, pulling open the door to the session and lowering his voice, "I thought you were just practicing your penmanship."

Mairead realized he didn't want the volume of his words interrupting the trial of *Commonwealth v. Dooley,* though from the look contorting Barbara Pitt's face up on the bench, interruption might have been a welcome thing. The judge was listening, jury absent, to Dooley himself. Shel motioned toward a row in the gallery, and the two of them sidestepped into it.

Mairead recognized some of the others sitting in front of her, even from the back. Bill Sherden, the victims' advocate; Donald Iverson, his opposite for the man/boy group; a woman Mairead took to be Amelie Cardon, the clergy's advocate; and assorted media representatives. Then she decided to focus on what Dooley was saying to Judge Pitt.

"And therefore, Your Honor, I need to call that psychologist who testified for the prosecution, to ask him about whether certain alleged 'victims' go on to lead perfectly normal lives."

"Mr. Dooley, as I've told you before, that issue is not material to the question of whether or not you committed certain acts on the many complaining parties in this case. And, even if it were, Ms. Yelverton, under our court's evidence practice of 'wide-open' cross-examination, could have inquired of the psychologist when he was here the first time."

"But I've fired my lawyer, Your Honor, and it is *my* decision to call this witness back to the stand."

"Mr. Dooley, if I were to allow that, Ms. Butler as prosecutor would simply object to your questions, and I would have to sustain her objections."

"I don't see how or why you would do that, Your Honor. This is very important information for my jury to have."

My jury. Mairead noticed the judge look away from Dooley, probably to keep from uncorking a primal scream of exasperation. Pitt's eyes lodged on Shel, and she nodded once. Shel nodded back.

Her Honor then said, "I will reconsider your request, Mr. Dooley, though I doubt my decision on it will change. And, as indicated earlier, we will now adjourn until Monday morning because of private business of mine."

As everyone stood up, Shel said, "I think I should see Judge Pitt by myself."

"I do, too," replied Mairead. "But could you ask Tommy Flanagan to come back out to me when he's free?"

"Yes."

As Shel moved toward the judge's lobby and the courtroom emptied, Mairead noticed Cornelius Dooley staring at her again. He gave that sick little finger wave, and she felt herself fighting not to shudder as he was led away past Flo Altamira's desk by Flanagan and another bailiff.

Mairead sat back down and took out the sheet of paper she'd been writing on during Shel's argument in the first session. Mairead had thought that maybe by repeating Dooley's copying she might tumble to why he was doing it. But other than "practicing penmanship," as Shel had jokingly suggested, Mairead couldn't see any purpose to it.

However, young lady, remember what Ms. Yelverton told you.

Okay. Dooley said, "I'm missing a letter."

Missing a letter for what?

Mairead took out a fresh piece of paper and listed the alphabet, A–Z, down the left-hand margin. Then she made an X next to each letter every time it appeared in the phrase "Defendant's Motion for Change of Venue is denied."

When Mairead finished, she tapped her pencil against the roll call of letters:

A   XX
B
C   X
D   XXXX
E   XXXXXX
F   XXX
G   X
H   X
I   XXX
J
K
L
M   X
N   XXXXXX
O   XXXX
P
Q
R   X
S   XX
T   XX
U   X
V   X
W
X
Y
Z

In all, forty characters, with all vowels represented, and "E" appearing the most, at seven times. The letters of the alphabet "missing" were B, J, K, L, P, Q, W, X, Y, and Z.

Mairead shook her head. It made no sense.

Then again, it could be that Cornelius X. Dooley was simply crazy—not incompetent to stand trial or claim insanity as a defense—but just plain nuts.

"Ms. O'Clare?"

So, Shelly, how did we do?"

Barbara Pitt had taken off her robe after Tommy Flanagan had shown him into her lobby. She wore a white, ruffled blouse that reminded Shel of a man's tuxedo shirt, the suit jacket on her coat tree as black as a tuxedo one would be. And her breasts seemed to press urgently against the material of her blouse.

"Earth to Shelly?"

"I'm sorry, Barbara." He sat down across the desk from her. "I just thought . . . You look terrific in that outfit."

Pitt glanced up at her coat tree. "I'm wearing this 'outfit'—and canceling the rest of today's session—because Chuck's wake is this afternoon, up in New Hampshire."

Shel felt himself wince, having thought that the "private business" Pitt referred to in the courtroom must be his own representation of her. "I didn't know."

"No reason you should, I suppose. At least the drive will be a relief from Cornelius Dooley. You heard his argument just now?"

"Enough of it." Gallina Ekarevskaya's comment about a "coup" came to mind, but Shel said, "From what Dooley was babbling, I agree with your analysis."

"I just don't understand what that sick little scorpion hopes to show the jury." A dismissive wave. "But enough of him, for today, anyway. What happened on the contempt before June Smith?"

"Well, we didn't get trounced, but we didn't exactly win, either."

"Tell me."

He did.

Pitt looked down at her desk, then squinched her eyes shut, as she had in Shel's office what felt like a month ago. "When Murizzi testifies Monday morning—"

"*If* he testifies."

She opened her eyes again, her mouth following suit before any words came out. "You think he . . . You really believe he might still refuse?"

"I don't know, Barbara. The Pope's got his own code on things. If he thinks you're innocent, and he's told me he does, then he might do almost anything. I've told him it's his call."

"Did he . . ." A pause, as though Barbara Pitt were eggshelling over her next words. "Did Murizzi ever tell you why it's important for him to know that a given 'client' he helps is truly innocent?"

"Yes," Shel not wanting to divulge the Pope's story about sending a wrongly convicted defendant to prison, only to see the young man commit suicide two weeks before the real killer was identified.

Pitt nodded. "Did he tell you who the presiding judge was on that case?"

"No," but, suddenly, Shel knew.

A heaving sigh. "The real reason I didn't want to involve Murizzi in this disaster originally, Shelly. I didn't want him . . . 'judging' *my* innocence in deciding whether or not to try helping me."

Shel wasn't sure he understood all that, then didn't think it mattered right then. "Well, the bottom-line alternatives are pretty clear, I think. If the Pope testifies on Monday, your affair with Mr. Vareika will probably leak, regardless of how otherwise 'secret' we'd hope a grand jury would be."

"And my personal life becomes fodder for the jackals of the media."

Shel didn't think "jackals" ate "fodder," but let it pass. "On the other hand, if the Pope refuses to answer Tina Murphy's questions, he goes to jail for the balance of the grand jury's term."

"Or until Murizzi agrees to talk in order to get out of said jail."

"He would have the key to the cell door in his pocket, yes. But somehow I don't see the Pope *not* staying the course once he embarks on it."

"At least, that's what I have to hope for."

Shel Gold thought that was about the best frame of mind in which to leave his current client/former lover for the drive to her dead lover's wake.

Pontifico Murizzi parked his Explorer in front of the dinky little house near the New Hampshire beach, thinking he must have set some kind of land speed record going northward from Boston. As he'd hoped, the same old but mint Buick Riviera was in the driveway.

When the Pope knocked on the front door of the ranch-cum-cottage, he was greeted by Eddie Vareika, wearing a tie and dress shirt over the slacks to a dark suit, but with the tie yanked down like Murizzi had his own back at the courthouse. Not all the way off, though, like Vareika believed he was going to have to snug it back up again after he finished the beer almost lost in his beefy hand.

Which is when it hit the Pope: Artie Chin had told him they'd released the body to the family.

"What do you want?" said Vareika, not waiting for Murizzi's answer before downing some of his beer.

"I'm sure this is a pretty bad time for you."

"Bad time?" Vareika's eyebrows arched like Jackie Gleason's used to, and the Pope got the idea that the beer he could see might not be the guy's first of the day. "We have to wake our son this afternoon and bury him tomorrow, otherwise the priest here says we'd have to wait till Monday. And I'm not gonna have Lina dreading that for another thirty-six hours. So, would you call this a 'bad time'?"

The Pope had been there before, hat in hand on a doorstep while some good citizens—who committed no crime worse than loving a child—were in their grieving. And his job then hadn't changed much: He had to drop water on the stone, like that Chinese torture, slowly eroding their unwillingness to cooperate.

Murizzi said, "If I could just talk with the two of you for a few minutes?"

"No way." A belch, the beer fumes carrying through the screen door and into the Pope's nostrils. "I'm not putting Lina through any more than she has to."

"Maybe then just a talk with you?"

"With me? What for? Chuck's dead, even before he got everybody else to call him 'Charles,' for Christ sake."

You've seen this a hundred times, too: trivializing the vic by tangential shit, make the deceased loved one seem less important, less real in the moment. "Mr. Vareika, please? I don't think I'd have to bother you again after that."

The father turned around, sloshing his beer a little. Then he turned back, wiping his hand against a thigh. "Lina's sleeping. Or trying to. Doctor gave her something, but it just makes her drowsy and weepy. So yeah, let's take a walk, get some fresh air."

Vareika put down his beer and came through the screen door. Murizzi decided to bide his time as they walked, mainly because the sidewalk was so narrow, they had to march single file toward the water.

Once on the main drag along the ocean, though, the sidewalk became boardwalk, about ten feet wide. Vareika turned south, sticking his hands in the side pockets of his slacks, the Pope falling in beside him.

Murizzi said, "I used to work Homicide in Boston, so I know how tough this can be on the family involved."

"Something you never think of, a kid dying before you do. I mean, after September eleventh, I read all the papers and watched that video of those fucking maniacs sending the planes into the towers I don't know how many times, and it's all the same: You can't believe it. But it happened to those poor people in New York, and now it's happened to Lina and me."

The Pope thought about the Sherdens on Beacon Hill, and their resolution to spend more time with *their* sons.

Vareika gestured toward the rolling waves, breaking hard against the rocks compared to the relatively quiet beaches that Murizzi knew in Massachusetts. "I remember the first time I ever took Chuck out there, to bodysurf. He was just nine, and I thought he'd never come out of the water." A small laugh. "It was so fucking cold, the poor kid's lips were blue, and I figured his teeth wouldn't be far behind."

A penny dropped for the Pope: He couldn't remember any family photos back at the Vareika house that showed "Dad" with "Chuck" before about that age. "The same year you taught him how to fight?"

"Huh?"

Murizzi stopped walking, touching Vareika lightly at the elbow. "When I was up here the last time, you told me Chuck was nine when you taught him how to fight, over a toy fire truck."

The big man stopped, too. "Hey, I taught him a lot of stuff, that first year."

"First year of what?"

Eddie Vareika looked at the Pope. "Got any kids of your own?"

"No."

"I wanted them, but," flicking his hand below his belt, "not enough sperm down there to do the job. Reason my first wife divorced me, tell you the truth. Then I met Lina. She was a little older than me, but since she already had Chuck—"

Jeez: The kid was adopted.

"—I tried to be the kind of father his own piece-of-shit moron never was."

Vareika started walking again, Murizzi still pacing him. "What was this other guy's name?"

"Lye-kow-skas."

"Could you maybe spell that for me?"

"L-Y-K-A-U-S-K-A-S. Jonas Lykauskas. Lithuanian, too. But that and Lina were the only things old Jonas and me had in common."

"Can you tell me about him?"

"Some, but not much. Drank himself to death before I came along. But according to Lina, the only thing he was good for was taking Chuck to church."

Let it happen, thought the Pope. Now you got him talking, let the guy tell it in his own words, at his own speed.

Vareika snorted once. "Lina had to work harder to support her and Chuck once she broke up with Jonas, so Lina handed Chuck over to him Saturdays and Sundays, when she covered this second job of hers. I can tell you this much: The moron didn't teach him anything the Church didn't."

"Do you remember where they lived at the time?"

"No, but Lina told me it was different towns, down in Mass."

Murizzi struggled to remember all the places the *Boston Herald* and the TV news had reported Dooley "serving" as a priest. "Smithfield, Calem, Wes—"

"Calem, yeah. That was it. Not Lina, but the moron." Now Vareika stopped walking. "Christ, you'd think a guy would be happy to have a son, you know? Somebody to look after, somebody to look up to you. But this Jonas, the stupid shit, I guess he couldn't see any of that."

Another snort, followed quickly by a third.

The Pope said, "Did Chuck ever mention any of the priests from his father's church?"

"Way back when. There were a couple things the kid *could* do without me showing him. Like pitch a tent, even cook a little. I asked him about it, and Chuck said this one priest took the kids camping, taught them some stuff."

"That priest have a name?"

"Of course. It was . . . Let me think a minute." Another snort, almost like a man with a head cold. "Yeah, Father Ned or . . . Neil. Yeah, that's right. Father Neil."

Short for "Cornelius." The son of a bitch.

"Funny thing was, I couldn't get Chuck to go camping with *me*. It was the one thing he knew how to do, but he always wanted to do something else."

Murizzi was trying to decide what to pursue when Vareika snorted twice more. "You don't mind, pal, I'd like to be alone for a while."

"Sure," said the Pope, grateful he'd gotten that far with the guy. "Thanks for your time, especially today of all—"

But Eddie Vareika was already stomping away, waving him off with one hand while the other went to his face, trying to put a muzzle on the tears and crying that went out over the sand toward the pounding, empty waves.

Mairead O'Clare had jumped a little at the sound of her name in the otherwise empty courtroom, and Tommy Flanagan apologized for startling her.

"No," she said, controlling her breathing, "No, that's all right."

Flanagan sat on the gallery bench in front of her, twisting his torso so he could face her.

"Mr. Gold said you wanted to see me, but Her Honor, Flo, and I have to leave pretty soon for the wake up in New Hampshire."

Mairead suppressed a shudder. "This won't take long. Flo told me that last Friday afternoon, Charles Vareika kind of burst in on her, clearly agitated."

A frown. "A week ago, this was?"

"Correct. Through the glory of hindsight, we figured out he asked her slightly odd questions while he was crushing an envelope in his hand."

Mairead noticed a little tic under Flanagan's left eye as she spoke the last few words, and he frowned more deeply. "Tommy, do you know anything about an envelope?"

He glanced around the courtroom. Less to refamiliarize himself with it, Mairead thought, and more to scan for eavesdroppers.

When Flanagan came back to her, he said quietly, "After we adjourned last Friday afternoon, I found an envelope on the courtroom floor, up near Flo's desk."

Mairead wanted to be careful. "Can you describe it?"

A shrug. "White, smaller than letter-size. The kind you'd use to maybe mail a check."

She nodded. "Did this envelope have anything in it?"

"I think so. There was some weight to it, and the flap was sealed."

"But you didn't open it."

"No, because there was a name on the back."

Mairead thought about where Flanagan had found the thing. "Flo's?"

"No, Her Honor's research clerk."

"Charles Vareika?"

"Right."

Mairead tried to stem the rush of anger she felt. "Tommy, why didn't you tell me this before?"

"Because it was the nickname only she used for him."

"She?"

"Judge Pitt." Flanagan waved a hand toward the lobby behind him. "She's the only one who called him 'Chuck.' So I figured, if Her Honor wanted you to know about whatever was in the envelope, she would have told you herself."

Mairead tried to process the bailiff's explanation. It made sense, if he suspected an affair between his boss and her research clerk, something that he wouldn't want to disclose if the judge's lawyer didn't already know about it from the client herself.

"Tommy?"

"Yes?"

"What did you do with this envelope?"

"I went to give it to Charles—the way he wanted to be called by everybody else—but he wasn't at his desk in Flo's office, so I left it on his chair, with a stapler as paperweight."

"Have you mentioned this envelope to the judge?"

A bewildered expression. "No, why should I? She's the one who put his name on it."

"How do you know that?"

"It was her handwriting," said Flanagan. "For sure. I mean, I've seen it a thousand times."

Mairead looked back down at her own second sheet of paper, the one on which she'd logged the alphabet as it appeared in Pitt's venue decision that Dooley had kept copying. The monster had told Kyra Yelverton, "I'm missing a letter."

The letter "K," to end . . . "Chuck."

"Ms. O'Clare?"

Flanagan seemed worried about her.

"Tommy, was there anything odd about any of the letters in that name on the envelope?"

"Odd? No, I— Well, kind of. It was like Her Honor's hand slipped a little at the end."

"Slipped on the 'k'?"

"Right. But you could still read it, no problem."

And Mairead O'Clare guessed that Charles Vareika could also have read whatever Cornelius Dooley had put in the envelope before sealing it. And dropping it on the courtroom floor, probably as he was being led away past Florinda Altamira's desk.

When nobody else was looking at the vile, smiling man with the rounded shoulders.

TWENTY-THREE

Billie Sunday, placing some documents for signature on Shel's desk in his empty office, heard two things at once. The sound of the suite door closing, and Shel's voice in the reception area saying, "Mairead?"

Aggravating man, all he has to do is *look,* and he won't see her. "She's not back yet."

"How long a walk is it from the courthouse?" Shel appeared in his doorway now. "*I'm* already back."

Billie gestured toward the answering machine on her reception desk. "Mairead called in on her cell phone while I was down the hall." Years ago, when Shel had first insisted they use that phrase for "going to the bathroom," Billie had thought it quaint, an opinion of hers that hadn't changed any since.

A troubled expression on the man's face. "What did she say?"

"Not much. Something came up that could help your judge's case, but it might take her a while."

"That's all?"

"From her, yes. But the Pope called, too. Told me he thinks there's a connection between the dead boy and that devil-priest."

"What connection?"

Billie regarded her boss as if he were the little child he sometimes could be. "Shel, if you went and splurged on a cell phone for your ownself, maybe Mairead and the Pope would call *you,* and that way you could ask both of them these things."

Sheldon A. Gold nodded, but somehow Billie Sunday didn't think the aggravating man was agreeing with her.

If Pontifico Murizzi thought he'd set a new track record for getting to New Hampshire, he figured he might break that driving back to Boston.

Thank Christ it's still early afternoon, and the Red Sox are in Chicago this weekend instead of Fenway, or it'd look like the morning rush hour into the city.

As it was, the Pope could leave the Explorer on cruise control and think. About what he'd learned from Eddie Vareika.

The kid wasn't his, but the mother, Lina, was in no shape to answer questions about her son's early years. On the other hand, the Calem connection—through Chuck's other biological parent—and the "Father Neil" created too much convergence to be coincidence.

Murizzi tried to figure why Charles Lykauskas—or Vareika—wouldn't have bailed out on helping Judge Pitt with Dooley's case. Some reasons came to mind. One, the kid probably hadn't seen "Father Neil" for fifteen, seventeen years, and Vareika would have changed a lot—including his last name—during the intervening time, which meant that the kid couldn't have expected Father Neil to recognize him in just a few minutes of courtroom facetime during jury selection. Second, Vareika would probably have felt at least embarrassed to tell Pitt why he was bailing, or risk her being pissed and maybe not helping him out toward other legal jobs once he left the clerkship. Third, maybe the kid really did have the hots for Her Honor, and he wanted to stay close the only way he could.

Or fourth, and the one that would have been the Pope's motivation if he'd been in Charles Vareika's shoes: Maybe the kid wanted to seek some vengeance, help get the sick bastard sent away forever on the baby-rapes currently charged against Dooley.

Four arguable motives. And maybe a half dozen others you're just not seeing. Only, with Vareika dead, you'll probably never know for sure.

One thing *was* sure, though: Given the big trial going on, not much chance Murizzi would get his own facetime in front of Dooley. But there was somebody else the Pope had met who ought to have a pretty good line on what was really going on with the defrocked priest.

Pontifico Murizzi kicked the sport ute up another five miles per hour, hoping he'd be able to find a parking space in Bay Village.

I must say, young lady, that when they told me you were here to see me, it was quite the surprise."

Mairead O'Clare sat across the small table from Cornelius X. Dooley in one of the attorney interview rooms at the Suffolk County Jail, where Tommy Flanagan had told her the defendant would be remanded until the trial resumed on Monday. She'd been to the jail often enough to know the routine. Mairead had entered the six-by-six room from a corridor door that a sheriff's officer locked behind her. Once that key was turned, the inner door to the jail could open on the other side of the tiny space, and the inmate would take the opposite chair.

Close quarters, with no guards present. However, there was a panic button on the right wall by the attorney's side, should he or she need to call for help.

Mairead didn't expect to be pressing that button. "Thank you for seeing me, Mr. Dooley."

"Must we be so . . . formal?" He extended his hands palms up across the table. "This little chamber is so much more . . . congenial than that screened window in the lockup, don't you think? Less the confessional here and more the . . . counseling table, Counselor?"

Mairead had no intention of touching the disgusting man, much less holding hands with him. "I'd like to ask you some questions."

"Yes," said Dooley, drawing his hands back slowly to his edge of the table and clasping them together. "Yes, I assumed you would." Then he half-stood, peering over toward her lap. "But I don't see it."

"You don't see what?"

"My diary. Remember?"

Mairead controlled her gag reflex. "I couldn't bring it, but I have read a copy of it."

A sneer. "A 'copy' is no good, as I told you before. The actual original is the . . . keepsake. I almost said 'heirloom,' because that's how I picture it, although, as a priest, I naturally don't have any descendants to welcome it as a legacy."

Mairead tried to swallow, couldn't, then tried again and succeeded. "Mr. Dooley, if I tell you how to access that original diary, will you answer my questions?"

The eyes behind the glasses glowed as though spotlights were shining upon them. "You can do that?"

"I believe so."

"Well, how then?"

"After you answer my questions."

Dooley came forward in his chair like a dog straining on an invisible leash. "No. Now!"

Having no intention of being cowed, Mairead leaned forward, too. "I think you called it a 'negotiated exchange'?"

Dooley's eyes jumped, but the emotion in them seemed to wane. "Oh, very good, young lady." At such short range, the foul breath whistling through his stained teeth was like a blowtorch. "Quoting me against myself." An assessment of some sort, his fingers fidgeting despite the hands staying clasped. "Very good, and very well. We've struck a second bargain." He slumped back into his seat. "Your questions?"

Mairead had given a great deal of thought to how she should start. "When did you first meet Charles Vareika?"

A sly smile. "Why, at the beginning of the trial, of course."

"I don't think so. I think you met him a long time ago, as chronicled in your diary. Only his first name back then was 'Chuck,' and somehow his last name didn't begin with a 'V.'"

"Ah, you haven't merely been reading my diary, you've been studying it. And study—of any kind—provides its own reward. However, I didn't lie to you just now. I can't recall his original last name—though it was very ethnic, nearly unpronounceable—but it began with an "L," and therefore I really *didn't* meet Chuck 'Vareika' until my trial began here."

Okay. "When did you first meet . . . 'Chuck L.'?"

A serenity washed over Dooley's features, smoothing them out. "During my ministry in Calem. I was relatively young, and poor Chuck was in the hands of his father, a devout drunkard. But he was also a devout Catholic, at least when he could rise for the eleven-o'clock Mass on Sunday morning after a Saturday night worshiping at the twin fountains of Jim Beam and Jack Daniel's. The man would bring young Chuck with him to church." A deep breath, slow exhalation. "The moment I saw that boy, I knew he would become one of my little gentlemen. His 'natural' role model for a male was unacceptable, something Chuck sensed despite his tender years. I groomed him into something quite special, even by my standards, before his mother remarried and he was taken from me by their moving to the new husband's town. 'Vareika' was obviously that new one's name, from somewhere in New Hampshire, I believe."

Mairead had no desire for the details of the "grooming," but she did wonder if perhaps Chuck's "swinging" attitude later in his life was somehow an outgrowth of what Dooley had done to him earlier.

Mairead said, "Chuck's name had changed to 'Vareika,' and you hadn't seen him in over ten years, correct?"

"Over fifteen, actually."

"Yet you recognized him in the courtroom, when the jury selection began?"

"Naturally." More serenity than Mairead felt she could stand. "My little gentleman had grown up. Tall and handsome and strong. I could sense his muscle tone, young lady, even through the suit he wore that day. And I believe, if somewhat immodestly, that he recognized me as well. His first . . . tutor, you might say?"

No, *you* might say. "But then you had no contact with him after that?"

A sadness now, and a shaking of the thinly haired head. "That first day of trial, I was overjoyed. I mean, the thought of having one of my little gentlemen there with me, in Pontius Pilate's den, while the prosecutor tore at my garments and flesh, rending both . . . Well, it was sustaining. But then, when he didn't appear after that, I asked Donald why Chuck couldn't—"

"Wait a minute. You told Donald Iverson about Chuck?"

A surprised look. "Why, yes. Donald was helping me with my defense. Not just the monetary side, but the strategic as well, in a way I obviously couldn't share with my Nubian attorney."

Nubian . . . Mairead shook her head. "Mr. Dooley, Iverson knows about Chuck having been one of your 'little gentlemen'?"

"Of course. How else could our defense strategy work?"

Mairead felt overwhelmed by a matrix displaying conflicts of interest. Could the private lawyer for a judge ask a defendant on trial before that judge of his defense strategy any more than the same judge's law clerk could? Would that produce a mistrial if the information ever came to light, as on an appeal? Would such a conflict be grounds for attorney discipline before the Board of Bar Overseers? Suspension from the practice of law, even . . . disbarment?

Trust your instincts, young lady.

"Mr. Dooley, what 'strategy' are we talking about?"

He seemed disappointed, as though his star pupil inexplicably started having trouble with elemental arithmetic. "The defense I outlined in the courtroom today: That many of my little gentlemen have grown into 'normal,' heterosexually functioning males. Like Chuck with his . . . 'roommate,' a woman named Klein, and therefore probably Jewish. Quite ecumenical of him, eh?"

Mairead was beginning to feel like Alice Through the Looking Glass. "How could you know about who Chuck . . . lived with?"

Another disappointed expression. "From Donald. After I told him about Chuck and me, Donald began to follow him."

"Mr. Iverson followed Charles Vareika?"

"Yes. And it was apparent, rather quickly, that Chuck was sharing more with Ms. Klein than merely . . . expenses." A conspiratorial wink. "Donald even told me he saw them enter a 'swingers' club,' I believe it's called."

Mairead's mind was reeling. Dooley hadn't mentioned Chuck and Judge Pitt, so Mairead dared not, yet she had to know. "Why did you drop the envelope with 'Chuck' on it last Friday, the handwriting your mimicking of the judge's?"

Dooley smiled broadly, unclasping his hands to applaud silently by tapping the three middle fingers of his right hand into his left palm, then returning his hands to the prayer position. "Oh, that's even better, young lady. You really are quite the detective, aren't you?"

"Mr. Dooley, what was in that envelope?"

"Just a brief note, asking Chuck to please attend my trial more often because I missed him terribly."

"And that was all?"

"That, and the fact that I was glad he'd be the star witness in proving my defense."

"Your defense?"

"Pay attention, please. The defense that my interactions with my little gentlemen didn't harm them, the way that Hector W.'s shrew of a mother and all the others seem to believe. No, Chuck was going to be my prime example for the harmlessness of my encounters over the years."

Mairead tried to weave this into what she'd already learned. "You told Chuck in that note that he was going to be called as a witness, to relate this alleged relationship with his roommate?"

"And his heterosexual prowess in general, à la the swingers' club. Oh, and we mustn't forget his fine maturing, too, from graduating law school to a prestigious job with a highly regarded judge." Another sly smile. "In fact, it was when I heard 'Her Honor' refer to him as 'Chuck' with one of the bailiffs that I had the idea of copying her handwriting as the conduit for his receiving my note safely. Frankly, young lady, I couldn't see any other way to reach him, since he wasn't attending my trial in person."

It then hit Mairead, just as Sister Bernadette's voice said, *He doesn't know, young lady.*

Cornelius Dooley doesn't know about Charles Vareika and Judge Pitt having an affair.

But Donald Iverson would know, would *have* to know, if "man/boy love" had really been following Vareika around.

Now a frown from Dooley. "Oh, my. You don't suppose that's why Chuck disappeared, do you? That he was too shy and modest to take the witness stand on my behalf?"

Mairead wasn't sure how much more she could stomach of this clueless madman's reckless behavior. And attitude.

She rose from her chair, Dooley nearly leaping across the table at her. Mairead found herself hoping he'd try something physical, because she intended some payback for a lot of innocent kids before pushing the panic button.

However, all Dooley did was look up at her from the tabletop, now more like a food-begging puppy than a leash-straining dog. "We do have a bargain, remember?"

It took a moment for Mairead to realize what the man meant. "The original of your diary."

"What else?"

"You've fired your defense attorney—"

"Donald and I agree that she never would have presented our planned defense with enthusi—"

"—and you're proceeding as your own counsel, correct?"

Dooley seemed confused by the question. "Correct."

"Well, then. As the 'attorney for yourself,' I believe you can view any documents entered into evidence at the trial, simply by asking the court clerk, Ms. Altamira, for them."

"Including the original of . . ." Tears welled in Dooley's eyes, but this time he made no effort to deal with them. "Oh, thank you, thank you. Perhaps it was obvious to someone trained in the ways of the law, but I didn't see it."

Mairead turned to knock on her side of the door.

"Young lady?"

She turned back. "Yes?"

"Do you think I could see my diary now?"

Mairead shook her head. "Probably not until court's back in session on Monday."

"That certainly doesn't seem fair." The moist eyes darted back and forth. "I should have been able to see my diary today, if Judge Pitt hadn't adjourned so early. Do you have any idea why she did that?"

God, let me be out of here. "I believe it was to attend the wake."

More confusion now. "Someone died?"

Could it be Dooley doesn't know that, either? Kyra Yelverton was fired Wednesday afternoon, before Vareika's body was discovered, so she probably never had a chance to tell him, and in the Segregation Unit, he might not have access—

"Well?"

She snapped out of it. "Mr. Dooley, Charles Vareika was murdered."

Dooley slithered back off the tabletop into his chair, recoiling like a snake now. But more a wounded reptile than a dangerous one. "What . . . what are you saying?"

"Someone shot Mr. Vareika to death. His wake is this afternoon, in New Hampshire."

"But who, young lady?" Dooley looked as though he was about to be physically sick, and Mairead certainly didn't want to witness that. "Who could have done such a thing to one of my little gentlemen?"

"That's what I'm trying to find out."

Mairead O'Clare turned back to the door and knocked, but she couldn't keep the sounds—or the smells—of Cornelius X. Dooley's apparent grieving from assaulting her senses.

TWENTY-FOUR

Sheldon A. Gold was staring at the telephone on his office desk when Billie Sunday stuck her head in the open doorway.

She said, "Okay if I take off for the day?"

Shel didn't bother checking his watch. "Mairead call back in?"

"If she had, I would have put her through."

Shel found himself nodding, but still staring at his telephone.

"Shel?"

"Yes?"

"You all right?"

He broke his trance, looked up at the kind, concerned eyes. "Fine, Billie. Just juggling a lot of things in my head right now."

"You want me to stick around, catch any of the balls that might fall out?"

Shel couldn't help himself: He grinned at her. "No, you go home to your family."

"You need me for something, call."

"I will. Have a good weekend."

"You, too."

Shel was vaguely aware of the suite door closing behind Billie.

Admit it: You're glad she asked to leave early. It doesn't help you with your decision; it just helps you execute it.

If you decide at all.

Shel shook his head. It had been a hell of a week. Barbara Q. Pitt, rising up from his past. Natalie, always a part of his present. And Gallina Ekarevskaya, perhaps a part of his future.

Shel's hand drifted toward the phone. Then, six inches away from it, he pulled back.

You have to ask yourself a question first: What kind of future could a chronically depressive, impotent, fiftysomething male—married to a memory—offer a woman like Ekarevskaya by way of relationship? The occasional lunch or drink? Dinner and a movie or even a play?

At least that would be something, better than take-out Szechuan or deli sandwiches in front of your television set.

Shel's hand drifted toward the phone. Again. Three inches away this time before he pulled back. Again.

And, after the public part of the "date" was over, then what?

Shel took a deep breath, held it, and let it out again.

Only one way to find out.

He picked up the phone in one surprisingly fluid motion, dialed the number he'd memorized half an hour before, and waited through three rings, expecting to get a voice mail message.

Instead though, what Shel heard was, "Gallina Ekarevskaya speaking."

He hesitated.

"Who is this calling, please?"

The coward dies a thousand deaths. "Gallina?"

"Sheldon. A pleasant surprise near the end of a long day."

"For me, too. Uh, I was wondering if . . ."

Fuck it.

Pontifico Murizzi drove around the block containing Donald Iverson's town house four times, but apparently nobody who lived in Bay Village ever moved their cars on a Friday afternoon. He swung the Explorer into the curb cut for a driveway, then put on his emergency flashers, pulled down his visor with the PBA shield on it, and locked up.

When he got to the front door, the Pope rang the bell, the chimes giving off that melody he couldn't place. Expecting somehow to see Ordell, the new sparrow, Murizzi was glad that instead Iverson greeted him.

"Ah," said the pervert. "The closet case himself."

"Great to see you, too. We need to talk."

"Certainly. Come in."

The Pope followed Iverson into the house and then up the stairs to the office floor, the guy's footfalls bringing back Murizzi's initial impression of the pervert's quickness. At the landing, Iverson called up to the third level. "Ordell, we have company, so be sure you're decent, sartorially if not morally."

As they entered the office, the Pope said, "Ordell knows what 'sartorially' means?"

"I'm teaching him." A smarmy smile. "Lots of things."

Murizzi took one of the sling chairs, settling into it comfortably. "Had a nice talk with the bereaved parents."

"Bereaved?" said Iverson, sitting behind his desk.

"Well, actually, just the father. That is, the stepfather."

The smile seemed to freeze on Iverson's face. "Who are you talking about, again?"

"Eddie Vareika, the guy who married Chuck's mom after her ex-husband drank himself to death. You know the ex, or at least your friend the other baby-raper does. Dooley was the parish priest in Calem, where the ex lived and used to bring Chuck to church. Where Father Neil took care of him."

The smile departed entirely now. "I don't know what you're talking about."

"Sure you do. Dooley's such a whack-job, he had to tell you about it, and I'm guessing he spotted his little victim all grown up the first time he saw Vareika in court, when the players are identified for the jury. The ironic twist? One of Dooley's victims gets to be a law clerk helping the judge trying him for other child rapes."

The Pope watched Iverson. The guy was just smart enough not to talk without thinking first, but you could almost hear the wheels churning in his brain and see the smoke from them coming out his pores. Asking himself the same question every killer Murizzi had interrogated had to face: How the fuck do I get out of this hole *whole?*

"Motive," said the Pope. "Somehow Charles Vareika gets wind of something you plan to do, to 'out' him as a victim, maybe to show baby-rape doesn't really 'hurt' the kids who suffered it. I mean, after all, Vareika grows up to be a good-looking guy, law school graduate, nice job with the courts as a springboard to his future. Unless, that is, you fucking blow that future out of the water by revealing him as not just one of Dooley's victims, but as a member of the bar who consciously continued helping the judge trying his molester. Now that might get Chuck in trouble, cost him a good job opportunity with a fancy firm, maybe even get him disbarred. And I think he would have been plenty pissed at the architect of Dooley's defense strategy. You, my friend."

A monumental sigh from Iverson, but Murizzi didn't like it. It wasn't one of fear, or even sadness. More just resignation.

Iverson said, "I think I've heard enough, Ordell."

The Pope wasn't even turned around before the room caved in on him.

Billie Sunday got home with the nice fillet of steelhead trout she'd bought at the fish market in the square. Neither Robert, Jr., her oldest, nor William, her youngest, was partial to fish, even though at least Robert knew it was good for him. But her oldest was away for an overnight with his friend Carmine and Carmine's father, who was nice enough to include Robert in some of the "guy stuff" they did together. And her youngest, William, was off camping with his Cub Scout troop.

And, Lord forgive me, didn't you think twice about signing the permission slip for *that,* all the things you've learned about what a bad priest did to the youngsters in his flock?

Billie shook it off. No, her two "sandwich" sons were off on their own for the night, which left the middle son, Matthew—who just *loved* his fish—to share dinner with his momma.

At least until she saw the note on the kitchen table, held up between the salt and pepper shakers.

Billie plucked the note and opened it. The thing read, *Momma, I'll be at Rachelle's for dinner tonight. Here's the number, you need me.*

Billie looked down at the number, Matthew remembering to put in the 617 area code, since all of Massachusetts now had to dial ten numbers, even just to speak to their next-door neighbors. Billie also liked that Matthew wrote *I'll be* instead of *I be,* which was the way he was talking until he had a falling-out with his hip-hop friend a few months before.

But now her middle son was fifteen going on thirty-five, with all those hormones stirring inside him like a nest of hornets. And he was having dinner with Rachelle, a nice girl Billie had met at a school function.

Then she eyed the fish. So be it. Cut the fillet in half, freeze the rest, and make a good corn chowder out of it another day.

So Billie took the sharp knife from the angled wooden block on her kitchen counter, divided the steelhead, and put one section in the freezer. She poked holes in the other with a fork, drizzled some Caesar salad dressing on top, then poked a few more times with the fork, let the marinade seep into the flesh some.

Billie Sunday covered the dish with a plastic bag, put tonight's dinner in the fridge, and decided, if she was going to have an evening alone, the best way to wash off the fish smell from her hands would be a bubble bath.

Mairead O'Clare had figured that walking to Bay Village from the jail would be faster than cabbing it, and, given the bumper-to-bumper traffic choking the narrow streets, she proved herself right. It was even easier for pedestrians, if not cars, once she hit the Boston Common, and beyond that, the crowds for the theater district hadn't yet started pouring into the neighborhood surrounding it.

Plus, the walk gave her time to think, to fit the pieces of the puzzle together.

Donald Iverson gets Cornelius Dooley to fire his attorney, Kyra Yelverton, in order to present a crazy defense that would hideously expose Charles Vareika—the former "Chuck L." in Dooley's diary—to all kinds of problems, from the lawyerly ethical to the personally shaming, certainly costing Vareika his privacy and probably his job hopes with the large law firms Barbara Pitt was, in her own way, "grooming" him for. The note from Dooley tips Chuck that his world is coming to an end, and Vivianna Klein said that when her roommate was faced with a problem, he analyzed it, then fixed it. "Analyzed it" here by trying to get Florinda Altamira and Kyra Yelverton to tell him which "defenses" Dooley would raise. Assuming the worst—that Dooley and his side knew about the affair with Judge Pitt—Vareika would have approached the only defense advocate left.

And with access to the judge's gun Saturday morning, and the knowledge through his job of Iverson's address for the splinter man/boy love organization, Charles Vareika would "fix" the problem his own way.

When Mairead reached Bay Village, she was reminded of her classmates at New England School of Law, complaining about no parking on the streets surrounding the campus. And for the hundredth time, Mairead gave thanks she lived and worked on Beacon Hill, where she didn't need a car to get around. But approaching the address Donald Iverson had on his business card, she noticed one vehicle blocking a driveway, plainly illegally even with its emergency flashers on.

A white, two-door Ford Explorer.

The Pope's? No, there had to be a million SUVs like it, all the yuppies driving them. But still . . .

Mairead walked up to the truck. It was locked, but she could just see through the smoked glass the orange anorak Murizzi had worn to view the place where Charles Vareika's body was found.

So, the Pope beat me here. But what made *him* want to see Iverson again?

Not wanting to cramp Murizzi's style, Mairead O'Clare crossed her arms and leaned her rump against the fender of the Explorer, trying to think it through.

The Pope opened his eyes, but he couldn't see Iverson. Ordell, though, was in plain sight, wearing athletic pants but no top, his bruised face getting better.

And his right hand leveling a small-frame revolver on Murizzi from ten feet away.

"Ah, you've rejoined us."

The voice came from behind him, but as the Pope tried to turn toward it, his head began pounding like a hammer on an anvil.

"I liked hitting you so hard," said Ordell in his twangy accent.

Iverson came around the Pope's chair, the same one he'd been sitting in when the lights went out. "Pontifico, we seem to have a problem on our hands."

"What you've got is blood on your hands, and the first one of you decides to flip on the other might get out of prison pre–Social Security."

A deep laugh from Iverson, a kind of high snickering from Ordell.

"Divide and conquer?" Iverson moved over to his sparrow, kneading the boy's neck muscles. "I'm afraid not, Pontifico. Ordell and I are in this together, for the duration."

The pounding in Murizzi's head reduced itself to a dull, rolling thunder. "Let me guess. That 'sartorially/morally' line was the warning, right?"

"Very good, Pontifico. Ordell and I did design a little code all our own. You see, when one is out of the closet, unafraid to trumpet a special status, there are always those who would stifle that joyous song by strangling the throat from which it rises."

The Pope spoke to Ordell's dull, vacant eyes. "You know you can't get away with this, right? Your sugar daddy's going to get you thrown into a place for life that'll make the streets look like the Taj Mahal."

Ordell said, "What's the Taj Mahal?"

Iverson laughed. "I'm teaching him, Pontifico, as I mentioned before." Iverson ruffled the boy's rust-colored hair. "But he still has a ways to go."

Murizzi needed to buy some time, sink into the kid just what he was facing. "That the gun you used on poor Vareika?"

"'Poor Vareika'?" Iverson shook his head. "Ordell, did you hear that?"

"Poor Vareika," said the kid.

Iverson took back the lead. "Poor Vareika, as you call him, came here Saturday night, ranting and raving about a note that idiot Dooley passed him somehow. A note that told the fellow most of what we had planned for him."

"Which was?"

"To have Dooley call him as a witness, make Poor Vareika testify, however hostilely, in a public trial about how his 'homosexual experiences' as a child had no negative impact on his torrid, *hetero*sexual later life. His 'roommate,' the swingers' club."

When Iverson didn't mention Vareika's affair with Judge Pitt, the Pope tried to deflect it with, "Baby-raping isn't 'homosexuality.'"

"We can debate that later, Pontifico. But something else you may not know is that Poor Vareika was also banging the living daylights out of the judge hearing Dooley's case." Iverson hesitated, maybe waiting for Murizzi to acknowledge the fact. "I held that back from our idiot priest because I didn't think I could trust him with it, and that note to his 'little gentleman' proved me right. But, once we were shed of Ms. Yelverton's cloying sense of propriety, I fully intended to put Poor Vareika up on that stand and have Dooley ask him to relate their adventures in the 'good old days,' culminating in the jury hearing all about the judge's *own* glass-house problems in the realm of sexual stone-throwing."

"I'm no lawyer, but I don't see how all that mudslinging at Vareika and the judge would get Dooley off the baby-rape hook."

"I doubt it would, Pontifico. In fact, the 'mudslinging,' as you call it, might not even be admissible in evidence. But then, who cares?" Iverson glanced over at Ordell. "That courtroom's been packed with media for weeks. Just having the information come out at a public trial and trumpeted by reporters, both print and broadcast, buttresses my own organization's arguments that society has nothing real or permanent to fear from man/boy love."

"At the cost of Dooley going to jail forever."

"Which was going to happen anyway. And, even if Ms. Yelverton as legal 'plumber' could somehow have hit the judicial 'pipe' in precisely the right place, gotten Dooley a deal for less than that, well," Iverson spread his hands like a priest performing a benediction, "certainly he, if anyone, should understand that every cause must have its . . . martyrs?"

You can't beat this guy at his own game: Iverson was willing to ruin the judge and make her clerk/lover into a victim all over again, just to advance the pervert's private agenda. "All right, so Vareika shows up on your doorstep . . ."

"More *barges in*, Pontifico. And not just to rant and rave. He had that gun with him as well. He even helped us—mightily, if unintentionally—by mentioning he'd taken it from the judge's own boudoir. Well, I'd called out to Ordell, as I did today with you, but Poor Vareika, perhaps because he was so much younger and stronger than you, gave us proportionately more trouble. He heard Ordell coming up behind him, and I barely got to Poor Vareika's hand before he could fire. Fortunately Ordell had his nightstick—"

"His what?" said the Pope.

Ordell reached his free hand around behind his back, pulling out a riot baton with a perpendicular handle for gripping and jabbing. "Took this off a fuck-brained railroad cop, tried to roust me in a yard last winter."

Iverson smiled proudly. "Ordell hit Poor Vareika with it very hard, and his gun fell to the floor. But, as I said, the young man was enormously strong, and enraged to boot, so he tore the nightstick from Ordell's grasp and hit him with it. I shouted for Poor Vareika to stop, but he didn't, and so I picked up his gun and fired once, causing him to turn and lunge at me. I fired twice more, and he toppled at my feet." Now Iverson stared at the Pope. "It was rather easy, Pontifico. And surprisingly enjoyable."

"Only it also canceled out your witness."

"Yes, it did that, to be sure. And I of course had to keep Poor Vareika's death from the loose cannon Dooley, for fear he'd do more than pen a note after hearing that this special little gentleman of his—not to mention the cornerstone of his defense—was off the playing board. But then I had a brainstorm, if you'll permit me that immodesty." Iverson looked down at the rug on the floor of the office. "We rolled Poor Vareika into the predecessor of this fine Persian, since his blood was already all over it. Then we wrapped both shower curtains around that, to prevent . . . Well, leaking, unless you have a more technical term for it."

"Weeping," said Murizzi, buying more time, he hoped. "Blood weeps from a wound."

"Thank you, Pontifico. See, Ordell? I teach you, and he teaches me."

"When do we teach him how to die?"

"Soon, soon." Iverson picked up his story line. "We had a devil of a time getting Poor Vareika downstairs to my car, but by waiting until three A.M. of a Saturday into a Sunday, even the clubs in this neighborhood were closed. We drove him to the Big Dig and lightly covered him in a trash heap of construction materials, calculating that he'd be found when the workers returned on Monday, thus nicely blurring the time of his death."

"And that was your 'brainstorm'?"

"Ah, no. But it's coming, Pontifico, it's coming. Well, Monday arrives, and the body somehow *isn't* discovered. By Wednesday, I was growing concerned, especially with that horribly blotched young lawyer—and then you—poking around Poor Vareika's disappearance. So, finally I ask Ordell here to call nine-one-one from a pay phone and report strange goings-on by dogs and cats at the site, resulting in the body finally being found." Iverson smiled broadly. "And, after an appropriate interval, the murder weapon will turn up as well. *Now* do you see the brainstorm?"

"The judge's piece will match up ballistically with the slugs from Vareika's body."

"Precisely. It would have been exquisite to gild the lily by allowing the judge's fingerprints to remain on the gun and its shells as well, but since both Poor Vareika *and* I had handled the weapon, it became necessary to wipe all of that clean."

Brainstorm? Not exactly. "So, nobody's prints are on the gun or the shells in the cylinder, except for the ones Ordell's applying right now?"

Iverson's smile lost a little of its candlepower. "Well, yes. But what difference will that make, once we wipe it clean again? It's Pitt's gun, and the serial number will match her registration of the thing."

"Afraid not."

Iverson now dropped the smile as completely as he had before, when the Pope had been interrogating him. "What do you mean, Pontifico?"

"Pitt never registered the gun."

"What . . . what are you talking about? She's a judge! Of course she registered it."

Murizzi risked swinging his head side to side, slowly. The rolling thunder inside it got closer and more insistent.

Iverson changed his tone, if not his tune. "How could she *not* have registered it?"

The Pope didn't see that his sharing any more information would help his situation. "I don't know the reason. I just know she didn't."

Iverson went back to the wheels-churning look.

"Ordell," said Murizzi. "It seems your sugar daddy just lost his trump card."

The dull, vacant eyes didn't waver. "Don't mean I won't get to kill you. Make my bones, just like Donald did with that fuck-brained lawyer."

At which point door chimes rang, the melody the Pope still couldn't place.

Iverson turned toward the front windows, but they were, Murizzi remembered, on the second floor.

Ordell said, "You want me to go see?"

"No," said Iverson. "Just ignore it."

The chimes rang again.

The Pope tried to bluff. "When the police respond to a robbery in progress—or a hostage situation, like this here?—they approach with bubble lights flashing but no sirens. You notice those flashing lights a few seconds ago?"

Iverson started worrying his lower lip with his teeth.

Ordell said, "I didn't see no lights."

The chimes rang a third time, and some part of the Pope's brain came up with the song. It was the signature theme from *Oliver.*

Iverson, you sick bastard.

Ordell said, "What'll we do, Donald?"

Murizzi mimicked him, accent and all. "What'll we do, Donald?"

"Shut up, the both of you," from Iverson. "Let me think."

Pontifico Murizzi was flexing his calf muscles, getting ready to try for Ordell and the gun at the next distraction, when he heard what sounded like one of the department's fourteen-pound sledges hit the front door, cracking the wood.

Jeez, maybe it really *is* the cavalry?

Pope?" yelled Mairead O'Clare from the foyer of the town house, her hockey-conditioned leg not feeling any pain from having blasted a kick at the lock on the front door.

"Irish, get—"

She heard what sounded like a gunshot, from the same general location as Murizzi's shout, and Mairead knew she'd done the right thing by crashing.

Mairead took the stairs two at a time, hearing a scuffle and a man's voice that sounded like Iverson's. "Kill her, too."

Jesus Mary, no. "Pope!"

As Mairead hit the landing, that early-teen boy from her courtroom meeting with Iverson came at her through a doorway, now wearing just a pair of athletic pants, some kind of black club in his hand. He tried swinging it at her head, but Mairead's years on the ice told her how to estimate the angle of the attack and parry the thrust of it. The boy—Ordell, right—collided with her, front to front, and from the look on his face, was surprised that she didn't budge. Gripping the club the way Mairead would a violent opponent's hockey stick, she twisted as hard as she could, not quite breaking Ordell's grip but sending him through the low, flimsy balustrade and over into the stairwell. He screamed, Mairead just hearing his body thud solidly into the steps, but not before a cracking sound punctuated the continuing rattling of the club making its own way downstairs.

Suddenly nauseous, she looked over the gaping balustrade.

Ordell stared up, eyes at the wrong angle, his chin squarely over the back of his spine, like Linda Blair, swiveling her head in *The Exorcist.*

His neck is broken, young lady. And nothing more you can do for him.

Mairead, operating solely on adrenaline, was already entering the room Ordell had left.

What she saw: The Pope, flat on his back on the floor, blood pulsing out from his chest, his face a mask of pain and rage. He was trying to punch Donald Iverson, who was straddling his waist, choking him. A handgun lay on the carpet ten feet from the struggling men.

Mairead instinctively dived for the gun, catching from the corner of her eye Iverson turning quickly toward her, then closing even faster. He kicked at her head, nailing her cheek enough to knock Mairead onto her back. He raised his foot again, as if to crush her throat.

And that's when her right index finger closed on the trigger.

Mairead's hand jumped, her thumb knuckle registering pain. Her ears rang from the incredible report of the gun being discharged in such an enclosed space.

Iverson pantomimed crying out before stumbling several steps, then lurching out of the room.

Mairead could see the Pope, trying to lever his torso off the floor on an elbow, coughing up blood. As she scrambled over to him on her hands and knees, Mairead felt more than heard another body tumble down the staircase.

"Irish," said Pontifico Murizzi, in what seemed to her a whisper from very far away. "You did just right. But nine-one-one, huh? Right now."

TWENTY-FIVE

Sheldon A. Gold was waiting outside the Congress Street entrance to the courthouse when the dark sedan with the telltale white-on-powder-blue license plates of a state vehicle screeched to a halt at the curb. Judge Barbara Q. Pitt exited the rear passenger's side before Tommy Flanagan could get out from behind the wheel. He went to the front passenger's door to help Florinda Altamira with her braces.

Shel halved the distance between them, intentionally reaching Pitt first.

She said, "You got my message on your office machine?"

"No," said Shel, "I was, uh, in a cocktail lounge, and I saw the news bulletin on the television set over the bar."

He didn't add that, as soon as Gallina Ekarevskaya saw it, too, she said, "You must go to your client, Sheldon. Immediately."

Pitt glanced behind her. "We were coming back from the wake. Oh, God, Shelly. It was awful. Closed casket, Chuck's mother almost catatonic, the . . ." She put a hand to her mouth, the dainty way she had. "Tommy got a call on his cellular from the jail, and . . . Shelly, what do you think it means?"

He tried to remember that Pitt had been under a lot of pressure, not the least of which would have been just attending a wake and masquerading as only the employer of a murdered young man who'd been her lover as well.

Shel said, "I think the death of Cornelius Dooley ends the trial."

Pitt set her jaw. "I'm aware of that. I meant, how does it impact my situation?"

Shel began losing his sympathy. "The man hanged himself, Barbara."

"Which I still find hard to believe. If ever there was a prisoner who seemed anything but suicidal . . ."

Shel waited. When Pitt didn't continue, he said, "Apparently Dooley left some kind of a note, but the television news didn't give any details."

"Fortunately, there weren't any details. Tommy reached somebody at the jail who read the note to him. Basically, Dooley just apologized for everything he'd ever done, any of his 'little gentlemen' he'd ever hurt. No mention of anyone specific, including me."

In its own way, some emotional, if not financial, closure for Hector Washington and the other victims. "Then I believe there'll be no real 'impact' on your situation, other than to muffle the media drums a bit."

"But, Shelly—"

"The police will continue to investigate Mr. Vareika's murder, and we'll still have to wait for Monday to know the Pope's decision on testifying before the grand jury."

Shel sensed something going awfully odd behind Barbara Pitt's eyes.

His client said, "You haven't heard, then?"

"Heard what, Barbara?"

"About Donald Iverson."

Shel thought, The woman's still distraught, not thinking clearly. "I think our man/boy love advocate has certainly lost at least this opportunity for advancing his cause."

Pitt shook her head. "We turned on the radio as soon as Tommy got that first call. We were looking for news about Dooley, of course, but they also broadcast what happened at Iverson's home."

Sheldon A. Gold, trying to be understanding, to live up to his image of "the good lawyer," patiently asked Barbara Q. Pitt just exactly what she meant.

Pontifico Murizzi thought about opening his eyes.

It seemed to be one of those major life decisions, like buying a new sport ute or houseboat. The kind of thing you didn't want to rush into, you know? Especially when it was all warm and fuzzy inside his body, like somebody ordered up a nice white cloud for him to float on, all through the night.

And the Pope figured it had to be after dark, even though the days in June were long fucking stretches of sunshine, the most they'd get in Boston the whole year. Because he'd been doing some time computations in his head, and it had to have been ten minutes till the EMTs arrived, him trying to fill Mairead in on why Judge Hot Pants was off the hook completely. Then another five or seven minutes to the hospital, his "golden hour" of trauma intervention ticking away. Murizzi remembered Irish riding alongside him in the ambulance, blood dripping off her face, more of it on her blouse, though he thought that might have been some of his.

Or that baby-raper's, Iverson. The son of a bitch.

Funny, over the years, the Pope had talked to a couple, three guys on the force who'd been shot. Never really raised it himself, just waited for them to open up, usually after a few belts. But once the guys started talking, Murizzi paid close fucking attention. Another sergeant compared it to being hit by a baseball bat, and that's what the Pope would have gone with, too, now that he'd had the chance to experience the sensation. Like somebody had knocked all the fucking wind out of him with a Louisville slugger.

But he had forced himself to keep going, stay focused on that fucking revolver in Ordell's hand.

In the academy, the instructors always said, "Watch their eyes. The skels who're gonna shoot, they'll telegraph it with their eyes. Flinch a little, they will, from anticipating the noise."

On the street, though, his first partner in uniform had said that was bullshit. What you did was you watched their hands. Eyes can't kill. Knives and guns can, and they'll be in a given skel's hand. That's what you worry about.

And that's what Murizzi had been watching, Ordell's trigger finger. When it started to twitch, then tighten, Murizzi went at him hard and kept going even after getting hit, knocked the fucking gun out of his fucking hand—

No, wait a second here. You were trying to figure out what time it is. Maybe open the eyes just a little, catch the face of a clock.

"Pope?"

No, no good. Too bright in the room. Maybe it was still daylight. Yeah—no. No, that can't be. Murizzi could remember the ambulance tear-assing into the Emergency Room driveway, the whole van swaying from the torque of going around the corner. Then the doors opening and him getting lifted out on the gurney before the wheels kicked in and they were going hell-bent through the doors, somebody holding a bag over him, zooming along like he was the prize in *Supermarket Sweep,* the cart with all the high-end items in it.

And Irish, tears streaming down her face, turning some of the blood on her cheek pink. A couple drops falling off onto him as she ran alongside the gurney, talking to him.

"Pope, you awake?"

Just like that, yeah. Nice, sweet voice she has.

"Mairead?"

At first, Murizzi thought he'd said something himself, but he had this big tube down his throat, the Pope could feel it even without seeing it, so he thought probably no, it wasn't him. Then the voice repeated her name, but different, like they weren't talking to each other exactly. More like muffling each other's words.

Mairead's voice said, "Oh, God, I thought he was going to die."

Well, thought Murizzi. That's certainly fucking nice to hear. How come I bothered to stay conscious the whole way into the hospital, that's how she felt?

Shel Gold's voice now. "I talked to his doctor. They say he was lucky."

Huh, Shel's who it is. Why didn't you recognize his voice the first time? Maybe account of it sounded so husky, like he'd been smoking or something.

Good fucking news, though, that "lucky" part.

Then something the Pope didn't follow, Shel saying, "No, both of them, I'm afraid. A terrible thing, especially for you, Mairead, but combined with the suicide, it does mean the judge is in the clear, her secrets as secure as they can be."

Suicide? Secrets?

Then Irish said, "I don't want to, though."

Want to what?

Shel said, "The doctor also told me you were lucky, too. That a plastic surgeon was in the building, checking on another patient when you arrived."

Murizzi missed what she said next because he was thinking about things.

Then Mairead's voice with, "But I'm all right. And I'd rather stay."

Shel said, "No, you've already done all you could. Go home and get some sleep yourself. I won't leave his bedside unless Sergeant Detective Chin or somebody like him arrives to relieve me. Promise."

Hey, thought Murizzi. Don't I get a vote in any of this?

But then the Pope felt one hand squeeze his own down by his thigh someplace. And then another hand—bigger, and lumpier in the knuckles—did the same.

After which Pontifico Murizzi decided that he could wait awhile longer on that decision.

The one about opening his eyes.

No sense rushing things.

No sense at all.

Billie Sunday stood at the sink in her kitchen, drying her hands, dressed only in the chenille robe Robert, Sr., had given her for Mother's Day that last year he was alive. The red robe was tattered at the cuffs and hem now, and, truth be told, Billie would have been ashamed to be seen in it by just about anybody but her boys, the two older ones remembering who'd given it to her, and never commenting on its condition.

Billie had just finished washing the last of the plates from her steelhead trout dinner. Nothing that fancy: just the fish and a green salad, a glass of wine from the jug she kept in the refrigerator—always making a little Sharpie mark on the glass, be sure the level of the stuff didn't change any with two teenaged boys in the house.

Ah, but that bubble bath had felt good, too. It'd been a tough week, what with—

Her doorbell.

Billie glanced up at the clock over the sink. Probably just some solicitor. Jehovah's Witnesses, vacuum cleaner sales—

The doorbell again.

So, maybe Matthew forgot his key. Only it's a little early for him to be getting home, unless things went south with Rachelle.

Or unless something else went wrong, and—

Billie was halfway to her front door before the third bell sound died in the air.

When she looked through her peephole, though, she didn't see her middle son, or a police officer—thank you, Lord. But what she did see she didn't understand, though that didn't keep Billie from yanking open her door.

Mairead stood there on the steps, tears flowing down the sides of her nose, a taxicab pulling away behind her.

At first Billie thought it was a trick of the light, but then she realized there was a big white patch on the child's right cheek, and stains like blood all over her blouse. "What in the world happened to you?"

"Oh, Billie. I'm sorry, but the Pope's in the hospital, and Shel's with him—

"Child, what are you talking about?"

"—and I don't have anywhere else to go."

"Mairead—"

"Oh, God, Billie. God in heaven. I killed two men tonight." The child's mouth just wouldn't stop running now. "I threw one down the stairs and he broke his neck and I shot the other and they're both dead and I killed them. Oh, God, Jesus Mary, I killed two human beings."

Mairead sagged into Billie and clamped her arms around her, the mother of three hugging back just to hold the child up. Then Mairead sank her face into Billie's left breast and began to cry. Huge, racking sobs.

And so Billie sort of eased rearward, bringing the child into her house. Shutting the front door with one foot, Billie Sunday started thinking it was just as well all her sons were gone for a while longer, so they wouldn't notice just how far the level of wine in that jug might drop before morning.